EXITUS

VOLUME I
THE IMPOSTOR

By

David Slattery

First published in German in Munich by btb Verlagsgruppe Random House 2019

1

PB ISBN: 978-1-7399137-0-0

EB ISBN: 978-1-7399137-1-7

HB ISBN: 978-1-7399137-2-4

Cover design by: John Brady Design

Scripture quotations taken from the New English Bible, copyright © Cambridge University Press and Oxford University Press 1961, 1970. All rights reserved.

Typeset in Adobe Garamond Pro by Coinlea Services

Front and back cover collages: John Brady. Swimming pool photo: Sam Moqadam (Unsplash). University old building photo: Vadim Sher (Unsplash). Angel image: The Cabinet of Dr. Caligari – Wikimedia Commons. Nietzsche photo: Wikimedia Commons. Man with box on head and Man falling: Dreamstime[dot]com (Stock Photography).

*To the memory of my father, Jack, from whom
I inherited my need to tell stories and other
weaknesses.*

Part I

Ecce Wallace

Behold Wallace

I

Ingressus
Entry

He told himself to count to ten. At two he was pounding the door with his fist. A stunning, but bizarrely dressed woman appeared holding an overflowing cocktail glass in one hand and clutching the doorframe with the other. He gaped at her wild, red-dyed hair that dangled over her left eye before disappearing in a tangle behind her incongruously wide shoulders. He stared down past the lurid blue satin shirt and thin strip of denim skirt and along her bare legs to the retro woollen leg-warmers piled up in layers above high-heeled cork sandals. His prepared words vanished. She smiled and waved him in with the glass, spilling its contents over her alien shoulders.

"It's the eighties!" she shouted.

She grabbed his tie and pulled him inside the hotel room, kicking the door closed behind them with a sandaled foot. He couldn't protest because his tie was choking him. Still holding on, she began to bob to the voice of Gloria Gaynor who was just then insisting that she would survive some traumatic experience. Behind her, a swarm of dancing people in the room joined in with impromptu support for Ms Gaynor, chanting that they too were confident they would survive.

He clawed at the knot of his tie. A disco ball hung from the bland light fitting in the middle of the ceiling. But he couldn't tell whether the lights flashing before his eyes were those, as custom had it, he was supposed to see before passing out or were visible to everyone else in the hotel room.

The woman let go her grip.

"What?" he managed to croak.

"It's a back-to-the-eighties party," she screamed into his face above the throb of the music and collective singing. "Come on in and boogie. That's what you do in the eighties. Get down and boogie."

She whirled away between a gyrating couple who were part of the forest of dancers before him and disappeared. He was spun around to face a woman who waved her hands in the air and screamed at him again that she *would* survive.

He had come there as an annoyed neighbour, but now he too began to dance, sucked in by the throb of the pounding rhythm. A part of him was dancing because he didn't want to offend; he wanted to fit in. He found it easier than he would ever have imagined to go, in less than two minutes, from sulking alone in his room to disco-dancing with screaming strangers.

"I hate disco," he shouted at no one in particular on the packed dance floor as he followed the example of those next to him and punched the air.

Now he was on the ground with his feet pointing in opposite directions. The pain reminded him why he was here. Through the jumping and kicking legs around him he saw a table in the back corner of the room loaded with bottles. Alcohol would kill the ache in his over-stretched leg muscles while he recovered his breath to deliver his protest, which thus far, had gone unheard.

He raised his arms above his head in the hope someone would lift him up. Willing hands lifted him to his feet. He shouted his thanks and hobbled to the table of bottles. He poured whiskey into a glass and searched for the woman with the enormous shoulders amongst the dancers. He couldn't even guess how many people were squeezed into the hotel room: definitely more than the fire regulations permitted. At least eight were dancing on the bed, splashing their drinks onto the ceiling.

He studied the wall of sweating flesh just a few feet in front of him, now jumping up and down to the sound of Men at Work's "Down Under". He imagined himself an invisible witness to other people's lives. But he didn't mind because up until then he had been perfecting the art of living invisibly.

As he sipped the whiskey, he was already nostalgic for room 513 next door.

II

Exitus
Exit

No one took any notice of him as he drank one glass of whiskey after another in the corner of the packed room. The pulse of the music interrupted his thoughts as he tried to formulate a new plan of action. He had lost his enthusiasm for complaining to his neighbours who clearly outnumbered him. How would it look asking them to stop when he had already danced his way across the floor? Accepting failure was the easier path. He decided to be gracious in defeat. He would go back to his own room, pull a pillow over his head, and try to sleep. For the sake of politeness, he should find the woman with the wide shoulders, whom he assumed was his host, and say goodnight. He didn't feel right about just sneaking off, even if he could find the door in this crush.

While he was abstractly working out the details of his retreat in his head, he found himself examining what he took for his own reflection in a full-length mirror. Water droplets of light from the disco ball bounced off the shiny surface, illuminating a plump figure in a grey suit holding a glass in his raised hand staring straight back at him. He was disappointed that he appeared to have put on loads of weight in the short time since he had last seen himself in a mirror. He only realized that he was looking at someone else through a nearby balcony door when his reflection began to make independent gestures.

I must be drunk, he thought.

What he had taken to be his reflection started mouthing at him to come outside. He slid the glass door open and stepped onto the balcony.

"Come out quick and close that fucking door behind you," his reflection shouted above Michael Jackson's protest that he wasn't Billie Jean's lover. "I have a private supply of booze out here."

There was indeed a collection of bottles in the middle of a round iron table and two chairs from which, on a different evening than this, a couple of hotel guests might enjoy a romantic drink while watching the sun go down beyond the city horizon spread out in front of them.

"Wallace. My name is Wallace," the man roared as the balcony door slid firmly shut. The wall of glass reduced the noise to a point where they could hear each other without screaming.

"I'm not going back in there," Wallace said. "What a racket. I hate fucking disco."

Our hero recoiled from the gratuitous swearing, but nodded. "So do I."

"So, we have something other than our taste in grey suits in common." Wallace spread his arms out wide. "Cheers," he said clinking, their glasses together. "Imagine, I came here to complain about the noise."

"So did I."

"See? We are kindred spirits. Speaking of spirits, have

another drink. Free booze is fantastic in any decade, even the eighties."

Compelled to fit in with any social scene in which he found himself, he agreed to have just one more drink with Wallace. They stood side by side in silence and drank as the autumn sun rolled down the sky like an old-fashioned bronze coin, throwing rectangles of yellow light onto the hotel room walls that turned the corporate-approved beige colour scheme a snug, deep orange. They watched the lights of the city come on along the horizon, forming amber strings and irregular mosaics of tiny yellow rectangles separated by large black patches.

Finishing his drink, he turned to go back inside and continue the hunt through the mass of bodies for the woman with the wide shoulders who had opened the door on this fascinating hell for him. "I must find our host," he told Wallace.

Just then there was a collective cry of delight from behind the glass door as Ian Dury began to demand someone hit him with a rhythm stick. With the music turned up even louder, the crowd echoed his demand to be hit.

"I love this fucking song," Wallace said, starting to sway to the chorus blasting through the balcony door. "From the seventies. Not the fucking eighties. A much better fucking decade, altogether."

He grimaced again at Wallace's wanton swearing and uninvited musical pedantry and poured himself a final inch of whiskey. Near him, Wallace shuffled from side to side with one hand pressed against his hip and the other holding his drink arched over his head in the posture of an obese bullfighter. He swallowed the liquid in one gulp. "I have to go," he shouted, putting his empty glass on the round iron table.

"Wait, wait! I want to show you something." Wallace grabbed him by the lapel as he turned for the door. "Just wait one fucking minute," he commanded and began to laugh. "I want to show you something … ammaaaazzing."

With drunken care Wallace placed his drink on the edge of the table, shrugged out of his jacket, hung it over the back of one of the chairs with frustratingly drunken slowness, and then stood in front of him in his shirt with his back to the city lights. "Hit me as hard as you can in the face," Wallace said, straightening himself up in preparation for the blow. "Go on hit me. Hit me!"

"I'm leaving now," our hero said, reaching for the balcony door handle.

The other man's face turned deep red and veins sprung up on his neck as if his head was controlled by an electrical switch. Wallace grabbed him by the tie – the tie, again; he should never have worn a tie to this party – and pulled his face close to his. "I said fucking hit me as hard as you fucking can!" Flecks of spittle flew from Wallace's mouth. Then he calmed down as suddenly as he had flared up, the switch in his head apparently having turned to a new setting.

Wallace let go of the tie and stepped back, laughing. "Look, amongst other things, I used to be a boxer. I just want to show you how tough I am. This song reminded me of a game I used to play when I was a student. Hit me in the face as hard as you can. I promise I won't hit you back. I swear it. Just fucking hit me," he pleaded. He started to giggle.

Our hero stood there trying to work out how to control a situation that was rapidly spiralling out of his control. Before he could think of anything to say Wallace was talking again.

"I know I'm fucking drunk and crazy, but that's my problem. Just one punch, and I'll let you go. I promise. Look, I am a professor of ethics. Therefore, I *know* the difference between right and wrong. You don't believe me? Don't I look like a moral authority? I am. It's what I do. I am telling you as a professional ethicist – is that a word? – it is right to hit me if I tell you to do it. Hit me in the fucking face as hard as you can. Here," he said, pointing to his chin. He stood with his back to the railing, grinning. "Just one quality dig. Give it your best shot, and who knows, you might win a fucking prize?"

Our hero could not remember ever hitting anyone in his life, let alone hitting anyone in the face on demand. His mother was right. He actually couldn't kill a mouse. He vividly remembered the time as a child that he failed to assassinate a mouse on his mother's instructions. She had handed him a biscuit tin in which she had trapped the mouse and a shoe with which she suggested he beat the captive to death. His terror changed to instant affection for the trembling creature when he peeped inside the tin. He lied to her that he would take care of it outside, hoping he was emulating a villain from the movies. Instead, he hid his new friend in his bedroom for six weeks until his mother found it and beat it to death herself.

Looking at Wallace now he blew his breath out between his teeth as he wondered how he was going to get out of this situation without causing offence. He was confident, despite what Wallace said about his being a moral authority, that he wouldn't let him go just like that. He was sure there would be repercussions: a fight, resulting in his own face being smashed in. Then he wondered whether, if Wallace meant what he said, hitting Wallace might be easier than trying to protest. What could he say? Sorry, I don't want to upset you by refusing to hit you in the face.

While this internal dialogue seemed eternal to his alcohol-soaked brain, in real time it took just a fraction of a second while Wallace swayed in front of him. The man was starting to turn red again.

He hit Wallace on the chin as instructed. Wallace's head went straight back, followed by the rest of Wallace as he disappeared over the balcony. He stared at the place where just an instant before Wallace had stood wobbling and grinning. Then he rushed to the railing and looked down. Wallace lay spreadeagled on the roof of a car in the hotel car park five floors below. His white shirt was visible in the glow of a neon sign advertising the original Italian pasta that Momma used to make back in Sicily. In the flashing light he watched as Wallace's shirt turned red. He couldn't make out Wallace's head from that height. Perhaps he was too far away, or perhaps, as he began to suspect from up there, it had been driven through the roof of the car.

If there ever was an apposite occasion for swearing, he thought, surely this was it. "Oh fuck," he said, putting his head in his hands. "Oh fuck, fuck, fuckety-fuck."

III

Pallium Praeditium Opibus
A Cape with Natural Powers

Killing Wallace was beyond the range of his usual worries when travelling, such as making sure his alarm was set; that he had a window seat on the aeroplane; that his rental car was the model he had ordered; that he had a clean shirt to wear in the morning; or how he was going to get an annoying tune out of his head.

At the exact moment Wallace vanished over the balcony, unknown to him and deep in the murky depths of his unconscious, a capacity for chaos slid open its eyelids, and with a flick of its prehensile tail, made its confident lazy way to the surface of his control-freak mind. His brain began to work with a guile he never knew he possessed. If he had ever imagined how he would have behaved had he killed someone, he would have visualized himself in hysterics. Here, in the moment, he was stunned but calm.

He looked through the sliding doors and saw the mob inside was still laughing and singing along to Ian Dury. Some beat their dance partners with invisible rhythm sticks while those partners knelt on the floor begging for mercy between bouts of uncontrollable laughter. It appeared everyone was drunk. The end of his blameless law-abiding life had come about in less time than it took to sing a hit single.

The car park below was empty. No one had noticed a bleeding headless corpse on the roof of a blue car. He picked up Wallace's jacket and searched the pockets. He found the large yellow hotel key fob to room 515 and a wallet with rows of credit cards and some money. He placed these on the round iron table beside the bottles. He took his own wallet, the key fob to room 513, his mobile phone and a bunch of keys from his pockets and held them in both hands over the railing of the balcony. He opened his fingers and watched them fall. His phone and keys crashed onto the car roof where Wallace's head should have been. His hotel key drifted in the wind, landing in the soundless street. His wallet bounced off the canopy over the entrance to Momma's Pasta House and settled on the footpath.

He stuffed Wallace's possessions into his trouser pockets, opened the sliding door, and went inside. He danced his way across the floor in the direction of the door. Twice he had to fend off attempts by drunken women to make him dance to New Order's "Blue Monday" that had everyone gyrating in a sweaty frenzy.

As he was reaching for the hotel room door handle, the woman with the wide shoulders appeared in front of him, blocking his escape. She rubbed her back against the smooth white wood of the door in time to the music, like a cat marking its territory. "Where are you going?" she shouted at him.

"I'm going home. Next door," he shouted back. He waved in the direction of the hall.

"I'll come with you," she shouted back.

"No need. I can find my own way. It's not far," he protested.

"Don't you find your neighbours attractive?" she screamed, moving closer to the rhythm of the music.

"It's not that," he shouted, stepping back. "I think I am going to be sick."

"What you need is a little nursing. Let's go."

In his entire life no woman had ever come on to him in this way, and never in his wildest tame fantasies one as beautiful as this flesh-and-blood version. Who knew, he thought. Kill just one person, and women are all over you within minutes. Had he read somewhere that some women were attracted to danger? Maybe he was radiating menace – which would be novel for him. But then, with a sudden shock of fear, he wondered if she saw him killing Wallace. Of course, that must be it, he thought. Women don't throw themselves at me. Not beautiful women with huge shoulders. Not even ugly ones with tiny shoulders. Not even his wife.

With his new-found cunning, he decided he had better find out what she knew and what she wanted. Maybe he should kill her too.

"Okay," he said. "Follow me."

Outside in the hall he instinctively turned for his own room before remembering he had the key for room 515 in the opposite direction.

"It's this way," he said, turning around. She followed him along the corridor to Wallace's room where his new skin was hanging in the wardrobe, waiting for him.

IV

Cubiculum in Contraria Versum
Room Reversal

In room 515 he stood with his back against the door, listening for the sound of a siren, or at least, a scream from the street. He decided not to go out on the balcony to see what was happening below. What had he been thinking throwing his wallet, phone and keys down into the car park after Wallace? Breaking a lifetime habit, he had acted on a mad impulse; just to make time to decide what to do next without any thought whatsoever for the consequences. No planning. No control. Nothing. Now a consequence was standing in the middle of room 515 facing him with the largest shoulders he had ever seen.

"What's your name?" she asked.

"Wallace."

"Wallace what?"

"My friends just call me Wallace."

"Hmmm …You mustn't have many friends."

"I don't have any."

"These aren't real," she said, unbuttoning her blue satin blouse.

"Wh … at?" he stammered, staring at her breasts, beginning

to sweat.

She reached inside the blouse. She pulled out one shoulder pad, and then the other, and threw them on the bed. "Sooo eighties," she said. "I just love the eighties. Don't you?"

"I can't decide. Make yourself at home," he told her, before lunging through the bathroom door.

Shock seemed to have caused his heart to leave its usual place in his chest because it was now beating behind his ears. He imagined the boring calm of the bathroom in room 513 which looked just like this one but without the reflection in the mirror of a man whose world was falling apart. He didn't laugh at the sour irony that his life had been turned around.

I can't go on the run, he thought. I've never even had a parking ticket. I'll call the police and explain everything. He rehearsed in his mind an account of what had happened. It was an accident. He insisted I punch him in the face because he is some sort of moral philosopher carrying out an experiment. No, I didn't take his wallet for the money. Were there witnesses? Oh, yes: a mob of drunken dancers who saw nothing.

A momentary hope: maybe *she* hadn't seen anything either. Then back to despairing again. What if she was the *only* one who had seen him kill Wallace? How was he going to do her in? He wondered if he would be able to strangle her? He tried to remember if she had a thin neck that he could get his puny hands around. He was confident he would never manage to strangle anyone with a thick neck. He began to look around the bathroom in search of something he could use to throttle her. He saw the towels stacked in a neat pile on a shelf. A towel would do, he thought. He remembered his pet mouse in the biscuit tin looking up at him with its mousy eyes begging him not to do it.

"Oh my God, I have gone insane," he groaned at his reflection. "I have become a homicidal maniac. Just because I killed one person doesn't mean I have to murder everyone I meet from now on."

He slumped to the cold, tiled bathroom floor and vomited whiskey into the toilet. At that moment, with his burning cheek resting on the cool rim of the bowl, his newly awakened cunning deserted him. He hoped it was a temporary relapse if he were going to survive. "Think. Think!" What am I going to do?" he asked himself out loud.

He had no idea how long he sat on the floor before he remembered Wallace's wallet. Propped against the tiled wall, he studied the contents. He read the two words "Rik Wallace" on a bank card.

He stood up and washed his face at the sink. The vibration of the bass disco music throbbing through the walls stopped with an ominous suddenness. The party screams also stopped and were replaced by the wailing of sirens coming from outside. He left the bathroom carrying a towel.

She was naked on the bed watching the news channels on the television. Oh Christ, he thought, first murder, now gratuitous nudity.

"My name?" she asked.

"What?"

"You haven't asked me my name. Don't you want to know?"

"Ahem, yes." He hesitated. "I suppose I do." He studied her neck, relieved. He would never get his fingers around that beautiful, thicker-than-average neck. He looked at the towel dangling from his hand. He didn't know how to strangle someone with a towel.

"It's Della."

"What?"

"My name is Della."

"Mine is Rik. Rik Wallace." He could tell her now that he knew.

"Does that mean we are no longer friends?"

He gazed at her in confusion. Then he remembered his earlier comment.

"Yes. I suppose it does." He smiled, relaxing.

He walked towards the bed to get a better view of her neck, and her breasts, and her—

Someone knocked on the door.

Two men stood outside facing him in the hall, now filled with people hurrying away to their own rooms. The younger of the two men flashed an ID and pushed past him while still asking if he could come in.

"This is Detective Inspector Jackson," the younger man said, flicking his chin at the older man. "There has been a homicide," he continued, as an explanation for their presence.

"An accident," Jackson corrected, bring up the rear. He was tall and thin with a permanent sad expression even when he smiled because his lips curled downwards. He unbuttoned his wrinkled coat with one hand and ran the other over his bald patch as if checking to see if his hair had miraculously grown back since he had last studied the pace of its retreat from his forehead earlier that morning in his bathroom mirror, pulled out a notebook and began to study it.

"Someone went off a balcony,' the younger policeman declared. "We think he was staying in room 513. A complete mess. Head like jam." He paused for his imagery to take effect before continuing with rapid-fire questions. "We were wondering if you saw or heard anything, sir? Is this your room, sir? Or yours, madam?" he asked turning to Della who had gotten off the bed and was gliding towards the two policemen.

Jackson looked up from his notebook to stare at her.

"Ah, this is Detective … what did you say your name is? He's new," Jackson explained, waving a hand in the general direction of his partner without taking his eyes off Della.

"Sullivan, sir. Freddy Sullivan. I've told you at least six times already today."

"Yes. Freddy Sullivan. How could I forget?" He tore his eyes away from Della and pointed at his colleague with his pencil. "This is Detective Sullivan. He is new on the job. Try to be helpful to him by answering his endless questions."

Sullivan was shorter and even thinner than Jackson. He was wearing a light grey suit that looked like his mother had bought it him for his first day as a detective. He was clearly impatient to get back to his questioning. "Is this your room, madam?" he asked again, resting his gaze on Della's forehead.

"It's his room," Della replied. "I'm staying next door. Room 514."

"It seems there was a party in room 514. An eighties party. It appears the victim fell from above or below room 514 or from room 514 itself. Did you see or hear anything, sir?

"I neither saw nor heard anything, Detective."

"Your name, sir? Can you confirm your name?"

"Yes, I can confirm my name. It's Rik Wallace."

"Why are you here, sir?"

"What do you mean?"

"He means nothing existential. Just why are you here in the hotel?" Jackson sighed, apparently more used to dealing with morons than his new partner.

Before he could think of a response, Della said, "He is on his way to a department of moral philosophy."

"Rik Wallace" gaped at her, and it was not because she was naked for no apparent reason in front of the three of them. Any residual thought of strangling her had vanished from his mind. She shrugged her now normal-sized shoulders and continued.

"I went through your letters which I found on the bed while you were in the bathroom. I had to do something you were in there so long. I thought you had fallen down the toilet."

She glided back to the bed, indifferent to both her nakedness and reading other people's private correspondence, picked up a letter from a bundle, and handed it to Jackson. "See for yourself. He starts the day after tomorrow. The college will provide him with accommodation. I assume that is why he is here in this hotel tonight," she theorized, pleased to assist the investigation.

A dribble of cold sweat ran down now-Rik-Wallace's spine as Jackson held the letter in front of him and read it. He rocked over and back on his toes until he could no longer endure the suspense.

"Can I see that?" he said, plucking the letter from Jackson's hand to read:

Dear Professor Wallace,

I am delighted you have agreed to join us as a lecturer in moral philosophy at Commerce, Arts and Technology College (CAT College). As you know we are a small group of colleagues who are confident you will fit in amongst us to become the leading light of our modest research and teaching efforts. Though we met only once at interview, and for such a short time, the positive impression you made on both my colleagues and me, remains with us.

The provost informs me that your academic transcripts, social security, bank, and medical details have all arrived safely in her office. Everything is ready for your commencement. To help you settle in we have given you a light teaching schedule for this coming term.

We expect you here on campus on the 5th. The provost has arranged convenient accommodation for you, which the Head of Psychology recommends as the perfect place to live, just a short distance from campus. If you come to the provost's office around noon, I will meet you and escort you to the department where we have planned a small soirée to introduce you to your new colleagues. (Don't worry. How could we forget you are a public anti-alcohol campaigner? We have arranged for non-alcoholic refreshments to be served).

I cannot tell you how excited we all are that our students will soon be enjoying the benefit of your considerable learning and extraordinarily nuanced ethical judgements. Until the 5th.

Yours sincerely,
Professor Maurice Spencer
Head of the Department of Philosophy
CAT College

"Can I read it, sir?" Sullivan asked Jackson.

"No need," Jackson barked. "I think I have seen enough. I am not an expert on moral philosophy but I believe, madam, you should put on some clothes while you accompany me to the station to make a statement."

"Do I have to?" Della asked.

"Get dressed or make a statement? Both, please."

It seemed the presence of a naked woman in room 515 removed any suspicion that might have attached itself to Rik Wallace in Jackson's mind.

"Shouldn't we also bring him with us, sir? Take fingerprints, DNA samples, check his story, that sort of thing? Make sure he is who he says he is. I learned in the police academy that a lot of people aren't who they say they are. You would be surprised."

"I suppose I would," Jackson replied. "As I said, he is new," he told Wallace. He turned to Sullivan. "I realize I shouldn't suppress your enthusiasm, but on this occasion I will. I would enjoy hearing her side of the story more than his if I must listen to someone at this time of the night. I'll make sure she isn't hiding anything – which I doubt," he said, still staring at her breasts. He made an upside-down smile. "Sullivan, you go down the hall and gather more … evidence. And try not to fingerprint anyone by accident."

"Yes, sir."

Sullivan departed.

Della dressed, using the unhurried movements of a striptease artist. But this was a strip show in reverse that left her audience more disenchanted at the end than at the beginning. She kissed Wallace on the lips. "Maybe I'll come and visit you at CAT College to see how you are getting on," she teased before leaving with Jackson.

Alone in room 515 he emptied all the tiny bottles and cans out of the mini bar and piled them on the bed. He sat beside them and began to drink. The indiscriminate mix of alcohol made him pine for the predictable, suffocatingly mundane, controlled existence that he had enjoyed up to what seemed to him to be just an hour ago. In fact, it was an hour and thirty-five minutes since his life changed, but he was no longer the kind of person who could keep an accurate track of time. He looked down at the semicircle of tiny empty bottles radiating out from his feet. He kicked out at them, scattering several across the beige carpet.

"Fuck it. Fuck it. Fuck it!" he said over and over as if practising the dialect of his new life. "What are you going to do now?" he asked his new self. There was no answer. At least he was still at liberty. He knew he wanted to stay that way for as long as possible.

He was surprised at how quickly he became bored with his worries. He opened the wardrobe and took out a grey suit that was obviously too large for him and laid it across the pillows at the head of the bed. He knew that if that detective – the younger one, whatever his name was – measured the body on the roof of the car in the car park against this suit he would be in trouble. Then he picked up Wallace's briefcase and opened it. He had better find out as much as he could about himself now that he was Rik Wallace, Professor of Moral Philosophy at CAT College and a highly qualified expert on right and wrong.

V

Habitus Habilis
A Fitting Disguise

He dozed in bouts of drunken torpor on the hotel bed before finally lurching fully awake to the kind of extreme headache only possible from mixing beer, wine, and spirits in reckless proportions. At first, he remembered nothing of the events of the previous night. He remembered that Wallace was a fat man, fatter than him, when he saw the large grey suit laid out on the pillows. Details flashed back in a sequence of mounting dismay. From the various documents he had found in the briefcase he discovered Rik Wallace had travelled a long way to take up his post at CAT College. After an hour of reading through the paperwork, along with his name, he knew his place and date of birth, how much he was worth, his credit card balance, social security number, and bank PIN numbers, which were helpfully listed inside the back cover of a notebook with the words "PIN numbers" written beside them.

He learned that he had been interviewed at the college nine weeks earlier. He knew Wallace was a hypocrite who drank alcohol on at least one occasion while boasting to his new employers about his public anti-drink campaigning. Perhaps he had been on a final binge before taking up his new post?

From the photograph in the passport, he hoped that he might pass for Wallace if he told those who had seen him at that interview, he had been ill and had lost forty pounds in just nine weeks. He decided to invent a wasting disease just embarrassing enough that no one would make too close an enquiry. He made a mental note to look up embarrassing wasting diseases on the Internet.

From a copy of the CV – which he imagined Wallace had printed to remind himself which version of himself he had sold to his employers – he learned where he had gone to school and college, the subjects on which he had written essays, theses, book chapters, conference papers, and lectures. He read that he, Wallace, was now an expert on something called consequentialist ethics, the Greeks, and post-modern ethics. Worst of all, he had written several books he should now borrow from the library to see what it was about morality he propounded. He made notes of the titles in Wallace's notebook. He also made notes of the general topics he needed to look up later in the library to pass as a moral virtuoso. He had most of one day in which to become an expert.

He had no mobile phone belonging to Wallace and no contact numbers. He hoped it was in a squish of Wallace's blood and guts in the mortuary. He didn't know if he was married or single. He didn't know if he was in a relationship or had children. He didn't know if he was gay.

He found just one photograph amongst Wallace's documents in the inner pocket of the briefcase. It was a black-and-white picture of a woman in her forties, twenty inches square. On the back was written in neat handwriting "Rik, With Love, Mum". No name, no endearments: just "Mum".

He imagined the photograph could have been taken anytime in the last twenty years. He hoped she was dead.

He skipped breakfast to avoid risking meeting Della, Detective Inspector Jackson, that other detective, or any other of the guests from room 514. He dressed in the grey oversized suit and a tie enclosing the collar of a shirt that hung loosely around his neck, emphasizing the impact of his wasting disease. He packed the rest of Wallace's clothes into a suitcase he found in the bottom of the wardrobe, put all the letters and papers back into the briefcase, and went downstairs to check out. He would spend his last night before becoming Rik Wallace in another hotel.

"Did you enjoy your stay, sir?" the blond woman on reception asked him. She was staring at the distance between his collar and his neck. He realized he should have discarded the tie and gone for a casual look.

"Yes. Thank you. Everything was wonderful," he lied.

"Did you sleep well, sir? I hope the minor incident we had last night didn't disturb you."

"No, not at all. I slept like the dead. I mean, what incident was that?" he asked, feigning casual curiosity.

"One of our guests fell off a balcony. He landed on a car. Made a complete mess of it. They've moved the body, but you can still see the car, if you like. It's ruined. Blood spattered everywhere when his face went through the roof. You can see the hole on your way out."

"Who was he?" he asked twiddling the pen, trying to concentrate on forging his new signature.

"I can't say, sir. It's against hotel policy to reveal details of any guests who are killed on the premises. But I can tell you that his wife's lawyer has already been in contact to inform us she is suing. It's going to cost us a fortune even though it seems he was pissed when he went off the balcony. John on breakfast service says he may have been at an orgy in room 514."

At least, he thought, his wife would be compensated for the shock of learning about the orgy.

"Have a nice day, Professor Wallace. I hope you will come back again and stay with us soon."

"No chance," he muttered under his breath.

In the city library, one of the several identical, thin, pale women behind the desk sighed deliberately before informing him that the library stocked topical non-fiction, crime, history, romances, books of general interest but not obscure titles in moral philosophy of no public interest such as those he had asked for. With condescension, she recommended he look for those titles in a university library. From this rebuff he realized his appreciation of his own writings must wait until he arrived at CAT College.

He sat down at one of the computer terminals and Googled Greek philosophy and consequentialist ethics. He decided to ignore post-modernity because it seemed too complicated from the huge number of related sites. He had one day in which to become a passable expert so something had to go. He made notes of terms and key words he hoped he would find useful if he found himself trapped in a conversation about his work. On the Internet he came across a moral sentiment, expressed in different ways but each amounting to the same thing: people claimed they relied on their belief in God for their morality because if they didn't believe, what according to them, was to stop them slaughtering their neighbours? He thought he would not want to live beside such people. But then, who would want to live beside him? Look what had happened to his neighbour in room 515. But he was now a moral authority. He didn't need God to tell him the difference between right and wrong.

He also read on the Internet that Consequentialists, such as he now was, believed the consequence of their actions was the basis for judgement about the rightness or otherwise of those actions. He understood that to mean that before he could say killing Wallace had been wrong, he needed to see what the consequences would be. He could make everything better by being a good Wallace and making a positive difference at CAT College. He left the library as calm as he had been since he had killed Wallace. He would find a hotel room on the ground floor tonight.

VI

Primo Die Ad Scholam
First Day in School

The taxi carrying Rik Wallace to his new life drove through a rundown suburb, unfashionable even with the bohemian set that tend to settle around a campus like expectant children encircling the deathbed of a parent, before stopping under the first of a sequence of arches that gave access to a series of enclosed quadrangles beyond.

"This is as far as I can go. You can find your own way from here," the driver told him.

Wallace paid the fare, got out, and studied the facade of the building erected in an age obsessed with symmetry. The name of the college was spelled out, in full, in large blue plastic letters above the archway that divided the long wall of windows into two even sections. A row of pointed railings ran along the front of each side guarding the college from any curious passer-by who might have hoped for casual enlightenment by looking through the rows of tall windows. A pedant – not our Wallace – entering the college who counted the railing spikes would have discovered an extra one on the eastern side of the archway. The expansive plains of grey stone on the front walls belied the general intellectual environment of the college, which was decidedly black and white.

He approached a hatch, beneath a large white sign with the word "Reception" spelled out by hand in black letters, set into the wall of a timber office built under one side of the archway. The glass panel flew open. A red face topped by white frizzy hair appeared from within.

"What do you want?" the porter asked, clearly in despair that people would keep turning up to the college with questions and would not just leave him alone to get on with his job in reception, which, as he conceived it in its ideal form, was a role akin to that of a hermit. Wallace took a step backwards.

"I'm looking for the provost's office."

"What do you want with her?"

Wallace paused. He wasn't expecting to be found wanting in his understanding of college protocol at his very first attempt. Was this interrogation by the porter of the provost's schedule normal practice in academic life?

"I am starting work today," he volunteered.

"Oh, you're the new professor. Why didn't you say so? I'll take you over there myself."

Seconds after slamming the glass panel shut, the porter appeared in front of the hut. Wallace walked beside him on the path that ran around the neat square of grass in the quadrangle beyond the entrance archway. At the first corner the porter stepped off the gravel path onto the lawn in the direction of a door in the opposite corner, past the small sign carrying a warning to keep off the grass. He hauled Wallace by the arm after him on his shortcut.

"It's supposed to be bad luck to walk on the grass," he announced. "At least that's what we tell the students to keep them off it. But I'll walk on it if I want because I have to cut it. I would tar over the lot but the provost is particular about her grass. She gets a lawn if she wants a lawn, even if she doesn't trim it herself. But then she is a woman of considerable style, and I'm not."

"I know this place used to be a hospital for wounded soldiers in the early nineteenth century, and after that a lunatic asylum for those considered insane by the standards for madness back then," Wallace told the porter, pleased to demonstrate his knowledge from his online research of the previous day.

"If you ask me, it still is an asylum. They have just swapped one set of nutcases for a different variety," the porter said and burst out laughing at his own unoriginal insight. He muttered something to himself that Wallace couldn't hear, though he did catch the words, "bloody academics".

"The college has been here since the fifties," Wallace said, practising a little pedantry for the pedantic trials that he was confident lay ahead. The porter stopped in the middle of the lawn, turned to Wallace and poked him in the chest to emphasize his point.

"You don't need to tell *me* anything about this college. I have been here all my life. My father worked for the provost's grandmother who started this place as a secretarial college for ladies of good breeding. I have witnessed it grow to what you see here today. You can't imagine the miles of grass I have mowed during those years. What will you be teaching here apart from the history of the college?"

"Moral philosophy," Wallace told him, surprising himself with his confident tone.

"Moral philosophy," the porter repeated. He looked

Wallace up and down, as if weighing in his mind the potential value of the new arrival's contribution to future generations of CAT College students the way an unsentimental farmer might assess the potential value of a neglected old donkey deposited on his farm by a society for the protection of cruelty to animals. "I'm confident we need a lot more of that, whatever it is. I am all for progress as long as it does not involve me. Anyway, what do I know about these things? I'm just the bloody dogsbody porter who has to trim the grass and keep everyone happy. Here we are."

They had arrived at a heavy door in the far corner of one of the four walls that formed the symmetrical quadrangle. The opposite wall had the exact number and style of doors and windows. The wall facing the archway had its own arch leading into another quadrangle of lawn beyond.

"Go straight through here, down the corridor to the end, turn right, and it's the first door on the right. You will see the sign for the provost's secretary, Pandora. Take it easy on the provost. She has a lot of troubles. She is not as strong nor as young as she used to be," he said, tapping the side of his head in an amateur psychiatric assessment of his employer. "But then none of us are, I suppose" he added. "And watch out for that boyfriend of hers. He is one of those psychologists. A complete lunatic, if you want my opinion; which I suppose you don't because I'm only the porter. Don't bother with any of those academic idiots, just go straight to my missus, Rose, if you need anything. She looks after all the cleaning round here. Knows everything. Ask Rose if you need to get the low-down on anyone. By the way, my name is Jim. Jim the porter."

He held out his hand. Wallace took it and felt his fingers

being squeezed in the strong grip developed over a lifetime of clasping, holding, grasping, and crushing things.

"Good luck. I'm sure you will be fine," Jim said and laughed as he turned away and walked straight back across the trimmed grass. Wallace felt as if a grim butler had led him into the middle of his sinister master's dreaded empty castle before vanishing behind a moth-eaten tapestry, leaving him alone to his fate in front of a large table set for one because the host did not follow an orthodox diet. "I've being staying up late watching too many scary films," he told himself before remembering that that habit was part of his past life.

In the corridor behind the door the cold air was imbued with the impermeable smell of years of the life of the building as a hospital that the fresh breaths of generations of students had failed to dilute. Wallace flexed his squeezed fingers as he followed the directions the porter had given him along the cold marble floor. White paint had been applied to the walls in a vain attempt to make the old building look inviting. A line of heavy doors punctuated the high walls of the corridor he imagined were rows of nineteenth-century padded cells. Even though Wallace was prepared for the absolute silence to be broken at any moment by a maniacal scream from anywhere, his heart did jump when a distant door banged. He heard laughter – not the laughter of a lunatic on the loose but easy sociable laughter. Then a group of students appeared in the corridor. They ignored him as they passed by in animated conversation.

A voice shouted at him to come in when he knocked on the heavy timber door. Inside, a woman of an unknowable age sat at the far side of a desk flooded with cold bright autumn light pouring into the room through a row of high windows, unhindered by either blinds or curtains. She wore black sunglasses that made it impossible for Wallace to know where she was looking. He wondered if perhaps she was blind. A smouldering cigarette dangled from her mouth, which had a semi-circular moustache of wrinkles radiating out from it as if she had been caught halfway through the act of swallowing a hundred-legged spider. A sign on the wall above her head read "No Smoking".

"Pandora?"

"Yes. What do you want?" she snapped in a gravelly voice, perhaps without looking at him.

"I'm here to see the provost. I have an appointment. My name is Rik Wallace. I am the new lecturer. I am a professor. Of moral philosophy."

He told himself to shut up.

She turned the plates of black glass in his direction. As she dragged on her cigarette something went wrong with the smooth flow of smoke through her tarred respiratory system, causing her to cough. She leaned over the wastepaper bin, slapping the desk with the hand not holding the cigarette. Wallace thought perhaps he should go around behind her and attempt the Heimlich manoeuvre, which he didn't know how to do. Just as he was about to panic, he had to turn away in horror as he glimpsed what was either a pink-green hairball or part of her lung on its way into the bin. She was gasping for air, and so desperate was her plight, she removed her sunglasses from her streaming eyes. She had gone from her standard paper-white complexion to a deep red. She took a drag on her still-smouldering cigarette, wedged it back between her lips, and blinked her bloodshot eyes at him. At this point Wallace realized she could see. As she put back on the sun glasses, she told him to sit down while she informed the provost of his arrival.

But she didn't move as he perched on one of the straight-backed wooden chairs lined up against the wall facing her, ready to flee. Then the phone on her desk rang only once before she snatched up the handset and said, "Oh, hello. I was thinking about you this minute. No. Not necessarily with pleasure. Maybe just a little. You won't be free this evening? Because of the damned new lecturer? Yes. He is sitting here now in front of me." The dishes of her black glasses were trained straight at Wallace. "Tomorrow? Yes. I suppose I can last until then. Don't overestimate my desire for you. Since your most attractive feature is your convenience, try not to make a habit of disappointing me. What's the theme?" She listened. "If that's what you want, fine, but I would like to get to decide sometime. As long as you bring the props. No. I don't have time to buy stuff, and you know I don't find those shops appealing. Okay, that's a date. I'll see you then."

She hung up and told Wallace that that had been a private conversation and was none of his business. The phone rang again. She grabbed it once more before the second ring. This time she covered the receiver with her hand, informing Wallace it was the secretary from the faculty of commerce on the line. Wallace listened in on the ten-minute conversation that followed. He learned that Pandora shared a particular interest with her colleague in the topic of health, especially her own. Her side of the conversation involved offering an assessment of her illnesses brought on, she had no doubt, by being overworked at CAT College.

While exhausting all possible symptoms and offering diagnoses of symptoms related back to her over the phone, the door behind Pandora opened and the provost stepped out of her office. Her immaculate blond hair formed gentle waves that flowed above her broad forehead as if a light breeze circulated around her head. While her make-up hid the few wrinkles that she may have had underneath, her startled expression suggested her youthful looks were man-made rather than natural. She was dressed in a severe but expensive two-piece blue suit, a look which seemed inspired by the kind of management course advice that insisted that employees were more likely to take advantage of a friendly boss. She seemed to be trying hard to give the impression she wasn't kind, despite her obvious warm nature and, in Pandora's case, regularly undermined this illusion by telling her at least once a day that she was her favourite employee. But for everyone else, to reinforce an uncongenial effect, she attempted to remind herself not to smile, which was her first instinct. In more recent years, her efforts to avoid smiling were helped by Botox injections.

"Pandora, dear, you must quit smoking," the provost said, using her hand to fan a cloud away from her face. "If not for my sake, at least for your own. You will ruin your beautiful skin."

"I must go. I will continue our important discussion at another time," Pandora told the secretary of the commerce faculty before hanging up. "I do have beautiful skin," she confirmed rubbing the back of her fingers over a wrinkled cheek. "Professor Wallace just got here this minute, Provost," she lied, looking at her watch as if this gesture was proof of his lack of punctuality.

"Now, now, Pandora. Not everyone can be as conscientious as you. Especially with the excitement of their first day." The provost placed her hand on the shoulder of her pet employee before turning back towards her office.

Pandora lit another cigarette. "You can go in now, but you should try to be on time in future. It doesn't make a good impression to keep the provost waiting."

Wallace would not have been surprised if Pandora stuck her long, tarry, pink tongue out at him.

VII

Agnus Dei
The Lamb of God

The provost's spacious office was decorated in the style in which an undertaker on an extravagant budget might have embellished their coffin showroom. Sombre shades, whatever the original intention, evoked the idea of mortality, which was not to be treated with a frivolous palette. The carpets were profoundly deep. As Rik Wallace entered this shrine to existential angst, the provost held out the fingers of her hand in greeting, pressed together into a tight cone as if holding an invisible thermometer to gauge the temperature of her visitor.

"Professor Wallace, welcome to CAT College," she purred with the reassuring tones of a psychiatric nurse. "I'm the provost, Patricia."

He hesitated for a moment. Did scholarly protocol demand he speak in alliterations? Did academic convention demand he kiss her outstretched fingers? Or perhaps the huge diamond ring sparkling on one of them? He settled on holding on to just her index finger and moving it up and down.

"I cannot tell you how excited I am you have finally arrived amongst us," she said, revealing no trace of excitement. "May I call you Rik?"

"Yes. Please do."

"You may call me Provost. This is the Reverend Professor Stephen Lambe," she said waving in the direction of a tall grey-haired man dressed in black behind an enormous desk. "Stephen is our college chaplain and the head of our counselling services. He is also the head of our psychology department, and my rock. I rely on him for everything. He is the Richelieu to my Louis XIII; the Samson to my Delilah; the Antony to my Cleopatra." Wallace didn't try to keep track of the names or roles. He was just relieved to realize being introduced meant that he hadn't met Lambe before.

As they stretched towards each other to shake hands across the desk Lambe said, "Just so you know where I stand; because I believe in people knowing where I stand, Rik. In my opinion all of this moral philosophy is a load of bollocks. God can be relied on to let us know the difference between right and wrong, and for those who forget, he wrote it down in the Ten Commandments. We would all slaughter each other without belief in God. Where would we be then?"

"I have come across that point of view before," Wallace said.

"Drink, Rik?"

"What?"

"Will you have a drink?"

Wallace turned red with the effort of trying to remember whether or not he was supposed to drink. He had a sudden raging desire to guzzle the entire bottle of wine that Lambe was holding towards him. After a long pause, in which he was being scrutinized with what he imagined was a professional psychological gaze, he said as casually as he could muster to disguise his enthusiasm, "I don't drink but I'll have just a small one to celebrate being here."

"Please do sit down" the provost commanded, indicating a cluster of leather armchairs around a glass coffee table arranged on one side of the room.

They sat facing each other in a circle. Wallace and Lambe each held a brimming glass of white wine. Patricia the provost sipped a coffee.

"I read your CV," Lambe said between gulps. "I can tell you are someone who is easily bored. You will enjoy it here because there is always too much going on at any time. No, you definitely won't be bored. I can promise you that. Too much going on," he muttered, before lapsing into silence.

"Stephen is an exceptional student of the human condition," Patricia the provost said, patting Lambe on the inside of his leg. "I would be lost without his advice on how to manage everybody. Stephen has convinced me I'm not a wonderful judge of people. I have made countless mistakes in the past. But not anymore, now I have Stephen to guide me."

"I try my best, darl— Er … Provost."

"Rik, you know CAT College was founded by my grandmother as a commercial school for respectable young ladies of superior breeding. Back then it was called The College of Commerce. She added business degrees to the secretarial and language courses because the ladies wanted the opportunity to become professionals. Then she even enrolled young gentlemen of unspecified breeding. After that she started a liberal arts faculty. I added technology when I took over. Consequently, we are now Commerce, Arts and Technology College. We chose commerce rather than business. We prefer cats to bats because you rarely come across a bat person. We used to—"

"You should know we don't do art for art's sake here," Lambe interrupted, obviously bored with the oft-repeated history of the institution. "We do art for the sake of business. You need to make moral philosophy relevant to our business students who are the lifeblood of this college. Mind you, our commerce students have no interest in arts, while our arts students despise anything with commercial opportunity. God only knows what the technology students are interested in."

"I have learned a lot about psychology from Stephen," Patricia the provost told Wallace, reprising her earlier theme. "Thanks to him I am now aware you can think you are one thing but, in reality, be something different. You need to be a psychologist to know what is real and what isn't," she said patting the inside of Lambe's leg again. "In my case, before I met Stephen, I thought I was happy, but I wasn't. I needed Stephen to show me how wrong I was. It took me five years. Yes. Five long years of patience and constant sacrifice on Stephen's part to help me see how miserable I actually was while, all that time, I thought I was happy. But it was just an illusion: nothing like the real joy I have now."

She smiled, and even though it took physical effort, Wallace was certain the staff of CAT College looked forward to seeing that smile: a treasured act that fleetingly revealed her kindness before her mouth collapsed again into despondency.

"Many people think they are happy," she continued. "They think laughing, smiling, sleeping soundly, enjoying life, not having a care in the world is happiness. But real happiness doesn't involve joy: real happiness demands suffering and pain. But Stephen has also taught me the opposite is true. You can have all the outward signs of misery but be cheerful deep down, unknown to everyone else, and even unknown to yourself. In fact, humans are the last people in the world who know who they really are. 'To thine own self be true.' That's Shakespeare's advice to us. Wouldn't you agree, Rik?"

"Yes. I do. I don't know who I am or who I am going to be here," he laughed. He put down his empty glass in alarm and stood up to leave.

Patricia the provost stretched her palm in the direction of Lambe, grasping his hand in hers while not taking her eyes from Wallace, who thought she was about to burst into tears.

"Don't you believe happiness is the most important thing we can strive for, Rik? More important even than truth? More important than moral philosophy?" His old self would have agreed – if by happiness she meant paying the mortgage, blending in, being left alone to watch television. Just being left alone. Before his new self could form a new lie, the provost was speaking again. "It is really all too complicated for me because I am just a simple woman. My qualifications are in sales and marketing. I took one of my grandmother's commerce degrees."

Wallace looked at his watch. "Excuse me, Provost. I have an appointment with Professor Spencer who is picking me up here at noon to take me to the philosophy department to introduce me to my new colleagues."

"Bloody philosophers. Bunch of crackpots if you ask me. God's not intelligent enough for that lot," Lambe slurred. He remained sitting as he poured himself another glass of wine. Wallace suspected Lambe would find it difficult to get out of the comfortable deep armchair without resorting to rolling across the floor. But Patricia the provost stood up without effort.

"Thank you for coming to see me, Rik. I wish you luck and happiness amongst us. Remember. We are here for you whoever you turn out to be."

She smiled the way Frankenstein's well-meaning monster might have smiled, while trying to give the doctor the impression he was pleased to have been brought back from the dead.

VIII

Philosophia
The Philosophy Department

The man Pandora was talking to leaned a few inches further back when he saw Rik Wallace come out of the provost's office. Professor Maurice Spencer was tall, thin, dark, and handsome. He looked intelligent, but he wasn't because, according to some philosophies, we can't have everything. His intellectual weakness was a willingness to mistake quantity of learning for knowledge. In practice that meant he didn't know when to stop studying. He never felt he had attained his goals, but if asked, he couldn't have said what those were except something to do with knowing the truth when he saw it. He had made it to head of department because he was a wise-looking fool, which is a form of idiocy that his colleagues found impossible to take seriously.

Spencer's marathon pursuit of truth had cost him his marriage. His wife disappeared, citing neglect in a note she left on the mantelpiece. It was two days before he found it. Two more days in which he searched for philosophical enlightenment instead of her. However, it seems she also abandoned a child because, soon after her disappearance, Spencer began to talk about his daughter for the first time.

She could be heard stomping around the bedroom overhead soon after Spencer, making some excuse, had left the room. Even obtuse visitors noticed that the sounds from the daughter always stopped just before he reappeared downstairs. She was seen, if ever, by third parties as a silhouette behind the blinds of the window. He would have been surprised how easy it had been for those who knew him to conclude that the daughter was, in fact, Spencer glimpsed out of the corner of an eye wearing a dress and voluminous wig. But no one demanded solid proof of her existence; no one insisted on bursting into the bedroom when they had glimpsed her shadow on their way up the garden path; no one attempted to force the bedroom door to catch him crawling around on his hands and knees when he thought his guests were gathered below. That was not the way moral colleagues would act. Perhaps morality had nothing to do with it. Maybe it was because, in general, while people liked Spencer, they liked his imaginary daughter even more.

He cited his daughter as a reason to abruptly leave college events. She was always doing this or that. He would quit a reception to pick her up from swimming. He would exit a meeting to drop her off at the girl guides, or baking classes, or horse riding. For a child that no one ever saw, she was unnecessarily hyperactive. She even had imaginary friends who caused confusion amongst those who gossiped about her behind Spencer's back. Her age was the single inconsistency in the chronicles of her life. One week she would be twelve and going on her first camping weekend. The following week she would have aged four years, preparing for her first date. The week after that she would be in primary school again.

Spencer was studying Wallace, clearly sensing something was wrong. Then he got it. "Good God! You've lost weight since we met at your interview."

"Yes. I have been sick," Wallace said, prepared for this moment, having learned his lines from the Internet. "I've had a wasting disease. Chronic Wasting Disease, in fact."

Spencer withdrew the hand he was holding out.

"Chronic Wasting Disease? Isn't that a disease in deer?"

Wallace paused before replying. "Yes, I suppose. But I got it, and I'm not a deer."

"But isn't it fatal?" Spencer asked, upset he was going to lose a new recruit so soon after the trouble of assessing all those candidates and organizing an interview. He was thinking he should have gone with his instincts and hired his second choice. He tried to recall if that applicant had appeared healthy. He did remember that, while less qualified, he had struck Spencer as a more empathetic moral philosopher than the fat Wallace who had turned up for interview.

"It might be fatal in deer, but not in my case." Wallace replied, annoyed with his peculiarly bad luck that the head of the philosophy department seemed to be an expert in animal welfare.

"I hope you are feeling better now," Spencer said, distracted by the effort of trying to remember Wallace's original merits as a candidate. He did recall an attractive metaphysician who had been discounted because the panel couldn't imagine what use she might have been to the college apart from her looks. Now he remembered: Wallace was regarded as potentially more valuable as a specialist in business ethics. By now Spencer was thinking perhaps a live good-looking metaphysician would have been a more rational choice than a dying ethics lecturer.

"I have made a full recovery, thank you. A miracle."

"Yes. It must be a miracle you caught it in the first place and then recovered. But that's excellent news. I don't mean excellent you were ill, but that you are on the mend; excellent for our department after all the trouble we had hiring you. It would have been annoying for us if you had expired from a wasting disease hitherto found exclusively amongst the deer population." Spencer felt it was now safe to shake hands.

Pandora removed her sunglasses to examine the biological phenomenon that was Wallace, unhindered by the panes of black glass. She was dying to tell the commerce secretary about him because they competed with each other in sourcing campus-based obscure medical disorders. She was confident the commerce secretary would not have come across anyone with a wasting disease – animal or human – in her faculty where they were notoriously conservative even in their choice of fatal illnesses. But since she retained her doubts about the possible full extent of Wallace's potential recovery from a disease that exclusively afflicted deer, she retreated behind her desk to establish what she hoped was a safe distance – a space she then filled with sanitizing cigarette smoke.

"I'll take you to meet your colleagues. We can walk and talk," Spencer said. As they were leaving, he asked Pandora if she wanted to come to the departmental reception for Professor Wallace.

"Thanks for the last-minute invitation, but some people around here have to work," she told him. While Wallace was wondering to whom she could be referring, she clarified the matter. "In particular, those of us who aren't lecturing. Some of us have *actual* responsibilities." Then she sat down behind her desk and began to re-arrange files and move her collection of pens from one desk tidy to another, waiting for them to leave before picking up the phone to inform the commerce secretary about the potential for an extraordinary outbreak on campus of Chronic Wasting Disease. She remembered the name because she had an eidetic memory for medical terms.

As they strolled through the quadrangles in the direction of the open meadow bordered by individual buildings hidden behind trees at the far side of the college, Professor Spencer told Rik Wallace about the philosophy department and the approved curriculum with a frankness Wallace doubted was part of the original interview for the job. He understood now that he was safe on campus the practical challenges of the task ahead could be imparted without the idealistic embellishments that he was confident had been used to attract the real candidate in the first place.

"I assume you were treated to Lambe's line on not-art-for-art's-sake. I say not-the-Reverend-Lambe-for-God's-sake." Spencer laughed at his own humour. He continued in a conspiratorial tone. "The Reverend Lambe has the provost under his thumb, and she isn't even a religious woman. But one has to admire his single-minded determination. He applied himself to the task of getting her to fall in love with him, and now she defers to him on every decision. He controls the college through her. He has ideas about what everyone should be teaching on their courses, especially in the areas he knows nothing about, which is everything including his own field, psychology." Spencer laughed again. "He made a name for himself a few hundred years ago amongst a particular group of scholars in evolutionary psychology, which you might think is a strange field for a churchman. I assume he was trying to convince his clerical colleagues he was progressive and his academic fellows he was tolerant, neither of which is the case. In reality, wherever that means for us philosophers, he is a narrow-minded bigot."

"I understood from the provost he is an expert in happiness," Wallace put in, anxious to gather as much information about anything to do with the college as fast as he could.

"Closer to an expert in unhappiness because he has a natural talent for making everyone around him miserable. Pandora is jealous of his Svengali influence over the provost, a role she used to enjoy before he came along. She is one of the provost's rescue animals: her most successful good cause. Patricia is not bad. It's just that, since she has no basic instincts, she needs to study the difference between right and wrong – same as us moral philosophers. Pandora met all the obvious requirements as a case in need of help: dropped-out of school early; hung out with the wrong crowd; dabbled in this and that; unpleasant boyfriends, etcetera. Patricia took her on as a project. Got her into one of her grandmother's secretarial courses with the result that Pandora ended up running the place. Despite appearances she is efficient. Things happen without her seeming to do anything. Maybe they would have happened anyway. I'm not an authority on administration. She is a formidable woman. A stimulating – I mean – interesting woman; a complex woman. She has benefitted from the provost rescuing her even if she resists showing gratitude. She has her pride, you know. It's natural for a rescue animal to bite the hand that saved it every now and again just to show there are no hard feelings."

He stopped talking for a moment to concentrate on his thoughts. "I suspect the only creatures Pandora has real feelings for are her cat and the provost, and even then, I don't know in what order. She loves that cat." He paused again. "Pandora and Lambe cannot go on forever competing like children for the provost's affection. Lambe may be ahead now, but I wouldn't write Pandora off. She is resourceful. And she still has her street-fighter instincts."

"What age is Pandora?"

"Somewhere between twenty-five and sixty-eight, but I'm only guessing." He returned to the topic of the provost. "Patricia thinks she is happy because Lambe tells her that being with him is the definition of bliss. She is the saddest-looking happy person I have ever seen."

"Was her mother also a provost?"

"God, no. Her mother was a model. Education can skip a generation, you know."

"I felt obliged to join Lambe in a glass of wine," Wallace confessed, afraid Spencer might smell the drink on his breath on his way to the non-alcoholic reception arranged to accommodate the supposedly abstemiousness original Wallace. "He forced me."

"You emphatically told me you didn't drink," Spencer said, his instant anger giving way to regret that he had ordered only tea, coffee, and apple juice for the reception.

"The specialist treating me recommended I might take it up as part of my ongoing therapy for Chronic Wasting Disease," Wallace blustered, pleased that he seemed to have evolved a spontaneous capacity for lying.

"I see," Spencer said, disappointed at the lost opportunity

for a midday drinking session. "Obviously part of your miracle cure."

"Obviously."

They walked on together not sharing their thoughts. Spencer eventually broke the silence. "It was better back in the days when Pandora controlled the provost. She had no opinions on what we should teach. She confined her influence to what she considered to be the vital issues of staff and student dress codes, what colours the halls should be painted, and the font we should use when communicating with each other. Pandora's only intellectual interest is medical research. She wanted the provost to establish a Faculty of Medicine with her in charge. However, Lambe will have plenty ideas about what you should teach your students. We are not allowed to even mention Friedrich Nietzsche since the incident with the cardboard box."

"The cardboard box?"

"It was my first year here. I wanted to shake things up for the commerce students. I put Nietzsche's *Beyond Good and Evil* on the curriculum. When you combine Nietzsche with no philosophical training and a little cost-accounting you get the cardboard box incident."

"The cardboard box incident?"

"One day during a lecture I looked out the window, and there's one of my students strolling by with a cornflakes box on his head. At least he was rational enough to have cut eyeholes in it to see where he was going. Probably his practical business solutions classes coming to his aid. According to Pandora, who got it from the provost, who got it from Lambe, that is the sort of thing can happen to commerce students who read Nietzsche without the appropriate safeguards."

"What safeguards are they?" Wallace asked, worried that there might be some well-known philosophical prophylactics against the hazards of Nietzsche he should be aware of as a teacher of philosophy.

"No one seems to have worked out what they are, and in the meantime, Nietzsche is banned from the curriculum. The parents of that student went crazy and blamed the provost. She blamed me after consulting with Lambe. They removed him from the college but not before he spent the rest of the term wandering the campus with that box on his head to make the best possible legal case against us."

"But what has Nietzsche to do with cornflakes?" Wallace asked, hoping to learn of any established philosophical connection.

"Oh, not a thing. I can assure you Nietzsche has nothing to say on the topic of cornflakes. I even made that argument in court to no avail. As Lambe is fond of quoting the judge in the case: 'You cannot predict the effects of Nietzsche's writings on an impressionable mind.' The point with Nietzsche is not cornflakes apparently, but that he undermines the foundations of our traditional morality. For some people, those who are not professors of moral philosophy, that leaves them without moral principles, and as a consequence, they go off the rails. Look at the Reverend Lambe: despite his evolutionary theories he would be lost without his God for personal guidance. He believes something is ethical if it arrives on a floating cloud, with wings, strumming a golden harp."

"Who does he recommend amongst the philosophers?" Wallace asked, developing a tactic of distracting Spencer from worrying about *him* by getting him to fret about Lambe instead.

"There is Socrates, of course, who is a favourite with students everywhere because of his proclamation that the only thing he knew for certain was that he knew nothing. That idea is especially popular amongst first years who identify with the literal interpretation, even if it wasn't what Socrates meant. It's the fate of all great philosophers to be interpreted by others in whatever way suits their purposes best. You know Plato wrote down everything Socrates said after the fact. If only Socrates had killed Plato first and then himself – in that order – we would never have heard of either of them. But you can't go wrong with Socrates or any other of the ancient Greek bores because they have never incited any of our students to wear a cardboard box on their head and never will."

By now they had arrived outside a detached three-storey building set back on its own patch of grass and separated by a gravel road from the open meadow behind the last of the linked quadrangles. The structure, which had been designed as two semi-detached homes for resident psychiatrists in the days of the asylum, had been made into one edifice sometime in the past by replacing the two front doors with a single oversized one, which opened under the centre of a veranda stretching between the wings, topped by windowed eaves that ran into the roof forming a third floor. The smooth rendered walls had been painted light blue years ago. In the interim the paint had faded to white in large patches producing the effect of a sad, pale, sick-looking building.

"Here we are. You remember this dump from your interview? I don't know how we managed to persuade you to come back once you had laid eyes on this place. We need a refurbishment, but the provost will never agree while Lambe holds what we do in contempt. Here we are. No matter how decrepit, there is nowhere like your new home: the Department of Philosophy in CAT College." Spencer bowed in mock ceremony towards the building.

The melancholic face of the department saddened Wallace who was, of course, seeing it for the first time. "I enjoy DIY," he told Spencer with a direct confidence absent until now in their conversation. "I can help you make the outside look more cheerful if you get me a few buckets of paint and a ladder. How about yellow?" he asked, studying the building through a photograph frame of his fingers. His old passion for fixing things up made him indifferent to whether he had mentioned anything about DIY at interview.

"Jim the porter would never allow you to climb up his ladders," Spencer replied, ignoring his enthusiasm. "And he won't climb up them himself."

"I'll persuade him to hold the ladder while I splash on the paint," Wallace said, gratified he had something he could contribute to the Department of Philosophy.

Wallace saw a group of people inside the bay window on the left of the doorway. They were laughing and talking together, glad to be distracted from the routine by his arrival. He took a deep breath and plunged into the building through the battered, oversized front door. Inside, the walls of the hallway were covered with notice boards overloaded with posters of all sizes announcing examination results, timetables, advertising concerts both impending and long over, guest lectures, public and student protests, club activities, and health and safety notices. A large poster pinned on top of others announced his inaugural lecture just three weeks hence. A sign informed him the stairs at the end of the hall led to staff offices and lecture rooms on the floors above.

The door to the seminar room was open. Wallace could hear the hubbub from the crowd inside waiting for him. He was handed a glass of apple juice as he walked in. He followed Spencer through the throng, nodding and smiling when introduced to random people in turn. He was relieved to learn he seemed to have never met most before. But a few he assumed he had met at interview stared at him with expressions that indicated they were struggling to remember what was different about him now.

"I've lost weight," Wallace repeated as he shook each hand. Most were students or lecturers from other departments who had gathered for the party and were trying to come to terms with the absence of alcohol. He smiled and repeated how thrilled he was to be there and how much he looked forward to enlightening everyone. Most ignored him in favour of resuming their animated conversations with each other as soon as he had passed.

Two young women stood together in a small clearing inside the window as if a force field was keeping the crowd around them at bay. They appeared translucent in the yellow sunlight that bounced off their silhouettes. They bobbed their heads on their long necks like gossiping swans. But just then the distracting image evaporated because Spencer was introducing him.

"This is Sally Doolittle. She is a graduate student and one of our college counsellors," he said of the shorter of the two swans.

"I've lost weight," Wallace announced. "Aren't you a bit

young to be a counsellor? Do you have qualifications?" he added, manically initiating conversation.

"You're so conventional. People always ask me that. No. I haven't qualifications in counselling *per se* but I can offer advice based in my own experience: drugs, drink, stupid sexual relationships, gambling, overdoses, and failing exams. You name it; I've done it. The students know I can relate to them."

"Sally is exceptionally empathetic. She hasn't lost many of our students," Spencer put in.

"Just four to date." Doolittle confirmed with pride.

"Lost?"

"It's a counselling term," Doolittle explained.

"Better record than her predecessor who was qualified. We lost him too which proves you can never tell in advance what approach to student counselling will work," Spencer said. "The Reverend Lambe, who you may have been told is our chaplain, head of counselling services, head of—"

"Yes. Yes. I know. Anthony, Samson, and someone else."

"He decided to try something new and have Sally here, with less qualifications, do the job."

"Less as in none," Doolittle clarified. "My record is impressive when you average it out over years and years. My quotation marks in the air with my fingers 'clients' are satisfied, so it seems to be working."

"Aren't you supposed to do the quotation marks thing with your fingers and not say quotation marks as well?" Wallace asked.

"It's post-modern irony, but then there is no irony in the fact that you're not a post-modernist even though Professor Spencer told me he hired an expert in post-modern ethics. I knew this place would never employ a real one of those."

"She is cost-effective," Spencer explained, ignoring her criticisms of his recruitment tactics.

Doolittle looked into her empty glass of apple juice and turned away, having lost interest in Wallace.

"This is our most outstanding graduate student, Julie Progress," Spencer said introducing Wallace to the taller of the swans in the window. "Julie is writing a doctorate thesis on ethics."

Progress was holding a glass of apple juice as far away from her as possible as if it was a bad-tempered pet rat a younger brother had asked her to hold on to while he tied his shoelaces. She looked into his eyes. "I am a huge fan of your work, Professor Wallace," she told him.

"Specifically, which aspects of my work?" Wallace asked, picking up the habits of an unprepared student gathering hints for an impending examination.

"I have read everything you have written. I enjoyed your arguments on the assessment of business managers in your article on 'Living with The Consequences of Other People's Mistakes'. You remember that one?"

"Oh yes. I do," he lied. Wallace knew this moment would come. He had tried to prepare, but now he realized planning was in vain. He began to sweat. He wondered if this was an appropriate moment to stage a blackout. Instead of falling to the floor Wallace heard himself saying, "Maybe we can discuss my genius over a real drink later on."

"Spencer warned us you don't drink real drinks."

"It's a long story."

"I have read your criticisms of the drinks industry."

"It's a *very* long story."

"Why not tell me at your place this evening?"

"I haven't even unpacked yet."

"If you haven't unpacked the glasses by then, we can drink from the bottle."

"Eight o'clock?"

"Wine?"

"Red."

"Is that a real drink?"

"It's real. Trust me. I'm a philosopher. I know these things."

Spencer, who was listening in on their conversation, said, "I would love to join you two, but I must take my daughter to the cinema this evening."

"Oh. You have a daughter? What's her name?" Wallace asked.

"Samantha. She is turning thirteen next week."

Spencer turned away.

"Children are a lot of work," Wallace said with a sigh.

"I imagine pretend ones need even more effort," Progress said.

Wallace's eyes widened a little with curiosity.

"That is also a long story. We will have much to talk about this evening if we don't find something else to do. I will bring two bottles," Progress concluded.

IX

Progressus
Progress

The greasy bulb in the lamp managed to produce a romantic sludge of circular light around the bed while keeping the unattractive features of the room hidden in shadow. Julie Progress pulled the sheet over her naked breasts and held it in place under her chin as she used her hands to remove a cigarette from a red-and-white packet.

"Smoke?" she asked Rik Wallace, who lay beside her studying the ceiling, which he had noticed earlier required plastering followed by at least two coats of paint.

"Why not?" he asked.

"Do you have an ashtray in this dump?"

"I don't have one of my own because I am not really a smoker, but there might be one somewhere from the previous tenant. I haven't had a chance to look around to investigate what's here."

"What do you mean you don't really smoke? You either do or you don't?"

"I mean, I don't know if I smoke." He hesitated. "Okay. I have decided I am a smoker. Give me a cigarette."

"You are strange, but I suppose philosophers are a bit

weird. I think I'm becoming a bit weird myself from my own research."

Progress was the opposite kind of philosopher to Maurice Spencer. She was willing to accept anything as the truth if it put an end the tedious search for it as soon as possible. For her, philosophy was the excitement of arriving – anywhere – rather than the boredom she experienced on the journey. If Spencer was an idiot, didn't it logically follow that Progress was the antithesis to an idiot, whatever that might be, ontologically speaking? And Wallace, he seemed to be different again. Imagine not knowing who he was. Maybe that was why he was a philosopher in the first place?

"I'll use a saucer if I can find one," she said, climbing out of bed. She moved, swaying her rounded buttocks to show off her fabulous figure to best effect, as if she was a well-practised cow at an agricultural show. She flicked her long straight blond hair over her shoulders to make it lie iron-flat on her naked back as she disappeared into the gloom beyond the feeble range of the grimy bedside lamp.

In the dark kitchen Progress swore when she banged her toe on something sharp. She wondered why she hadn't sent Wallace to look for a saucer. She opened cupboards and used her fingers to feel for anything saucer-shaped. She was annoyed because she wasn't used to doing things for herself. As the eldest of three siblings who were raised by their divorced mother, she had learned to manipulate her younger brothers, whom she had come to realize were equal parts predictable and fickle. Her embittered mother had assured her this was because they were males. By the time she left home she was convinced that matriarchy was the natural order of things despite what any man might claim, even a philosopher. This was a conviction she carried into her life at CAT College.

In first year she was attracted by the idea of power she found in a book in the library, but she wasn't encouraged to read more because, apparently, it fell between disciplines. The Reverend Professor Lambe asked where would the established division of intellectual labour end up if first years were allowed to study whatever fired their imaginations. Lambe assured her that the distinctions between disciplines and departments existed for reasons, which, he also assured her, were beyond her undergraduate comprehension.

During the terms that followed, despite his warnings, she evolved her understanding of power, coming to believe that she possessed a natural authority best articulated through her animal sexuality, while men were more successful at articulating ideas because they didn't believe them. Progress suspected the ancient Greeks, who were all men to a man, had invented the idea of being rational because it would allow everyone to aspire to it, safe in the confidence that no one would ever achieve this ludicrous abstract goal while they got on with what was important: the exploitation of the many by the few. Oh, but Progress could pretend she was trying to be reasonable like all the other sheep if that's what it took to succeed.

Her fingers landed on a column of saucers under the leaking sink.

In the bedroom, Rik Wallace thought for the first time since becoming Wallace he was experiencing a moment of happiness. I could learn to enjoy this academic life, he thought, leaning back on the pillows while reflecting on what could be done technically to improve the walls. He heard Progress rummaging in the kitchen before she reappeared in doorway carrying saucers, one in each hand, held out in front of her to reveal her breasts. It was obvious to Wallace that Progress was proud of her body.

He propped himself on an elbow and puffed smoke like a settler trying to appease a hostile Indian chief who had handed him a peace pipe to prove his *bona fides.* Progress now sat on the end of the bed, playing with her hair, burning through her cigarette in just three fierce inhalations.

"That was great, Julie," he said. He decided not to comment in detail on her loud exclamations of encouragement during sex, which made him think someone might be secretly filming them: perhaps Spencer, or Lambe, or Pandora, or even all three together. In the circumstances, he felt the sanest response was to be paranoid.

"Thanks, but it's not free, you know," she informed him without hesitation. She was prepared for this conversation while he was not.

"Oh. I didn't realize," he said, turning red and coughing on the smoke. "That's okay. Um … how much do I owe you?" he asked, reaching for the wallet in his trousers on the floor.

"It's not about money. I'm not some kind of whore. I want help with my doctoral research. I need your superior guidance to make sure it reaches the required standard."

"But how can I do that?" he stammered. "I don't understand." He was panicking again about yet another obvious failure in his preparation for his new academic life. How was he supposed to equip himself for the unknown?

She sighed at how obtuse he was being. "By doing the research with me. *For* me. Haven't you ever had a research student before?"

"No. You are – will be – my first," he confessed.

"I can't believe you haven't supervised doctoral students. Didn't you say you did in your CV? We have all read your CV, you know."

"I didn't mean no as in what you mean by no. I mean, I haven't supervised a doctoral student in exchange for sex before."

"Where have you been? Listen, I am fed up with my current supervisor. He is a complete jerk. Stinking breath, never washes, and he doesn't have your international publications profile. I've decided you would make a much better supervisor all round. I'll dump my current one if you agree. Won't be the first time."

"It's not Spencer, is it? I couldn't do that to him. Not on my first day."

"It's not Spencer. It's Bacon. You met him this morning. The one with the ceramic hair that goes straight up like this," she said, pushing her palms in parallel above her head.

Wallace missed the impression her hands made because he was following the movement of her breasts.

"Bacon is one of those people who wakes up on their twenty-ninth birthday with white hair and looking sixty-five years old. You know him. He interviewed you."

"Yes, him. I remember," he lied. "Seems pleasant."

"Pleasant, yes. But no influence."

"How long have you been … what can I say … uh … researching for your doctorate?"

"Almost three years. I am sick of it. But now you're here, it might be fun again. What do you say? Will you supervise my thesis?" She was jumping up and down on the bed on her hands and knees in excitement. "I have finished the first draft. All you need do is rewrite the thing. Six months tops, and you will be free of me. What do you say? Please, please." She began to tickle him.

He did know he hated being tickled. Instead of laughing, he shouted at her to stop. "Okay. Okay. I'll do it," he said. "But I'm sure you will be disappointed."

"I think you might turn out to be a brilliant supervisor." She paused, remembering an important aspect of the contract, which was exclusivity. "But if you are helping me, I don't want you sleeping with other students, especially undergraduates. Remember, I got in first, on your first day. You should respect that sort of initiative."

As he lay beside her, he was saddened that someone so young and so beautiful could be so pragmatic. "Wow. You are incredibly practical. You must be a utilitarian," he joked, gratified to be able to mention a philosophy he had found on the Internet. "Do you think I'm worth the effort for a career in business ethics which isn't even business? Wouldn't you be better off doing something else? Maybe even running an actual business?"

"You're typical of people who have achieved their goals and look down on the rest of us. It's all right for you, now that you are Mister Hotshot Professor of Moral Philosophy. I'm sure you did some things to get where you are now that you're not going to boast about."

"Yes. But I never had a deliberate plan for this career. I am an accidental moralist."

"Oh no! The celebrated professor of moral philosophy has judged me. I am officially a bad person."

"I am not in a position to judge anyone. I just think what you are doing takes a lot of effort for little reward."

"Do you think having sex with you takes a lot of effort?" she asked, coyly.

"Hopefully not."

She looked at him through a cloud of cigarette smoke.

"Come here," she said, grinding his cigarette out on the saucer that she placed on the floor beside the bed. "I think it's time for an advance on my first chapter."

She kissed him on the lips and climbed back under the sheet.

"Will you help me straighten this house out in the morning?" he asked.

"How did you end up in this slum anyway?"

"It belongs to the college. Lambe recommended it. Spencer says I can renovate if I want. I'm into DIY. I plan to knock down a few walls, build new ones, put up shelves, do a little rewiring, plaster that ceiling up there, repair the walls and maybe put down a new patio out back. But the location is good."

"Enough of boring me to death with DIY. Shut up and kiss me." She lowered her long smooth naked body onto his. "Is this what you call a dovetail joint?" she asked rotating her hips.

X

Domus Dulcis Bibliotheca
Home Sweet Library

The round-topped windows of Jim the porter and Rose the cleaner's house formed a pair of raised architectural eyebrows that gave their home an expression of resigned despair. Inside, sitting on the couch in his living room, Jim was listening to J.J. Cale's *5* at maximum volume, while Rose prepared their dinner in the kitchen.

Halfway through his after-work-four-inch joint he was beginning to substitute hidden connections in the music for those he discerned around him during the day. He believed cannabis helped his paranoia, while Rose believed it caused it. But he was against the legalization of marijuana because he couldn't imagine dealing with a student population legally high on dope. He was sixty-four years old and was hoping he could get to retirement without another major incident in his life. The joint helped him relax; that and the cans of beer. In the last few years, he was finding it harder to tolerate the students and their ever-increasing demands. They stayed forever young while he got a year older every year.

He came to CAT College because his father, the porter before him, secured him part-time work to support his own studies in another college. He was going to be a dentist. The casual power of being his father's son on campus went to his head and undermined his commitment to dentistry. He found it difficult now, years later, to remember why he was once interested in teeth. He started working full-time for his father when he failed his examinations at the end of his first year, which resulted in a life-sentence at CAT College. He was due for parole next year if the provost would let him go. She insisted the place couldn't function without him. Despite intermittent hopes, he had reconciled himself to the belief that he would die before gaining his freedom.

Jim resented everyone at CAT College because he believed that even though they were thick, they were in positions of power just because they had qualifications. Everyone bossed him around. He had more brains than any of them; definitely more brains than that new philosopher. A real imbecile if ever he met one. But the provost had always been kind to him even in difficult times. Despite her reluctance to let him go, he was unflinchingly loyal to her.

The entire wall space of the room was covered from floor to ceiling with bookshelves, every inch of which carried books with the white Dewey Decimal System tabs from the college library still on the spines. At first, he had tried to peel off these labels, but the damage caused in the effort made him change his mind. As a compromise, he planned someday to produce his own catalogue if he could only work out how to do it. If anyone walked through the house, which no one did, they would see that the walls in every room, including the kitchen and tiny bathroom under the stairs, were smothered in books that Rose had taken from the college library and staff offices during her night shifts as cleaning supervisor. Jim and Rose had long ago stopped inviting anyone from the college around to their home, despite accepting invitations to staff parties, dinners, and social occasions. There were several popular theories to account for this anti-social behaviour that the college staff exchanged amongst each other behind Rose's and Jim's backs, but none involved the possibility of a secret stolen library.

The unplanned weight of the books put an enormous strain on the old house producing a lattice of cracks in the walls behind the shelves. Floorboards made their increasing discomfort known through louder and more frequent groans. When they first moved in, the sun had lit up the white walls as if they were living in a villa on the Mediterranean coast. Now the solid dull books absorbed the light, turning the house into a labyrinth of inter-connecting caves.

Rose wasn't particular about the type of book she took from the library: she wasn't compiling a comprehensive collection in a single subject area. She justified her actions by persuading herself, as there was no one around in the middle of the night to ask, that she was merely borrowing books. While her taste was catholic, she knew Jim appreciated thick hardbacks because they filled the spaces more efficiently. Their hobby of book collecting had exhausted all possible shelf space years ago. By now there were books under tables and chairs, stacked in corners, and leaning, in the style of idle students, against doorframes. A neat cube built from a uniform multi-volume edition of nineteenth-century masters was supporting the television. Surrounded on all sides by so many books, they felt compelled to make use of some of them. Jim was reading his way through twentieth-century literary criticism, while Rose dipped into physics, marketing, advertising, and PR.

He stood up, stubbed out the joint, turned off the music and made his way to the kitchen table when Rose roared at him over the noise of his singing along to "Lou-Easy-Ann" that dinner was ready.

Rose was small and thin. The bones of her joints were visible through the sheer covering of skin on her elbows and knees, but her death-head face did give a slight impression of flesh. She dyed her short hair a shoe-polish brown not found on any animal in nature. She felt a commitment on principle, because she was a cleaner outside the house, to neglect as much as possible all domestic activities at home. The few chores she could not ignore she performed out of a sense of fondness for Jim. She knew he would have allowed himself to starve to death before washing a plate because she recognized that he was an independent spirit. However, her love for Jim, which was intuitive and not learned from the books that surrounded her, did not stretch to ironing. Both Rose and Jim were known for their wrinkled look on campus, which was the ironic sign of their mutual devotion.

Every weekday, before her night shift of supervising the cleaning of the college, Rose cooked dinner which the couple ate together in the kitchen with the radio playing in the background to drown out the sound of Jim's open-jawed chewing. She didn't enjoy cooking. She didn't relish what she cooked. And she took no satisfaction in watching her poor culinary efforts revolving like damp clothes in the dryer of Jim's gaping mouth. But their shared meal was the one time they had to gossip about college life when he had finished his day's work and before she commenced hers.

"Did you find out anything about that new philosopher, Wallace?" Jim asked.

"Not much rubbish in his wastepaper bin yet. He spends most of his time in the library reading, which I suppose is odd."

"Anything at all of interest in the bin?"

"Just a few pages of scribbles. Doodles, lists of this and that, including building supplies, diagrams, and sketches of some woman called Della. Also, he was reminding himself that he had to try to stop smoking and drinking."

"He staggered across my lawn to reception today, asking if he could borrow my ladders."

"On his desk there was a list of questions he seemed to be addressing to himself on what Wallace would do. I suppose philosophers write to themselves if no one else will. I heard he wrote to Maurice Spencer asking if it was all right for him to supervise that Julie Progress."

"She must be at it again. She doesn't waste time," Jim chuckled.

"He was calculating how many paving slabs he would need for the back of that house on Love Street that Lambe has put him in," Rose said, remembering the sketch of small squares on the large rectangle he had drawn in pencil. "Lambe must have it in for him moving him in there. The place is a wreck. But if he fixes it up, it has a huge sunny garden, and it is convenient. It's a great location."

"He must be burying people out back. Wouldn't be the first. Keep an eye on him. He is a queer fish."

"Why do you say that? He isn't any stranger than the rest of them in that department. That reminds me. I must buy a birthday present for Spencer's daughter Samantha? She is thirteen again."

"What did you get her last time?"

"I can't remember, but it would be embarrassing to buy her the same present."

"Anything new in other bins?" he asked, bored with Samantha Spencer.

"The provost is on a new prescription. Lambe seems to be practising her signature. She must have refused to open a joint bank account yet again."

"That's going to end badly. Very badly."

"It's not the same as it used to be with everyone using computers and e-mailing each other these days. It's not easy to follow what's going on. Time was when everyone was using paper."

"You could sit in on those computer courses in the technology faculty and learn how they work."

"I couldn't be bothered. They use passwords and all kinds of security. You'd think they had actual important secrets to keep. I'd be all night in just one office trying to break into a file. Isn't that what they're called?"

"People write down their passwords. You'd soon get to know them all, love. You're a clever old girl."

"I'll think about it. Still. I'm getting old. Hard to keep up."

"The golden age of paper is over. Do you remember when Pandora used to write all those anonymous threatening notes to Lambe? You couldn't do that with e-mail. You can't do better than a note made from letters cut from a newspaper if you want to frighten someone."

"Pandora would kill me if she ever found out how much I

have learned about her so-called secret life over the years."

"She would kill us both."

"But we're not judgmental. We are students of the human condition. When you think about it, we are disinterested anthropologists gathering research from everyone's bins."

"They were great days when everyone used paper."

They ate without speaking for several minutes.

"Do you need anything from the library?" Rose asked. "Last night I saw that the librarian put up another huge notice warning the students about the unacceptable level of book losses. Those students should be ashamed of themselves. Most of them aren't even interested in reading. No curiosity about books. It's all websites with them. The librarian is old school though. She likes to use the written word."

"If you see anything substantial on the eighteenth-century Romantic poets you might pick it up. It would fill a gap."

"We don't have a gap."

"I thought we might bring a few books from the attic over to Young Rose and her fella at the weekend. It might improve their minds to read something historical."

"I'll have a look, but I might not have time tonight. Nothing but parties, functions, and meetings on campus these days to clean up after."

"I don't know why they bother. It's a total waste of energy, if you ask me. Don't forget to check Wallace's bin again, and if you find anything exciting bring it home," Jim told her as he kissed her on the cheek when she stood up to leave the table. "Will you rinse the plates? I thought I might take a look at some Keats before catching the nine o'clock news."

XI

Nobiles Barbari
Noble Savages

Pandora was wearing a pink-and-white cotton dressing gown with the collar clutched in her hand under her chin, a work file balanced on her knees. Her cat clawed at a page with his sharp nails, meowing, competing for her attention. Marlboro was his competition name, but at home, Pandora called him Marley. She stroked the fur on his back while exhaling plumes of cigarette smoke.

"Stop it, Marley. I need to read this. I've told you before, I don't want the provost to think I do any work. That's why I sneak these files home. I'm sorry, but that's how it is. I don't want to give her the impression I'm grateful to have such an important job, which means I can afford those delicious pouches of cat food you love."

For the last week Marley had been experiencing difficulty breathing, but then everyone and everything had difficulty breathing around Pandora. She had scheduled an appointment with the vet next morning. Marley didn't know, and she wasn't going to tell him because she knew he would worry. She would do the worrying for both of them.

Just then the doorbell rang. "Now who could that be?" she

asked Marley – rhetorically, of course, because she had been waiting for her visitor with a level of excitement that surprised her. She threw the file aside and gently placed Marley on his feet on the floor, put on her black sunglasses, and went to open the front door. Spencer was standing outside clutching a large black plastic bag.

"Do you have much time?" she asked.

"Yes. I have all night. Samantha is on a sleepover."

Behind her sunglasses Pandora rolled her eyes skywards.

She closed the door behind Spencer as he walked down the hall. He turned around when he reached the bedroom door, opened the plastic bag, and took out a large off-the-shoulder fur dress. "This is for you. And these," he added, handing her a pair of sandals, a worn leather rope, and a white plastic dog bone.

She stared at the dress. "The Flintstones? We're doing the Flintstones. You didn't tell me on the phone it was the Flintstones."

"It's not the Flintstones. We're cave men. I mean, cave *people*. Technically, we are Rousseau's noble savages. Not the Hobbesian savages whose lives are solitary, poor, nasty, brutish, and short. Not those ones. We are the more idealistic version. If you want to be historically precise, perhaps Rousseau didn't invent the idea of the noble savage, but for the sake of our role play, I thi—"

"I warned you before. If you make this philosophical, you will turn me right off, and you can go home now. I'll settle for the Flintstones."

"I told you on the phone we are going back to our primeval roots."

"I didn't know what you were saying. I heard something about our evil roots."

"Here. Take this," he said, pulling a large rubber club from the bottom of the plastic bag. You get ready in your bedroom. I'll get dressed, or should I say undressed, out here. Then I will burst into your cave, and we will take it from there. Okay?"

"Fine. But no philosophy."

Pandora placed her cigarette between her lips, tucked the dress and sandals under her arm, took the rubber club from Spencer, and went into the bedroom, closing the door behind her.

Outside in the hall Spencer pulled off his clothes. He wrapped a leather rectangle around his waist that formed a skirt hanging just below his knees. Next, he put his hands through two holes in a large fake bison skin. He raised his arms and jiggled until his head came through a larger hole in the middle. Then he sat on the floor and bound two strips of leather around his shins, tying them in place with rough laces. By the time he stood up, he heard Pandora shouting through the door that she was ready.

Marlboro began to wrap himself around the irresistible scratching post that was Spencer's leather-bound left leg.

"Piss off, Marley," Spencer hissed, kicking out at the cat with the bare toes of his free right foot. Marlboro howled before lapsing into a fit of coughing.

"What are you doing out there?"

"Nothing. I'm ready now. Are you rigged out?" he shouted through the door. "Go away, Marley," he told the cat under his breath. "Don't screw things up for me this evening."

"I'm ready, Igor," Pandora shouted. "Come and get some

furry mammoth."

Spencer decided to throw himself against the door – as any self-respecting caveman would. He bounced off it, landing on his woollen back on the carpet. Cursing, he got to his feet and turned the door handle. Inside, Pandora was jumping up and down on the bed waving her rubber club. She was wearing the one-piece fur dress bound at her waist with the leather rope. Her hair was tied up around the plastic dog bone. She was wearing her sunglasses.

"Lose the glasses, Pandora. We must get completely into the cave mood. It has to be authentic. We're supposed to be savages."

"Spencer. I warned you about philosophizing. Just shut up."

"Is the camera going?"

"Yes, the camera is going." She swiped at him with the club, missed, and laughed. She leaped into the air making a noise she thought sounded primitive and landed in front of him on the bed with her fur dress riding up her buttocks. "Stick your bone in there, Igor," she told him.

Spencer stared between her wide-apart legs.

"A Brazilian? You got a Brazilian," he shouted. "You are supposed to be a hairy cave woman."

Pandora sat up. "I didn't know I was going to be Wilma bloody Flintstone. When you said evil, I thought it would be something Satanic. A Brazilian is … well … evil."

"Prim-e-val. I said *prime*-ee-val. Not *ev*-il," Spencer shouted each syllable. "Cavemen were our noble savage ancestors. They were good guys. You never listen."

"I was hoping we would do something contemporary. I'm

sick of all this historical stuff. You made me be a nineteenth-century farmer the last time."

"We were astronauts in space last month. That was your idea. I supposed you washed too," Spencer moaned. "What did I say before about washing? Most people in history never washed. Hygiene is a recent phenomenon. Cavemen … people … didn't wash. How can we get into character if you smell of soap? You're not in earnest about our relationship."

"I could wash if we were Satanists. I'm sure Satanists are hygienic. I have to wash. I go to work every day. People would talk."

"They don't talk about me."

"That's what you think. They're not going to tell you that you stink, are they? I have been trying not to wash my feet. Do you want to smell them?"

"No," he said sulking. "I'm not into feet."

"Pity. I think that's a corn. Is that a corn? You could lick it if you want."

Spencer didn't respond. They sat together in silence on the end of the bed.

"Anyway, you're not hairy enough for a caveman," Pandora said. "Look at those legs. And you have no chest hair. How would a hairless person come up with the idea of being Fred Flintstone?"

"A noble savage! Noble savages don't have to be hairy."

"Oh, yeah. But I'm supposed to be hairy. Did you even put on a chest wig? No. Typical. That bitch in the salon enjoyed ripping off those strips of wax. Look. You can still see how red my skin is down there. You wouldn't believe the pain. I wouldn't give her the satisfaction of screaming just to gratify her sadism. You should try it sometime."

"Was it unbearable?"

"Yes."

"Do you have wax?"

"I'll look in the bathroom. Stay there. Don't move, Igor."

XII

Domus Dulcis Domus
Home Sweet Home

Three weeks of cloudy days had scudded by since Rik Wallace's first appearance in CAT College. On each grey morning in his office in the philosophy department, while studying to catch up on the missing years of knowledge, he expected to find Inspector Jackson and his partner standing side by side in front of him every time he looked up from his books. Instead, he could now see the top of the aluminium extension ladder through his window where he had left it leaning against the wall outside. He had covered a large square with yellow paint before his arm began to ache. The intensity of the pain measured against the enormous expanse of still unpainted wall persuaded him to abandon the project. Jim the porter had carried the ladder to the department, happy to loan it to him on the condition that he promised to fall off and break his academic neck. Now he tried to ignore the ladder, which was making him feel guilty, to concentrate on other worries. When not panicking about the police, he worried that Maurice Spencer would burst in, waving his CV in his face, shouting that he was an impostor.

That first post-coital cigarette with Progress had ignited

a forty-a-day habit. His routine included visiting Pandora at noon to smoke a cigarette with her, enquire after her health, and the health of the secretary of the commerce faculty. He convinced himself he was winning her over as an ally through a shared interest in smoking. She even confided her worry about her beloved Marlboro's cough. He received this news with an over-elaborate straight face and asked that his best wishes be passed on to the cat. Despite this conspicuous confidence, most of their time passed in silence, exhaling nicotine-laden smoke, while each pondered their separate unshared troubles.

Wallace was drinking two bottles of wine each evening with Julie Progress who, having dumped Bacon as her supervisor, moved in with him on Love Street. She was supposed to await the formal permission of the Academic Board to approve the change of supervisor but she wasn't anticipating a problem with her application, this being her fourth such request. Besides, as she explained to Wallace, she hadn't been able to live with Bacon who shared his house with his wife and six children. This new arrangement would save her rent. She expressed surprise that he didn't appear at all interested in how rational she was being in her approach to supervision.

He had found the college library by following a sequence of blue signs. The head librarian was on sentry duty behind the issuing desk and not, as usual, sequestered in her office surrounded by columns of books piled on the floor queuing to be catalogued. She was tall and skeletal with her hair cut in a fat bob that cast a mushroom shadow. She chose her woollen clothes with care to give the impression that she was a hundred years older than she was. When he asked her for a copy of everything that he had ever written, she shattered the silence by exclaiming that he must be the vainest member of staff, a position for which, she assured him, the competition was intense in that institution.

He had looked around the library while she shouted at him. Large signs hung above the few huddled heads demanding that patrons refrain from eating, drinking, and talking either to each other or to persons not necessarily present in the library at that time via mobile phones. Those bored with their own studies could distract themselves browsing the various notices setting out the library regulations that were placed strategically for maximum visibility. Patrons were reminded the library was a place of study and not of socialization. Rules specifying the number of books that could be borrowed at the same time and the intervals for which they could be removed from the library depending on how far aspirant borrowers had progressed through their studies were printed in large letters on signs attached to every exposed surface. Fines, punishments and threats were detailed on long posters on the backs of doors. Only the head librarian had a perfect memory for all of the regulations, which she could recall when needed against anyone attempting to subvert the order of things without even resorting to the thick rule book she made available each year to first-year students.

Wallace sat in the library on the damp afternoons reading his books. In his own uninformed criticism, he felt he should have written less, and more to the point. He promised himself that, once he had familiarized himself with his subject matter, he would take his writing in a new direction, which would involve fewer rambling asides and footnotes and shorter titles. When he told Progress, she laughed and reminded him that long-titled research was *de rigour* amongst the leading researchers in his field. He spent time preparing his lectures or attempting to rewrite the first draft chapter of Progress's doctoral thesis when not studying himself in the library. She was trying to convince him she needed a real moral problem to form the basis of her research rather than just an abstract philosophical analysis of morality. She informed him it was now his responsibility, as her supervisor, to identify a suitable moral dilemma for him to work on for her.

He delivered his first lecture ever on the third day of his second week to the first-year commerce students. He was relieved that it had gone better than he expected because, surprisingly, the students seemed to know even less than him about either business or ethics. For most of his allotted hour he improvised on details of Socrates' suicide by hemlock which he had looked up online. He hoped that by drawing their attention to the form of his discourse he would distract them from its lack of content. The students didn't seem to notice his lecture was really a one-man play with a lot of arm movements.

He had also begun to renovate his new home. His order of plasterboard, plywood, lengths of wooden batons, bags of plaster, filler, tape, screws, nails, glue, bricks, cement and sand, paving slabs, and gravel, along with a variety of copper pipes and electrical wires had been delivered on the first Saturday morning from the local builder's merchant. He used his credit cards to pay for a large box of tools, a variety of power saws, drills, and a router. He began in the kitchen. While the powerless cooker stood in the middle of the floor, he ate in the college canteen at lunchtime, while he and Progress shared takeaway food in the evenings, which they washed down with wine. He was also drinking a half bottle of indigestion medicine a day to deal with his heartburn, which had started the moment Progress appeared at his door with her belongings in black plastic bags.

Sometimes, when heartburn woke him, he got out of bed to work on the kitchen. In the dead of night, he would pause in his sawing lengthwise through a sheet of plywood, light a cigarette, and allow his thoughts on tile cutting and wooden flooring to float in front of him on the smoke while the complexities of thesis supervision, Socratic philosophy, Nietzsche and cornflakes, and arguments on the pros and cons of euthanasia drifted to the back of his mind. He conjured up a spectral sense of his old self when labouring under the feeble glow of the weak bulb that illuminated his night shift in the ruins of the kitchen on Love Street: the details were fading in direct proportion to the growth of his nostalgia for them. But, when he woke to the virile daylight of each new morning, he felt relieved that his attempts to saw and hammer his way back home were less and less effective with each day of philosophizing.

XIII

Publico Auditorio
A Public Lecture

The hall allocated to Rik Wallace's formal inaugural lecture was furnished with rows of wooden seats with ledges running along the back of each to support the notebooks and computer tablets of those behind. Light oak panelling covered the walls halfway to the ceiling. Its old-fashioned sombre décor made it a fitting venue in which to launch a pedagogic career.

It wasn't the largest lecture hall in CAT College. Pandora, confident he wouldn't fill the biggest on a Wednesday night, or indeed on any night, had put him here. Nevertheless, despite her doubts, the room was crowded. Students who had given up their seats to ingratiate themselves with lecturers were sitting on the steps on the aisles. From his chair behind the table at the top of the room Wallace could scan the faces in the crowd. He was relieved to recognize only a few. Patricia the provost was sitting beside him, waiting to make the formal introduction. The Reverend Professor Lambe sat holding her hand for moral support. Wallace couldn't tell who was supporting whom. Maurice Spencer was in the middle of the front row smiling at him and waving in the manner of an overexcited schoolboy. Earlier, in the hall outside, Spencer had reminded him not to mention Nietzsche. Progress sat between Pandora and Spencer. She was becoming complacent in her proprietorial role in his new life.

A woman sat in the middle of the fourth row wearing a headscarf and a blue woollen coat buttoned up to the neck despite the rising temperature in the room generated by the crush of bodies and the ancient iron radiators under the windows. The woman in the headscarf looked familiar. He was convinced he had seen her before, but he couldn't remember where. Was she someone from his former life?

Wallace looked up towards the emptiness of the ceiling to calm his nerves. High up in the corners the small black spiders went about their business indifferent to what was happening below. From the blackness, number, and density of their webs they appeared to have been up there since the hall was first built. Wallace imagined these must be the wisest spiders in the world if learning was just exposure to thought. If only he had access to a fraction of the knowledge that they ignored every day in favour of concentrating on trapping hapless flies. He empathized with those flies, gripped in a sticky web. But his web was of his own weaving.

His arachnid reverie was interrupted by the commotion made by someone insisting a half-row stand up in the narrow stall to allow her to squeeze past into an empty seat near the middle. His heart lurched when he recognized Della. She smiled, revealing perfect white teeth, and blew him a kiss when she saw that she had caught his eye. "Good luck," she mouthed.

He scanned the rest of the crowd expecting to see Inspector Jackson with his enthusiastic partner waving a pair of handcuffs at him from the back row. Then he noticed the woman in the headscarf was staring intently at him. Where had he seen her before? He needed a cigarette. Wasn't she boiling in that coat? He was roasting in his shirt and jacket. Had he time for a cigarette before he was supposed to start? Maybe he still had time to run away. What was he doing there in front of the entire college about to be unmasked as a philosophical fraud and a murderer? Had Della come to expose him in public because she thought that would be more fun than a discreet arrest? The new professor of moral philosophy hauled off to jail in handcuffs!

He had just made up his mind to run when the thrumming crowd went silent as the provost stood up. He had learned during his social cigarette breaks with Pandora that if the provost wore blue it signified that she was in a compliant humour. If she wore red, it meant she was completely stressed. Tonight, she was wearing a bright red suit with a red scarf and red shoes. Lambe held her by the elbow as they made their way together to the lectern. Wallace still couldn't tell who was supporting whom. Lambe stood beside the provost smiling at the audience as she spoke, nodding here and there for emphasis. He vigorously nodded whenever he was in agreement with a particular point in her speech, the entire of which he had written himself.

"Respected guests, colleagues, my dear students, ladies and gentlemen, welcome to the inaugural lecture of our newest member of staff, Professor Rik Wallace." She sounded bored, almost asleep from the tranquilizers she used when called-upon to speak in public. "I am excited at the prospect of his talk entitled 'Measuring the Consequences of our Actions, a New Approach'," she said, without any evidence of excitement.

"Professor Wallace is an expert on moral consequences. He has published widely on the topic and enjoys a growing international reputation. But morality is not just an abstract concept for him; he has embodied it through his behaviour. He sets us a high moral example by his tireless campaigning for animal rights and his veganism."

Wallace recalled with horror the beef stew he so publicly spooned into his mouth at lunchtime in the canteen. He wondered if anyone in the audience remembered. Thank God, he thought, neither the provost nor Lambe ever took their meals in public.

"He is also an outspoken critic of both the drink and tobacco industries." He gulped water from the glass in front of him to suppress his new tobacco-induced bronchitis. His hand moved to his pocket to smooth the bulge of his cigarette packet. "Rik Wallace came to prominence as a graduate student under the supervision of Professor Amanda Wearing."

Another one I have to look up online, he thought.

"Professor Wearing praised him as the most original of her crop of brilliant graduates. He rose through the ranks of academia, relentlessly building his reputation in moral philosophy. At the pinnacle of his moral powers, he chose to come here to enlighten our students in business ethics when he could have gone anywhere. While we may never understand his motives, we can rejoice in his decision. I want you to join with me in extending him the warmest CAT College welcome. I give you Professor Rik Wallace."

The crowd applauded while the provost and Lambe helped each other back to their seats.

Wallace stood at the lectern.

The woman in the blue coat removed her headscarf while everyone else was clapping.

Wallace recognized her from the photograph in the briefcase back at the hotel: she was his mother. The entire content of his lecture vanished from his mind as the strength abandoned his legs.

The applause lasted several minutes as it was motivated by a general desire to appease the provost in her red outfit rather than to make Wallace feel welcome. Everyone in the college, even the dimmest student, understood the semiotics of the provost's clothes. The crowd expected Wallace to begin when the noise subsided because that was the well-understood convention of public lectures in CAT College. But he didn't. Minutes passed in a silence broken by the random coughing of the few smokers peppered here and there throughout the audience.

Wallace dared not look in the direction of his mother. Even without understanding any epistemology he knew she would know he was not the son she thought she knew.

He began to speak when, finally, the non-smokers joined the smokers in a general barrage of coughing.

"My philosophy is guided by a simple imperative: do as I say, not as I do because behaviour should be judged, not on what I seem to be doing, however that may appear to you, but on the consequences of that behaviour. We must measure outcomes and not what we thought we were doing – or what you thought I was doing, which cannot be measured anyway. How would we even know what our intentions are supposed to be? We would need to consult a psychologist every time we decided to do something to check if we knew what we thought we were doing. We can be mistaken about our intentions. We can forget what we thought they were. We can lie about them. We can discover new ones to justify our actions after the fact. Okay. Yes. I have taken up smoking, drinking, and eating meat. But I did that to discover first-hand what the consequences of those habits are, rather than relying on someone else to suffer those consequences on my behalf. In other words, my smoking, drinking, and eating meat are my moral sacrifices for the benefit of mankind. My death will deter others if I die as a result of my new habits, and in that way, will produce a morally good consequence from my behaviour. I plan to document my decline. In particular, I plan to drink for research. It's all right for me. I'm not some ordinary drunk. I am drinking for philosophical reasons."

A scattering of meek applause from the audience mingled with some murmuring. Wallace was unable to tell if the murmuring was the sort that signified approval or the type that preceded a riot because he was no expert in the sorts of noises that emanated from audiences.

"Measuring the consequences of our actions is very complicated. Not the same as gauging the length of a piece of timber or weighing out aggregates. There are countless variations involved in calculating behaviour because moral philosophy is difficult; not an exact science like engineering. By the way, you would be surprised how much I know about engineering. Anyway, if an action results in an unplanned benefit for society we think of it as a good, even where the person performing it could not have foreseen those consequences. If an action, by convention regarded as evil, avoids a significant amount of suffering and pain in the future, is it morally good conduct?

For example, if someone strangles a child, that person would be condemned as a villain by the law, religion and society. To me it seems strangling some young people should be regarded as good, and I imagine most of you would agree, because we don't know whether we will be better or worse off that the so-called victim is no longer with us: we can't tell what they might have done to society had they lived. This is true even for the killing of a professor of moral philosophy. Who can say if we would have been better off without him? Same as strangling a child who would grow up to be a monster, killing a crazy academic might be regarded in a future possible world as a good thing. Therefore, if it's morally acceptable to kill a child who would grow into an adult monster, isn't it also right to kill a professor if we could see into the future. Just because we can't make accurate predictions doesn't mean we can't make an intelligent guess about the moral consequences of every so-called murder. It seems obvious on the basis of statistical probability alone we would be better off without at least half the population. In practice, I am not condoning strangling children; I am just urging us not to rush to judgement." He paused to slurp water from the glass in front of him. By now he had departed from his prepared notes and was improvising. "What am I talking about?" he asked his audience as a trickle of sweat ran down his spine.

"Child murderer," someone shouted while the rest of his audience stared at him in silence. He thought he recognized Pandora's hoarse tobacco voice. He continued to improvise on his theme hoping to start making sense soon. "Some consider ending the suffering of those who are terminally ill by euthanasia to be a morally justifiable act, even if it goes against the commandment 'thou shalt not kill'. Likewise, many think that killing someone who threatens us, or our loved ones, is justified as self-defence. If the state takes the life of someone who has killed an innocent person, we don't punish the state. We debate whether capital punishment is a good act based on its effect as a deterrent. From these few examples, we can conclude nothing is good or bad in the act of killing in itself. The consequence of killing is what makes it right or wrong."

"Godless maniac," someone shouted from the audience.

Wallace thought it came from the direction of his mother. By now, he felt he was defending himself in the dock. Stick with your notes and stop improvising, he told himself. But by then he couldn't find the page he was supposed to be on. He couldn't focus his eyes to read through the film of sweat that covered his face.

"How long should we wait before deciding whether killing someone is a good or bad act based on its consequences? While we can't wait forever, surely, we can hold on longer than it takes to make an arrest and convene a trial? We should use our own judgement and not that of the church, law or state. Moral philosophy is not interested in what is practical. Yes. The law, society, and religion can all be practical, but are they *philosophical?* These should be changed or abandoned if they don't take into account the particular circumstance. I am not talking about what is right or wrong in the eyes of the law – we are all familiar with the law – or in the eyes of God. I am only concerned with the abstract basis of our actions. Where our motives are pure, by acting in a way we think is correct, we are behaving in a morally justifiable way even when we don't know what our motives or intentions are, which we wouldn't know anyway in another system of morals. Look, you can't say it's wrong when we don't even know what we are doing." He trailed off into mumbling.

"Speak up for God's sake," someone shouted from the back of the audience.

He wondered where these ideas were coming from? He was fascinated that he couldn't stop talking. Swathes of the vast amount of moral information he had read online were percolating through his consciousness like methane rising off a swamp.

"We should be guided by the principle that by our individual and collective actions we are trying to improve the quality of life in our society by removing evil people, even if we don't know for certain who they are," he shouted.

A member of the audience too impatient to wait for the scheduled question and answer session yelled back "Are you a vigilante?"

He leaned forward over the lectern and persisted with his argument even though he had long since ceased to know what he was saying. He would have been more relaxed had he realized he was making a favourable impression on a sizeable minority of the audience, including Pandora and Spencer. The latter had put aside his notebook, listening and nodding with enthusiasm. Spencer felt that, at last, he had found one of the elusive truths where he hadn't expected it to be, which he then realized was where he should have been looking in the first place. Pandora took off her sunglasses, polished the lenses, and put them back on before anyone could catch sight of her varicose eyes. She was studying Wallace closely with a new interest.

"It is good if a horrible person dies and is replaced by a nicer person. Surely it is also good if anyone, good or bad, is killed and replaced by someone who tries to be a better version of that person. What I am trying to say is this: if you kill someone, say by accident, even if it doesn't appear that way at the time, that's not necessarily wrong because it depends on what happens afterwards. It's good if that death benefits society. Just don't be quick to judge."

He looked out at his audience and saw his mother looking back at him through slitted eyes. Della smiled and held up both her thumbs when he caught her eye. Meanwhile Progress was taking notes she hoped would pad out her thesis. He exhaled and continued with his improvisation.

"If, for example, a lecturer let's say, ah … dies … and is replaced by someone who at least tries harder, that's good, isn't it? If an incompetent academic is killed to allow the majority of lecturers to do their jobs better, and in turn, inspire their students to live happier and more productive lives, we can see that the measure of the good moral consequences outweighs the bad. Even if the judgement that led to the original killing is faulty; even if alcohol was involved, and the intention was misguided or unknowable, the good outcome justifies it."

"Lunatic. Dangerous lunatic," was bellowed from the crowd.

Wallace couldn't tell but he hoped it was one energetic critic rather than a majority. "Take Socrates," he persisted without pausing. "Socrates could not have foretold his suicide would have catapulted him into countless books all over the world for the benefit of generations of students. That makes his killing himself a good thing which at the time in ancient

Greece no one realized, except perhaps Plato, who wanted to cash in on his ideas anyway."

Lambe was on his feet, swaying from side to side. "Stop this nonsense," he cried. "I mean, we have heard enough, Professor Wallace. Thank you. That is plenty for us to be going on with. That is sufficient for anyone's mind to have to assimilate on a Wednesday night. Thank you very much. Can we have a round of applause for Professor Wallace?" He let go of the table he was using to steady himself and clapped his hands together starting a ripple of applause that crawled out of the room like an embarrassed iguana.

Wallace left the lectern without waiting for questions because he was ignorant of the academic protocol of allowing his audience to recover from the indignity of having had to listen to him by subjecting him, in turn, to their ideas. He abandoned the frustrated questioners, who had been composing and rehearsing their questions in their minds from the moment he had begun to speak as a satisfying distraction from what he had been saying. He marched straight into the room next door where the post-lecture reception was laid out. Along one wall there was a table loaded with glasses of wine and plates of canapés. The wait staff, who were huddled talking in a corner as he approached the table, spread out in panic, running to take up their posts when they realized the lecture had ended ahead of schedule. He picked up a glass of white wine, drank it down in one swallow and picked up another.

Students in search of free food and drink streamed into the room and fanned out, ignoring Wallace. Spencer appeared next, while a large knot of academics formed outside to tell each other how shocked and outraged they were that Wallace had not taken questions. What in the world was academia coming to, they asked each other? Spencer crossed the room to Wallace, ignoring one waiter who was holding a tray of canapés out to him and another who was trying to hand him a glass of wine. "I thought it was extraordinary, and the audience's response was positive. They listened, which is encouraging. I was delighted you mentioned Socrates. That should put the Reverend Professor Lambe in a good mood."

Pandora came in next. She was out of breath. "I was more interested in your views on killing incompetent academics than what you had to say about philosophy. Too much talk and not enough action in your department," she said looking at Spencer.

"I must go," Spencer said. "I am already late for Samantha's parent–teacher meeting."

When Spencer had disappeared, Pandora reached into her handbag and pulled out a silver cup mounted on a black plastic base crowned with a gold medallion. "I liked what you said about killing people. I want you to have this as a memento of your lecture. I had it in my office. I ran over there and got it just now. Marley won it in a competition two years ago for coming third in his breed. It has his name on the plate on the bottom but you can take it off and put your own name on. He won't mind." She handed the trophy to Wallace. They both blushed.

By then the rest of the audience had started to flow into the reception and gather around Wallace. He turned to face the woman in the headscarf.

"Mother? What are you doing here? I mean. It's wonderful to see you." He leaned over and kissed her on one wrinkled cheek and then on the other in the manner of a Latin generalissimo greeting a long-standing rival whom he had just realized had not in fact been shot by firing squad, as rumour had it.

She pushed him away and said, "I came here because you didn't write or call. It's obvious you have changed since you took up this job. Changed in ways I would never have imagined possible, even by your standards." A menacing smile produced even more wrinkles on her crinkled face.

"You had better come home with me, mother dear, where I can explain everything."

Then Progress was at his elbow. "Who is this?" she enquired.

"Julie, this is my mother … aah, Mrs Wallace. Mother this is my … erm … graduate student, Julie Progress."

"Oh, it's good to meet you. You must be proud of your son," Progress said in the condescending tone she reserved for talking to undergraduates, the sick, children, domesticated animals, and the elderly.

"Another whore you have picked up?" Mrs Wallace asked her son in her only tone, which was curt.

"You are coming home with me now," he said, shoving Marlboro's trophy into his pocket to allow him wrap his fingers around her skinny arm. He forced his way through the crowd, shaking hands with his free hand, and explaining he had to leave unexpectedly due to the domestic crisis caused by the sudden but always welcome arrival of his dear frail mother. While dragging her towards the door, he was looking around in vain for Della. He hoped to avoid the provost and Lambe but, distracted by his search, he walked straight into them standing in the doorway.

"I enjoyed your talk, Rik. It was … erm … *thought-*

provoking," the provost said, ending her sentence decisively.

"A load of bollix, if you ask me," Lambe said. "Typical of the kind of non-sense you philosophers come out with. But I was glad to see you didn't ignore Socrates, who was the only sensible philosopher ever, including all living ones I might add. But the idea his killing himself was a good thing – what rubbish will philosophy come out with next? If I had my way," he said, emphasizing his point by poking Wallace in the chest with a long bony finger, "I'd have the whole lot of you—"

"What is that in your pocket? Did you win a prize?" the provost interrupted before Lambe could inform Wallace of the details of his resolution to the problem of philosophers.

"It's a present from Pandora," he said, wriggling it free and raising it to eye level. "It seems my talk affected her."

"That is impressive. Pandora is not easily affected."

"It belonged to her cat, Marlboro."

"Oh. That means so much to her. I am delighted with her attitude. What a lovely gesture."

Lambe rolled his eyes.

"Come and visit me in my office," the provost said. "Just a social call. I haven't seen you since you got here," she added, seeing he looked alarmed at the suggestion.

"Come in the mornings," Lambe said. "I am always there in the mornings."

With Wallace's mother clamped in his grip he thought it unlikely he would ever be able to take up the invitation. "I'll call by the first chance I get," he lied. "I need to take my mother home. She's tired. You know mothers. She could say anything to anyone."

"I'm not crazy," Mrs Wallace snapped.

"See what I mean?"

Lambe scrutinized her as if she was a candidate for a yet unoccupied stage in his taxonomy of human evolution. "I never imagined someone with your moral outlook would be concerned about their mother. Nothing can compare to the love of a son for his mother. God's most precious blessing. Cherish your mother and hold her tight to your bosom and never let her go. I never had the privilege of clasping my mother in my arms," Lambe said, plaintively. "She died giving birth to me. She was fifty-three. Selfish bitch."

"You told me she ran away with the milkman," the provost said, annoyed at his long-standing deception.

"Yes, she did. But by then she was metaphorically dead to me, anyway. Imagine having a baby at that age. She should have died."

"Your mother must care for you very much if she came all this way to see you tonight," the provost told Wallace, ignoring both Lambe and Mrs Wallace.

"Yes, she must," Wallace replied squeezing Mrs Wallace's arm. "We have to leave now. Goodnight."

The academics had looked forward to arguing with Wallace at the reception. He was unaware that he had inadvertently made an outstanding contribution to his intellectual reputation by his early exit. As they drank and argued, the noise in the room got louder. The effects of alcohol produced a collective conclusion amongst them that, had Wallace been there, he would have had the genius to recognize the brilliance of what they would have said in the lecture if they had been him.

XIV

Para Exitum Tuum
A Do-It-Yourself Exit

Mrs Wallace spoke only to say she had left a suitcase at the porter's lodge for safekeeping. After collecting it, they took a taxi on the short journey from the college to Love Street. The trip passed in silence except for the repetitive swish of the windscreen wipers. However, the moment the front door closed behind them, she said, "I was disappointed when my son became an academic. One day he tells me he's becoming a moral philosopher. Just like that. I was totally unprepared. Our family has always kept as far away from both learning and morals as possible. What a disappointment he was to his poor father when he was alive. Didn't care that generations of Wallaces before him have invested so much effort in building up the family business. Pah. Ungrateful bastard."

"What business is that?"

"Crime. Crime," she shouted at him, waving a clenched fist. "Where is he? What have you done with him?" she asked, changing the subject. "Who are you anyway? Is this one of his cons? Doesn't matter what education he has because he will always be a conman. It's in his blood. Has he gone skiving off somewhere and got you involved in one of his swindles?

He's my own son but he's a bastard," she spat. But then her mood changed. "I always said he was the smartest one of us. A chip off the old block," she said, pointing to her own chest. As suddenly as she had become angry, she was calm again, seemingly anxious to reminisce on her prodigal son. "We did overindulge him, his father and me, when he was growing up. We gave him everything he asked for. We even allowed him go to school, and then university, just because it was what he wanted. And that was how he repaid us: he became a bloody moral philosopher."

"Can I take your coat?"

"No. I'll keep it on. This place is freezing."

"Do you want a drink?" he asked, trying to buy time, but for what he couldn't imagine.

She hesitated. "Yes. Tea would be fine. Milk and two sugars."

"I am sorry about the mess. I am putting in a new wall to separate the kitchen from the living room. After that I plan to redo the bathroom and renovate the garden. It's going to look fantastic. *Was* Rik a DIY enthusiast?"

She was now confident she was dealing with an idiot. "No. He was useless with a hammer and nails." She stopped to change direction again. "What do you mean *was*? Is he dead? What have you done with him?"

He ignored her questions.

"Sit down while I make tea."

He put two teacups, two saucers that didn't match each other or the cups, an unrelated sugar bowl and a bottle of milk on a battered tin tray in front of her on the table. While waiting for the kettle to boil on the floor in the kitchen he shouted a question from behind the half-built partition. "How did you find me?"

"It wasn't difficult. Even though I don't approve of Rik's choice of career, he keeps me informed about how successful he is. Just to annoy me I suppose. He told me he was starting work at CAT College. I rang when he didn't phone or text, and a helpful man called Jim told me he was speaking tonight. I decided to come here and see for myself. I thought I'd surprise Rik, but it seems I was the one got the bigger surprise. I'm moving in with him. I'm too old and tired to make my own way anymore. I brought my things with me," she said, tilting her chin in the direction of her suitcase. "Such as they are." She sniffed and dabbed a tissue against the tip of her nose. "I can't trust anyone left back there. No one cares about me anymore."

"It's a long story but for reasons I can't explain I have taken over his job and …er … identity. He is not here, and I don't expect to see him soon. You can't stay with me. As you can see this place is falling down. I have a live-in student I'm supervising. There is no room for a mother, my own or anyone else's."

He put the teapot down beside the tin tray. She didn't respond. Instead, she began to fill one of the cups with pale hot liquid.

"You might want to leave that brew."

"I prefer it weak. Same as the men in my life." She paused for effect before continuing outlining her business plan. "I want half of what you are paid by the college. I am going to live here with you in this house, which I am sure will be great when it's finished. I want you to fix me up a bedroom. I'm too young and active to stay in that place where they put me, surrounded by all those crazy old people. Nothing but bloody bingo. This house will make a perfect headquarters and later a retirement home when I'm good and ready. I can't think of a better location than CAT College because from what I saw of that crowd tonight, the place is full of suckers."

He was standing beside her but slightly behind. He watched her slug-shaped lips curl around the rim of the cup to suck up the tea. He picked up a yard length of un-planed softwood timber that stood beside the half-built wall he designed to separate the dining area from the kitchen in an attempt to modernize the internal layout of the house. The short beam was intended to brace two uprights that he had installed the day before. He took aim at the grey spherical bun of hair sticking out of the back of Mrs Wallace's head. He hit the bun so sweetly that, if it had been a ball, it would have sped off into the distance to loud cheering from an appreciative crowd. But there were no sports fans present.

Mrs Wallace's head pitched forward onto the table as the cup of tea she had been holding to her lips broke against the far wall.

He stood over her body for several minutes wondering what to do next. He looked around. He saw the wires hanging from the ceiling and remembered that he had been working in the attic; or rather, the musty loft where Mrs Wallace's drying-apple body could now shrivel, losing its moisture over time.

He grabbed her by the large lapels of her blue woollen coat and heaved her to her feet. He threw her across his shoulder and tottered to the rickety wooden stepladder under the open loft trapdoor located at the end of the dark hall that led to the two bedrooms in the single-storey house. Progress and he occupied the room on the right. The door on the left opened only a few inches because it was filled with old furniture.

He carried Mrs Wallace up the nearside of the ladder as if he was a fireman who had changed his mind and was returning someone he had just rescued to the blaze. He squeezed through the narrow opening, and when his waist cleared the frame of the trapdoor, he pushed her into the pitch black. He went back down the ladder to find a flashlight. Returning along the hall, he saw her stockinged legs dangling through the dark square in the ceiling. He noticed she had worn sensible laced shoes for her journey.

The floor of the attic was made of narrow uncovered beams with no insulation between them. Just a few loose boards allowed access to the far corners. With his feet balanced on adjoining beams and holding Mrs Wallace under the arms, he dragged her away from the trapdoor. He laid her between two joists that were far enough apart to accommodate her lying on her back with her arms folded across her chest. He went down the ladder to retrieve her belongings. He wedged her handbag under her elbow and covered the reposing corpse with her suitcase, which she might find useful for her onward journey to the next world.

Back on the stepladder, he shone the flashlight into the attic for a final overview of his work. The beam picked out a dense tangle of webs. The cousins of the small black spiders who had ignored him earlier in the lecture hall were also indifferent to him now as they hung their nets like dirty laundry across the beams of the low roof. "Rest in peace, mother," he whispered before closing the trapdoor on Mrs Wallace's dark tomb.

He carried the stepladder to the far end of the house,

swept up the fragments of broken china, washed the floor with a bucket and mop he remembered seeing earlier in the corner of the hall. He changed the mucky water several times, emptying the scum of years of dirt that had accumulated on the floor, tea, milk, hairs, and a small amount of blood down the kitchen sink. He found an ancient vacuum cleaner that he used to suck the dust from every surface in the house. He cleaned in an hysterical attempt to remove any stain of memory of Mrs Wallace from his mind. After an hour and a half of uninterrupted purification therapy, he collapsed in exhaustion.

Fortunately, when Julie Progress showed up she was too drunk to notice his attempt to sterilize the house following his abrupt exit from the reception for his lecture.

"You should have stayed," she slurred. "You missed a super party. Everyone thought you were brilliant. You should have been there." Then she remembered why he had gone home. "Where's your mother?" she asked, looking around on unsteady legs.

"She left," he lied.

"Left? Pity. She was such a lovely woman," she mumbled sarcastically.

"Yes, lovely."

"Oh God. I need to lie down. My head is spinning. Excellent party. You should have stayed. You have no idea what you missed," she repeated drunkenly.

Later that night Wallace lay awake in bed drinking wine straight from the bottle. At least, he thought, he could afford a decent label now he was a depressed professor. Progress was snoring beside him. She lay on her back with her mouth wide open. He pushed her over onto her side into what he hoped was the recommended unconscious position for drunks. The beautiful Julie Progress farted in thanks for this health and safety intervention.

A full moon shining through the curtain-less window decorated the bedroom with a macabre black and silver palette. Wallace studied the map of fine cracks running across the ceiling. He thought he would be in jail before he had a chance to repair it. He felt resentment towards Progress that, after his frantic effort to hide the body, she was too drunk to even notice how clean the normally filthy house was. Even when sober she didn't share his interest in renovation. She was a slob: more evidence they had little in common beyond an athletic sex life.

Lying there, he realized that he wanted her to share his pride in the great job he had been doing trying to be Rik Wallace up to the point where he killed Rik Wallace's mother. He wondered how he could describe their relationship. Lovers? Maybe, but it was too contractual for that. Partners, perhaps? It was a term he disliked, but felt its commercial connotation might better describe their particular alliance. He was confident their bond, whatever it was, would be tested if the police showed up. Progress groaned in her sleep, unconsciously acknowledging the difficulties ahead for them.

He couldn't believe how stupid he was to have stood in front of a room crowded with witnesses and told them that, in his idiotic opinion, intentions didn't matter. He had started to believe he might have been able to persuade Inspector Jackson that he had just panicked after Rik Wallace's death; convince him he hadn't intended to kill him. Up until a fraction of a second before he hit Mrs Wallace across the back of the head, he hadn't intended to kill her either. He just needed to shut her up; stop everything just for a minute so that he could have time to think. But his was a permanent solution to a momentary problem. Who would believe him now: first the son, and then the mother? According to him, it was the outcome that mattered and not the intention. That's what he told a room full of people a few hours ago. The outcome was that Mrs Wallace was beginning to mummify in his attic. He was embarrassed to be such a useless philosopher. He couldn't get his ideas straight or in line with his actions. After weeks of study, he had hoped he would have been more moral by now.

He was suddenly terrified by a novel self-awareness that an historical force he could neither control nor understand possessed him: a power that had prevailed for over two thousand years against greater opponents than his ignorance. He was being consumed by the might of philosophy. How had he imagined he could have gotten away with challenging such a monster to a life-or-death contest? Nausea caused a coating of icy sweat to condense on his skin. It was clear to him now: in less than a month he had become a homicidal maniac, not just espousing the strangling of children, killing the sick and elderly, half the population and anyone who got in his way but actually putting his theories into practice. Where would it end? He just wanted to go home. But it was too late for that now.

A plan formed in his brain in a flash of inspiration that most academics would pray for. He knew he should cease all thought and reflection. He must stop the what ifs, whys and hows. It was time for pure action stripped of all thought. His reason hadn't yet benefitted from his short philosophical training to allow him the critical insight that acting without thought had, in fact, been his guiding principle since beating on the door of room 514. But why stop now?

Wearing the wine-stained white vest and underpants he had worn to bed, he walked into the bathroom carrying his only tie, which he plucked from the back of the chair as he passed. He stood on the side of the bathtub and knotted one end of the tie around his neck and the other around the shower rail. Then he jumped into the bathtub.

XV

Exitus Iterum
Exit Again

A cumulus cloud in the sky above Love Street, which was acting as a stage curtain for the sun, lifted causing a spotlight of cold white light to shoot through the bathroom window and bounce off the tiles in search of a drama to illuminate. It settled on Rik Wallace's swollen purple face. His head was wedged between the toilet bowl and the wall. The blood had drained from his elevated feet resting on the edge of the bathtub. The toilet seat had broken free and lay under his head on the floor. The light pried his eyes open.

He unwrapped an arm that was trapped behind his back and loosened the tie around his neck with numb fingers. With these he next explored the egg-size lump on the middle of his forehead where he hit the rim of the toilet bowl on his way to the floor. He couldn't get his legs to work when he dragged them down off the tub. He crawled across the floor using his swollen arms to pull himself along, and into the bedroom beyond where Julie Progress lay flat on the bed holding her head in her hands. Propping himself against the edge of the mattress, he managed to roll in beside her.

"What are you doing with that tie on over that vest?" she

asked looking at him through her fingers. "You are really letting yourself go." Before he could answer she continued, "I think I am dying. Actually dying. Oh, God. I remember something about tequila shots on top of all that free beer and wine."

Several minutes passed as Wallace and Progress struggled with pillows to prop themselves up in the sagging bed. Tiny flakes of white paint and plaster dust from the ceiling snowed onto their aching heads. Their loud groans drowned out the whimpers of the house. They covered their inflamed eyes against the glare of the morning sun pouring through the curtain-less bedroom window. Then Wallace's blood started to flow again, bringing pain into his numb legs.

"I have to tell you something," he told her, wincing as he patted the bump on his head. "Something happened here last night before you got home. I—"

"I met Bacon last night," she blurted out. "He was drunk and upset that I dumped him as my supervisor. We went for more drinks together after the reception. Oh, God. I'm going to be sick."

Progress ran to the bathroom holding her hand over her mouth. When she was gone, he lay still, contemplating the confession he was determined to make as soon as she got back. He heard the sound of retching echoing off the bathroom tiles. He heard the house croak in sympathy. She was trying not to move her head when she finally reappeared.

"What did you do in there? The toilet is wrecked. Don't tell me you have started working on the bathroom. Not today. I can't deal with any more DIY. I am dying." She gingerly lowered herself onto the bed. "I think I have a brain haemorrhage. Do you have an aspirin? Oh, God. Why can't Bacon leave me alone? I don't want you to be jealous. After your lecture last night no one else can supervise my thesis. You are the only one, despite what Bacon thinks. It was the tequila made me—"

"I need to tell you something," Wallace persisted, ignoring both her request for medical assistance and her competitive confessing.

"Where is your mother? I remember she called me a whore. I remember that even if I can't remember anything else. She called me a whore. I'm sorry to tell you this. I know she is your mother, but she is also a cow. Your mother is a cow." Progress started to snigger, but her laughter soon turned into a series of moans. "I think I'm still drunk."

"That's what I'm trying to tell you. I killed her last night."

"Killed who?"

"Killed whom. It's killed whom, I think. My mother. I killed my mother."

"Jesus Christ, Rik. Why?" Progress asked, clearly trying to show more interest in the confession of murder than the hangover, which was killing her. She was starting to feel sick again.

"She was blackmailing me."

"Blackmailing you? How? I mean, what was she blackmailing you about?"

"She was going to tell the college authorities I wasn't her son."

"Jesus Christ, Rik," she repeated in exasperation. "No one gives a damn these days about that kind of thing, not even moral philosophers. No one cares who your real mother is. How can you kill someone over such bourgeois crap? Oh God, I can't believe it. You kill your mother because she tells you she's not your biological mother, and she is going to blackmail you over that, and you think anyone in the department gives a shit. We have students with lesbian mothers. We have students with lesbian fathers. No one cares if you are a test-tube baby. That is so passé. Do you think Lambe ever had a mother? And you do this the one time I am in real danger of dying from a hangover. That is so selfish. You are a pathetic self-centred Freudian. Killing your mother just because you feel betrayed by her. At your age."

Just then some of the alcohol evaporated in her pickled brain. "What do you mean you killed her?" she asked, lifting her face from her hands and struggling to sit up in the bed.

"I don't mean she wasn't my real mother. I mean, I'm *not* her son. She was going to tell Lambe that—"

Progress groaned.

"It's complicated. I … ah … I hit her—"

His explanation was interrupted by the sound of a loud crack above their heads followed by a muffled ripping that drowned out the end of his sentence.

The ceiling over the bed burst open.

Mrs Wallace, in her blue woollen coat and her arms crossed, fell through the air, landed on the bed, bounced, and rolled onto the floor. Her suitcase landed at her feet. The series of explosive detonations was followed by a moment of complete silence while Wallace and Progress stared at Mrs Wallace where she lay face down beside the bed, panting. Between gasps and wheezes they heard indistinct muttered curses aimed at all philosophers in general and Wallace in particular.

Wallace and Progress were on their feet without being conscious of having moved. Blood, dust, and hair had formed a balaclava of gore around Mrs Wallace's head. She stood up, swayed and glared at Wallace through swollen bloodshot eyes under a veil of cobwebs. She was still clutching her handbag under her arm.

"What kind of a bastard son are you?" she snarled at him when she recovered her breath. "Trying to kill your own mother."

"But you're not my mother," Wallace stammered, regaining the power of speech.

"That's not the point, you moron. It's the principle," Mrs Wallace shouted. "What kind of a moral philosopher are you? Killing your own mother."

Wallace lunged at her.

"Oh God. You're alive. Thank God, you're alive," he said, hugging and kissing her as any son should. "You're alive. I never meant to kill you. I'm sorry. It was an accident. I don't know what came over me. I just panicked." He picked up a length of timber from his building project stored upright against the dressing table in the bedroom in anticipation of the next renovation phase. "I hit you with a plank similar to this one. Except I used a softwood," he explained, as if she shared his enthusiasm for wood species and their uses. "Thank God, it was a soft pine. This one here is a hard oak. If I had hit you with this you—"

"Get the fuck off me," she said, shoving him away with her strong skinny arms.

"No need for that kind of language. You know I don't approve of swearing." He was jumping up and down on the floor in front of her as if he was her cheerful child.

"I don't know anything about you," she told him. "Fuck,

fuck, fuck. That's what I think of you and your fucking likes and fucking dislikes. Even if you were my son, you would be the most ungrateful fucked-up son any mother ever had."

Wallace hugged her again. "You don't know how glad I am I didn't kill you."

"Get off me, you maniac," she said pushing him back.

"What in God's name is going on?" Progress asked, a tide of vomit rising from the dregs of the cocktail of tequila, beer and wine still sloshing around in her stomach.

"I was trying to explain before she burst through the ceiling," Wallace said. "She was blackmailing me because I am not her son and … it's complicated … so I hit her with a length of timber from the new kitchen wall. She wants to move in here with us. She brought her suitcase. She wants half my salary or she will tell Lambe that—"

"She wants to move in here with us?" Progress shouted. "Where? You are knocking down the whole fucking place."

"There's the spare bedroom across the hall," Wallace suggested meekly.

Mrs Wallace straightened herself up, adjusted her handbag under her armpit, smoothed her wrecked overcoat, wiped the mask of cobwebs from her face, stuck out her chest, picked up her suitcase, and facing Progress said, "I'm willing to overlook this poor start to our relationship. I'm moving in, and after this fiasco your boyfriend here will be lucky to have anything left at the end of the month to support a whore like you."

"Move in here with us? No way! I'm not having some hag in this house whom by their own admission isn't even related to Rik."

"It's who."

"What?"

"It's *who* by their own admission," Wallace corrected her.

"You are becoming such a pedantic asshole. My head is killing me. I don't need a tutorial in grammar right now," Julie Progress screamed with a double-barrelled blast of both lungs.

Mrs Wallace turned on her heel. "I need to get cleaned up. Where's the bathroom? And show me to this spare bedroom because I can't stay in this one with the ceiling falling in."

She walked towards the door carrying her suitcase by her side. Progress spent a moment trying to get her limbs to respond to her will. "Give me that," she said, ripping the hardwood plank from Wallace's grip. With both hands she swung the joist over her head in a wide arch and brought it down on top of Mrs Wallace's blood and dust-soaked head.

Mrs Wallace dropped straight to the floor.

Wallace knelt beside the body while Progress stood over him panting from the effort of having poleaxed Mrs Wallace.

"Thank God, I didn't kill her," he said, holding onto one of the corpse's hands. "I'm not a homicidal maniac. You cannot imagine how relieved I am. I'm not a danger to society after all. Oh, thank God, I didn't kill her. It's not my fault she is dead. It's not my responsibility."

Wallace wasn't aware that existentialist philosophers wouldn't agree in principle with his arguments made while kneeling on the floor beside his dead-again mother. But they – who admittedly form only a tiny minority – are aware that the majority who are not existentialists are desperate to blame other people for their own actions. This is understandable in stressful situations. Furthermore, they wouldn't be overly critical of Wallace just because he wasn't an existentialist himself. After all, they would appreciate that he had more than enough philosophical trends to catch up on without including the demanding existentialists on his list. Therefore, in this unique moral circumstance they might forgive him for not taking responsibility for his part in his own enterprise. On the other hand, existentialism is not characterized by forgiveness. Inversely, the existentialists also know that the world is filled with those willing to take the credit for other people's actions when they work out unexpectedly well. Maybe that was Progress's thinking in this case?

"Can you put her somewhere she will stay this time?" Progress asked him calmly. "I can't go through this again. I need an aspirin. I can't help you with this mess. I have to go back to bed. Wine, beer and tequila may cause brain tumours. You don't know. You're not a *medical* doctor."

Wallace's DIY instincts kicked in. He picked his mother up off the floor where she lay in a circle of blood, dragged her into the kitchen and stood her in the cavity in the half-built partition wall. He held her in place with the softwood baton he had used to hit her the first time wedged across her chest between the two uprights he had installed earlier. He was pleased that by shoving her sideways in a standing position she was such a good fit he could not have done better had he measured her in advance.

He broke up her suitcase with a hammer and placed the pieces in the cavities, using her few clothes to insulate the spaces between the timber and the sheets of plasterboard he had already nailed in place on the far side of the partition. Using the table as his workbench, he laid a new sheet of plasterboard across it, made careful measurements, and cut through the gypsum with a handsaw producing one L-shaped and two large rectangular pieces. These he nailed over the timber frame. He put tape on the joints and went outside into the garden and mixed a large bucket of plaster. He carried this inside when he was satisfied with the consistency. He placed a plastic sheet along the floor where it met the bottom of the new wall. Then he trowelled the plaster onto the plasterboard. He spent over an hour smoothing and touching up the surface because plastering wasn't one of his better DIY skills. He rinsed out the bucket with the garden hose and replaced the dining table in its original position against the wall.

"I never meant to kill you," he whispered to the new plaster. "I knew it. I knew I hadn't killed you. I couldn't have," he said, running the tips of his fingers over the slight undulations on the surface. "The mother and son were both accidents. It's not my fault. From now on, if I must kill anyone, it will only be to help others. That is what a moral philosopher should do."

XVI

Vigiliae Intempesta Nocte
The Night Shift

Patricia the provost was sitting in bed between the Reverend Professor Lambe on one side and her immaculate hair on a manikin head on the dressing table on the other. Lambe was making notes for the next morning's ecumenical service in the college that was regularly attended by the provost, Pandora, and a few psychology students, who were not motivated so much by piety as by the hope that their presence would influence Lambe's marking of their psychology examinations.

Dark blue walls and heavy velvet curtains enclosed the over-heated bedroom. A portrait of the provost's grandmother wearing a bright red academic gown hung above the headboard. She looked down with a fixed expression of apprehension at what she was forced to witness at night in the bed below. The provost was studying the few remaining natural strands of hair still clinging to her skull in a hand mirror propped on her knees. "My God, I look horrible. Do I look horrible?" she asked Lambe, vainly seeking consolation.

"What's that dear? I'm trying to concentrate on my sermon. I'm writing about the evils of drink. Rose the cleaner told me our new anti-alcohol philosopher, Wallace, is – in fact – an alcoholic. Typical. You see it all the time. It's reverse psychology: Wallace campaigns against the drinks industry because he is an alcoholic. His anti-drink crusade is what has driven him to drink in the first place. He is obsessed with alcohol. Obviously, he is enabling his vice by moralizing against it. I think I will mention that in my homily. The road to hell is paved with good intentions, etcetera, and etcetera. That's brilliant." To celebrate his insight Lambe waved his whiskey glass in the air and made a toast. "Cheers to all those in darkest denial. I hope they come to see the light."

The provost was crying.

"What's wrong now, dear?" Lambe asked, not waiting for an answer but writing again under the irresistible force of his epiphany on alcohol.

"I look awful. I need to go back to Doctor Harmon's clinic. I don't care what you say about the cost. I'm worth it. Tell me I'm worth it."

"I have a feeling Wallace may have normopathy. He seems obsessed with fitting in. I can't grasp who he is, which isn't typical of me because I can always see beyond a person's mask. For some reason, he strikes me as being desperate not to call attention to himself, which is what attracts my interest. He is hiding something in plain sight. I know it. Drink? A drink will do you good, dear."

"Oh, God. I'm getting old. I look old. Tell me I don't look old," she pleaded stretching the skin on her face with her fingers.

"Speaking of old, Julie Progress must be at least twenty-three by now. I heard through the grapevine she has shacked up with Wallace, the lucky bugger. Bacon was in my office today screaming at me that Wallace was poaching his students. He is an exceptionally insecure man. I haven't seen Bacon on campus so often since he first starting lecturing here when he was trying to make an impression. He asked, as compensation, if he could supervise Sally Doolittle. He isn't going to take my students if he can't hang onto his own. He told me Sally wants to develop her psychology thesis into philosophy – some obsession she has with post-structuralism. I told him to sod off. I will supervise Sally's thesis whether she— I mean, *he* likes it or not. You know Sally is already working with me in the student-counselling centre. I am halfway there. I remember Julie was interested in psychology when she was an undergraduate. She read a lot of Freud. I thought I would have her … erm … in the department; I mean, as a graduate, but she was seduced by the philosophers."

"My teeth are loose. I need more implants," the provost said, depressing her cheeks.

"It's your gums. Your teeth are fine. Here, have a drink, dear."

In one lithe movement the provost leaped onto the floor. Her skull shiny and white under the bulbs on the chandelier that hung above the bed. She screamed that she didn't want a drink.

"You bastard. I'm falling apart – literally – and the only thing you can think about is young women."

"What young women? What are you talking about?"

"Sally Doolittle and Julie Progress. You're pathetic. Still chasing students around the college at your age. Get out. Get out of my bed, you lecherous bastard."

"Calm down. I don't know what are you talking about."

"Don't tell me to calm down," she screamed. "You have

ruined my life. I was happy before I met you, but I didn't know it. You and your bloody psychology."

"You're upset. It's not me you are angry with. You are just transferring your resentment *onto* me. I understand that. Anyone else wouldn't, but I do. Look. I'm putting the drink down. Look." He gulped the remaining whiskey and placed the empty glass beside the bottle within easy reach on the bedside locker. "Come back to bed, dear."

Later, when the lights on the chandelier were out and the room was pitch black, the provost lay crying, thinking about Sally Doolittle. What did Lambe mean he was halfway there? She could remember when Doolittle was an innocent enthusiastic first-year sitting in the middle of the front row for induction. She had asked Lambe who the striking student with the long mane of red hair was because he knew all of the new female students, arguing that young women needed the support of an experienced chaplain when away from home for the first time. She remembered helping Doolittle in her second year with a difficult landlord and something she couldn't remember now – maybe debts or drugs? Doolittle told the provost she would be grateful to her forever. She would never forget how obliged she was. The provost had even agreed to make her a student counsellor at Lambe's urging. Was Doolittle's memory poor even by the standards of CAT College's students?

There in the dark the provost was suddenly overwhelmed by one of the abrupt blasts of reality that, for some reason, had been assailing her with more frequent urgency in the last few weeks. These waves of existential angst would break over her with the unannounced impact of a seizure that left her conscious, nauseous, and exhausted. She tried dosing herself with more and different combinations of pills to halt these unbidden episodes of supernatural lucidity. Pressed into the mattress under the invisible hand of certainty she saw that her attachment to Lambe was desperation rather than affection. He was a shit! Everything else was an elaborate mirage. Her one regret was she might have gotten through the rest of her life without ever discovering the truth if he had been a better psychologist or a better liar.

Lambe lay awake beside the provost in the black silence with his separate thoughts of Sally Doolittle. He too remembered seeing her on her first day in the college. He didn't get a chance to talk to her for over a year, but he often saw her passing outside his office window, flicking her long hair over her shoulders as if she lived in an advertisement for shampoo. She attended his classes in psychology in her final undergraduate year, but he finally lost her to the philosophy department because of her attraction to that ludicrous French philosopher, Derrida. He should have pretended to be a fan, but he didn't think of that move at the time. He wasn't half as clever back then. Not as cunning as he was these days. Making her a student counsellor brought her into his sight almost every day. What did it matter if a few students ran screaming out of her office? Small collateral damage for a significant strategic victory for him.

He would have total control over her if he could only supervise her thesis. He knew after a lifetime of struggling for domination he was in danger of falling under her power: falling under her. He didn't care. Let her control him. She could whip him if she wanted to. His heart beat faster as he recalled his meeting with her earlier that day. Why had she arranged to see him in his office tomorrow to discuss her unhappiness with her supervision in the philosophy department if it wasn't to persuade him to be her supervisor? Why come and talk to him about Derrida when she knew he hated everything to do with French philosophy? He knew she wanted him, despite what she said, because he knew what women wanted even if they didn't know themselves, which was always the case with women. For the first time in his life a disturbing sensation made him feel reckless. With a tremor of excited horror, he realized he might be in love. He didn't give a damn what either Freud or God would think. He would be the judge of what was right and wrong when it came to important moral matters, such as his own lust.

Lambe's thoughts switched from Sally Doolittle to the half-full bottle of whiskey that stood on his bedside locker just within reach in the dark. He imagined his fingers closing around the smooth glass, as smooth as the flesh on Sally Doolittle's thigh. He held his breath and listened for the tell-tale rhythmic breathing of sleep in the dark beside him. He heard nothing because the provost lay awake holding her breath listening for his.

Far away in another part of the city, Sally Doolittle flicked her long red mane that any shampoo manufacturer would be willing to sponsor, unaware that, at that moment, a fantasy version of herself was holding her flaming hair out from her face as she lowered her naked body down onto the Reverend Professor Lambe's drunken penis, where he lay in the enormous bed in the pitch dark in desperate rigid silence beside the despondent provost.

XVII

Silentium, Placet
No Talking, Please

Rik Wallace and Julie Progress were perched, with one buttock each, balanced on a single chair in a study booth in the library. A sign above their heads advised them that the recommended number of persons per booth should not exceed the number of chairs. They were whispering. By now, two days after Mrs Wallace's reappearance through the ceiling, both had recovered from their respective headaches. Wallace had passed the time adding finishing touches to the kitchen while waiting for the bump on his head to subside enough not to be a topic of conversation amongst his colleagues. He painted the partition a summer sun yellow, a shade he chose on his own because Progress had emphatically indicated her continued disinterest in all DIY projects from the bed where she lay groaning for a day and a night.

Now that Progress had recovered, she felt the time was right to get Wallace to come to terms with the consequences, both moral and psychological, of his recent behaviour towards his mother. Following a search of the college, she had found him in the library where he had been half-heartedly trying to hide from her. Just before she turned up, he had been hoping that perhaps he could skip the ancient Greeks in his lectures. After all, what more could he add to the already enormous collection of reflections and commentaries on reflections on the origins of Western thought? He was thinking current philosophy must have all of the answers to everything by now.

"Shove over and make room," Progress said when she appeared beside him, having sneaked up on him where he was sitting with both buttocks planted on the middle of the single chair.

"I know what you're thinking," she told him.

"Really?"

"You're thinking: why did I kill my mother? Are you impressed?"

"Not really. I was actually thinking about the Greek philosophers."

"We need to talk about her," Progress whispered, loudly.

He groaned.

"It's not good to keep things bottled up. You need to explore how your mother's rejection of you makes you feel."

"With whom am I supposed to explore that? You?"

"I took classes in psychology when I was an undergraduate. I'm sure I can help."

"I'm not keeping anything bottled up," he hissed. "She wasn't my mother."

"You really *do* need help."

"Look. At an unconscious level, I didn't intend to kill her, and that is why I didn't hit her hard enough or with the appropriate species of timber in the first place. It was a softwood. Unlike you, who hit her with a hardwood."

"Oh. This is good. Can I take notes?"

"For God's sake, don't. Do you want us both to end up in jail?"

"The notes would be confidential. Doctor–patient privilege."

"You're not a doctor."

"I will be soon, with your help."

"You'll be a doctor of moral philosophy if I ever finish your thesis. And philosophy isn't covered by client confidentiality. *No* notes. Are you crazy?"

"We are discussing your mental problems, not mine. A real psychiatrist would ask what your mother was doing in the attic in the first place?"

He rubbed his hands over his eyes. "Look. I didn't kill her. You are the one who *really* killed her with that incredible blow. What brought that on?"

"I don't want to talk about it. This is not about me. It's about you. I won't go mad, which you will, if I don't talk about it, because she wasn't my mother."

"I'm not going mad," Wallace shouted in frustration.

"Can you please stop whispering so loudly?" the librarian interjected over their shoulders. She had slunk up on them undetected using just a few well-practised moves from shelf to shelf to hide her approach with the skill of a lion stalking a couple of unwary gossiping antelope. "Everyone in the library can hear your entire conversation," she said, exaggerating slightly. Wallace turned pale. "Are you still reading your own books, professor?" she asked, leaning over the low partition to see what was on his desk.

"Ah … no. I'm reading Plato on Socrates."

"Can you please do it in silence. I am aware our students

don't read in the library, but I insist they not read in a quiet environment." She glared at both of them before turning on her heel and striding back to the front desk.

Progress, ignoring the librarian's warning, resumed whispering. "You are storing up trouble for the future if you repress your feelings about your mother."

"I am not repressing my feelings. She wasn't my mother," he shouted.

The librarian stared at him, placing a finger over her lips.

"Look at what happened to Oedipus. He ended up killing his own father and having sex with his mother. A disaster for his whole family," Progress said.

"More bloody ancient Greeks!"

"Stop changing the subject. We are discussing your psychological problems. You are in denial. All of this DIY you do – it's what we call a form of sublimation."

"We who?" he asked.

"Isn't that we whom? Never mind. We analysts. I also took classes in psychoanalysis when I was an undergraduate. I really got Freud. It's as if he is talking to me. You are transferring your sexual desire for your mother into building a home. Yes. That's it. A home the two of you can share. Mother, home, nest – get it? The DIY is a front for incest. Oh, this is good. I should write it down, or I'll forget it. I wonder if I can get it into my thesis? And naturally, you no longer desired her, at an unconscious level, of course, when she told you she wasn't your mother. That's why you killed her. My God, sometimes I frighten myself I'm such a genius."

"Rubbish. I didn't desire her at a conscious or unconscious level. Not at any level. My mother didn't disown me. She died in a car crash when I was ten." He was shouting again.

"That's awful. I know how you feel. My mother also died when I was a child." This from the librarian who had sneaked up on them again. "I am sorry to interrupt your confidential counselling session but a Detective Inspector Jackson and another detective whose name I can't remember are here to see you. He says it's an emergency. If you insist on whispering, can you do it just a little bit louder because I don't want to miss out on hearing what kind of trouble you are in, Professor Wallace."

He didn't reply because his heart had started thumping when she mentioned Jackson. He didn't hear her sardonic request. At last, the fateful moment had come: his arrest. The librarian walked back towards her desk where Jackson and Sullivan were waiting and pointed them in the direction of Wallace and Progress crouching in the booth in the corner of the library.

Inspector Jackson squeezed in and settled both his buttocks on the desk in front of them. Sullivan asked Jackson where he might sit.

"Just stand there and be quiet," Jackson told him. "As an officer of the law, you should want to obey the rules hanging all around you." He shook hands with Wallace and whispered a hello.

"Inspector Jackson. I remember you from the hotel," Wallace murmured with studied casualness. "And you. I'm sure I remember you too."

"Sullivan, sir. The name is Sullivan."

"Yes, of course, the new detective. How are you settling in?"

"Fine, sir. Just fine. I haven't made an arrest yet but I'm sure I will soon, though the inspector doesn't share my optimism."

"When did we met in the hotel? Over a month ago?" Wallace asked, hiding the fact that he had been counting each day ever since.

"Thirty-three days, sir," Sullivan said, revealing that he had been counting too.

"This is my graduate student, Julie Progress. I'm supervising her doctorate thesis. She is writing on business ethics. Been at it about three years now, but we are hoping for some progress soon. Progress, that's good – get it?" He stopped talking when he realized he was babbling.

Jackson shook Progress's outstretched hand. Sullivan and Progress ignored each other.

"Yes, that night in the hotel. A terrible tragedy. I remember you from the room next door. You were with that gratuitously naked woman. I knew I would find you here. I remembered your letter from the college. Something has come up," Jackson said.

His blood pounded under immense pressure as it passed through the tiny vessels in Wallace's ears. Now that the long-expected police had at last arrived, he felt disappointed he had managed only thirty-three days at liberty. He thought about making a dash from the booth. He was on the wrong side of Progress and Sullivan, but he could get past Jackson by shoving him backwards over the partition, past the librarian, and out the door before anyone could react. He had started to transfer his weight forward onto one leg and lift his buttock from the seat when Inspector Jackson said, "I am worried that you might be in danger."

Wallace replaced his buttock and gasped, "Oh, thank God. I mean … Oh God, that's terrible."

"My colleagues contacted me last night. It appears your mother has escaped again."

"Escaped?" Wallace and Progress repeated the word together.

"Yes, escaped," Sullivan confirmed. "Oh, I see he didn't tell you," he said to Progress. "I appreciate why a hotshot moral philosopher might not tell his students his mother is a jailbird. Well, maybe she is not a real jailbird because she was in one of those do-gooder open-prisons. Criminals can come and go there as they like, and three days ago, she went, as she liked. Carried a suitcase out the main gate and into a waiting taxi."

"Prison?" Progress asked.

"I knew he wouldn't tell you. I told the inspector before we came here that he wouldn't tell anyone his mother is a gangster." Sullivan laughed with smug satisfaction at his insight into the nature of moral philosophers. "I took psychology courses in the police academy. That's standard practice these days. Which wasn't the case back in the dark ages when the inspector here was training."

"I studied psychology too when I was an undergraduate," Progress boasted.

"I came here to warn you she has been making threats against you for the last few weeks. The prison doctor says she is suffering from early-onset dementia. Deranged people are liable to do anything," Jackson said, consulting his notebook. "The Reverend Professor Lambe told me she was here a few nights ago, and that you departed arm in arm with her after some talk. It appears she didn't mean you any harm as you seem to have survived the encounter," he said lifting his eyebrows at Wallace. "I was worried she might do something given her criminal past; but maybe she is just losing her marbles after all."

"Was she dangerous before she … er … lost her marbles?" Progress asked.

"We could never make much stick, but according to our file, which is that thick," he said, spreading his thumb as far from his index finger as he could, "she was involved in the disappearance of a lot of people, most of them no good."

Progress looked at Wallace but said nothing.

"So, you know where she is now?" Sullivan asked.

"She went back to my place with me for a cup of tea. Then she left."

"What time was that?"

"About eleven o'clock."

"Did she threaten you?"

"No. We had a pleasant conversation about old times. You know, normal mother and son stuff."

"Such as?" Progress asked.

Wallace glared at her. "You know? Stuff. Asking me if I was looking after myself. When was I going to settle down? If I found a woman she could think of as her daughter? Complaining about the women I dated in the past. How they were all whores. That sort of thing. Standard family chit-chat."

"Did she tell you she was on the run? Are you hiding her?" Sullivan asked.

"She didn't tell me she was on the run and, no, I am not hiding her," Wallace lied, turning red.

"Do you know where she might have gone?" Jackson asked.

"She didn't confide in me, ever. We weren't that close. I know nothing about her … uhm … business affairs. You should understand, Inspector; I'm the white sheep in my family."

"Try not to worry. We'll catch her. We have done before. Where can a crazy bird like her hide anyway? She is bound to create a stink somewhere."

"I'm sure she will."

"Can we fingerprint him this time?" Sullivan asked his boss.

"No," Jackson sighed, before turning back to Wallace. "Give me a ring if she does get in touch again. Here is my card. I don't think she poses a real threat to you since she has already come and gone. But I can't say the same about that brother of yours."

"Brother?" Progress and Wallace repeated the word in unison.

"Oh, didn't he tell you about him either," Sullivan asked Progress. "No surprise there – between us psychologists."

"Why don't you tell her since you know so much about my family?" Wallace muttered, disguising his own curiosity.

"Okay. I will. His brother, Larry, is a real psycho. He lost the head when he found out his mother had gone missing. He has that gang of his working on finding her."

"Gang?" Wallace and Progress said once more in chorus.

"Yes. Gang. He has even offered a reward for information leading to her whereabouts. We didn't tell him your mother came here. The inspector says we don't need the reward, and besides, he imagines you have enough excitement settling into your new job without that psycho showing up amongst these sensitive scholars. But I think if he finds out he will come straight here and beat the shit out of you. But you don't need me telling you that. You know him better than anyone."

"It seems that those two brothers don't get on. Never have,"

Jackson told Progress.

"Wait. I have a question," Sullivan said, consulting his notes. "Now what was it? Ah yes. How did your mother leave the other night?"

"What do you mean 'leave'?"

"I mean how did she leave your place? Did she walk, get in a car, cycle a bike, get a taxi, or what?"

"I … ah … don't remember. Oh yes. We walked to the end of the street and hailed a taxi. Yes. That's what we did."

"Do you remember anything about the taxi? Number? Company? Colour? Anything?"

"No, it was dark."

"That's enough questions, Sullivan," Jackson interrupted.

"Why did she come here if she didn't mean to harm you? Why did she just leave again without doing anything?" the librarian asked, once more reappearing undetected to listen in on the interrogation.

"They're impressive questions," Jackson said. "Have you ever thought about becoming a detective?"

Sullivan scowled at the librarian.

Jackson couldn't remember why he had decided to become a policeman. Maybe, he thought, he could have become a librarian if his career guidance teacher had suggested it. Librarianship wasn't one of those careers – such as being a fireman or an astronaut – that children thought of doing when they grew up.

"Thanks," the librarian said, blushing. "I am interested in laws and rules in general." In school, the librarian had wanted to become a judge, but lost interest when she discovered she would have to become a lawyer first.

"My mother was proud of my inaugural lecture, she told me," Wallace lied, when he got a chance to interrupt.

"Really? That's dementia for you," the librarian said.

"You will let me know if she shows up again," Jackson said. "And let me know if you see that crazy brother of yours around here."

"Your brother loves his mother a little too much, if you know what I mean. He says he will break the legs of anyone who says his mother is mad, including the prison doctor," Sullivan said.

"That's a Freudian observation," Progress told him. "Did you study psychoanalysis as part of your police training? I read Freud when I was an undergraduate. You can learn a lot about families from Freud. I am sure it would be a tremendous help in your detective work. He has loads to say about mothers and sons. It's not good for a man to be too close to his mother. Do *you* live with your mother, Detective?"

Sullivan blushed. "At the moment, yes; but only because I have just started my police career. I'm going to move out as soon as possible."

"She buys his clothes for him," Jackson told her.

"I'm too busy to go shopping. So what if my mother helps me?"

"Mothers. You can't live with them, and if you kill them you have to deal with me. I would be out of business if families stopped killing each other," Jackson said.

After a moment of stunned silence, everyone laughed hysterically, including Jackson and the librarian.

"It's funny meeting you again like this," Jackson told Wallace when the laughter subsided. "A coincidence, perhaps;

but policemen don't believe in coincidences. There are always some hidden links joining the dots no matter how unconnected they may appear on the surface. We should investigate what lies beneath."

"Freud says it's all about motivation," Progress declared with enthusiasm.

"Yes," Jackson said. "Supposedly when you find the motive, you will find the culprit. Impossible to solve a crime without motivation. Fortunately, we can usually find a motive even if we have to make one up."

"Make one up?" Sullivan asked.

"You see, Sullivan, here is something you won't have learned in your academy. To find a motivation behind a crime you need to be dealing with competent criminals. For most people there is a huge gap between their plan for getting from A to B and how they get there, ending up at P or somewhere else in the alphabet. You are concerned in your imagination with criminal geniuses. I deal with the majority who are morons. Therefore, I find it simpler to make up a motivation for them. For example, when you come across a dead mother, you cannot rule out the possibility that someone was aiming at the father and missed. Can happen. Does happen."

"How is Della?" Wallace asked in an impetuous attempt to change the subject.

"Who?"

"Della. The naked woman who was with me in the hotel room. You took her away for questioning."

"Oh her. I don't know. I haven't seen her since that night, though I doubt I will see that much of her ever again." Jackson laughed and winked at Wallace. Progress and Sullivan stared at both of them. Then Jackson caught the librarian's eye and reddened. "Why do you ask?" he asked, clearing his throat.

"Oh nothing. Speaking of coincidences, she showed up at my talk the night my mother was here."

"That is curious." Jackson wrote something in his notebook.

Wallace regretted mentioning Della. He instinctively felt he had betrayed her in some way he didn't understand.

Jackson put his notebook in his pocket and squeezed past them out of the booth.

"Can't I just practise taking some fingerprints? Or a DNA swab?" Sullivan asked.

"No."

"I am the same as you, Inspector. Involved in the constant struggle to maintain law and order. Are you married?" the librarian asked him as they walked side by side towards the main issuing desk with Sullivan moping along behind them like an unhappy child on holiday trying to come up with the most effective sulking strategy against his uncooperative parents.

Wallace and Progress couldn't hear his reply. They watched Jackson and the librarian lean their heads towards each other in conversation. Jackson handed the librarian a card.

"I'm glad we killed her," Progress murmured.

"Speak for yourself. I didn't kill her. You did," Wallace hissed.

"Why didn't you tell me you had an immoral brother? What are we going to do if he turns up here?"

"Is it okay if we never talk about my family ever again?"

"Who is Della, this naked woman you are seeing? Is she a past student of yours? Are you related to her?"

"I'm not seeing her. No, she is not a student. I not related to her, and I don't know who she is."

"What do you mean you don't know?"

"I mean, I don't know, that's all. Isn't it possible to *not* know someone?"

"Yes. I suppose. You, for example: I don't know who you are. But I learn something new about you every day. That must be what makes you such a gifted teacher," Progress said as they squeezed out of the booth together.

Wallace was no expert, but he thought what made him a passable teacher was being one lesson ahead of his students. A good educator would be an entire course ahead. Perhaps next year – if he survived – he would be good.

XVIII

Certamen Singulare
A Close Encounter

Yet another miraculous day passed at CAT College in which Rik Wallace was not exposed as a fraudulent matricide or a fake moralist. He was sitting at his desk in his office planning how to extend that record indefinitely. An almost soundless tap on the door broke his fragile concentration. He thought he only imagined it because the knock was so tentative. He waited to see if it was repeated: a gentle tap-tapping followed.

"Come in," he said, pushing his books away, and realizing he was relieved rather than annoyed by the interruption. Nothing happened. "I said come in," he shouted.

Patricia the Provost's blond head appeared from behind the opening door.

"Am I interrupting?" she asked. Without waiting for a reply, she stepped inside and closed the door behind her.

"No. You're not interrupting. I thought you were a timid student."

"Oh, are you disappointed I'm not?"

"I am always pleased to see you," he lied. "Come in and sit down. I don't have anything to offer you to drink. I haven't unpacked yet because my boxes only arrived this morning. I

141

don't know which box contains what because the outsides are blank. I can't imagine what I was thinking when packing." He pointed to a curtain of cardboard boxes along the wall behind his desk.

"Are you glad to see me?"

"Ah … yes," he lied again. He noticed that she was dressed entirely in green. He wondered what mood that colour signified. He couldn't remember what Maurice Spencer had said about green.

"You look … uhm … intriguing … I mean … nice … in green. Is that outfit … eh … new?"

"How sweet of you to notice. I decided I need a fresh look."

She sat into the empty chair in front of his desk.

Green signifies fresh, he noted.

"I wanted to tell you how much I enjoyed your inaugural lecture. I'm sure all the women on campus must be in love with your mind by now."

"Yes. It seems they are. I mean, I can't understand why they would be. No one was ever in love with my mind – or really any part of me – before I came here."

"I knew CAT College would be your spiritual home. How are you settling in?"

"Everything has been perfect," he lied.

He realized that he could lie fluently if he told her only the opposite to what he was actually feeling. He was pleased that this insight might be his first genuine philosophical idea. He tried to formulate this new axiom in his head. Wallace's first law of lying: to be an effective liar one should be in touch with one's honest feelings in order to be able to invert them. Maybe he could get his law on lying into one of his lectures.

Perhaps he could get it into Julie Progress's doctoral thesis. He decided to look it up before claiming it as his own because, even from his scant reading, he suspected that after more than two thousand years of philosophizing every possible thought had already been had by someone, somewhere, at some time, about everything.

"What?" he asked as he came out of his philosophical reverie.

"I said I am glad you are having a good time; because I'm not."

"I am sorry. I was distracted. Philosophizing in my head. You know once you start thinking it is difficult to stop. I am organizing my … er … ideas for my lectures. Yes. That's what I'm doing. Preparing my lectures. I want to be as engaging for my students as possible."

"You are so conscientious. I admire you. Still enthusiastic about your pedagogic mission."

He said nothing because he was trying to work out what his actual feelings about his pedagogic mission were so that he could lie about them too in accordance with his new axiom. Was it dismay he was experiencing? His theory about lying might need more work before he could take it public.

"I said I'm not having a good time," the provost reiterated.

"What did you say?" he asked. "I was having another philosophical thought. I missed what you said."

"I understand. Brilliant men have penetrating thoughts that take them away from the mundane rest of us. Lambe is the same. I said I'm not doing fine."

Looking at her, he knew she wasn't lying. Now he felt bad about his own lies. He decided to compensate by sharing her frankness.

"I am not sure how I can help with other people's emotions because I am not even an expert on my own feelings. And I'm not brilliant. I don't have original philosophical ideas. I can't think on demand. There are so many things I should be doing right now. In fact, I have had a stressful time settling in, if you must know."

"Nonsense. It's all right for you. You *are* a genius. You showed the entire college that in your lecture. Lambe is a fraud, but he's *my* fraud. He is not a real intellectual like you. You are willing to follow your ideas wherever they might lead. That's what makes you brilliant. That's what women find attractive."

Wallace blushed. "I don't know where my ideas will take me. I don't even know if they are my ideas. It's a real mystery."

"I'm sure. But I didn't come here to talk about you. I want to talk about me. I feel you are someone who will listen without telling me how *they* feel, or how *they* think I should feel, which Lambe does all the time. I just need to tell someone how *I* feel. People babble on about themselves all the time. Me, me, me" she screamed at him across the desk, standing up without warning. "I want to talk about *me*. I want some *me, me, me time.*"

Wallace decided to stay silent. He now hypothesized that green might signify a fresh start in terms of a break with reality. He hoped it didn't signify a dangerous break.

"Is that awful? For once in my life thinking about what *I* want and *who* I want?" the provost asked Wallace. She was calm again.

"Who?"

"Yes, who."

She was around the desk and on top of him so fast he hadn't time to recoil. She was sitting on his lap. His arms were wedged by his sides. She held his cheeks between her palms, and kissed him on the lips, crowbarring them apart with her tongue. Then she began to massage his scalp with her pointed fingernails.

Wallace screamed.

"What's wrong, darling?" she asked, leaning back to look at him.

"Your hair. Your hair is moving on its own."

"Oh, this thing," she said pulling off her wig. "I hate it. It's hot and itchy." She threw it on the floor. "Is that better, darling? With you I feel I can be myself. We don't need to hide our real selves from each other. I know the real you. Now you can see the real me."

Wallace squirmed to get out from under her. The chair fell sideways throwing them both across the carpet. The provost rolled over, crashing against the wall of packing boxes. Wallace lay face down with his mouth pressed into the carpet.

The door opened and a student walked into the office. He was reading something from the screen of his phone that he held at arm's length in front of him. He looked up. The eyes behind his jam-jar glasses moved from Wallace to the provost propped against the curtain of boxes and back to his screen before settling again on Wallace. "I need a course outline," he announced.

"Come back later," Wallace gasped, blowing carpet threads from his lips.

"I'll be busy later. I just want to pick up a copy now."

Wallace dragged himself up by the side of the desk and searched through a pile of papers.

"Here," he said, handing the student a page.

"I was wondering if you could go through it with me. Show me the topics that will be on the examination."

"No. I can't go through it with you now."

"It will just take a minute. Then I will get out of your hair … er … your office." He was trying not to look at the provost.

"I haven't worked out the exam questions yet."

"You mean you don't know what questions are going to be on the paper? What kind of a course is that? Doctor Bacon doesn't need to see us, ever, because he tells us all the questions and answers in advance. You can see the advantage of that, can't you?" He had his fingers on the phone, hoping to get a clear photograph of the provost. Wallace stood into his line of fire.

"Come back next week. I might know what the questions are by then."

The student blew out a long breath through his open mouth. "It's unfair. Couldn't you think of just one now?"

Wallace put his hand on the student's shoulder, spun him around and shoved him through the door, closing it behind him. He picked up the provost's wig and sat down on the floor beside her.

"Here. You might want to put this back on," he said, handing her the shiny blond hair. She held it in her hands, rotating it until the tag on the back was facing her. She pulled it over her head like a ski cap.

"I'm sorry about freaking out," Wallace said. "It's not because you're bald. My nerves are shattered since I got here. Women keep throwing themselves at me since I … er … became a moral philosopher. I can't get used to it. One crazy woman at a time is enough."

"Julie Progress?"

"Now? Yes. Julie Progress. And I'm worried that Pandora is starting to have feelings for me. You saw the cat competition trophy she gave me."

"I think you are safe from Pandora. I don't think *she* is into the mind. Pandora doesn't have intellectual appetites. But she does have her own hair," the provost said, falling silent and smoothing her wig with her palms.

After a few minutes in which neither of them shared their thoughts – if they had any – the provost smiled and spoke. "You were saved from me by a student. I am sorry for attacking you. Lambe would put it down to hormones. I would rather you believe I am bad. I hope you have more imagination than him. He doesn't allow me to be plain old-fashioned bad because he explains everything away with a psychological theory that he hasn't even thought about in twenty years. Lambe is terrified of thinking because it might undermine his precious faith. Any thought that might come into his head is banned. I can't remember the last time he was disturbed by an original idea, unless it's his thoughts of Sally Doolittle. I just want to be bad. Is that asking too much? Am I shocking you even with my hair back on?"

Wallace stayed silent.

"Pandora knows Lambe for what he really is. She is an excellent judge of character, unlike me. With those sunglasses of hers, it's as if she can see right through a person, like X-ray glasses. I often tell her how much it means having her beside me as I make my way through this maze that is my life. I hope she believes me, but with Pandora you can't tell what is going on in her head."

"I wonder what she sees inside me?" Wallace mused. "I have noticed that when Pandora is looking at me, she keeps taking her glasses off and cleaning them, as if they don't work on me. Interesting."

"Lambe is an expert on feelings because he doesn't have any. I'm an idealist. I want everyone to be as perfect as they are in my imagination. I used to think Lambe was my ideal man. I didn't try to change him, but he changed me. Now I am stuck the way the Lambe of God has made me. He will destroy this place with his righteousness if he has his way."

Patricia the provost wedged her fingers into the gaps between the boxes and pulled herself onto her feet. She held out her hand to help Wallace up.

"Maybe if we had met years ago or before Progress found you—" She left the thought unfinished. "But perhaps you will turn into Lambe if you stay here long enough. Did this place change him, or was he always a shit? I don't know. Don't try to change Progress."

"I won't."

"I am sorry for frightening you."

"That's okay. It wasn't just you. There are too many scary women in this college."

"I made Pandora promise to look after you if anything should happen to me. The only way you can tell Pandora is on your side is if she isn't actually trying to harm you. Neutrality is Pandora's version of affection."

"Now you are scaring me again."

XIX

Fugit Tempus?

Does Time Fly?

The end of term came around so fast it seemed to those on the worn-out campus that the hands on the yellowed face of the old clock that stood in the corner of the Aula Maxima had rotated at a pace even faster than last year. The clock retained its status as CAT College's official marker of the passage of time by being an object of affection rather than a respected chronograph. The illusion of a speeded-up term was even more pronounced for those students unprepared for examinations that the lecturers vainly hoped, for the sake of their progression rates, were a minority.

It seemed Rik Wallace would survive his first ever philosophy term with his secret intact. He had been busy. He was preoccupied writing Julie Progress's doctorate thesis; preparing and delivering lectures; learning how to set and mark assignments; and how to compose examination papers. By mid-term, the top of the aluminium extension ladder was still visible from his office window. However, he had unpacked the wall of boxes and Blu-Tacked a sign to his door advertising the times at which he was willing to meet with his students. He was astonished, and then disturbed, that they formed a long queue at the appointed hours to seek his advice on a range of topics: from what he thought of the practical value of medieval metaphysics in the contemporary world to his views on whether long- or short-term relationships helped to foster an idealized existential angst. With practice, he felt he could become a punctilious moral authority on almost everything if only he could remain at liberty.

In the evenings and at weekends he continued to work on the decrepit house on Love Street he now thought of as his home. Sometimes, he even put down his glass of wine to take up a brush to paint a wall or a hammer to nail down a loose floorboard. He was less startled by how quickly time appeared to pass than at how easily he found himself fitting into his new life. He had lost his obsession with being in control, concentrating his entire mental effort on acquiring the basic knowledge he needed just to survive in his new identity.

When he woke on the last day of term, he blinked his eyes into focus and took in the scene. The debris of his existence surrounded the bed as if his new psyche was building a levee to keep his old self at bay. This fortification was built of empty bottles, overflowing ashtrays, tools, and both Progress's and his unwashed underwear and discarded clothes intertwined on the floor where they had fallen together in a fumbling embrace.

Behind these defences Progress lay face down sprawled across the bed sound asleep with her head dangling over the edge of the brown-stained mattress, her twin bare buttocks sticking out from under the once-white sheet, her mouth hanging open. She woke with a loud snort. She sat up. "What are you looking so pleased about?" she asked, still grumpy from sleep.

"I was just thinking that the academic life has its

attractions."

"Oh, I would love to be a lecturer. Do you think it will ever happen?" she asked, extending both her arms into a yawn.

"You must wait for a vacancy to arise. I am sure you will get a position, if one comes up."

"Will I get Bacon's job?"

"Bacon is still with us."

"True. Pity he wouldn't just … die."

"Don't say that, Julie. Something is bound to turn up soon."

"Sometimes we must give destiny a helping hand. I'll make breakfast now that I'm awake."

He lay on the bed listening to her muttering curses against Bacon through the open door as she dropped plates and cups onto the table. He smiled. He believed that at some ontological, epistemological, and even ethical level that he wasn't yet philosophically competent to understand, he might *be* Rik Wallace. Being superstitious, he imagined if he admitted he liked this new self his current way of life would end suddenly and badly. But despite his best efforts to suppress his positive feelings, as each hour rolled around the yellowed dial of the old clock in the Aula Maxima, he became more comfortable and more confident as this creature, Rik Wallace. He felt that, whoever he was, he was contented, even happy. It seemed a new term might come and go without anyone else dying on campus.

XX

Exitus Dramaticus
A Dramatic Exit

Patricia the provost was trying to focus her eyes on a series of alternating dark and light concentric rings projected onto the ceiling by the bedside lamp. Jim Morrison was assuring her that this was the end. But she sensed that anyway without him having to croon it at her. But why was the music so loud and where was it coming from? Was it inside her head? She stretched out her hand and pressed her palm into Lambe's side of the mattress. The sheet was cold. She was alone in bed. Maybe he was downstairs playing music. She peered at the alarm clock. Two hands pointed towards the top of the round face and two more pointed towards the bottom. She covered her right eye as her stereoscopic vision seemed to be impaired. It could be four or six o'clock in the day or the night. She couldn't tell because the heavy velvet curtains blocked out the natural light.

Lambe played only classical music, so who could be down stairs? Maybe he had decided to raid her vinyl collection. Maybe it was Jim Morrison back from the dead – if he had ever died. She reached for her pills. She didn't care which of the little flock of bottles she picked up. The cap was already off the one her fingers had found. She spilled some pills into her palm and threw them into her mouth. She pushed in two more from another open bottle and washed them down with a mouthful of clear liquid from the half-empty vodka bottle.

Her feet landed on the deep sheepskin rug that slid across the polished wooden boards leaving her sitting on the floor when she swung her legs out of bed. Her fingers sunk into the comforting soft pile.

"I could lie here," she told herself, rolling onto the fleece.

"You will get cold. Let me help you up, Patricia."

"You are kind to me, Pandora, but I don't see you as the nursing type. Are you sure you are not feeling unwell yourself?"

"I have worn a nurse's uniform on occasion. It was one of my better roles. Hold my arms and I will lift you up."

"Thank you, Pandora. Where would I be without you?"

Pandora's arms became the bedcovers that wrapped themselves around Patricia's waist. Her assistance turned to a struggle. Now Patricia lay face down, bent over the mattress with her feet planted on the ground. Pandora's helping hand turned into a cylinder of white sheet that ran down the middle of the bed.

Patricia's grandmother in the red gown in the picture above the headboard sighed and asked her something when she straightened up.

"What? I can't hear you, Grandmother. The music is too loud. What did you say?"

"I said, have you remembered to do your homework? You must study hard, Patricia, if you want to get on. Not like your mother."

"Yes, Grandmother."

"Don't call me that."

"Yes, Grandmother. I mean, Your Majesty."

"Are you still wasting your time daydreaming, Patricia?"

"I don't know, Your Majesty. I may be dreaming now."

"Why don't you ask him?"

"Who?"

"Him. Doctor Freud. He knows about dreaming. After all the money I spent on doctors, you might at least talk to one. Not like your mother."

Patricia the provost turned her face from the picture. Sigmund Freud was standing at the end of the bed. She recognized him from his famously judgmental expression, refined by years of pursing his lips around his phallic cigars.

"I suppose you are going to tell me I need a penis to be happy. I have one downstairs, and I'm still not happy." She fell flat on her face on the bed laughing.

The noise outside Patricia's head increased. She straightened up and turned around to face the door, which was wide open. There was a light in the hall. Maurice Spencer stood in the doorway smiling at her.

"I heard you were in trouble. I want to help."

"Who told you that?"

"My daughter, Samantha."

"Oh dear. I must really be in trouble."

"Have you met Samantha?"

"I imagine she is flawless, unlike real children that ordinary people have. Everyone in my imagination is perfect. Is she perfect?"

"Yes, she is perfect."

"You should be proud to have a perfect child."

"I am."

"Is there a meeting downstairs I should attend? You must

send around notification in advance. I need to be prepared."

She moved her hand to check that her hair was in place. Spencer had disappeared when she reached the corridor.

Patricia held on to the wooden handrail that ran from the bedroom doorway to the first of two carved cherubs who sat on top of a pair of newel posts that marked the steep downturn of the banister into the chequered black-and-white tiled hall below. In the dark at the bottom of the stairs, a rectangle of yellow light lay on the floor outside the open door of the living room. She was certain that the music was coming from there – or from inside her head. Wherever it was, she felt she was closing in on its source. She put her hands over her ears and screamed for silence. The cherub stood up on his post and pissed a broad stream of hot slippery urine onto the floor. His twin brother laughed. Patricia hadn't seen them do that before.

"You are very naughty," she scolded. "You should talk to Doctor Freud about the size of your penis. He's in the bedroom."

The cherub turned his back on her.

Rik Wallace was standing at the top of the stairs. "*Is this my fault? Has my coming here started something?*" he asked.

"Lambe is jealous of your relationship with Julie Progress."

"*Are you happy, Patricia?*"

"I don't know. I might be, if I could wake up."

"*You are awake. Look, I will prove it. Kiss me.*"

He reached out towards her. She stepped forward with her eyes closed and her arms opened to embrace him. She waited for the feel of his lips on hers. She opened her eyes in time to see all the way through Wallace before he disappeared in a light green glow.

She ran her tongue over the cracked sheets of skin on her dry lips. A flash of lightening illuminated the stained-glass window at the top of the stairs, throwing a metal-clad rider with a long lance through the neck of a red dragon down onto the chequered floor below just as the thunder shook the house. She saw Lambe standing with his back to the wall. She had forgotten why she was standing there.

"Patricia."

"You are not here. Go away. I can wait until you disappear too."

She turned around with her back to the stairwell. Lambe stepped in front of her.

"Patricia. Why are you out of bed?"

She felt his fingers sink into the flesh on her upper arm. She tried to pull away. "Music. Someone is playing loud music. It woke me up."

"I don't hear music," Lambe said.

"Stop shouting."

She struggled to raise her arms and put her hands over her ears. She turned to break free of Lambe's iron grip. "None of the rest of them touched me. Get away from me," she screamed. Her feet slipped on the warm damp floor at the top of the stairs. When her head hit the fifth step down, Jim the porter, who was walking across the trimmed grass in CAT College, asked her if he could retire now. As she watched him turn away, she felt the tide of her life run back out to sea.

"Ah, the end," she said.

Patricia the provost rotated in the air. Her neck broke when her head hit the eleventh step down. The music stopped.

Part II

Wallace, Omnia Nimis Wallace

Wallace, All Too Wallace

XXI

Manducate Viridi Legumina
Eat Your Greens!

"Not cabbage again," Jim the porter moaned when Rose the cleaner thrust the dinner she had prepared without care in the book-lined kitchen onto the table in front of him. "I'm still in shock. I need cheering up. You know cabbage doesn't raise my spirits."

"I don't have time to shop for all kinds of vegetables to combat your depressions. Cabbage looked fresh in Everything Fresh Today on the corner. There are reporters everywhere spilling tea on my floors and throwing litter wherever the mood takes them. And of course, everyone is waiting for news of the funeral. It seems ages since she died. How long has it been?"

"A week already. The police released Lambe just this morning. That Inspector Jackson and his assistant don't have enough evidence to hold him. It seems that they cannot prove that he pushed her down the stairs. Lambe is sticking to his story that it was an accident, but he would, wouldn't he? Everyone knows he did it. I don't care what the police say. I never liked that creep, the Reverend Professor Lambe."

"What was that poor woman doing wandering around that cavernous old house in the middle of the night when she should have been tucked up in bed sound asleep? She should have been knocked out from all those pills she was on. I don't understand how she could break her neck with enough drugs flowing around her blood stream to stun a medium-sized elephant. I hope she didn't suffer in the end."

"She was kind to both of us, and Pandora. We were her pets. If Inspector Jackson can't prove Lambe killed her, I doubt *we* can, even with your resources."

"You had better stop that talk about murder, love, or you will get us both into trouble with Lambe. He will be in charge from now on, suspect or no suspect."

"According to Lambe, she was sleepwalking, and it was not the first time. He says she was out of bed every night. The wonder is she didn't fall down the stairs long before this. Curious the way the provost sleepwalks down the stairs the same time Lambe starts supervising Sally Doolittle."

"Keep your opinions to yourself if you want to avoid trouble with Lambe because he will be the provost now. Anyway, he is not supervising her because she hasn't agreed yet. She must have some hidden intelligence I can't see because she doesn't seem to share his enthusiasm for that arrangement."

"He is in love. He has been studying French philosophy just to impress her. He was reading someone called Derrida in jail. I'm told Derrida deconstructs things. Was he trying to break out? Is Derrida some kind of escapologist?"

"No, he's a French philosopher. We have some of his books here somewhere. I'll try to find one for you tonight. Whether or not he is in love with Doolittle, he was tiring of the provost and she knew it. Patricia craved attention, and he wasn't going to give it to her. He is too self-obsessed to concern himself with the needs of others, especially someone as needy as the provost. He will deliver the eulogy at the funeral service. After all, he supposedly knew her better than anyone else."

"Pandora is devastated. I have never seen her this disturbed about anything. She just sits there outside that empty office chain-smoking and muttering to herself. She can't even talk about her depression with the commerce faculty secretary she is that upset."

"It must be real rather than her usual hypochondria."

"It's a worrying sight."

"Pandora was never able to express her emotions in a normal way. I wonder what form her expression of grief will take."

"We have to wait and see."

"The funeral will be packed because everyone will want to hear what Lambe has to say."

"Tomorrow, can you try?"

"Try what?"

"To find something for dinner other than cabbage. I'm going to turn green if I eat any more cabbage."

"I'll try, but it's not easy to clean up after all the excitement caused by a death *and* do the shopping as well. I haven't seen so many students in the library in the evenings since I can't remember, even during examinations. I promise I'll try, love. How about spinach?"

"No. Not spinach. Something that isn't green. Maybe cauliflower."

"I will look out for cauliflower, but don't complain if it isn't fresh. I was too distracted to bring you home a book, love."

The floorboards stretched in relief at being spared the

additional burden. The old house groaned like Atlas exhausted from bearing the weight of a world of books for what seemed an eternity.

XXII

Requiem

Requiem

Patricia the provost's coffin rested on a stainless-steel trolley in front of the altar. Wreaths covered the ground along the front benches, which were empty except for Sally Doolittle who sat alone in the first pew. By now, mid-morning, the college chapel was overflowing with a few sincere mourners and a large number of curious spectators. Pandora the secretary, Jim the porter, Rose the cleaner, Maurice Spencer the philosopher, Progress the postgraduate, and Rik Wallace – whatever he was – sat together in the second stall on one side of the nave. Rows on the other side had been reserved for representatives from other colleges and universities who used the time away from their own campuses to reflect on the existential impact of the death of one of their peers, disturbing their habitual conviction that they were immortal. A few of these provosts, vice-provosts, deans and chancellors resolved to think about changing their ways: a resolution they would soon forget. Extra plastic chairs had been arranged in the transepts beside the altar and along the walls just behind the row of stone pillars for this popular service. The Reverend Professor Lambe was high above the crowd in the carved wooden pulpit that wound its way up the pillar at the junction of the nave and the sanctuary as if it was the original snake climbing the tree of knowledge in the Garden of Eden. He was waiting for the stragglers and disorientated atheists to settle.

Wallace had looked up the history of the building the night before. Now he knew the floor plan of the original church had been cruciform. However, when the population of pious lunatics in the original asylum increased when there was a fashionable outbreak in religiously-inspired manias in the nineteenth century, various extensions had been added to produce a rectangular space with a parallel row of bare stone pillars supporting a central nave. In the transition from asylum to college the congregation shrunk from a herd of insane believers to a few rational devout undergraduates.

Lambe nodded in the direction of the organist in the choir stall above the front porch when he was satisfied everyone who could squeeze into the old wooden pews, onto the new plastic chairs, or just along the walls behind the pillars were in place. The crowd was bludgeoned into silence by the wheezy gasps and roars of the organ undertaking the opening bars of Bach's "Sheep May Safely Graze". When the music stopped abruptly after three minutes as if the organ had been shot, Lambe addressed his dazed audience. "Esteemed guests, colleagues, students, reporters, the police, and dearly beloved in Christ, we are gathered here this morning to pay homage to the provost of CAT College. I know that everyone believes that I murdered my wife but—"

The audience gasped with one collective breath.

"What wife?" someone shouted. "Who else have you killed besides the provost?"

"My wife, the provost, you idiot. We were secretly married just a few months ago."

"Why didn't you tell me they were married?" Jim whispered to Rose who was squeezed into the pew beside him.

"Because I didn't know," she replied. "I don't know everything."

"I didn't know they weren't married," Wallace said loudly, sewing epistemological confusion amongst his neighbours.

"Yes, my beloved wife." Without pausing to allow his audience to absorb this revelation of their nuptials or to even give them time to inform each other how surprised they were, he plunged into reciting the 23rd Psalm: "The Lord is my shepherd. I shall not want. He maketh me to lie down in green pastures; He leadeth me beside the still waters."

Sitting amongst the mourners Detective Sullivan, who had never heard these words before, made notes. Pandora's black sunglasses were focused on Lambe high in his ornate eyrie. He raised his voice and shouted at the roof to subdue the rising steam of murmur coming off the crowd. "Yea, though I walk through the valley of the shadow of death, I will fear no evil; for Thou art with me; Thy rod and Thy staff, they comfort me. Thou preparest a table before me in the presence of mine enemies."

Pandora muttered to herself that he was definitely in the presence of at least one of his enemies.

Lambe continued, "Thou anointest my head with oil; my cup runneth over."

"For now," Pandora growled.

"Surely goodness and mercy shall follow me all the days of my life, and I will dwell in the house of the Lord forever."

"You will. Don't worry. Sooner than you think."

"He means dwell in the house of the provost forever," Progress whispered to Wallace.

Doolittle in the front row turned around to face the congregation. "I knew they were married," she mouthed to Progress. "He told me," she lip-synched. "Coun-sell-ing con-fid-ent-i-al-i-ty." She was dressed in black from her shoes to her veil, which was obscuring her pantomime lip movements.

Lambe raised his eyebrows to the organist who caught the signal in the motorbike mirror screwed to the side of the organ to help him follow the musical cues from the pulpit. The racket drowned out the rising hubbub from the congregation with the opening bars of Schubert's "Ave Maria", music which Lambe had selected himself to demonstrate both his grief and his erudition. A second-year sales and marketing student, who had won the Student's Union singing competition, sang the words. Doolittle cried, from envy at having lost that contest. Being a counsellor, she was in touch with her feelings. She was experiencing frustration that students from the commerce faculty seemed to win everything that mattered.

When the final notes died away with honks and rasps from the old organ, putting the throng in mind of the death throes of a disgruntled camel, Lambe had already stretched out his arms in the direction he felt heaven to be located. After all, he was the most pious authority available on where the gates of Paradise might be opening at just that moment to receive Patricia the provost.

Wallace hoped she would be allowed in after the balance of her life was taken. He wondered what colour outfit she might be wearing for her appointment with her maker. He hoped it was her new green suit and that she had her wig on straight. No point in frightening Saint Peter. He moved his hand to his face to trap a tear as it ran down his cheek. He felt others were present who should do more crying than him. He had known his new friend a short time, but he realized he had lost a potential old friend. He suspected his future on campus would have been easier with her around. Maybe he should cry for himself, he thought.

"I hate funerals," Spencer whispered to Rose. "I was at a funeral just last week. Samantha's classmate died. She was devastated."

Rose ignored him.

Lambe was ready to continue with the service. "God knows, I know more than most that the Lord works in mysterious ways. Few can divine his greater plan for us. Fortunately, I am one of those chosen few. Just when we had achieved our greatest happiness together, sharing in the destiny of the college, He saw fit to cast the provost down the stairs."

"Who did he say pushed her down the stairs?" Rose asked Jim. She hadn't been paying attention because she was looking around, enjoying the rare experience of being on campus during daylight hours. If anything, she thought, the old college looked gloomier when illuminated by the unflattering sunlight.

"He says the Lord pushed her down the stairs."

"That's awful."

"It's a lie."

"Shush. I want to hear this," someone sitting behind them said.

"The Lord giveth and the Lord taketh away. When he closes one door, he opens a window."

"I missed that. What's he saying about ventilation? Did he say the provost got up in the middle of the night for a breath of fresh air? Wouldn't be surprised. That old house is stuffy."

"Will you shut up and listen."

"My beautiful wife was taken from me in her prime. I woke when I heard her cry out. Her exact words were 'Oh Jesus Almighty', just before I heard the sound of her rolling down the stairs. She was a pious woman to the end. We should be pleased she died with the Lord's name on her lips. But don't grieve, because the provost's death is not an end but the beginning of a new life – here in CAT College with me in charge. At an Extraordinary Meeting of the Academic Council this morning, convened at my request, the provost's powers were transferred to me on an interim basis until my appointment can be ratified at the next scheduled formal meeting of that august body. I must accept my divine fate."

There was a communal gasp from the front rows of the church accompanied by an outbreak of uncomfortable buttock-shifting amongst the grey-haired council members sitting together in the two back rows.

"Not one of those relics is under eighty," Spencer said to no one in particular. "I doubt any of them know what century we are in. Some of them could have been tutors to Napoleon."

"I know there are some amongst you who are hoping my recent tragic loss will mean I am free now to pursue matters of the heart over those of the head." He stared in Pandora's direction where she sat upright still holding him in the glare of her black sunglasses. "But I am not free. Apart from my responsibilities to answer the call of duty, my heart lies elsewhere." He shifted his gaze to Doolittle on her own in the front pew. There was a groan of disgust from a large section of the congregation on the right of the nave, largely formed from postgraduates.

Lambe continued, oblivious of the impression he was making on his audience. "The provost had a dream for CAT College. I have a vision. As a man of God, I know the divine plan for this academy. As a man of science, you know I know that most of you have serious psychological problems that are holding this college back from taking its rightful place amongst the elite business schools of the world. Change involves pain, a great deal of pain – for you." He paused to steady himself against the book rest. "My darling departed provost was too tolerant of some so-called disciplines, such as literary criticism, economics, geography, modern languages, classics and moral philosophy to name but a few, because she was a kind-hearted person who saw the best in everyone, and was thus easily exploited. But from today we can look forward to a new dawn in learning here at CAT College. There must be improved financial controls, less waste in the library and reductions in other unnecessary resources. Next year there will be no more departments of—"

When he raised his hand to wipe the sweat from his brow, the organist, misconstruing the signal, blasted the opening bars of Bach's "Toccata and Fugue in D minor" into the nave below. The organist had been dying to play this piece. He knew it wasn't on Lambe's list, being more suitable to horror movies, but he felt he might take Lambe's advice and implement changes for the better, as he saw them. The irony of music more suited to a Dracula film than a sombre funeral was not lost on Lambe's audience. They were lamenting less the death of their now universally and inconsolably mourned provost, Patricia, than the prospect of life under the terrifying reign of the acting provost, the Reverend Professor Stephen Lambe.

XXIII

Luctus Consolabilis
Consolable Grief

The scary musical interlude caused the funeral for Patricia the provost to lose its vital momentum and fizzle out. If he had planned more for the service, the Reverend Professor Lambe's sudden rage against the organist had made him forget what it could have been. He descended from the pulpit holding on to every available carved surface on the way down. Back on the floor of the chapel he supported himself on the end of the coffin while it moved on the trolley down the central aisle of the overflowing church. Sally Doolittle linked her arm into his.

The provost was to be cremated in the city because the tiny chapel graveyard was overflowing with expired incarcerated lunatics whose families hadn't wanted them back, dead or alive. Lambe wept, stopping only to exchange greetings with the influential academic delegates from other colleges who offered him their condolences and business cards. His audience couldn't tell whether his tears were flowing from genuine grief or from humiliation at the ignoble end to his public performance that he had meticulously rehearsed during his forty-six hours in jail. Doolittle dabbed at her eyes with a large white handkerchief she thought contrasted with her all-black ensemble and waved to her friends and clients in the crowd.

As she walked behind the coffin, Doolittle daydreamed about the male brain. She believed it was the most erotic organ. She fantasized that she had invented the technology to remove a brain in working order from its protective bone armour. She would kiss and lick the meninges while talking to them in a French accent, because she didn't speak French even in her imagination. But she loved French brains, literally. Her fondness for that organ and her genuine desire to help the student body through counselling set her apart from her friend Julie Progress.

Doolittle broke away from Lambe when she met Progress at the tiny congested front porch. She prattled on to distract from her secret inner life, which gossips often do.

"Hi Julie. What do you think?"

"Of what?"

"Of my outfit?" She pushed those around her in the crowded space back far enough to execute a single whirl to show off the full black effect before the space filled up again with bodies. She bumped against several cursing people who were trying to escape from the church. "Pretty cool, isn't it? I borrowed the dress, the veil, and the eyeliner from my sister who is a Goth."

"What are you doing dressed as a grieving mother? You barely knew the provost."

"This is true, but Lambe suggested someone had to support him today because she has no family of her own except for him since her mother's modelling accident, and he had to be up in the pulpit. The all-black was my idea because I've never been chief mourner before. My parents won't die or anything. What do you think? Too much?"

"Way too much. What now? *What* are you going to do now?"

"First thing is to get out of this black. Do you know it's starting to bring me down? All this crying is starting to depress me."

"I meant after today. Are you going to move in with the old goat now that he is free?"

"God no. He gives me the creeps, and he's always pissed. Didn't you notice he could hardly stand up there in the pulpit? He fancies me. Okay. He has promoted me in the counselling services centre, but I deserved that anyway. He has been begging me to let him supervise my doctoral thesis. He's ancient and has no stimulating ideas. He hates Derrida. Julie, you're not a romantic. You're a pragmatist. A cold-hearted cow, if you ask me. No offence. I need a man with a sexy mind. I'm waiting for a real French deconstructionist to sweep me off my feet. I'd even settle for a post-structuralist – or a post-anything for that matter. I'm getting desperate. Fat chance of my ever finding one of them in this dump. Lambe is just a boring psychologist. What I need is a stimulating psychoanalyst. I want to finish my doctorate and get out of here as soon as possible. I want to go to Paris. Maybe I will meet Doctor Post-modern there."

"Do you think he did it?"

"Did what?"

"Pushed the provost down the stairs."

Doolittle laughed. "No. I'm sure he didn't do it. He was at my place pissed out of his head. I couldn't get him to leave. He told me he would read Derrida's *Of Grammatology* in the original French if I agreed to have dinner with him. He made me swear I wouldn't tell anyone he wasn't there when the provost fell. I won't. He said if it came to it and he was put on trial, I could tell the police, but in the meantime, I was to say nothing because he doesn't want the story of her suicide to get out because the scandal would destroy his reputation in the college."

"Reputation for what?"

"I sigh. I thought you understood the mind. You would know it's all in the mind if you read more French philosophy: all in *his* mind. God only knows what goes on in his head because I don't – despite my counselling skills."

"Maybe he crept home in the middle of the night when you were asleep and killed her. Were *you* unconscious?"

"I was not. I only had a few."

"Yeah, a few bottles. You're not a reliable alibi. Maybe he is just using you because he knows you will tell everyone anyway."

"What do you mean? I'm not a gossip. I don't believe he could sneak out without my hearing him. He was pissed. I'm sorry I told you. I'll never tell you anything again. Despite what she believed, she was actually unhappy, he says."

"Why didn't she kill him?"

"I don't know. Look if you are going to ask me difficult questions, I'm not telling you anything else. Ever again. I swear it. Do you know Lambe says the provost sacrificed having children of her own for an ungrateful college and says he won't make the same mistake? That may have contributed to her suicide, he says."

"Is he planning to have children? With you?"

"Ugggh. No. He will have to buy children if he wants them because I am not having them with him. I must go. He wants me to sit in the chief mourner's car beside him. And don't say anything to anyone that I told you that he told me he didn't kill the provost, and that she killed herself because she didn't have children."

"Don't worry, I won't."

The mourners were squashed together in the central aisle as they followed the coffin out of the church. Spencer was squeezed up close against Pandora.

"Someone has to do something, and soon, about him," she said nodding in the direction of Lambe's retreating back.

"Who do you think it will be?" Spencer asked.

"You, you idiot. You and me."

"Leave me out of this. I don't know anything about revenge. That topic wasn't something we studied on our philosophy courses."

"I've warned you about talking philosophy. I can't think when you start philosophizing."

"Yes, but we're not – you know – doing anything. This is a church, Pandora. Come on, you can't be thinking about that now, can you? Imagine me as a priest and you a nun, confessing your sins. Or we could both be dressed as monks. We could meet on the altar in the middle of the night."

She turned to face him in the crush. "Shut up," she hissed. "Lesson one in revenge – if you don't help me, I will put our collection of short but engaging films on the Internet."

"But ... but ... everyone will see you doing ... oh God."

"I don't care. I'm desperate. If you don't help me, I will embarrass both of us; or, more precisely, *you*, because I don't do shame. I need this. I need your help." Pandora ground her teeth. "I need a cigarette."

"You need more help than just me: you need people who understand revenge."

Jim overheard this conversation because he was pressed against Pandora's shoulder from the crush of people behind him trying to leave the airless church.

"I'll help," he volunteered. "Whatever you need, I'll do it."

Pandora considered his proposal for a full half-minute of silence. "We can't talk here in the middle of this crowd," she shouted over the din. "We need to discuss our plans in private."

"Come around to my place. We can meet there," Jim said, without thinking through possible consequences because he was anxious to prove his commitment. Spencer looked at Pandora whom he assumed nodded in agreement when he saw a faint glint of light reflect from the slight movement of the black lenses of her glasses moving up and down.

"You know where I live."

Jim turned to Rose, who was pressed into his side. "Can you take a night off and join us?" he asked her.

"I was hoping you would leave me out of this. If the police have nothing against him, neither have I. I don't admire him, but then I don't admire anyone in the college."

"But think what the provost did for us. You owe it to her memory."

"But what use could I be?"

"You can be our intelligence officer: our eyes and ears."

"I do have an apple, raspberry, and almond cake I baked for you to make up for all the cabbage. Maybe it's a sign, because that's the first cake I've made in five years. I could serve it with tea."

Wallace saw Inspector Jackson standing against the wall behind a row of pillars searching the crowd with his eyes. He waved at Jackson before thinking perhaps it was an immature way of greeting a policeman on whose list of suspects for indeterminate and unknown crimes, he was confident he featured, doubtless at the top. Jackson waved back and smiled before resuming his search for the librarian.

Outside, Progress caught up with Wallace as the hearse was passing under the neo-gothic arch on which a blackened headless angel was being an ineffective sentinel over the proceedings below.

"Lambe didn't kill the provost. He believes she killed herself because she didn't have children. Doolittle told me. He was blacked out on her couch the night she fell. But Doolittle was also passed out at the time."

"Why didn't he give that alibi to the police?"

"He wanted to protect his reputation?"

"What reputation?"

"It's a French philosophical thing. Deconstruction."

"I see," Wallace said, not seeing at all.

XXIV

Scopae Novae
New Brooms

The Reverend Professor Lambe, acting provost of CAT College, sat behind the mahogany desk in the leather swivel chair in the funereal office where only days before Patricia had ruled. In Lambe's lobbying of the majority octogenarians on the Academic Council he was blissfully unaware that his own merits had much less influence than his vanity allowed him to imagine. The choice of provost had been made easier by what the council perceived as the disturbing attributes of Lambe's few rivals for the post.

The head of the commerce faculty, Professor Mathilda Maddox, routinely wrote to the council to complain of her treatment as a female member of staff. Her unhappiness was not helped when one of them wrote back to advise her that if she didn't remind everyone on every possible occasion that she was in fact a woman, no one would suspect. After all, the council member added, she must be aware she was known throughout the campus as Maddox the Man.

Lambe's other rival was Maurice Spencer, who took every opportunity possible to avoid any administrative responsibilities. He had become Head of Philosophy against his will, but then philosophers are divided on the role of will in our achievements. Historically, and for reasons no one could remember, commerce and technology were run as faculties, while arts was a collection of independent departments forming powerless fiefdoms dependent on a mighty monarch: the provost. No one in arts cared, because nobody understood the organizational structures anyway. Pandora managed some of the administrative duties of the arts in general by distributing them amongst the frightened department heads, doing them herself when unavoidable, or in most instances, just ignoring them while remarking to herself how the world had once more not stopped because some inane administrative task hadn't been done.

The head of technology, Casper Wall, who was small, thin, and prematurely balding, lead the procession into Lambe's office for the first inter-faculty meeting of the new regime. He had been a child prodigy and was now merely a genius with no qualifications. The Academic Council was unanimous in agreeing that in rewarding brains rather than qualifications lay the destruction of everything they held dear. But Casper Wall was too absorbed in promoting his online second-life avatar self to have time to advance the interests of his offline real-life self. For this, the first meeting of the new epoch, he was wearing a tracksuit to emphasize his indifference to the traditional semiotics of authority and to communicate his anarchic pride in his lack of formal qualifications, which he once more reminded anyone who would listen, he didn't need because he was a genius.

Next came Spencer, who felt overdressed when he saw Casper Wall. He had bought a new suit for the occasion, spending more money than he had ever done before on a single item of clothing, even for his daughter, Samantha, who always demanded the latest fashion whim.

Next came Maddox the Man, who was wearing a bespoke handmade broad pinstriped suit, handmade shirt, silk tie, and tiepin large enough for anyone to make out at twenty feet that she was a member of the Real Grass Golf and Country Club. Spencer felt under-dressed when he saw her.

There was room for everyone around the giant desk: the acting head of psychology – a hand-picked lackey known as Sidney the Sycophant, who had taken over from Lambe after his elevation – as well as the heads of the departments of classics, economics, geography, and literary criticism, the bursar, the head of student recruitment, and the chief financial officer. Pandora sat in the corner taking notes in her official role as secretary to the provost.

Lambe cleared his throat. "May I have your attention, gentlemen?"

"And lady," Maddox the Man put in.

Lambe ignored her. "I asked you all here today to inform you of my plans for the College. For far too long we have been drifting without a clear strategic vision. Look at our name: CAT College. That may have been sufficient for the past but is inadequate for the future. We need a new name that people will recognize and immediately understand what it means. But which comes first? The subjects we teach or the name? Ha! Now that is the challenge. Let's begin by reviewing the value of our current appellation. Let's start with T for technology. What use is technology to anyone?"

Casper Wall looked up from his smartphone for a longer-than-usual interval. "Younger people expect to find technology in a college, even in a falling-down ruin. A fossil like you can appreciate that they won't enrol to use only pen and ink – or maybe velum and quills, in the case of your classes. Tell your fellow dinosaurs on the Academic Council that, as a prodigy, I don't need recognition from this obsolete offline establishment. I can purchase whatever online qualifications you think I should have." He lost interest in the conversation when a notification pinged to tell him he had received a text.

Lambe glared at Casper Wall. "I accept that T is a good letter. It's a strong letter. Let's move on. A is for arts? I think we can all agree that arts are not needed these days. The meaningless search for meaning, for answers to questions that no one in their right mind would ever think of asking, is as obsolete as the quill our younger unqualified colleague was referring to just now. What ordinary man on the street would ever come up with a philosophy question on his own? And that isn't just my opinion. The illustrious Ludwig Wittgenstein *proved* that philosophy was complete nonsense. He didn't just believe it as another opinion amongst the billions of worthless opinions in philosophy. No. He *proved* it. I appreciate that his proof is too complex for your weak minds to grasp. If anything, Wittgenstein is more difficult to understand than even Immanuel Kant. You will just have to take it on faith from me. The same can be said for politics, history, sociology, economics, and anthropology. I mean, economics is just philosophy with numbers. Who even knows what anthropologists do? You are not going to meet a cannibal in a restaurant around here, are you? Let's face it. Nowadays no one is interested in questions about what it's all about, where we came from, where we are going, the meaning of life. And we already have the answers for those disturbed few who are interested. Or at least I do. I propose to get rid of the arts faculty and replace it with divinity."

"Will this cost us more money?" the chief financial officer asked.

"No, it won't. It should result in a saving because divinity is one of the most cost-efficient disciplines. It has all the answers. We just need a few idiots like Spencer here to come up with some questions to go with them."

The chief financial officer was satisfied, because he cared nothing for the choice of subject matter the academics decided to deliver as long as it remained within budget.

"Are you planning to get rid of all the arts, Reverend Professor Lambe?" Sidney the Sycophant asked nervously, anxious that his new-found power was slipping away before he even got to exercise it.

"No Sidney. Don't worry. You are safe. Psychology is a science when properly practised, unlike all the other nonsense I am talking about. And we may hold onto the classics for the sake of tradition, which looks good. And maybe geography also because we need to know where we are and how to find our way around. But everything else is going," he shouted, cutting through the air with the edge of his hand, fantasizing he was lopping off academic heads with a scimitar.

"But what am I and the rest of us in philosophy supposed to do?" Spencer whined.

"I will allow you all to transfer into divinity studies. You will thank me in the end. Where are all the grand theories in philosophy? Religion is where you will find big ideas. All the answers are there. Your students don't realize it yet, but they will be happy in divinity because they are only interested in the answers. You should be creative with the questions. They won't care what they are as long as they know the answers. Can you manage to do that much?"

Spencer was too upset to respond. He looked over to Pandora in the corner who had stopped taking notes, not because she was concerned about the proposed fate of philosophy, but because she was preoccupied with her own plans.

"What about commerce?" Maddox the Man asked. "What are you proposing should happen to us?"

"Thus far we have a D for divinity and a T for technology. Therefore, we need a vowel to make a good name that will be vital to our success. Can you do something with a vowel, Maddox?"

"You're crazy. You can't run a college in this fashion. We are intellectuals. We should base our decisions in reason," Spencer protested.

"I can run this college whatever way I choose. I am in charge now."

"How about women's studies?" Maddox the Man asked.

"That's not a vowel," Sidney the Sycophant told her, finding his confidence again now that he was reconfirmed in Lambe's favour. "You need an a, e, i, o or u. They are the vowels."

"Are you sure w isn't a vowel. Or s?"

"You have all gone mad," Spencer lamented.

"You can't talk about me in that manner. I am going to complain you to the highest authorities," Maddox the Man said. "I am complaining you to the … the … provost … here. You heard him, Lambe. You are a witness. I'll need you to sign something. Everyone picks on me because I'm a woman."

"It's your own fault for being a woman," Spencer told her.

She glared at him, gritted her teeth, and hissed, "I'll get you for that."

"Not if I get you first."

Lambe stood up by leaning on the desk. He pushed the swivel chair with the back of his legs, making a space in which he could jump up and down, clenching his fists, and screaming, "Obey me. Obey me," before sitting down again.

A full minute of silence followed, and then the chief financial officer said, "Can we please do what the provost asks and get back to the serious task of finding a value-for-money commercial topic that starts with a vowel. How about organization? That would give us DOT College. That has a ring to it."

Lambe's blind-crab fingers, that had now apparently achieved independence from his brain, scuttled across the polished surface of the desk on their manicured nails searching for a drink that wasn't there. He looked past his team to the cluster of armchairs around the glass table where he had spent hours alone with Patricia, sipping gins and tonic. A sudden freak wave of loneliness threatened to drag him out to a cold rough sea where he knew he would drown. He clung to the edge of the desk with all of the strength in his bony fingers. He remembered snatches of his conversations with Patricia. Looking at the empty chair where she used to sit, he addressed her. "There has to be some meaning to life, doesn't there?"

His audience remained silent, not attempting to answer his existential question nor even breathe. Instead, they waited for their boss's next words, which came almost at once. "What about education? If life is meaningless, training for it is doubly pointless. If that is the case then we can't do real damage, can we? Maybe it has some beneficial effect on the profoundly stupid. Who knows? I don't. What is the point in worrying how to regulate something that makes no fundamental difference in the first place? But that's what we do. We put more and more rules on our useless endeavours. I told you that time and time again. No point, I said, but you wouldn't listen." He rubbed his hand over his forehead. "God will show us the way. He has to, because if he doesn't, what is to stop us slaughtering each other?"

Lambe eyes tried to focus on the audience sitting around him at the desk. After several seconds he discerned his blurry colleagues.

"You will destroy our academic traditions," Spencer was saying. "You are undermining our intellectual practices."

"Nonsense. You are living proof that you don't need to be intelligent to be an intellectual. We will always be able to produce intellectuals like you. Why do you think the term was invented?"

"Oh. You're such a cynic."

"I am many things but not a cynic. Call it a special form of self-deprecation where I deprecate everything except myself." Lambe loosened his rigor mortis grip on the edge of the desk, banged on its shiny surface with both palms and shouted, "Right. What about a drink to celebrate?"

Sidney the Sycophant stood up and almost ran to the drinks cabinet. "What are you having?" he asked when he got there.

Pandora, even without training in critical self-reflection,

was aware she wasn't an intellectual. She didn't understand what was being said. However, she knew she didn't like it.

Meanwhile, in an office in another part of the college, Sally Doolittle was holding a counselling session with a distraught third-year technology student. Doolittle lay back on a worn dark-brown sofa flicking through the photographs in a magazine that documented the nuptials of a celebrity couple. At the other side of the room, facing her on a straight-backed chair the student sat clutching a fist of tissues that she had pulled from a box on the table beside her.

"I can't show you: it's too embarrassing. I'd rather kill myself," the student said, sniffling.

"Trust me. I've seen everything. You couldn't shock me if you tried. Can't be done." Doolittle turned the magazine sideways to study one of the guests at the wedding as if he was in a horizontal position.

"I thought he was the one this time. I had no doubts. I didn't think I could love again when James dumped me. Then I met Stan, and I knew it was forever until this new guy, Michael, I met on work placement. Oh God, what am I going to do? If – when Michael sees this, it's all over. Who knew that stuff doesn't come off?"

"Most people on the planet." Doolittle threw the magazine on to the table and said, "Come on. Let's see. I haven't got all day. A queue is forming outside. Drop your pants and give me a look."

The third-year student of technology stood up. "You're not to criticize me. I get enough of that from my mother. It wasn't my fault." She unbuttoned her jeans, slid down the zip, dragged them down over her large thighs, and while holding on to the waistband of her knickers spun around to expose her backside to Doolittle. "There."

"I can't see anything." Doolittle caught hold of the elastic and bent it downward in the middle exposing the top of the third-year's buttocks. In ornate Germanic lettering a solid black sentence running across the top of her haunches read "Ich liebe dick – mein kleiner Standard ewig."

The elastic whipped back against the soft flesh when Doolittle released it.

"Who did you say did this artwork?" she asked.

"My friend Tracy from commerce. We share a room."

"You trust Tracy to tattoo permanent messages onto your arse?"

"I do."

"Who is this Standard?"

"Standard? That's short for Stan. I mean, Stan is the shortened form of Standard, my ex-boyfriend. I didn't know that. Tracy told me."

"Why German? Is Stan— Standard German?"

"No. Tracy took German classes last year – German with business studies. She said Stan would appreciate it."

"What did Standard say when he saw it?"

"He just laughed. He's not romantic. What am I going to tell Michael? Do you have any advice?"

"Yes. I do. Stick with English when getting tattoos. That is better advice than you appreciate. If you must, try dating this Michael guy without showing him your arse. Tell him you have an arse complex. If that doesn't work, and he wants to take the

relationship further you could have the dick – I mean, 'dich' –
along with the … er … name 'Standard' professionally burnt
off and replaced with 'Michael'."

"Tracy says you can get tattoos off with a curling tongs."

"Have you ever had a major falling-out with Tracy – over a
boyfriend, for example?"

"No. Never. I mean Stan *was* going out with her before he
met me, but it's not as if she was in love with him or anything.
Stan told me she wasn't."

"She's a real friend. A keeper. Maybe you should let her
try that thing with the curling tongs. Or acid and sandpaper.
Maybe you should consider staying with Stan … erm …
Standard, if only for convenience; or better still – fall in love
with another Standard."

"Wow. That is such a coincidence. I had that very thought
myself, and it would save me so much pain if I could find
another Standard."

"In psychology we prefer to talk about synchronicity rather
than coincidence because we believe that things are connected
by meaning rather than by being merely causally related. You
would need to look into your unconscious for an explanation
as to why you wrote Stan's name on your arse in the first place.
Perhaps you are saying at a deep level that you always want to
be with a Stan? Or maybe you want to be standard – whatever
that might be. But that's a Jungian idea, and I am more
Freudian-slash-Lacanian. You would need a lot of sessions to
get to the bottom of that. Get it? *Bottom.* God, I'm good at
this. What is your father's name?"

"Alexander."

"Okay. That's not it. Pull up your jeans and get out of here.

I have more desperate clients waiting to see me."

"Thanks for the advice. It's refreshing to meet someone who is not judgmental."

"I know. What's the point when you have been through it all yourself?"

"Do you have a tattoo on your arse with your ex-boyfriend's name?"

"Yeah, but in French not German."

"Oh. That's not the same thing."

"It's not at all the same thing. Next," Doolittle shouted into the corridor through the open door.

XXV

Conlegium Unanimorum
A Society of Like-Minded People

The habitually loquacious Professor Maurice Spencer was speechless when he saw the books lining the walls all the way into the kitchen and beyond from the hall in Jim the porter and Rose the cleaner's house, which had been chosen as their operational headquarters. Rose had set out mugs for tea, milk and sugar. Her apple, raspberry and almond cake sat on a plate covered in cellophane. Pandora, who had arrived before Spencer, was sitting at the kitchen table, smoking.

"Where did you get all these books? Has the librarian seen this place?" Spencer managed to ask Jim. The front door bell chimed just as he took his place at the kitchen table.

"Who is that?" Jim asked Pandora and Spencer.

"It's the librarian," Pandora said. "I asked her to come. That was before I knew about your … erm … hobby," she said, holding her hands out towards the walls of books as if she was a priest admiring a congregation.

"You let her in," Rose commanded Jim.

"No. You do it. I'm afraid of her."

"What a bunch of cowards. Someone had better open the door. I'll go," Pandora said, standing up and stubbing out her cigarette on the top plate of the stack Rose had put on the table for her cake. Rose, Jim and Spencer looked at each other when she left the kitchen. They could hear Pandora greeting the librarian at the front door and asking her to come in. "Thank you," they heard the librarian say as she stepped into the hallway. "Where can I leave my coat?" In the kitchen they held a collective breath as they waited for a scream. It never came. Rose hurried out to intercept them. "I'll take your coat," she told the librarian.

The librarian shook hands with Jim and Spencer in turn before taking a seat. They hadn't yet fully abandoned the possibility of an outbreak of screaming. However, the librarian seemed free of book-related concerns.

"Tea?" Rose asked, coming back into the kitchen after balancing the librarian's coat on an unsteady column of books in the corner of the hall.

"We should sample Rose's cake or she will be upset," Jim announced trying to break the tension. He unwrapped the cellophane as Rose poured tea into mugs.

"Yes. Let's have tea and cake," the librarian said. "Jim, do you have a copy of Lombardo's translation of Ovid's *Metamorphoses*? I had someone in last week enquiring about it? I don't have it on the shelves. Perhaps you could loan me a copy?"

"I might have it somewhere, but it could take me a day or two to find it; that is, if I have it; and if I haven't, it might take me a week to find out it's not here."

"It might take you longer," Spencer said. "In philosophy we say the absence of evidence is not evidence of absence. Evidence you have a particular book because you found it is not the same as the lack of evidence that you have it, because you couldn't find it after a search; that is, if it had been here, which it might not be. Some philosophers find it reasonable to take the absence of proof of the existence of a book as positive proof of its non-existence, if you see what I mean?"

"And we were wondering why Lambe is planning to close down the philosophy department," Pandora said, lighting a fresh cigarette.

"This is why I always emphasize the management of books make a library and not the books themselves. That is why a catalogue is essential," the librarian said. "Your library is useless without the means of accessing your collection. You should have an issuing desk over there with a sign overhead. And a computer", she added, pointing to a relatively uncluttered corner near the cooker. "Ideally two terminals: one facing inwards for yourself and one facing out for users."

"But we don't have users," Jim protested.

"That is not the point. The principle of a catalogue is still valid. And I can loan you some of the better warning signs from the library I produced over the years. How large is your collection?"

"I have no idea," he said, turning red.

"I would guess you have at least sixty thousand items, give or take a book or two in a house this size using the attic space as a closed access stack." Jim was nodding. "You probably don't have enough journals and nothing online. Still. Impressive. I am pleased to find someone who shares my interest in books," she said, before falling silent and staring wistfully into the middle distance, daydreaming of her perfect partner: a bibliophile. Yes, the librarian was thinking how lucky Jim and Rose were when

Pandora interrupted her reverie as if she could see inside her head with her sunglasses.

"Aren't you screwing that policeman who came to the college looking for Wallace's mother?" Pandora asked.

"Oh him. Inspector Jackson. I loaned him a few philosophy books, but I haven't seen him since. I hope I didn't scare him away. A strange man, but I think he might be fascinating. Yes. I suppose I find him attractive, but we're not *screwing* each other as you put it."

Jim asked if anyone minded if he had a beer instead of tea. There was no dissent.

Spencer cleared his throat. "Pandora and I had a chat about what we should do about Lambe. We decided to form a group of like-minded individuals. We agreed – I hope you don't object even if I don't know if we have a quorum present – to kill Lambe and replace him with a more enlightened academic. Have I put that the right way, Pandora? That is what we agreed?"

"Yes."

"Pandora and I cannot imagine what will become of CAT College under his leadership without the humane influence of our dearly departed Patricia the provost."

"Should I take minutes?" the librarian asked.

"What?" Pandora snapped.

"I brought a notebook with me."

"We should also appoint officers if we take minutes. We should have a chair, a secretary and ordinary members," Jim suggested.

Following a thirty-minute discussion about the appropriate structure of their group, Spencer was elected chair, the librarian secretary, while Rose and Jim were deemed to be ordinary members. Pandora's role remained undefined. She aimed smoke rings at the bulging kitchen ceiling. A further twenty minutes were given over to the matter of recruiting new comrades. It was agreed that candidates' names should be forwarded to the secretary for full-committee consideration. It was also settled, to Pandora's relief, that a new member must be approved by at least 75% of the committee to be allowed join.

Pandora looked at her watch. "It's getting late. I think we should get on to our main agenda item: the assassination of the Reverend Professor Lambe," she said.

"In this matter I take inspiration from the moral leadership of our new colleague, Professor Rik Wallace. I'm proud to have had a small part in his potential brilliant contribution to CAT College by being on the interview panel that recruited him," Spencer told his fellow conspirators.

Pandora continued to study the ceiling and blow smoke rings.

"Should we ask him join our committee?" the librarian asked.

"No. Wallace is a creative theoretician," Spencer replied. "He is not the kind to get involved in practical undertakings such as the one we are proposing. That's the nature of his genius. Our group needs an inspirational figure who guides our decisions from a theoretical distance: from on high. You heard what he believes when he spoke so movingly at his inaugural lecture. I'll never forget his words and the impression they made on me that night." Spencer broke off to wipe a tear from his eye as he stared into the space above the librarian's head, recalling the feeling of the weight of stress lifting from his shoulders that fateful evening when he realized Wallace was speaking to him alone: someone to share the burden of the search for the truth. "Wallace is a champion of pure academic integrity. We cannot – should not – ask him to get his hands dirty implementing his own ideas. That is our task. Our duty is to put his thoughts into our actions. According to Wallace, we are morally obliged to kill Lambe before he turns us all into divinity lecturers."

"Is that what he said at his talk?" the librarian asked. "I wasn't there. I was at home. On my own."

"Not in those exact words but more or less. As I am the only one here qualified to explain what he meant, you must leave the interpretation, or hermeneutics as we philosophers call it, to me. According to Wallace, killing Lambe will be proven to be a good act when the benefits of his death reverberate throughout the college. Literary criticism, economics, history, moral philosophy, and the library, amongst others will benefit from his being sacrificed."

"Apart from the so-called moral justification we need to revenge the death of our dear, departed provost," Pandora added.

"I don't remember Wallace saying anything about revenge killings being morally acceptable," Spencer protested.

Pandora groaned with impatience. "Am I not entitled to my own view or is our noble leader Wallace the only person with an opinion that matters?"

It was now Spencer's turn to sigh in frustration at being surrounded by such obtuse students of philosophy. Why was it his bad luck, he wondered, that his discipline was one of those where everyone felt they could contribute their own worthless opinion? For the sake of the harmony of the new federation he resolved to stay calm. "Well, yes. I concede that while he didn't explicitly sanction revenge, it could be seen as an extra moral bonus on top of the general beneficial consequences of getting rid of Lambe permanently. But in general, leave the interpretation of Wallace's words to me. That is why I spent years at university studying the philosophical greats. I now realize it was to be ready for the unpredictable momentous occasion such as this when a new order emerges under the influence of an inspirational leader: the coming of a philosophical messiah."

"What new order will we put in place when Lambe is gone?" the librarian asked.

"Of course, the library will be expanded, particularly the philosophy section. The cleaning staff will be issued with the most up-to-date cleaning agents, mops, and dusters. Jim, what do you want?" Spencer asked.

"I want to retire, and I want two of those library computers the librarian mentioned. I also want Rose to be our intelligence officer. She has a natural aptitude for that kind of thing."

"So be it," Spencer said. "All in favour of Jim retiring this year say aye." Everyone said aye.

Spencer assumed Jim's nomination of Rose for intelligence officer was just a patronizing concession to his wife. He was unaware his own wastepaper bin had been forensically examined every working night since he first came to CAT College. He was also unaware that Rose, and consequently most of the college, knew that his wife would leave him before he did. He didn't suspect the general assessment of his mental balance propagated by Rose on the basis of the discarded notes between him and his daughter, Samantha. He could indulge Jim by agreeing to such a harmless request. He gave the matter no further thought. "All in favour of Rose becoming our intelligence officer say aye." Everyone said aye again. "That's unanimous."

"Who is next in line to become provost?" the librarian asked.

"I didn't think of that," Spencer said.

"From the documents I have seen from Academic Council meetings, the current preferred candidate is Maddox the Man. She is the most senior and qualified of the heads of faculty and the Academic Council do favour business people in general," Rose told them.

"She is as mad as Lambe. What can we do?"

"We have to kill her before we get rid of Lambe," Jim said. "Who are the other potential candidates, love?" he asked Rose.

"Spencer is next as the most senior head of an arts department," Rose confirmed.

"No. I won't do it. I don't want to be provost if it means voting to kill myself. I am a natural kingmaker rather than a king. Who is after me?"

"Casper Wall doesn't count because he has no qualifications. After him it would be an open competition between the heads of departments and the other senior lecturers. Sidney the Sycophant has no experience. As philosophy is the largest department, my money would be on either Wallace or Bacon. Wallace has more publications if that counts for anything, but Bacon has been here forever."

"Isn't he close to retirement?"

"No, he isn't," Pandora said. "He is only about thirty. He just looks old. It's the hair. Let's not go that far down the list of possible candidates or we will be here all night. Even if he is our spiritual leader, I think we can control Wallace. In the event someone else is offered the job we can deal with them at that time. Spencer, you could blackmail the council; you could tell them that it was Wallace or you. They would choose anyone instead of you."

"Wallace is a genius. He would be the perfect symbolic leader for the college."

"It sounds as if he is too caught up in the abstract concerns of the world of ideas to be bothered with anything practical," the librarian said.

Spencer was experiencing a rare bout of optimism. "Wallace will be assisted by Pandora when he becomes provost. It will be the good old days for philosophy again. I will maintain a behind-the-scenes position befitting my role as philosophical *consigliere*. Furthermore, with Maddox the Man gone, the commerce faculty will lose influence and their budget can then be reduced in favour of the humanities. We will ignore the technology faculty because, as Lambe says, what use is technology anyway? We will concentrate on growing the A in CAT College."

"The what?"

"The A. Commerce. Arts. Technology. A is for arts," he sighed. "Must I literally spell out my plan?"

"Yes, you must."

"We will prioritize the arts because abstract thought alone constitutes a proper education and not practical training. I am confident the overall consequences of our actions will be beneficial for the whole college proving we're morally justified in killing Lambe. Isn't that the point Wallace made? Are you in agreement with that, Pandora?"

"Yes. You can dress it up whatever philosophical way you want as long as it involves killing Lambe."

"If that is agreed, then the first thing we must do is get rid of Maddox the Man. All in favour of bumping her off say aye."

Everyone said aye.

"Through the chair, may I ask how we will do it?" Jim enquired.

"Do what?"

"Kill Maddox the Man."

"We should put that on our agenda. At our next meeting there will be no hopping from one topic to the next because we will circulate an agenda in advance. We will have minutes with minutes approved, etcetera," the librarian assured them. Everyone except Pandora supported the ideal of a well-run committee.

The hour that followed passed in a wide-ranging discussion weighing up the pros and cons of a variety of plans of attack on Maddox the Man. A proposal was approved as a consequence of fatigue rather than prudence – and after Pandora told them to get on with it because she was running low on cigarettes. Rose assured them she could determine Maddox the Man's whereabouts to within a twenty-minute window and design a plan to eliminate her that would appear to be an accident. Spencer ignored her assurances. He was already living in his imagination under the benign reign of the new provost he had created. The librarian asked if there were any AOBs. There weren't. She proposed that, once the committee was properly functioning, it would meet every Tuesday and Thursday evening.

"Tuesday and Thursday?" Spencer asked. "I'm not sure I

can get away from Samantha on both nights."

"I'm sure you can," Pandora said. She seconded the proposal. Then the members departed, exhausted by their efforts.

Alone, Jim and Rose sat watching a programme about ancient forms of torture on the Discovery Channel on television. Jim drank beer from a can.

"Is this the kind of rubbish you watch in the evenings while I am out working?" Rose asked.

"Yes. This is the kind of rubbish I watch."

"You need to find something useful to do with yourself when you retire. You can't spend the rest of your life learning how to pull a medieval heretic in two with a pair of plough horses."

The long-suffering house shuddered around them as if dismayed by what had been agreed earlier amongst the visitors in the kitchen.

XXVI

Exitus Electricia
An Electrifying Exit

Popular psychology has determined beyond doubt that those who drive white vans are independent trades people running their own enterprises who have above average indifference to the needs of others. While Rose the cleaner hadn't consciously thought about the colour, she had considered the size of the van she rented for the nocturnal outing of the secret society of assassins. Jim the porter drove, while Rose navigated from the front seat using Google maps. Pandora, Maurice Spencer, and the librarian sat on sheets of cardboard in the pitch-black load area in the back.

Rose directed Jim to the physics laboratory of the Technology College at the other side of the city. She had borrowed the keys for the laboratory from the head of that college's hygienic services, Maggie Murphy, who had started her cleaning career under Rose's tutelage twelve years before. Jim reversed the white van as near as he could to the large double doors at the far end of the long single-storey building. Rose selected a key from the ring of keys Maggie had given her and opened the lock as her conspirators shivered in the chill dim circle of light from the naked bulb above their heads.

Inside, they used their torches to make their way past the rows of long wooden benches to a storage room at the back that Maggie had assured Rose contained what she was looking for.

On the fourth attempt, Rose found the key on the ring that fitted the lock, while the others squeezed together as if terrified of what physics might lie behind the door. She stepped inside the windowless room and turned on the light. The conspirators switched off their torches and gazed in scientific wonder. A mechanical extra-terrestrial loomed above them in the middle of the floor. A flying-saucer-shaped steel dome formed the skull of this metallic creature. An eight-foot coiled neck ran down to a horizontal disc of copper pipe shoulders above a short body of white ceramic cylinders.

"What is that?" the librarian asked.

"That is a Tesla coil," Rose explained. "The dome-shaped part on top is the toroid. The column in the middle holding it up is the secondary coil. That wide disc on the bottom is the primary coil," she said pointing with pride to each part in turn. "Maggie Murphy – do you remember Maggie? No? She was a cleaner at CAT College. Never mind – Maggie says this is one of the biggest Tesla coils in the country."

"I've seen a picture of one of these in Samantha's science book," Spencer said.

"But what does it do?" Pandora asked.

"It's a transformer that massively increases voltage from the standard domestic current just by plugging it in to a normal socket. Maggie says this machine produces half a million volts. We can use it to create our own lightning, just like you see in a Frankenstein film. The electrical charge leaps off the toroid here and …" Rose was lost in her physics lecture.

"Why do we need our own lightning?"

"We will get Maddox the Man to stand under this Tesla coil with a golf club over her shoulder like this," Rose said, swinging her arms over her head in a practical demonstration. "We should consider dousing her with water to improve conductivity, I think. Then *kaboom* – a bolt of lightning comes off the top and fries her brain. Then we take her out to the Real Grass Golf and Country Club in the middle of the night, lay her in a bunker, and we have an accidental death. Simple."

The others stared at her where she stood dwarfed by the metal mushroom towering above her shoe-polish brown head. "Any questions?" Rose asked.

"How do you propose to get Maddox the Man to come all the way to this laboratory, soak herself and then swing a golf club under this giant doughnut?" Spencer asked.

"I haven't worked out all of the finer details yet. We need to move this coil to somewhere more convenient."

"Where have you in mind, love?" Jim asked.

"First let's get it into the van. It's on wheels. We can push it outside. Maggie says no one will notice because no one ever comes into this storeroom. After that I need to check the voltage and amperes. We need high voltage for an ideal scorching finish, but we also need enough amps for a frying effect; we don't just want to make her hair stand on end. But I haven't worked out the exact mathematical relationship between the two yet. I think it has something to do with Ohm's law, which gives you the ratio between current and volts as a relationship of resistance. What? Why are you looking at me like that?"

"How do you know all this?" Spencer asked.

"Talking with my colleagues in the hygiene community.

Jim, look in the boxes on those shelves for chainmail suits."

"Are we going to have a sword fight with Maddox the Man?"

"No. We need them to keep the operators safe. Whoever throws the switches will be protected from electrocution by wearing a chainmail suit because the current will be conducted over them rather than through them. And we do not need a Faraday cage because that is used to screen people from shocks – which we don't want."

"If you say so, Rose."

"We also need a potentiometer to adjust the resistance, thereby increasing the amps to the required level. That will give us more flexibility."

"A potentiometer? What do they look like?" Jim asked, searching a shelf.

"According to Maggie the linear sliding models are stored in one of those drawers over there. Come on. Let's get what we need and get out of here." Rose clapped her hands together to hurry them up.

The conspirators found themselves obeying without asking more questions.

Three days later the Tesla coil was set up and wired to Rose's satisfaction. The librarian had designed, composed, and printed an invitation following Rose's instructions. Rose herself placed the bait on Maddox the Man's desk just before midnight. It was a simple lure. Large black letters ran across the top of a white rectangular card that read: "Real Grass Golf & Country Club". Below this a message addressed to Mathilda informed her that she was warmly invited to the launch of an indoor driving range for real women the following Thursday evening at 8 p.m. The card specified that complimentary refreshments would be served, and she should come alone dressed to golf with her own clubs. In case Maddox the Man was concerned that the venue was a warehouse in an industrial estate, a footnote explained that the course deployed the latest technology while repeating the fact that the invitation was strictly limited to female members of the golf club. Leaving nothing to chance, a second footnote required Mathilda to text an RSVP to the librarian's private phone number. In a third footnote, she was reminded to bring the invitation with her.

On the appointed Thursday at 7.55 p.m. Maddox the Man parked her car outside the warehouse, heaved her clubs from the booth, and slung the bag over her shoulder. She followed the painted white arrows on the walls around a corner to the door where a large cardboard sign indicated it was the "Official Indoor Driving Range of the Real Grass Golf and Country Club". A smaller sign underneath reminded patrons to make sure they were wearing their golf shoes before coming inside. Maddox the Man looked down at her feet to check she had her spikes on. She was also wearing a light blue beanie, a navy-blue long-sleeved lamb's wool sweater with a grey-and-white diamond pattern and a tiger-striped golf skort with black shorts underneath. In this costume she felt ready to face any golfing challenge imaginable. But then her imagination was less vivid than Rose's.

Inside, she found the librarian sitting at a desk behind a pile of brochures for the Real Grass Golf and Country Club. Behind the librarian was another door with a sign with the words "Driving Range" written on it.

"What are you doing here?" Maddox the Man asked.

"I need the extra work. I have expensive habits. Take a five iron from your bag, leave the rest of your clubs over there, and go on inside."

"Where are all the other real women?"

"They're inside. Keep in mind this driving range is the latest in golfing technology, so follow all instructions precisely."

Maddox the Man opened the door and stepped into a large room constructed from unplastered blocks. The Tesla coil stood in the middle of a concrete floor. A scene of rolling hills had been crudely painted onto the end wall. Her legs carried her on their own volition until a metallic scrape from her spiked shoes halted her on the middle of a sheet of steel. A thick cable soldered onto its edge snaked across the floor and out a side door to an iron bar that Jim had hammered into the soft ground. Someone in a chainmail suit clanked across the floor and threw a jug of water over her without either explanation or warning. She was thinking that had she known to expect weather effects indoors she would have worn her wet gear. Then the room was plunged into darkness. When she heard someone yell, "Drive", responding to years of shouted lessons, she swung the five iron over her shoulder. In the millisecond between the command and the swing she thought she recognized Pandora's voice. Then she heard another voice shout, "Throw the switch now, Jim."

A stream of ragged snakes of fire, accompanied by a sound resembling the droning of bees, came out of the darkness. The horizontal strands of electricity leaping off the toroid coil bent at right angles, forming a series of elbows on the legs of a giant electric spider. One of these legs stood on Maddox the Man. In the blue-green-flashing light she saw a figure dressed in a chainmail suit standing against the wall holding a lever. Then she had to squeeze her eyes closed to protect them from the stinging light that seemed to be coming from inside her skull. She felt elated as the electricity slowed her thoughts to the point where she could think about what she was thinking, which, when she thought about it, was actually nothing.

After a minute it was dark again as Jim turned off the current. Rose shone a flashlight on Maddox the Man who was still standing with the club raised above her head. Her light blue beanie had come off and her hair was standing straight up.

"More amps. We need more amps," Rose shouted at Jim.

"What's the formula? What does Ohm's law state?" Jim pleaded. He was flustered.

Rose clinked across the floor towards him in her suit of gleaming chainmail.

"Give me that," she said, grabbing the potentiometer. "Quick. Mental arithmetic. What is a half million divided by twelve? That's twelve into fifty goes four times and ..."

Maddox the Man stared at the two knights muttering together about mathematics with their helmets almost touching. Why weren't they discussing maidens like all good knights should? She wanted to ask them to rescue her, but she wasn't able to speak.

"I will increase the resistance to there," Rose said, sliding the knob of the potentiometer along the comb of wire to the halfway point. "That should do it. We haven't time for fine calculations. Stand back."

Jim closed the gate on the lever switch.

The abrupt bang of electricity was louder this time, and the swarm of bees around the toroid coil angrier. Maddox the Man was intermittently visible as the giant electric spider stamped again and again on her head with the same large leg of electricity. Jim held the gate of the lever down on the switch for twenty seconds, his counting to himself drowned out by the noise.

The world seemed to be suspended in an amber haze when he finally opened the gate. Maddox the Man was still upright. She was making a humming sound. Smoke rose from her hair and from the armpits of her lamb's wool golfing sweater. She stared at Rose and Jim with unseeing eyes because her brain was boiling. Her feet began to stagger towards them while her arms still held the club above her shoulder.

Without the benefit of more scientific calculations, Rose pushed the knob on the potentiometer all the way to the end. Jim slammed down the gate to reconnect the circuit. They were of one mind. Maddox the Man's feet began to dance. Over the noise Jim could hear Pandora, who was standing as far back as she could because she didn't have a chainmail suit, screaming, "Stop. Stop, for God's sake! We want people to be able to recognize her."

Maddox the Man, who was welded into a single inflexible post, fell sideways, hitting the floor like a felled tree.

They put Maddox the Man in the back of the rental van still holding the club that was fused to her hands. Jim drove the van to the Real Grass Golf and Country Club where Rose knew the cleaner. Spencer followed in Maddox the Man's car, which he left in the car park. Pandora, Jim, and Rose carried

Maddox the Man out onto the course. Spencer carried her bag of clubs wondering what anyone saw in the game of golf.

The next morning Betty Nolan, aged eighty-three and a half, was first out onto the course with her playing partner, Clarissa Butterworth, aged eighty-seven and a quarter. They liked to get an early start because they weren't as fast as they used to be and were annoyed when overtaken by the impatient younger players – which was all the other members of the club. Betty Nolan was confident she had seen everything someone who was three-times Lady Captain, Honorary Treasurer and Vice-President of the Real Grass Golf and Country Club might expect to see on a golf course during fifty-two years. She had seen two-inch putts missed; fist fights in the ladies' locker room over gimmes that hadn't been given; Waterford Crystal lost and won; semi-naked couples in the rough just off the fourteenth fairway including ex-Captain Higgins in the embraces of the seventeen-year-old son of ex-Captain Smyth who had been playing off eleven; cards mismarked; and drop shots not recorded. However, she had never seen such a favourable lie as this on the edge of the eight for a chip and run to make her par for the first time ever on this hole. But Clarissa Butterworth, twice Lady Captain, was lying in her line of fire: not Clarissa's ball but Clarissa herself.

It was the experience that comes with age rather than medical qualifications that made Betty confident that Clarissa had had a fatal myocardial infarction on seeing the body in the bunker behind the eight, which, while not visible from the tee, was noticeable from where Clarissa had been attempting to putt from this side of the green. A man. Yes, Betty was confident it was a man, even if he was wearing diamond earrings and a golf skort. He clutched a five iron in his hands. Smoke rose from his hair. Why he chose to hit a ball out of the bunker with a five iron and not a sand wedge before being hit by lightning she couldn't understand. But then she had seen everything. Clarissa was dead, as was the man with the diamond earrings in the bunker. There was nothing she could do for them now. Betty knew she was running out of potential rounds of golf and might not get such a shot again with the pin in this position. She decided to drag Clarissa to the edge of the green to take her chip shot. She was sure Clarissa would have done the same for her. She would call for an ambulance when she holed out.

The ambulance, when it arrived, called for backup, because by then Betty Nolan was lying on the green having put out her disc dragging Clarissa by the heels out of the line of her shot. Betty wept with frustration at missing what was her best ever chance of making par on the eight after fifty-two years of trying. Who knew when she would be back in action again? The smouldering body was loaded into one ambulance, while Clarissa and Betty were put in the other for the sake of their golfing partnership. As the paramedic closed the back door, he heard Betty muttering, "Damn you Clarissa. Why couldn't you have died in the rough," before his colleague driving the ambulance hit the siren.

XXVII

In Optimum Propositium
The Best-Laid Plans

The college chapel was almost empty for Professor Mathilda Maddox's funeral service. The students of the faculty of commerce signified their grief by vanishing from campus when given a day off classes to concentrate on mourning the passing of their business mentor. A few mourners were scattered over the front pews, an empty gap behind them, then Rik Wallace and Julie Progress sitting together in the middle of an otherwise empty pew; behind them, another gap to the back row occupied by the satisfied assassins.

The Reverend Professor Lambe was in his eyrie on top of the pulpit. "We are gathered here together, this time to commit the remains of our *female* colleague, Professor Mathilda Maddox, Head of the Faculty of Commerce, and CEO and Principal Mobility Officer at Maddox Management, to everlasting peace. We have the consolation of knowing that Professor Maddox died doing what she enjoyed most in life: playing golf; second only to her love for complaining. She didn't know what hit her. Better known to her colleagues and students as ..." he droned on.

"I'm sorry I doubted you, Rose," Maurice Spencer said.

"You did an excellent job. Highly scientific."

"Thank you. I am pleased everything worked out so well. My one regret is that Betty Nolan, who found Maddox the Man, may be facing charges for moving her golf partner's body. The ambulance crew saw heel marks on the green. Also, I admit I could have studied Ohm's law with more attention."

"It's good for the environment that Maddox the Man is being cremated, considering she is more than halfway there already," the librarian put in.

"In case you are having any ideas about me, I want to repeat my disinterest in becoming provost. Wallace can have that job. Do you hear me, Pandora?" Spencer asked.

"Stop worrying about yourself. We must decide what to do about him up there," Pandora said, nodding her black glasses in the direction of Lambe. "It's time we dealt with him."

"Do you have a plan, Rose?" the librarian asked. "I would prefer if we didn't have to lift heavy machinery this time or travel around in the back of an airless van."

"Yes. I have. In fact, it's Jim's plan. We will go to Lambe's house in the evening in Spencer's car. We will jump him, knock him out with chloroform we can buy online, and tie him up with duct tape. To avoid leaving marks on his ankles and wrists we should wrap the tape around bandages. Then we put his head in the oven, turn on the gas, leave a note in which he confesses to killing Patricia the provost and declares he is unable to go on because of his feelings of guilt. We remove the tape and bandages when he is gassed, and we have a suicide. Simple."

"That sounds good," Spencer said, nodding while running over the steps in his head. "A straightforward plan leaving little to go wrong. Maybe we should order some gasmasks for ourselves."

"I'll make a note of that," Rose said.

"Yes. That plan seems reasonable," the librarian mused. "It doesn't involve moving bodies in the middle of the night or heavy lifting."

"Does anyone have other ideas?" Spencer asked looking along the row. "No? If there are no other suggestions can all those in favour of Rose's plan say aye."

"Wait a minute. I appreciate Rose is some sort of homicidal genius, but I have an idea you might want to consider before voting," Pandora said.

"Okay. Tell us if you must," the librarian sighed, reopening her notebook to take more minutes.

"Rose's plan is too humane. We can't even bruise Lambe. He won't feel a thing because he will be unconscious. He won't even know it was us or why we did it. I say, we kidnap him, chain him to a wall and—"

"Whose wall?"

"Any wall and—"

"Your wall?"

"I don't have a basement. We can find a basement and chain him up and every day I – we – can go there and burn him with cigarettes and—"

"Did I tell you, Pandora, I don't want to be the provost? You will remember that, won't you?"

"We could plant a bomb under his desk with a note that popped up just before it exploded explaining to him that he was going to die and—"

"You work in the office beside his."

"I would be out at lunch. There are such things as timers or remote control switches."

"Do you have a bomb?"

"We can get one on the Internet. Same place Rose is planning to buy her chloroform. They must sell bombs."

"Why don't we use the Tesla coil again?" Jim asked.

"Lambe doesn't play golf."

"We must decide now. The service is coming to an end," the librarian put in. "Let's vote on Rose's original plan."

The conspirators at the back of the chapel, including Pandora, all said aye at the exact moment the few mourners at the front of the chapel said amen in response to the prayer for the departed.

"Is there any other business?" the librarian asked, scribbling in the notebook that she balanced on her knees.

"I could sort this business on my own if I had a basement in my house. An enormous basement with a lot of chains," Pandora said, lighting a cigarette.

Spencer leaned towards her as he stood up to follow Maddox the Man's coffin out of the chapel. "Remember, Pandora, I don't want to be provost. Are you doing anything this evening? Prison guards and prisoners? I am free all night because Samantha is camping out with the Girl Guides."

XXVIII

Onus Discipulorum
The Burden of Followers

At night before going to bed Rik Wallace had developed a compulsion to inspect the kitchen wall for signs of cracking to satisfy himself that Mrs Wallace wouldn't be staging another resurrection. Now he was sound asleep dreaming that the real Rik Wallace was sitting on his chest with his stubby fingers wrapped around his throat, while he lay on his back on one of the college's immaculate lawns. He couldn't lift his arms to defend himself. Mrs Wallace was trying to push her son aside saying, "Let *me* strangle the bastard." Then he was running. The Wallaces were chasing him across the quadrangle that had grown into a meadow since Patricia's death. The provost was waiting for him on the other side of a prairie that expanded as he ran. She was pointing him out to the Reverend Professor Lambe who was kneeling beside her in prayer. A grave opened up in front of his feet. He couldn't stop his momentum. He tumbled into the black pit. While falling through the darkness, he heard a voice demanding he wake up.

"Wake up. Wake up. For God's sake, Rik, wake up," Julie Progress was hissing into his ear.

"What? What is it?" he asked, his brain coming awake

with a jolt while his body continued to fall through the lumpy mattress.

Progress put a hand over his mouth. "Shissssh," she said. "Shut up. I hear voices."

"Oh Christ. You're not going mad, are you?"

"No. They are real voices – outside my head. There are people in the garden. Someone is digging up the patio. Maybe the previous occupants have come back for treasure they buried out there years ago. Go and see what is happening."

He looked at her in the dark. Even for a doctorate student, he thought, she had an overactive imagination. He listened for sounds from outside. He heard a cough, followed by the grating rasp of metal scraping stone, which, in turn, was followed by cursing. "Maybe we should call the police," he whispered.

"Are you crazy? We can't call the police. I don't think we are police-calling kind of people, do you? They might even *be* the police out there searching for your mother."

"Don't you think they would turn up in daylight with warrants?"

"Maybe. I suppose. Take a gun and see what is going on?"

"A gun? A gun? Where would I get a gun?" he was almost shouting. "I'm a professor of moral philosophy."

"Shut up. They'll hear you before you're ready for them."

"I'm never going to be ready for them. Let's ignore whoever they are and go back to sleep."

"We can't go back to sleep."

"Speak for yourself. I'm exhausted from the same recurring dream every night."

"I'll analyse your dream some other time. You must have a hammer. There are all kinds of tools lying everywhere around this house. I keep tripping over them. You never put your tools away. That's not a sign of a skilled workman. Get a hammer."

"I'm not going to hammer whoever is out there." He paused in defeat. "I suppose I could take it with me for protection."

"There's more than one person out there. It sounds like a crowd."

Wallace got out of bed and groped his way around the untidy mounds of clothes, discarded tools, and lengths of timber to the living room where he searched with his fingers in the toolbox on the floor. He found a hacksaw that he gripped in both hands as he tiptoed towards the patio doors. He stood just behind the doorframe and peeked out. The cold weak light from a half-moon illuminated a black and grey drama being played out in the garden. He recognized Maurice Spencer who was up to his knees in a trench in the middle of the patio removing soil with a spade and depositing it on the stones beside him. Pandora was standing back a little, supervising the dig while smoking a cigarette. Beside her the librarian was holding a torch, directing its light into the hole in which Spencer was working. Wallace unlocked the door and stepped outside into the ensemble without thinking through the possible consequences. "What the hell is going on out here?" he demanded to know.

"Told you. Told you he was in there. Told you we would wake him up. What did I tell you?" Spencer asked no one in particular. He climbed out of the trench by leaning on the spade. "We would have knocked, but Rose assured us you were attending the international interdisciplinary conference on the Application of Moral Brains to Emerging Technologies at the Freedom Centre. We thought the house was empty."

"I didn't say anything to Rose about that conference. Besides, I changed my mind. I realized I didn't want to leave the campus at this point, or perhaps ever. Progress was supposed to go in my place, but she doesn't want to leave me alone with the graduate population. We are at that stage in our relationship."

"You mean Progress is here with you? Inside? Damn Rose's so-called intelligence. Pandora insisted on this amendment to our initial plan," Spencer offered in explanation, pointing to the hole with the shovel.

"What is going on?" Progress asked. She was standing in the doorway holding a hammer. Wallace looked at the hacksaw in his own hand and passed it back to her. "I don't think you want to know," he said. "Take this and put it in my toolbox along with that hammer."

"We are the CAT College Federation for the Improvement of Society and Hygiene, CATfish for short," the librarian explained. "The hygiene was Rose's idea; which is understandable, I suppose, because she is a cleaner. We took your advice and killed Lambe," she continued. "But because I missed your inaugural lecture, I had to rely on what Spencer calls his hermeneutics to know what you wanted us to do."

Before Wallace could find his voice, Spencer began talking to himself. "Damn it. I *knew* Maddox the Man was beginner's luck. We should never have listened to Rose. People influence me too easily. That's my problem."

"One of your *many* problems," Pandora clarified.

"Maddox the Man? Do you mean you killed her?" Wallace asked, momentarily forgetting about Lambe.

"Yes, we did," Spencer confirmed.

"But she was hit by lightning."

"Rose organized everything," Pandora said with reluctant pride. "She has power over nature."

"Can we focus on the current body?" Spencer asked. "There was a complication in our original plan. We had to make an impromptu committee decision to bury Lambe here because no one will search the home of a respected moral authority for dead bodies. That's him in the bag."

Just then, Wallace heard gasping from the direction of an overgrown flowerbed. Jim and Sally Doolittle came staggering from behind a large shrub each carrying one end of a body-sized black plastic bundle that was dragging along the ground where it sagged in the middle.

"I didn't tell you to kill Lambe," Wallace shouted.

"Shissssh. You'll wake the neighbours. We in CATfish have already unanimously agreed I am the best judge of what you said and what your utterances mean. You did say to do as you said and not as you do. Or was that the other way around? We understand and appreciate you couldn't kill Lambe yourself because of your need to remain theoretically morally pure, but you did say the rest of us could do it. You told us the college would be better off without him. You instructed us to kill every bad academic who stood in our way."

"I thought I was talking about the college being better off without me. I need a drink."

Wallace went back inside the house and turned on the lights.

"What are they doing out there?" Progress whispered.

"It's some sort of federation of psychopaths from the college. I don't think they mean us harm. Me, at least." Wallace poured wine into a beer glass and went back outside to supervise the burial. "That looks deep enough," he observed, peering into the trench.

"Maybe you are right. We don't want to be here all night," Pandora agreed.

"I'm not coming out," Progress said from the living room. "I'm not coming out," she repeated. She stepped out onto the patio when she caught sight of Doolittle. She was holding the hammer out in front of her. "Sally. What are you doing here?"

"Oh, hi Julie. Isn't it exciting? I was having dinner with Lambe when the members of CATfish showed up. I was there against my will – sort of. Can you believe Lambe is a good cook – *was* a good cook? I would have gone home earlier when I had finished eating, but he kept speaking French and reciting passages from Derrida's *Of Grammatology* from the original French. Or should I say *De la grammatologie*. I couldn't follow it. Difficult enough in English. But the food was delicious."

"Sally. Can you get to the point? Why are you here?"

"The members of CATfish said I could either join their federation or become collateral moral damage. So here I am. It wasn't a difficult decision because I am a counsellor."

Spencer interrupted to explain the situation to his guru, Wallace. "Sally was at the house having dinner with Lambe when we arrived to … ahm … remove him from the moral equation of the college. I distracted him while Pandora sneaked up behind. The chloroform that Rose bought online didn't work, which I suppose is just typical. Good job we didn't buy a bomb, which Pandora wanted. We should have known we couldn't trust anaesthetics bought on the Internet. I'm going to demand a refund. There was a struggle, and Pandora hit Lambe on the head with a champagne bottle. Sally wouldn't stop screaming. Pandora wanted to bump her off too, but we put it to a vote. Pandora doesn't have much patience with students because she doesn't deal with them on a daily basis like the rest of us have to. In any event, as Sally wasn't included in the original moral calculation of consequences, bumping her off would have complicated our moral totting-up. We thought about including her as a neutral zero because, according to your teachings, she had a fifty per cent probability of being a force for evil in the future anyway. We didn't intend to kill her when we arrived at Lambe's place. It's not the intention that counts, as you preach, it's the consequence. But you know that better than I, as you are the master."

"Will you shut up?" Pandora asked.

Spencer leaned towards Wallace and whispered in the hope of not upsetting Pandora with more philosophizing. "Overall, I felt we needed more time to think about killing Sally. As it turns out, we made the correct decision because she has proven useful. We planned to leave Lambe with his head lying in the oven, but after Pandora hit him, we couldn't work out how to make it look as if he killed himself with a champagne bottle. So here we are. Plan B."

"Teachings? Preach? Master? I don't preach. You all need help. You need to see a psychiatrist, or an exorcist, or a psychologist, or any kind of an 'ist'."

"Like this one here?" Jim said, dropping Lambe's feet onto the patio. "I don't think he can help us. We understand your attitude," he added. "Spencer explained it to us. Your role is to provide the theoretical guidance, and ours is to implement it in practice. You are a person of the mind. We are a federation of activists."

"Don't get involved in this, Julie. Go back to bed," Wallace told Progress.

"Will she be all right?" Pandora asked.

"She can join our federation if she likes," the librarian suggested.

"That would be okay. I could do that. I would like that," they heard Progress say, now back inside.

"Oh, that would be fantastic. We could have fun together." Doolittle told her through the door.

"I am glad you joined, Sally" Progress said, coming outside again.

"I'm glad that creep won't be chasing me around the campus anymore, which has to be a moral positive. But I'll miss his cooking. I hope I keep my job in the Student Counselling Services."

"We're not joining anything," Wallace told Progress.

"You are eligible for honorary membership, being our inspiration. However, Progress must apply to our secretary, the librarian here, for consideration of her application. But, in the circumstances, I would be confident she would be accepted," Jim told Wallace. "We have everything worked out. Rose is back at Lambe's cleaning up any evidence. She established Lambe would be home tonight, but there was what we call an intelligence failure because she was unsuccessful in determining Sally's whereabouts. It was a last-minute date. It's no one's fault. We're not blaming Rose, are we?" he asked, looking around at the others. "Just an intelligence bungle. That sort of thing happens in the best secret organizations."

Spencer looked down at his feet and asked, "Is it normal to have two bungles in one night?"

Jim didn't say anything. He was disappointed Rose had made mistakes. He knew how much she wanted to impress the members of CATfish. Yes, he thought, in hindsight shopping online was a mistake. He resolved that in future they would keep away from anaesthetics. Better to stick with the laws of physics.

"But my patio is ruined. I just finished laying that yesterday and you come along the very next day and dig it all up. What are the police going to think if they show up and find a body-shaped hole in my patio?"

"Why would the police show up?" Pandora asked.

"No reason," Wallace lied.

"Don't worry about it," Jim told him. "We will leave it looking the same as we found it. You can rely on me. I know what I am doing when it comes to building jobs. Not like you and my ladder, which hasn't moved once since the day you leaned it against the philosophy department and you haven't broken your neck as promised."

"The paving stones will subside leaving a grave-shaped hollow above them on the patio when the body settles."

"Listen to Mister Expert-in-hiding-bodies. I have thought of that. We are digging down deep, compacting the soil and adding dry cement to the gravel base. It will be a perfect job. One shower of rain, and even you won't know we have been here."

Pandora and the librarian rolled Lambe into the hole in the patio.

"Do you want to say a few words on behalf of CATfish?" Spencer asked Wallace.

"No, I don't."

"Okay. I'll say something." Spencer clasped his hands together, stood at the edge of the hole and bowed his head. The others, except for Pandora, gathered around bowing their heads in turn.

Spencer began his graveside panegyric. "Dear members of CATfish and our esteemed inspiration," he said, glancing at Wallace. "And potential new member," he added, moving his gaze to take in Progress beside him. "We lay the Reverend Professor Lambe to rest under this patio. Lambe was a father figure to me when I first came to CAT College. I looked up to him for guidance. But I was soon disillusioned. I was left with a feeling of aporia." He stopped because Pandora was staring at him from the far side of the hole in the patio. "What? That's a feeling of emptiness when something you believed turns out not to be true," he explained. "I experienced aporia when I realized Lambe was a bollix. That's all I'm saying."

He now addressed the hole. "Lambe, you told me I was an intellectual sheep in search of a shepherd, and I shouldn't look to you for inspiration. Socrates perhaps, but not you – nor French philosophers. Do your own thinking, you used to say. So I did. This is what happens to those who disappoint an intellectual like me on the long and winding road to the truth. You deserved this for what you did to the provost; not that we did this for revenge because that would be a breach of the Wallacian principles."

"You don't know what he did to the provost," Progress said. "Her death was an accident or suicide. Tell them Sally what you told me in the church."

"My God. You're such a gossip, Julie. I'm saying nothing."

"What are these Wallacian principles?" Wallace asked.

"I am writing up a codex of your ideas."

"What ideas? I don't have ideas!" Wallace was shouting again.

"Can we get on with the burial service?" Pandora asked. "We can discuss your theological position some other time."

"It's not theology. It's philosophy. The two disciplines are often confused, but they are very different," Wallace explained.

"I agree," Spencer said.

"Please don't agree with me about anything."

"Okay. Anything you say. You are the authority."

Pandora rolled her sunglasses towards the sky, which was clouded with balls of black cotton.

Spencer bowed his head again. "Amen." The others, except Pandora, echoed his amen.

Wallace went back inside while they filled the grave where he found Doolittle standing at the table with Progress, who was still holding the hammer. Wallace sat down beside them and pressed his tired eyes with the heel of his thumbs. "Imagine. Once upon a time I couldn't live without trying to have complete control in my life. Now crazy people surround me on every side and I don't seem able to worry about it anymore. Maybe I deserve this for what I did. I should have just handed myself over to the police and gone straight to jail. Maybe it's not too late."

"What are you talking about? No one is going to jail," Progress said studying the hammer.

"Why don't you put that down? I should be paranoid, but I know I'm not because those people out there are actually trying to ruin my life."

Progress sat down beside him. She placed the hammer on

the table before taking his hand in hers. "You see, it is good to talk. What you are experiencing is pronoia, which is the belief people are conspiring on your behalf. There are only a tiny few who have ever been able to have that feeling. Those people out there on the patio burying Lambe are doing that *for you*. They are conspiring *for you*. They want to make the world a better place *for you*. They are promoting your moral vision for mankind."

"That's amazing." Doolittle said. "I'd love to suffer from pronoia."

"They would be helping me if they just left me alone. I'm not a moral authority on anything."

"You understand ideas, but I understand people, which is just as important. That is why we make such a super team. I am convinced your natural modesty appeals to Spencer. That is what inspires him. Imagine how far we can go in the college now we are part of their group. What are they called? Cat flap? Cat nip?"

"CATfish. We are called CATfish," Doolittle reminded her.

"Whatever. Now that we are part of CATfish, we can go straight to the top. I might not even need to bother finishing my doctorate. Imagine, Rik, you could be off the hook as my supervisor. You would enjoy that, wouldn't you?" she asked, teasing him.

"I don't want to be off the hook. I have already written fifty pages for you: some decent stuff too. You can get there if you can just keep focused. I know it. I am confident I will be able to finish it in a year, eighteen months at the most. Don't quit on me now."

"Yes. But you are still writing only about moral theory. I

need something morally practical for you to work on for me; for example, the body in the garden. Do you think you could get what happened to Lambe into my research as, say, an example of applied morality?"

"No. I don't think so. Sometimes it's better to leave things out no matter how absorbing or relevant they may seem at the time to avoid being distracted from the primary thesis. Sound research involves knowing what to omit as much as knowing what to put in. 'A lot of doctoral work is ruined by poor editing'," he said, quoting from website advice.

Spencer came through the patio doors. "I've left Jim to get on with the finishing touches."

"I'll help him," Wallace volunteered. "I don't trust him not to leave a dent in my patio." As he went outside Pandora and the librarian came in.

"Why are you two involved in this?" Wallace asked, stopping them in the doorway.

"Gets me out of the house," they said together. They looked at each other and smiled at their shared motivation.

"Tea for everyone!" Progress piped as she filled the kettle with water from the new kitchen tap. They sat around the table listening to Jim cursing at Wallace to stop interfering.

"Can I join Cat flap … I mean, CAT*fish*?" Progress asked.

"I suppose you should. It's that, or join Lambe out there under the patio," Pandora said without smiling.

"I think we can unofficially inform you that your application for membership will be endorsed at our next meeting; following our established rules and procedures, of course," the librarian told her. "We plan to meet every Tuesday and Thursday night at eight because Pandora thinks we will be busy. We hope to get Wallace elected as provost while Pandora and Spencer help him to run things from behind the scenes."

"Rik, the provost? Wow. I think that's an excellent idea. But he might get upset. I had better tell him when you are gone. He already worries you are trying to do too much for him."

"You didn't tell me it was both Tuesdays and Thursdays," Doolittle protested. "I have Pilates on Tuesdays and I always go out drinking with my student clients on Thursdays. You know – the ones whose problems I've solved during the week? It usually takes just one session with me for a student to be cured. They never come back. Can't I be an honorary member or something?"

"I told you we shouldn't have let her join," Pandora said between sucks on her cigarette.

"I am sure Sally can change her schedule to accommodate us," the librarian said.

They discussed their plans and hopes for the future of the college with Progress now that she was practically a member of their federation.

Jim and Wallace came inside as the sun was starting to lift off the horizon. "All done," Jim announced. "Better than it was before we showed up, if I say so myself. Your first effort was only okay because the edges of the stones weren't properly aligned. You didn't use a level," he told Wallace.

"I used a piece of string."

"I knew it. Not the same thing at all. You should use a spirit level. Don't walk out there until tomorrow to allow the mortar to dry. One shower of rain and no one will ever know we were here."

"I need to get home. Samantha will be out of her mind

worrying about where I am," Spencer said to no one in particular. "She needs her sleep because she has a school test in the morning."

"Why don't you phone her?" Wallace asked.

"I'll send her a text," Spencer suggested.

XXIX

Scrutatio Scaenam Sceleris
Crime Scene Investigation

Rik Wallace opened the door to Inspector Jackson who was standing on the red clay tiles of the garden path on which pools of rain had formed after a brief shower out of a blue sky just an hour before. Detective Sullivan was visible over his boss's shoulder.

"We called to your office. We were told you were working at home. Can we come in?"

"Yes. Come in. Can I get you something to drink? Tea? Coffee? Wine?" Wallace asked proffering the glass of red he was holding.

"No thanks. I want nothing to drink. I'll get straight to the point. The Reverend Professor Lambe has vanished. I thought that was a reasonable excuse to have one of, what I am starting to think of as, our regular chats. You have become my go-to-academic whenever someone goes missing or gets hit by lightning," Jackson said, smiling his upside-down smile.

"Hit by lightning? You've come to see me about Mathilda Maddox?"

"That was death by natural causes, sir," Sullivan corrected his boss.

"Either way the mortality rate in CAT College must be starting to become a concern to those of you still alive there," Jackson said.

"Everyone in college is talking about Lambe. Maybe he has run away with one of his students?" Wallace suggested.

"That is interesting. I learned in the police academy that suspects who offer up their ideas and theories are usually trying to send us in the wrong direction," Sullivan said.

"Am I a suspect?"

"Everyone is a suspect. Mind if we look around?" Sullivan asked. Without waiting for an answer, he walked down the hall.

"You appear to be doing a lot of work on this place. Imagine the college putting you in this dump," Jackson observed.

"It was Lambe's idea. Seems he doesn't appreciate philosophers."

"There's motive right there," Jackson said, smiling again. "Don't worry. This time there will be forensic evidence. I had to let Sullivan have his way. He went through Lambe's house with a team. That place was sterilized from top to bottom as if someone had hired a contract cleaner. I've seen the work of professional assassins, but I have never seen anywhere so clean afterwards: no blood, no signs of a struggle, and no signs of death. Not even signs of life, such as everyday dust and dirt. The house was spotless. Sullivan was disappointed. I told him it appeared a cleaner had killed Lambe."

"What's that?" Sullivan asked, breaking off his study of Wallace's house to pay attention to the conversation.

"I said it looks as if a cleaner killed Lambe."

Sullivan scowled at Wallace. "Since you have an opinion on this, don't you agree it's unlikely Lambe would have scrubbed the house before running away with a student? I think he would have been conserving his energy at his age. But they always leave something."

"Who?"

"The culprits. Forensic science nowadays is so precise we can build an entire case on the tiniest imperceptible particle of DNA," Sullivan explained, holding his thumb and index finger slightly apart to indicate exactly how small he meant. "I told the inspector that questioning people is a waste of time. This case will solve itself on forensic evidence alone. We will just leave the lab rats get on with their microscopic analysis of the invisible evidence and – hey presto – we will have our killer."

Jackson rubbed his fingertips along the greasy surface of the table, wiggled them under his nose, before wiping them on his coat. "You're not as hygienic as Lambe," he observed. "Forensics has taken a lot of the satisfaction out of my work. I enjoy getting out of the office, meeting people – including the suspects. I still believe, after all these years, that talk is the best method for solving crimes. I don't get enough opportunities to talk nowadays."

Jackson sat down on one of the old chairs that matched the worn table that had been a sought-after dining set several decades earlier. He stretched out his long legs and leaned back in the chair until it cracked its objections to the strain. He shared a house with three young offenders who were trying in vain to rehabilitate. He volunteered for the programme because he enjoyed being near crime – not because he was committed to reducing the overall total of world badness like Sullivan. "Being a detective isn't what it used to be. I suppose nothing is what it used to be. I imagine academics say that all the time."

"I couldn't say," Wallace said. "I only know the way it is now."

"I was young and naïve when I joined the force. I don't remember now what I was thinking back then. I suppose I wanted to do some good by helping to punish wicked people and get justice for victims. What they don't tell you when you start out is how being around crime everyday can have a corrosive effect on your ability to tell the difference between right and wrong. Or maybe I wanted to become a tireless vigilante delivering retribution. Perhaps if I had suffered a great injustice, I could have maintained a passion for punishment. Do you believe in punishment, Professor?"

"I am certain we are all punished for our crimes whether you catch us or not."

"Punishment is essential to deter others," Sullivan said.

Jackson ignored his colleague's opinion. "I used to be able to tell the bad ones from the good ones just by interviewing them. I know I am losing my touch. Nowadays we rely too much on CCTV, DNA, mobile technology, and psychological profiling to do our thinking for us. Maybe I should quit. A robot could do my job. I've gotten to the point where I could have a homicidal maniac in front of me, and I wouldn't know it. At least, I know that much."

"Socrates says we must acknowledge what we don't know," Wallace said. "You are a Socratic policeman, that's all."

"I'm not sure that's a compliment."

"Neither am I. Maybe life was never what it was supposed to be in the good old days. Even for policemen."

"Now that sounds philosophical."

"That's what I do: sound philosophical. Half the people

who were hanged in what you consider to be the good old days were innocent."

"As few as that? I thought it would have been most of them, but then, they were the good old days." Jackson smiled his upside-down smile. "In my job, whenever I solve a murder, another comes along almost immediately, and I never know if it will be more interesting than the last. I would like to stick with this case for a while. Something about this college – I can't put my finger on it – something sinister appeals to my instincts as a homicide detective. Any self-respecting policeman would wish to remain in the midst of a crime like this one for as long as possible."

"That's crazy, sir. We need to catch criminals fast, lock them up, and get back out there to catch the next lot. That's the way it works, sir. That's what we were taught in the police academy," Sullivan explained. "It is not our job to admire criminals and their work."

"I don't admire them, though sometimes I respect them: I feel I should give murderers a helping hand just to make the investigation last longer. Don't be horrified, Sullivan. Show them how it's done from a professional point of view. Nothing drastic, you understand."

Jackson turned to Wallace. "I don't mean what you philosophers would call a morally reprehensible killing; maybe just a little murder. Can you imagine such a thing?" He smiled. "Of course. I have learned everything I know about morality from the law, but you of all people should appreciate that the law tells us nothing about right and wrong. The law can only decide what is legal. We policemen chase people who break the law. We are not concerned with the immoral. But you know this already. Listen to me going on. It's time I thought about a new career before poor Sullivan here has a heart attack. I don't think I'd make much of a moral philosopher, though. Do you? Maybe I should sit in on your lectures. I could discover the difference between right and wrong before it's too late. The librarian loaned me philosophy books. I can't make sense of them on my own. I must remember to return them when I call to interrogate her. I feel comfortable talking to an attractive woman only when I pretend that she's a suspect. I'm not sure what I can accuse her of in this case. That's pathetic, isn't it? I'm sure if you were a psychologist, you would have something to say about that. I think the librarian likes me. Do you think I could persuade her that she is involved?"

"The librarian?" Wallace stammered. "According to Sullivan's theory, as a suspect I'm bound to say she is involved just to throw you off the trail."

"Okay. I'll tell her you pointed me in her direction. That might be a good opening line."

Wallace didn't respond.

Jackson stood up, stretched, and strolled through the house studying the patched walls and wires dangling from the ceiling. Sullivan tapped and rubbed his fingers along plaster finishes as if he was a master craftsman assessing the efforts of an apprentice. When he got to the bedroom, he noticed the outline of the plasterboard patch visible where it crudely joined the original over the bed without registering its significance as a clue. Jackson studied Sullivan studying the ceiling.

"I think Sullivan thinks that looks a bit rough," Jackson told Wallace.

"I find ceilings difficult. I am not a professional plasterer."

Jackson saw the unmade bed. He saw women's underwear and clothes discarded on the floor and across a nearby chair. He saw the grouping of jars, tubes, and bottles of make-up and cosmetics huddled together between a recharging cordless drill, a tool belt and a pyramid of screws on the dressing table.

"Unless you are a transvestite, my training as a detective leads me to deduce a woman is living here with you. Perhaps the enchanting blond you were with in the library. Am I correct in my deduction? What was her name?"

"You are correct. Her name is Julie Progress. I am supervising her doctoral research."

"Interesting venue for supervision, your bed."

"It's an academic thing. You wouldn't understand. I hardly understand it myself."

"I am assuming Lambe was killed by one of his colleagues, maybe more than one. Someone who believed he killed the provost, which seems to be the entire college, thus making all of you suspects. Lambe may have run away but I don't believe there has been another disappearance. With luck, we are dealing with a murder. Not that I wish Lambe harm. It's just a professional aspiration, you understand. Murders are more fascinating."

"What other disappearance?"

"Your mother. She vanished. Have you forgotten her already? Can't say I blame you. She hasn't been seen since the night she was here in this house with you."

"That is, unless you have seen her since," Sullivan put in.

"No, I haven't seen her."

"Anything from your brother?"

"Nothing, thank God. I mean. No."

"Impressive kitchen. What colour is this?" Jackson asked, standing beside the new partition wall and running his fingers over Mrs Wallace's tomb.

"It's called summer sun yellow."

"Stunning. Sullivan, make a note of the colour."

Sullivan wrote the words "summer sun" in his notebook while Jackson strolled towards the patio doors and looked outside. "Nice patio. Newly laid? Hard to get all of the paving stones to lie dead flat. The trick is, or at least homicidal maniacs of my acquaintance tell me, to make sure the ground underneath is well compacted. Popular place for hiding bodies."

"What's that?" Wallace asked from the kitchen where he was trying to control his breathing.

"I'm talking about bodies under your patio. But that is too obvious for a highbrow academic like you. Do you agree, Sullivan? No point in a mad digging expedition before we have the results from forensics. We need to conserve our energy; pace ourselves."

"If you insist, sir, but I could have it up in a flash. I see a spade out there."

"I insist. By the way, Wallace, your other girlfriend Della is back at that hotel: the one where we first met. At least, she is a regular guest every couple of months. Probably moved on again by now."

"She's not my girlfriend."

"Suit yourself. But I had a feeling that all you suspects might need to know each other's whereabouts. Since she knows where you are, I thought you should know where to find her sometimes. Just in case."

"Just in case of what?"

Jackson ignored the question. "Adds a little spice to your relationship. I don't think the police get enough credit for livening up people's love lives. You know. The desperate romance of people on the run, etcetera."

"No. I don't know."

"Okay. That's it. It was therapeutic talking to you. I'll miss our little chats."

"When? What? Are you going away?"

"No. I mean when Sullivan here solves this case. Pity, because I'm in no hurry to solve this one. I enjoy visiting the college. I get to meet intellectuals such as yourself." Jackson walked slowly towards the front door. "We'll see ourselves out. I hope no DNA turns up in Lambe's house. I hope whoever killed him is an experienced cleaner. Try not to look shocked, Sullivan; you should be prepared to see and hear many shocking things during your time as a policeman."

XXX

Exitus Philosophica
Philosophical Exit

Doctor Bacon sat at his desk in his office on the top floor under the eaves of the Department of Philosophy building. The three books he had on the day his hair first turned white sat unread on the empty shelves that they shared with the corpses of two mummified potted plants and a broken plastic radio. He was holding his left arm in the fingers of his right hand. He would have gone home ten minutes ago except he believed he was having a heart attack. Then pain shot from his arm into his neck. Vomit rose in his oesophagus. A few strands of his white ceramic hair stuck straight up so exceptional was his distress. His ambition was to never come into college. He hoped to reduce his participation to an infinitesimally small measurement approaching zero because, being aware of Zeno's paradox, he despaired of achieving actual zero time on campus. He had underestimated the effort involved in avoiding meeting undergraduate students. He applied for a sabbatical his first day back after his last one expired and waited to be away again, pretending to finish his monumental book on the complete history of Greek ethics, which he argued would be vital to a general understanding of morality when finished. Ideally, his proposed volume should take him forever to write. He knew he would rather die there and then than live long enough to discuss an essay extension with some idiot second-year. Perhaps no one's death would disturb the delicate intellectual Zeitgeist of CAT College less than Bacon's.

He groaned in pain and leaned his forehead over the desk. The door opened.

"Oh, what do you want?" Bacon asked. "At least you're not one of my students." He was torn between demanding an ambulance and allowing himself to die without asking for help because he couldn't locate the appropriate words to introduce his suspected medical condition. While trying to decide what to say, he thought that if he could just sit there for a few more minutes, he would get his breath back, and then he would be fine. After all, maybe it was just indigestion. He was under a lot of stress. He knew stress caused indigestion. His wife had been threatening not to leave him over his postgraduate student affairs. He could have a free house where he could entertain Julie Progress if his wife would only go and take those bloody children with her. What he heard himself saying was, "Your timing is bad. I would rather be alone now if this isn't important, if it can't keep until tomorrow." He groaned and gasped for air, hoping he appeared normal. He pawed at his pottery hair.

His visitor had seen the symptoms of acute myocardial infarction before but didn't phone for an ambulance or loosen Bacon's tie. Instead, his guest sat in the seldom-used chair at the other side of the desk and watched the sweat pour down Bacon's paper-white face.

"On the contrary," his visitor said. "It appears my timing

is perfect."

Bacon had reflected on death when he was a philosophy student. He was interested in the idea of dying when he was a younger man. As a postgraduate, inspired by his reading of Heidegger's *Being and Time,* he had even delivered lectures on the value of reflecting on mortality to a transient audience in a hospice. But the thought of death had not disrupted the slow smooth serene flow of his complacent imagination for years.

When at last Death came for him, while he was sitting there at his desk, it seemed to be both alarmingly tangible and in an undignified hurry. It was even wielding a knife. His final words before everything went crow-black were, "Wait a minute. I need time to think about this." He was a philosopher, after all. He would say that, wouldn't he?

XXXI

Homicidium Exiguum
A Little Murder

The corridor outside Doctor Bacon's office was cordoned off as a possible crime scene. Inspector Jackson saw Rik Wallace looking over the blue-and-white striped tape like a sheep appraising a greener pasture at the other side of a fence.

"Come on in," Jackson said, stretching the tape over his head and smiling his upside-down smile.

"Where is your partner – what's his name?" Wallace asked.

"I sent him to the library to practise taking fingerprints from students. Come and have a look at this," Jackson said, taking him by the arm.

From the doorway, Wallace saw that Bacon was still sitting at his desk, setting a new all-time personal record for a continuous length of time spent by him in his office. His porcelain hair was as smooth as ever. The wooden handle of a kitchen knife protruded straight out of one side of his neck, opposite the tip of the blade sticking out of the other side.

"A uniquely conscientious second-year decided to get here early and wait all day if necessary because he was desperate for an essay extension. He saw the open door. Despite the promising appearances, the medical examiner thinks from her preliminary observations that Bacon may or may not have been dead prior to being skewered through the neck because of the relative absence of blood from the wounds here and here," Jackson said, pointing to the knife handle and the tip of the protruding blade in turn with a pencil he had picked up from the desk. "She suspects he died from a massive heart attack just before he was impaled. Either way, I'm not complaining. It's another death on campus," he mused. "This college just keeps on giving. I have a theory. Do you want to hear it? I haven't yet worked out the finer details – such as who or what is behind these deaths and disappearances. The only thing they seem to have in common is they all involve philosophy in some way, except the Head of Commerce, and she doesn't count because she was hit by lightning. Sullivan is suspicious of any coincidence – like lightning hitting her at a time like this. But I don't share his view because Professor Maddox's death doesn't fit my working hypothesis because, as I said, she is not involved with philosophy, as far as I can see. From my limited reading of those books the librarian lent me, I can't determine yet exactly how philosophy is involved, but I'm confident I'll work it out. As you know I'm not in a hurry. I could ask you for help, but as you are my main suspect, I'm not sure that would be sensible or – can I say it? – ethical." He chuckled. "I'm on my own in this because all of your colleagues are suspects as well. But I'm diverging from my main point, which seems to be an important feature of philosophy. Where was I? Someone jumps from the fifth floor of a hotel, and there you are – a moral philosopher – staying in the room next door. Your mother disappears after she turns up here at CAT College for *your* inaugural philosophy lecture. The provost takes a dive down the stairs in the middle of the night, but she does die after meeting *you*. Okay. She isn't a philosopher, but you had started work here in the *philosophy* department. Her husband – yes, I know; also *not* a philosopher – whom no one knew she was married to, vanishes into thin air, but he is known to hate philosophers, and he did put you in that dump on Love Street."

"I enjoy DIY."

"Sullivan says we should look for your motivation. But I'm not sure that's the way to go. I can't imagine what your motivation could be. You don't strike me as someone driven by ambition. However, I'm sure you will benefit from Lambe's disappearance in some way. I admit my theory needs supporting evidence, which I don't have. I have no forensics from Lambe's house – cleaner than a space laboratory. But, happily for both of us, a philosopher turns up dead in his office where he is usually never seen. This is yet another link to philosophy, even though I have no idea how, except of course that he was a philosopher. Also, I get to continue my investigation of this intriguing case in your charming college. Reassuring for you, because I don't have a clue how you fit into Bacon's death either. Perhaps you have an accomplice or an imitator. I assume his post will be filled by yet another philosopher. That is something I can look into."

"You seem cheerful. You might have stuck that knife in Bacon yourself just to hang around here or, as you said the last time we met, to give the murderer a helping hand: what you called a *little* murder. You should enrol on a course in morality. It would be safer for all of us."

"Technically, this may not be a murder. Perhaps the perfect little murder, as you say. It might be a desecration of a dead body, which is not much of a crime – maybe my sensibilities are blunted from police work. He was dead or dying anyway. You can't murder a dead person. You see, I've been studying moral philosophy too. I'm going to draw up a list of those who would benefit from Bacon's death, and to satisfy you, I will put my own name on it along with whoever gets his job, his wife, and maybe even his children after I talk with them, even though they are all under ten. Still, you never know. What do they say in Hollywood about acting with children and wild animals? They can ruin your career."

Before Wallace could think of anything to say Jackson took two books from his bag. "That reminds me. I'm returning these to the librarian. She is a charming woman: intelligent; humorous; and attractive in a bookish kind of way. Reason enough, if I needed one, to hang around. What do you think?" he asked Wallace, stepping back.

"About what?"

"My outfit." He was wearing a new grey jacket with a light blue shirt and no tie. "Not too formal for a visit to the library?"

"Ah, so you haven't interrogated the librarian yet?"

"I'm on my way there now. How do I look?"

"You look dressed to kill."

Rik Wallace went in search of Pandora when Inspector Jackson left. He found her at her desk outside the provost's empty office. They stood by the wall under the "No Smoking" sign, blowing cones of smoke towards the high, brown ceiling.

"Unlike you, Pandora, I'm not comfortable breaking the rules. Rules exist for a reason."

"I can't imagine what they are. Thank God, I never studied moral philosophy. Ignorance is bliss."

"Ignorance is not a legal defence."

"You need a defence only if you're caught."

"Inspector Jackson is doing his best to catch us."

"I can't imagine what he has been doing. It seems everything except detecting."

"When he came to see me on Love Street, he told me he might give whoever caused Lambe to disappear a helping hand. I think he may have killed Bacon. Is that possible?"

"Anything is possible."

"It's just like old times, my visiting you for a smoke. Have you missed me?"

Pandora grunted.

"How is Marlboro? I haven't removed his name from the trophy you gave me."

"He's fine. That cough was just a hairball. It's a cat thing. I would die if anything happened to him."

The phone rang. Pandora snatched at it. She listened for a few seconds before holding her hand over the mouthpiece on the handset. "It's the secretary in the commerce faculty. I must get back to work." She sat down at her desk and swung her chair away from him, turning her back. "No. No I can talk," she said into the phone. "No. No one important."

As Rik Wallace walked towards the philosophy department his thoughts became more abstract with each step. By now, he knew that philosophers were interested in the moral *quality* of an action rather than the *quantity* of those actions. One reprehensible act seemed just as bad as ten to the likes of Socrates. It seemed unreasonable to be concerned that there might be some other maniac loose on campus that he didn't know about, apart from himself, Julie Progress, Pandora, Maurice Spencer, Sally Doolittle, the rest of CATfish, and maybe even Inspector Jackson. He speculated on how many lunatics were needed to make a difference to the moral fibre of the college? One? Ten? One hundred? He felt relieved that religion rather than philosophy was interested in quantifying badness. Fortunately, he had fallen into a subtle discipline. It could have been worse, he reflected; Rik Wallace could have been a sociologist.

XXXII

Meteoric Ortum
Meteoric Rise

Rik Wallace swivelled in the chair at the desk in the sepulchral office where the Reverend Professor Lambe had briefly reigned, and before that, Patricia the Provost. He hoped his rule might last longer than that of his immediate predecessor, not out of a lust for power, but from a new-found appetite for survival. He imagined his insecurity was what the last of the Roman emperors must have felt in the final days of that illustrious empire, conscious of the fact their own incompetence was contributing to its irrevocable downfall. The members of the Academic Council believed they had found in Wallace a person of as-yet-unproven moronicism, which they couldn't say of the other eligible candidate, Maurice Spencer, now that Bacon was no more. In Wallace's candidacy, the council held on to the promise of hope over experience with the desperation of drowning octogenarians clinging to an iron bedstead in the middle of the ocean.

The desk stretched out in front of Wallace as empty as his mind when it came to his ideas on what he was supposed to do next. On this, his second day in the latest manifestation of his new identity as provost, he was still in shock. When Pandora informed him of his promotion, she left him in no doubt that CATfish would not tolerate his turning down the honour they were bestowing on him as de facto rulers of CAT College. He was nervous of making a mess of being provost and terrified of Pandora's ambitions for him. He knew that Inspector Jackson would see this promotion as another brick in his theoretical forensic wall: that, somehow, he was behind the swelling crime wave in the college.

It seemed to Wallace that his second day would go the way of the first: in isolated contemplation of the unimaginable responsibilities of high office. But just then the door flew open. It was Pandora. This bursting in without knocking had been going on since yesterday morning. He imagined she spent her time listening outside waiting to spring in at what she hoped would be the most inopportune moment possible; but all moments had been opportune as he sat immobile behind the empty desk doing nothing. Now she informed him portentously that he had a visitor.

Before she could leave he said, "Oh. Pandora. Can you get me a notebook, some pens, and something to hold the pens? And pencils and sharpeners. That sort of thing. Oh, and a stapler, staples, paper clips, a desk tidy, and a huge blotting paper pad – the largest you can find. And an executive desk toy. You choose."

"Is that all?" she asked, holding him in the black plates of her sunglasses.

"Oh, a plant or two, and maybe an in-and-out tray. I thought that stuff would be here already."

"I cleared away all trace of Lambe for you, including his office supplies."

He could tell she was scowling from the wrinkles on her forehead above the frames.

As Julie Progress pushed passed her into the office, Pandora closed the door behind her.

"Isn't this exciting? Imagine what we could get up to on this desk?" Progress said.

"With Pandora launching unannounced into the office every other minute? No. I can't imagine what we could get up to on it."

"You are a prude. Oh. My. God. Look at the leather chair. Does it swivel? Let me have a go."

Progress sat on top of Wallace, who was too slow to jump out of the way, and began to revolve using one foot on the deep-pile carpet to build up momentum as they spun. Then she stopped suddenly.

"I'm going to be sick. You know, Rik, I am starting to be attracted to you – a lot. Not because of the desk, or the chair; or because you are running the college, and definitely not because of the vacancy in philosophy you will be in charge of filling. It's because you are different. I think I am falling in love with you. I mean it, Rik. Since you arrived here, my life has changed. Truly, Julie is in love with you. Wouldn't that make a catchy song? 'Truly, Julie is in love with you. Truly Julie'," she sang, before stopping to belch.

"Don't you think you should wait to get to really know someone before you start falling in love with them? Wouldn't that be the rational thing to do?"

"I don't want to be rational. I want to be emotional. Passionate. I'm tired of always being rational," she squealed, spinning again in the chair.

Wallace was trying to wriggle out from under her, while thinking of a single example of Progress's commitment to reason, when she jumped off the chair in the middle of a revolution.

"Maybe we would be safer over there," Wallace said, shepherding her towards the nest of armchairs around the glass coffee table where he had his first interview with Patricia the Provost on his first morning in CAT College just several lives ago. Before they were seated Pandora burst back into the room.

"Your inter-faculty planning meeting is scheduled to begin … *now*. The heads of faculty and departments are waiting outside."

"Why didn't you tell me about this? I have nothing prepared."

"I put it on your schedule on my desk. You didn't ask."

Progress kissed Wallace on the lips, holding the back of his head in both her hands. "I will go and leave you to get on with the important affairs of the college. I will see you tonight." She ran her fingers along the length of the edge of the desk as she strolled out.

Pandora had advertised her disinterest in the meeting by leaving his office when everyone was inside to take up her sentry post next door. She was talking with the secretary of the faculty of commerce on the phone when Wallace came out, discussing the probability one could die from a disease caught while in hospital versus the probability of dying from a lesser disease while refusing hospital treatment. She hissed at him, "Yes? What the hell do you want now?"

"Coffees?" Wallace was amazed to find within himself the courage to ask Pandora to organize anything.

"I'm busy."

"So am I."

"Not my job."

"Not my job either. Please."

They stared at each other, waiting for the other to blink first. Considering Pandora was wearing sunglasses Wallace felt he had no hope of victory.

"Got to go," she snarled into the phone. "Just coffee. No cakes nor biscuits," she said, standing up.

He realized with a renewed hope for his own long-term safety that all might be back in balance in Pandora's universe.

Maurice Spencer handed round a typed page while announcing to the group that Wallace had prepared a short statement of his vision for the future of the college that he would read to them. This was more of a surprise for Wallace than it was for the others clustered around the desk. He studied the print and wished Spencer could have at least shown him a draft yesterday when he had plenty time to rehearse. He crinkled his eyes for a better view and began reading aloud.

"CAT College's historical reputation lies in the renown of the commerce faculty. However, my vision for our illustrious future is to reposition the college's business courses away from promoting mere commercial competence towards fostering artistic achievements in our commerce students. Picture this: our future business graduates will have a unique grasp of the classics, literary criticism, media studies, sociology, psychology and, naturally, ethics. There are too many schools graduating business students who know too much about business. From now on, CAT College will no longer be numbered amongst these. Our graduates will benefit from having less business skills and a greater appreciation of the universal truths of philosophy. I know you may think I am mad. But this is my vision and I am in charge now!"

Wallace looked up from the page prepared to agree with anyone around the desk that he was indeed mad. However, in deference to their brand-new leader, they kept their psychiatric opinions to themselves. Besides, since Sydney the Sycophant alone understood psychology, he could have offered the only qualified diagnosis.

Maddox the Man's temporary replacement, Doctor Eddy Cashman, heard none of Wallace's speech because she was too busy texting her PA with a new complaint for the attention of the Academic Council: a habit she had picked up from her deceased boss. The head of technology, Casper Wall, was struggling to de-bug his latest application for his campus spin-off gambling company, CAT Bets. He was able to glance away from his smartphone long enough to endorse the new provost's vision with the word "whatever" when Wallace finished reading the prepared mission statement.

"What do you want me to do?" Sidney the Sycophant asked Wallace.

"What do you mean?" Spencer asked on Wallace's behalf.

"What kind of psychology do you want me to do in the department now that Lambe is gone?"

"I don't know. I'm not a psychologist. Psychological psychology, I suppose."

"Couldn't you be a bit more specific?"

"What kinds are there?"

"There are various types: clinical, counselling, educational, health, occupational, cognitive, to name but a few. Then there are different approaches within each field such as behaviourists and psychoanalysts."

"Just pick one."

"I can't pick one. I might get it wrong. You pick one for me."

"What about criminology? Couldn't your department specialize in studying the criminal mind?" Wallace suggested.

"Criminology? I don't know anything about that, but I could try. Where will I find criminals to study?"

"Inspector Jackson is on campus every day. You could ask him for advice. It's your department. You run it whatever way you want. I don't care what you do in psychology. Does anyone here care what the psychologists do?"

Those gathered around the desk shook their heads and muttered their collective indifference to psychology.

"Just don't spend money on fancy new experiments into criminals," the chief financial officer said. "Use the experiments you already have that I had to pay for."

Sidney the Sycophant was unhappy under the new regime. At least when Lambe was around he didn't need to think. Now he had to make decisions for the entire department. His head felt full. "I'll try my best, but I want to meet every day to discuss how I am getting on," he told Wallace.

"Once a month," Spencer suggested.

"Okay."

During the rest of the meeting the future of the college was arranged to the satisfaction of Spencer, who, by then, had turned a shiny red colour from excitement. Wallace soon lost track of the decisions that were made in his name. He did know he agreed to hire a new moral philosopher to replace

Bacon. Without thinking about it, he thought Progress would get the job, wouldn't she? He daydreamed about being able to continue being assertive with Pandora, despite his well-founded terror. It was also agreed to advertise for a prestigious new Head of Business who had a proven track record of being sympathetic to philosophy, and who should be recruited before the beginning of the next academic year. In the interim, the faculty was handed into the care of Doctor Eddy Cashman who being indifferent to metaphysics, epistemology and ethics was unlikely to secure the post permanently.

Spencer beamed in complete concord with his own sentiments. "I must leave now," he said. "I have to drive Samantha to her ballet class."

Following Rik Wallace's second day as provost, when time had slowed down to almost a standstill, it began to exponentially speed up again as his desk filled with office supplies and potted plants, which Pandora carried into the office and slammed down in front of him without comment, along with more and more files requiring his signature. He sent out e-mails; he attended parties, meetings, and sub-committee meetings; he opened on-campus exhibitions; launched a student magazine, and fell down stairs after a reception to mark Jim the porter's retirement. He had to ring back a producer to decline an invitation to appear on television – he had originally accepted, having momentarily forgotten he wasn't who he, or they, thought he was.

Pandora warmed to him in proportion to his drip-fed concessions. He agreed to all of her suggestions for new furnishings for offices after studying a dozen brochures, and to colour schemes for the decrepit lecture theatres after pretending to look through over a hundred colour cards while she stood over him. He also agreed to install new notice boards and to her inconveniencing out-of-favour lecturers on timetable schedules. Wallace approved an increase in the library budget of twenty-four percent that included the purchase of a book cataloguing system, a security gate, and two new computer terminals, which never arrived in the library. He presided at Examination Boards and expressed his official satisfaction at the college's embarrassingly low progression rates.

The night before the interviews for the new post in Moral Philosophy, Rik Wallace lay in bed beside Julie Progress, who was now convinced she was passionately in love with him. He was satisfied with the job he was doing as a moral philosopher, inspiration, and provost. It seemed to him he might have been born to his new role at CAT College he was doing such an excellent job – and that without any experience or training. Perhaps he should have studied the bible because Lambe would have known from the Book of Proverbs 16:18 that such pride goes before a downfall. Wallace's was about to begin the next morning.

XXXIII

Colloquium
Interview

The interviews to assess the candidates to fill the moral void caused by the ethically ambiguous death of Doctor Bacon were held in what was known as the "second-best boardroom" because Pandora was refurbishing the best in anticipation of a series of important committee meetings to promote the arts in the business faculty. The five members of the interview panel sat on green cloth–backed chairs arranged in a line down one side of a vast mahogany table that occupied half of the floor space on the puke-coloured carpet. Each candidate would sit, in their turn, on an isolated chair at the other side of the table.

The large pipes carrying hot water to other parts of the building, which ran around the top of the walls of the boardroom just below the stained ceiling, gurgled and burped giving the impression that the interrogations were being held inside a monstrous stomach. A feeble old man wearing an academic robe looked down on proceedings from a battered painting above a fireplace. Patricia the Provost's grandmother had bought the picture at auction to enhance the academic ambience of the room. The ancient scholar's achievements were long forgotten in the institution where he had been painted.

He hung there to make sure that what passed as fairness in his day at his alma mater, wherever that might have been, might prevail on this day in CAT College.

Rik Wallace, who had been bored throughout the day, was – for the first time since undertaking his crash course in moral philosophy – enthralled and moved by the fifth candidate's words and passionate expression of principles. Perhaps the drip-drip of ideas had filled a dam in his soul that had just burst open: not from the revelation of a single truth but from the accumulative pressure of novel concepts. There should have been an orchestra in the corner of the second-best boardroom to accompany these words and to underscore their effect on Wallace. He was now experiencing what he imagined Moses must have felt when he first heard the words of God. But these words weren't emanating from a burning bush, or even from a bearded face in a cloud. They were coming out of the thin mouth of a grey-faced academic with pointy yellow teeth and dangling wisps of greasy brown hair that hung down over the collar of a worn, tweed jacket, supporting a light shower of dandruff that had settled on his shoulders days before the interview.

"That is why Immanuel Kant's *Critique of Practical Reason* is the most important work in moral philosophy *ever.*"

Wallace didn't hear this conclusion of the summary of Kant's position on morality as presented by Doctor Ernest Fischer because he was still absorbed in the contemplation of the ideas he had just heard. "What?" he asked, coming awake to the realization Fischer had stopped talking.

"Kant. He's the best."

"Oh, yes. I agree."

Wallace forgot – that is, if he ever realized before – that he had been surviving by merely thinking he was thinking: a successful, if accidental strategy. Was now a good time to start having real thoughts and opinions?

Maurice Spencer didn't think so.

"What do you mean you agree? Your entire worldview is against everything Kant stands for," Spencer, sitting to Wallace's left, protested.

"Is it?"

"Anyway, whether Kant is right or wrong is irrelevant because he is too difficult for our students. What is the use in having any truth on the curriculum that can't be understood?" Spencer added.

"Isn't that what you said Lambe used to say about Nietzsche?"

"Not at all. I am in favour of censoring the difficult ideas: not the dangerous ones. It's a different argument. Thank you, Doctor Fischer. That was impressive. You have given us much to ponder. Do you have questions for the panel?" Spencer was asking, having already dismissed him from consideration.

"Are you all Nietzscheans in the department? I had no idea. I can't imagine you will be sympathetic to a Kantian like me."

"No way. We are not Nietzscheans. He is an anarchist. We think he is too dangerous for our students and your friend Kant is too esoteric. We are looking for something in between those philosophical extremes."

"What is the point in teaching only those ideas that you believe students can understand without effort? Aren't we supposed to be bringing them beyond where their current abilities lie?"

"Interesting point," Spencer said, looking to the stained ceiling.

"It was a question."

"An interesting question, then. Anyone this side of the table care to answer it? No? Thank you again, Doctor Fischer. Goodbye."

Fischer stood up, hesitated as if he might say something, exhaled, and left the room.

"Apart from his teeth, hair, and jacket, I thought he was impressive," Professor William Campbell said. He was the external member of the panel, present to guarantee proceedings would be fair by the standards of equity in his own college. He had reached a stage of intellectual maturity where he was no longer distracted by original ideas. This immunity to novelty allowed him to act as an ambassador for the superior learning of his college, which was free of dangerous innovations. Campbell represented the best tradition in education, which was tradition itself. He was seated on Wallace's right. "I couldn't follow any of it, but I got the impression he is some sort of genius. Extraordinary vocabulary. Haven't heard half of those words used in a sentence before. He has an enormous list of publications. Also, he is committed to research. You would find it difficult to find anyone better qualified than him. But I am not here to tell you what you should do, but what we would do in my college if we were you, which we're not."

"That's a very helpful contribution to our dilemma," Spencer said, dismissing it. "We have more candidates to assess. Let's not be unfair to those who have still to come. Who is next?" he asked, almost excited.

"Just one more. Local girl. Julie Progress. Let's see what

impression Ms Progress makes before we decide. We will review all the candidates at the end," Eddy Cashman said. She was chairing the panel, and the only female member. She read through Progress's CV to refresh her memory. "Progress? No doctorate. No publications. No teaching experience. She is almost as bad as you, Casper. I have no idea why she has been shortlisted for interview; except she is a woman, and we could do with a higher proportion of women on the faculty."

Casper Wall ignored the summary of Progress's achievements from where he sat at the end of the row of interviewers, reading his smartphone.

The ornate wooden door to the second-best boardroom crashed open. Seconds later Progress tottered into view on high heels, wearing an expensive black jacket over a white silk blouse, and a smart black woollen pencil skirt. She clutched a tiny glass-encrusted handbag rather than the practical briefcase favoured by the other candidates. She gave the impression that she had lost her way to an upmarket hen night. Wallace was, in fact, surprised that she wasn't giving the impression she was on the way to a gym because he had never seen her in anything other than tracksuits.

Wallace swallowed hard. Spencer and Campbell stared at her. Casper Wall put his smartphone in his pocket. Eddy Cashman cleared her throat and asked Progress to sit down. When perched on the chair in front of them, her skirt climbed up her thighs, exposing the suspenders holding up her sheer stockings.

"You look amazing," Spencer mouthed to her across the expanse of the empty table while Eddy Cashman was reading through her notes.

"I wanted to surprise you," Progress told Wallace. "I bought this outfit last week but kept it hidden. Cost me a fortune. I bet you thought I'd turn up in a tracksuit, didn't you?" She smiled, pleased with herself.

Wallace covered his face with his hands.

"Professor Wallace, as a conversation between you two has already started, would you care to begin with your questions?" Eddy Cashman asked.

"What do you know about Immanuel Kant, Ms Progress?" Wallace enquired.

"Ahm. Nothing. I'm not a Kantian. I'm a Wallacian. I know all about you."

This was followed by a long silence from both sides of the table interrupted by Wallace's groans as he put his face back behind his hands.

Eddy Cashman broke the ice. "We advertised this post for candidates with doctorates or those who are at the point of completing their doctoral research. What stage are you at in your research, Ms Progress?"

"We ... I mean, *I* ... am making progress. Ha, ha, ha. That's good, isn't it? Get it?"

"God, yes; we get it."

Wallace peeked out from between his fingers and saw Progress smiling with confidence into the silence.

"I will try a different tack. What makes you think you are an appropriate candidate for this job, apart from being a woman?"

"It's not as if I know where the bodies are buried. Ha, ha, ha. I mean, I do know. Ha, ha, ha."

At this point no one seemed to be breathing, not even

Campbell and Cashman who had no idea what was happening.

"My second-life avatar was almost killed last week. I wonder where the other avatars would have hidden his body online?" Casper Wall speculated to no one in particular.

"Are you trying to influence one or more members of this panel by exploiting some inappropriate connection you may have with them?" Campbell the extern asked, looking in turn from Wallace to Spencer who had both turned red.

"No. I am trying to influence them through blackmail. Ha, ha, ha."

Now Spencer laughed. Wallace hid his face again behind his outstretched fingers.

Following another silence, Campbell continued with the questions. Progress responded to being asked to clarify her lack of teaching experience by reading from an essay that she had written, with Wallace's unwitting help, on Wallacian moral philosophy as she understood it. She was prepared to show how much she adhered to the departmental position if she couldn't demonstrate actual relevant professional experience. She was confident Campbell would forget what it was he had asked if she read for long enough.

This strategy worked better than she could have hoped because Campbell did forget his question; Eddy Cashman forgot to thank her for coming to the interview; while the panel, in general, forgot what they were doing there. She stood up without asking questions when her uninterrupted soliloquy fizzled out. She made her unpractised way across the room on her high heels by holding her tiny bag out in front of her with both hands while sticking her backside out behind for counter-balance.

Twenty-eight seconds of exquisite silence passed after the door closed behind Progress before Spencer said, "I was impressed. I think she understands your views on the consequences of behaviour. Don't you, Rik?"

"Better than I understand them myself. However, I think we should do what is best for philosophy, the department and the college, no matter what the consequences. We should do what is right in itself. Just as Kant says."

"What Kant says? What about the consequences if we don't give Progress the job? Have you thought of that? Think of the consequences for the department of philosophy. Imagine the consequences for you and me." Spencer was on his feet shrieking. "Who do you think killed Bacon to get this job if it wasn't Progress?"

"I don't believe in moral consequences anymore. Objective right and wrong have nothing to do with consequences. That is what I have always believed, regardless of anything I have written or taught to the contrary. I don't care what I said before. I'm telling you now: I'm a Kantian and proud of it." He was also standing, shouting. "And I think Inspector Jackson stabbed Bacon who was already dead because he likes the librarian."

"You heretic!" Spencer shouted back, spraying spittle into the second-best boardroom. "You are destroying your own philosophy and risking all of our moral work, and for what? And what do you mean Bacon was already dead anyway?"

"For what is right. Bacon had a heart attack."

"Are you crazy? We're moral philosophers. We don't know what is right. Anyone would have a heart attack with a knife stuck in their neck. Jackson fancies the librarian. Interesting."

"I heard you philosophers take your ideas very seriously, but

I will have no actual fighting over candidates on any panel I am chairing," Eddy Cashman from Commerce said. "Discussion is allowed, encouraged even, where there isn't an obvious agreed candidate. I don't know what all the fuss is about. In my view Ms Progress was a poor applicant for a woman. In fact, I would go so far as to say she is thick."

"Being thick was never a fatal flaw in a lecturer. Anyway, some candidates don't show their best attributes at interview," Spencer said, getting his breath back. He sat down.

"I *am* a Kantian," Wallace told no one in particular. "With philosophy, it's impossible to know what you believe, but as far as I know, and I know I can't be certain because nothing is certain – I know that much from Socrates – I'm a Kantian. Why didn't I read Kant in college when I was a philosophy student? Maybe he was too difficult," he said, before remembering that he had never been a philosophy student. "According to Fischer, Kant believed in duty based in ethics. We have a duty on this panel to hire the best candidate. Our duty is to the college and not to saving our own skins. We should hire Fischer."

"But what about those teeth, that long greasy hair, and the dandruff? What kind of an example would that be for your students?" Campbell the extern asked.

"But you said he was the best candidate."

"Yes, but I didn't say we would hire him in our college."

Spencer was back on his feet again, shouting. "Kant is the polar opposite to the consequentialist position you preached at your inaugural lecture. What is the point in following someone if they keep changing their minds every time they come across a different point of view? Think of the consequences for all of us, Rik."

"I am the provost. It's my decision. I'm not going to make the prudent choice. I am going to do the right thing. Doctor Fischer is the best candidate. We must offer him the job. Look at the mess we are in from trying to produce a moral set of consequences from our actions. Kant is correct. Morally right action comes from duty. As provost I have a responsibility to CAT College I cannot ignore. Damn the consequences."

"You're mad. You have gone stark, raving mad. Power has gone to your head. It's always the same. All the provosts of this college eventually go mad."

Wallace ignored Spencer. "My motivation is the only moral thing that matters. Why didn't I realize this sooner? Why wasn't I a Kantian? I wouldn't be in this mess if that idiot Wallace had been a Kantian in the first place."

"Perhaps he is insane. Who is he talking about?" Campbell the extern asked Casper Wall who didn't know because he had his smartphone out again.

"Heretic. Traitor. Kantian," Spencer shouted at him, before slumping into his seat in despair. Tears began to flow down his face. "What's the point? Another guru reveals his feet of clay."

"Spencer, you heard what Fischer said Kant said: act as if our actions could become a universal law. We must run the college as a moral example to all other colleges by doing our duty. Trust me. You trusted me before this, and you didn't even know what I was talking about. What difference does it make now whether you understand what I mean or not? You should follow me no matter what. Don't you see where your talent lies? Just follow me whether you agree with me or not. Stop trying to think for yourself."

Spencer blew his nose in a handkerchief and dried his eyes.

"Maybe I don't always know what you mean because you are the brain behind our group as well as the moral authority. Maybe you are right. There are responsibilities to being a follower. I can't just abandon you every time you radically change direction. What kind of an acolyte would that make me? Good God, look at the time. I have to pick Samantha up at the crèche. Everyone will think I have abandoned her. Do what you want." He jumped out of his seat and ran out the door.

"I may be the moral authority, but I think Pandora is the brain," Wallace conceded to the space where Spencer had been.

Following a ten-minute discussion, the panel agreed to offer Doctor Fischer – adherent of Kant, free of the influences of dentists, barbers, and grooming products – the vacant post in the philosophy department at CAT College. The panel approved Campbell the extern's suggestion that they advise him in the letter offering him the post that he should wash and cut his hair as a moral imperative before appearing again in CAT College.

"I don't know what all the fuss is about," Casper Wall said to Eddy Cashman as they left the second-best boardroom together. "These interviews never succeed in securing the best candidates for a job. What we need is more online assessment."

"Oh, shut up you unqualified twit."

"I don't agree," Campbell the extern said. "In our college we find that staff recruitment has a way of balancing itself out in the end. It's only moral philosophy after all. It's not as if you are dealing with life and death."

XXXIV

Consequuntur Moralia
Moral Consequences

By the time Rik Wallace arrived at the semi-derelict house on Love Street that he now called home the novel impact of Kantian morality was already starting to wear off. Its full effects had lasted just over three hours. He couldn't tell any more whether he had done the right thing. However, he was certain he hadn't done the easier thing. Was it better if it was more difficult? he wondered. Was there a moral rule he hadn't come across yet that maintained the harder path was the superior one? Maybe Spencer is correct, he thought. Maybe I have gone mad. He was aware of the crushing weight of moral expectation he was experiencing. He was under pressure to learn what morality was, implement it, teach it, research it, supervise it, and inspire others with it. All this on top of running CAT College in a fashion approved by Pandora. While he was thus feeling sorry for himself, he heard a noise from the darkened bedroom. He made his way to the end of the corridor and turned on the light expecting to see Mrs Wallace up and about again. Progress was lying on the bed, immodestly alive. She was wearing the seductive lingerie she imagined a high-powered academic would wear beneath her conservative power-suit at interview.

She was holding a glass of champagne. She held the bottle between her suspender-belted thighs. Waiting for him to get home as the light faded, she had drunk most of the contents.

"There you are. I thought we should celebrate," she told him, patting the bed beside her with her free hand. "I have a glass here for you somewhere if you want to search for it." She rolled on the bed, spilling the champagne. "Ooops," she giggled. She was drunk.

He sat beside her, removed the bottle from between her legs and placed it on the floor. She threw her glass of champagne over her shoulder shattering it against the wall as if launching her new career. "Ooops. Thank God it's not the wall where that bitch of a mother of yours is hiding. Don't want to wake her up with the noise of our celebration." She knelt on the bed and began to approach him on her hands and knees. "Come here, colleague. Isn't it sexy? Inter-collegial fraternizing." She laughed. "I bet you thought I'd dump you when I achieved my life's ambition." She paused to hiccup. "But I won't. Because I love you. There. I've said it. I love you. I love you. I love you." Her momentum carried them both onto the floor when she threw her arms around his neck. As Progress kissed him over and over on the face, Wallace struggled to free himself from her arms.

"Julie. Julie. Listen. I need to tell you something."

"You love me too. I know you do." She stopped and sat up facing him. "God. I made a balls of that interview!" She hiccupped again and covered her mouth with her hand. "I thought that dragon Eddy Cashman was going to throw me out. But none of that matters now, because I am a member of a secret society, and that is more important than impressing a stupid cow in a pinstriped suit. She is the same as Maddox the Man. She should watch out. Maybe lightning will strike twice. But I did want to impress you. Did I dazzle you in my new outfit, darling?" She hitched her thumbs under the wire of her strapless bra and swayed her breasts over and back in front of him. She started to kiss him again.

Wallace pushed her away with both hands and held her at arm's length by her bare shoulders. "Julie. You didn't get the job. We offered the post to an extremely qualified academic who has written loads of books. His name is Ernest Fischer. He will grow on you as he did on me." He spoke as if he was a vet making a moot point to a dangerous wild animal. "Fischer is extremely qualified," he repeated. "We had to offer him the job. It was the right thing to do. You understand, don't you? As a department of moral philosophy, we must be seen to do the right thing."

Progress stiffened in front of him on the floor in her sexy lingerie. Her face darkened and then turned red. Veins appeared on her neck as if an army of worms was trying to break through her skin. She sprung to her feet. In front of Wallace's eyes, the crotch of her scant thong, now at the level of his face, changed from being an ornament of love to the girdle of an Amazonian warrior.

"Fair?" she screamed at him. "Fair? Did this delightful Ernest Fischer kill your mother for you and hide her in that wall?" she asked, pointing towards the spare bedroom.

"The other wall. She's in the kitchen."

"What?"

"It's that direction. She's over there."

"Did this fantastic Ernest Fischer help you bury the

provost in your garden and serve tea afterwards?" She was now pointing towards the patio. "That way? Yes?" She stuck her tongue out at him. "No. I don't think so. You overestimate the value of Fischer's formal qualifications compared to my broader knowledge," she snarled. "What did that moron Maurice Spencer say about this?"

"Spencer wanted you to get the job. He shouted at me. He even told me I was crazy. But in the end, he agreed that Kant was correct."

"Kant? What has Kant got to do with my job?"

"Kant says we should act according to our duty. Didn't you read Kant when you were an undergraduate?"

"No. Lambe said he was too difficult for us to understand. Stop changing the subject."

"I'm not. You asked me about Kant. I don't understand him myself, but Fischer explained his moral philosophy to me."

"Fischer – the person who got the job – explained to you why Kant says he should get the job." She emphasized each word as if making a point to an imbecile, which she now suspected he was.

"That's how interviews work. Candidates are supposed to persuade the panel to give them the job. I don't understand Kant, but I am going to read him as soon as I can get back into the library."

"What did Eddy Cashman say? She has a job, and she is the same age as me. It's not fair. All you need to do to get a job in that faculty is wear a suit. But they are loyal to each other in commerce, which is not the case amongst philosophers who don't even know what the word means."

"It wasn't Cashman's decision. It was mine. Don't blame

anyone but me. You didn't persuade me during your interview to give you the job. That's all. You will get a job when you finish your doctorate – when I finish it – and publish a few articles. I promise you."

"How long must I wait before another vacancy comes up?" She paused. "I can think of one philosopher I want to see being replaced."

"Don't go crazy. As soon as a new position opens up the job is yours, I promise. You might be waiting a while because everyone in philosophy is healthy now. Just try to be patient."

"Your promises are worthless. You promised me this job."

"I didn't promise you anything. We both just assumed too much."

"It's over between us."

"You mean I won't be supervising your research?"

"You won't be supervising anything." She turned her crotch away leaving him a clear view of her twin dimpled buttocks separated by the thin line of her thong as she went in search of her red tracksuit legs.

"Don't be hasty. We don't need to be friends, but I can still supervise your doctorate."

"Get out of here," she said, pointing at the door with an outstretched hand while holding her tracksuit legs in the other. "Get out of *my* room. Find somewhere else to sleep. Get out. Imagine, just a few minutes ago I loved you. Now that I know what kind of a fraud you are, I don't want you anymore. I have principles too, even if I've never read Kant," she shouted into the hall before slamming the door behind him.

Wallace sat alone on a chair at the dining table. He would improvise a bed on the floor when he could muster the enthusiasm. He thought perhaps he should read Nietzsche instead of the sober Kant because he couldn't imagine Nietzsche's writings could make his situation worse.

Meanwhile, in the bedroom Progress schemed revenge. Wallace could hear her muttered curses through the closed door. She wanted public retribution because she was an amateur. A master of the art of revenge would have appreciated that the best form is an anonymous act of malice that the victim might have imagined came about through bad luck alone. It would have been more depressing for Wallace to believe the fates were out to get him rather than merely an embittered Progress whose resources and imagination were limited compared to the gods.

Three days later Wallace had moved two more chairs into a row to improvise a bench. He wanted his bed back, but he didn't want Progress to leave. He hoped for a reconciliation, but he wasn't going to tell her that. She was too preoccupied trying to scheme how to get even to think about finding somewhere else to live. Perhaps she didn't want to leave because her unconscious self was an even lazier slob than her conscious self. Wallace was too depressed to face the chore of emptying the furniture from the spare bedroom in the hope of finding a bed under all of the debris. He refilled his beer glass with red wine to wash down his special fried rice for one.

XXXV

Custodientes Vigilias In Bibliotheca
Keeping Watch in the Library

Jim the now trainee librarian was on his hands and knees. A small amber light near the top of the twin white panels facing each other inside the front door blinked before turning a constant green to confirm that the system was armed when he plugged in the long white cable that snaked along the hall floor. He straightened up from the socket and stood beside the librarian who was supervising the installation of the security gate that would prevent books being removed from the house without Jim's authorization.

"I will leave now without checking out this book. You confront me outside the door when the alarm goes off. Are you ready? Do you have your ID and your Taser?" the librarian asked.

"Oh, it's so exciting. This is the first breach of my library rules. I will sit here and pretend I am just minding my own business while reading the paper as you go by. Okay?"

Jim sat on a plastic chair squeezed between two pillars of books while the librarian retreated to the kitchen.

"Are you ready?" she shouted into the hall. "Here I come."

"Ready," Jim confirmed.

The librarian walked by, casually holding a book down by her side away from Jim. She swung her free arm through a short arc and whistled. This was how she imagined students behaved when stealing books from her library.

"Excuse me, miss. Have you checked out that book at the issuing desk in the kitchen?" Jim asked, jumping to his feet in the narrow hallway.

"You're supposed to be reading the paper, Jim. You don't see me."

"Oh yeah. Sorry. It's my nerves." He sat back down.

"Never mind. Let's keep going. Where were we? Yes, I have checked it out at the issuing desk," she lied. "How dare you accuse me of trying to steal a book? I'm traumatized. I may sue this library for defamation."

"Ah, fine. Very good. Off you go then. Have a nice day, miss."

"Thank you."

The librarian walked between the parallel panels of the scanner. She braced herself for the blare of the alarm that Jim had set to maximum. But nothing happened, even by the time she was opening the front door. The librarian turned around on the footpath outside and looked back into the hallway.

"It's not working," Jim lamented, abandoning his security role along with the newspaper.

"Oh, we are such idiots," the librarian said, slapping her forehead with her palm. "We forgot to put the tags into the books we are using for our test."

"We were overexcited. I can do that now, and we can try again."

Jim and the librarian had set up an improvised issuing desk

in the kitchen. On the table columns of books leaned against each other like school friends. The librarian sat down at one of the pair of the back-to-back computer terminals while Jim sat in front of a single column of books. He tore the seal off a box of tabs and spilled the long thin paper strips on to the table top in front of him.

"While you are doing that, I will check we have an Internet connection," the librarian said.

Jim cracked open the book on top of the column at a random page. Holding a strip at each end he wiggled it until it was embedded in the spine.

"I'm going to Google Inspector Jackson."

"You fancy him, don't you?"

"Maybe. But I want to know who he is, at least according to the Internet?"

"He's a policeman. What else is there to know?"

"Let's see. Wow. There are pages of mentions of him here: stacks of newspaper reports. Here is one that says he was decorated for solving the Pasta Murders. The headline reads: *Brilliant Young Detective Solves Restaurant Slaughter That Confounded a Generation of Police.* Here is a more recent one: *Inspector Jackson Holds Station Record Third Year Running for Jailing Criminals.* Or: *Silent Sam Breaks Under Jackson Interrogation.* This is curious: *Homicide Detective Cleared of Suspicion in Homicide. This morning the Criminal Court threw out the case against Inspector Jackson, decorated* – blah, blah – *when the prosecution's witness failed to give evidence. The police are still searching for their star witness who disappeared just hours before being due to* – blah, blah. *Outside the court Police Chief—— said it was a disgrace that his finest officer had been dragged through the mud on the basis of the flimsy uncorroborated testimony of a well-known criminal with prior convictions.* Here's another. *Super Cop Bounces Back with Record Arrest After Charges Against Him Dropped.* It seems all that fuss was caused by criminals trying to make trouble for him because he is just too good at his job. He seems to be some sort of super cop, though we haven't seen any evidence of that yet in CAT College."

"Maybe he is toying with us."

"Maybe. But I sense some ambiguity in his attitude. I'm sensitive to those sorts of vibes. I thought, somehow, he was hoping we – *I* – was bad in some way. Maybe he is attracted to wicked women?"

"That's not you."

"What do you mean? I could be a villain if I wanted," the librarian mused. "It's disappointing. There is nothing on his personal life on these sites."

"Are you ready to try again," Jim asked standing up and handing her a tagged edition of Dostoyevsky's *Crime and Punishment.* "See if you can steal that."

XXXVI

Adde Unum Entrepreneurum Solum
Just Add One Entrepreneur

Professor Maurice Spencer and Pandora were walking together under a purple-and-yellow striped battle-flag sky fluttering above the college. They were discussing what, if anything, they might do about the growing rift between Rik Wallace and Julie Progress. While Spencer had sulked for a while over the outcome of the interviews, he had soon come to appreciate the virtue of Wallace's new position. He was once more committed to being the best disciple he could be. Pandora wanted the committee to consider bumping off Progress because her anger at Wallace was ruining the harmony of CATfish meetings. However, Spencer favoured a sympathetic attitude to Progress, whom he liked.

Pandora's feline instincts told her there was something unreliable she couldn't articulate about Progress, whereas she felt at least she could control Wallace because, deep down behind the academic genius, she believed he was a harmless idiot. For Pandora, the next plan was always perfect because it hadn't yet gone wrong. She didn't recognize her own role in her failed schemes because she was blessed with the gift of seeing only the fault in others. They were on their way to the reception hut to consult Jim the porter to see if he could break the deadlock. Spencer stopped. He pulled his hands from his pockets and waved them above his head, slapping his forehead. "We forgot! We are idiots! Jim has retired! He is no longer in his wooden sentry post. That spotty oaf who knows no one and nothing has replaced him."

"It appears he can't even use a lawnmower," Pandora said, pursing her lips at the lengthening grass.

"This college is going to fall apart without Jim. We should persuade him to come back. We need some of the old guard around here to maintain order," Spencer said.

"CATfish promised him he could retire. That's all he asked for. You and I should keep our promises otherwise we will have even more upset members of CATfish than just Progress. You realize she had a motive to kill Bacon even if Rik says he wasn't murdered. With him out of the way she had a chance of an academic position," Pandora said. "She has to wait until another vacancy comes up."

"But there isn't another vacancy coming up in philosophy. What? Why are you looking at me like that? She wouldn't come after me, would she? Do you think she would kill me?"

"No. Progress isn't capable of killing anyone. She is too weak. Besides. How could she be sure Wallace would give her the job when – she should know this better than the rest of us – he keeps changing his mind."

"Maybe she will kill Rik. That would make more sense than killing me. Would you mind telling her that when you see her? Do you think he did it?"

"Who?"

"Rik?"

"Did what?"

"Kill Bacon."

"Why would he? God knows he needs all the philosophers he has."

"That's true. He needs me. Would you mind telling him that when you see him? I think he likes me. I'm his most committed follower."

"You are his loudest follower."

"Did you kill Bacon?"

Pandora stubbed her cigarette out on the grass under the heel of her shoe. "I did not. We are not the only group operating on campus."

"What do you mean?"

"That wasn't our work. No meticulous planning. No team effort. I think it was an opportunistic killing by a loner."

They walked on together forming separate plans in their heads.

"Jim has nothing to do at home except catalogue his books on his new computers. He has no time for anyone since he got those machines from the librarian. The two of them are over there everyday borrowing books from each other and passing them through that security gate he has rigged up inside the front door," Pandora said.

"At least he is doing what he loves."

"You should ask Inspector Jackson what he likes doing with his spare time. Wallace told me that he thinks Jackson may have killed Bacon so that he would have an excuse to remain on campus. Perhaps the best way to get away with killing someone is to chase yourself."

"Oh God, I'm confused. How can I be safe if the police

are involved?"

"You think too much. Just stop for a while and see how the rest of us manage."

"I can't stop myself thinking. It's a lifetime of training. Maybe Progress could try to be a Kantian if another vacancy does come up, which would save us all a lot of trouble."

"I think she has lost interest in moral philosophy. I think she feels betrayed and that's dangerous for the rest of us."

"I hate these petty disagreements. Rik didn't promise Progress anything. She just presumed too much. They will kiss and make up soon. I know I'm right. We philosophers are either right or else we don't know. We're never wrong."

"I'll put you down as a 'don't know anything' then."

They walked on in silence again.

"We should stick together. Wallace should have stuck with Progress for the sake of CATfish and not betrayed her for some stupid abstract principle. Now she will destroy us all. She has to go," Pandora concluded.

"Rik has inspired me to cope with all the unexpected upheavals in my life plan. Yes. It would help my nerves if he didn't keep changing his core beliefs, but that's the proof of his genius. I'm sure he wouldn't want anything to happen to Progress."

"What is the point in the search for the fundamental meaning of life if you philosophers won't stick to it when you think you have found it? Where's the consolation in flitting from one idea to the next? You need to settle on something, and soon or you will drive me crazy. At least Progress doesn't appear to believe in anything except improving her own life. That I can understand."

"Your problem, Pandora, is that you are not a follower. You want to be the leader, and there can be only one of those. Who knew being a follower could be this stressful? Maybe Rik will leave. There are colleges out there where he would be worshipped as a prophet."

"Leave? Wallace will never leave. No one leaves here except in a box. I don't understand Wallace, but my instincts tell me there will be trouble in CAT College because of him. Everything was fine before he turned up."

"Pandora, you are not an intellectual. You should leave the thinking to those of us who are trained to think. Instincts can be dangerous."

Dangerous or not, Pandora's intuition was accurate on this occasion because trouble was just then arriving in the back of a black limousine that was pulling up under the main archway into the college. A hulk wearing a black suit, white shirt, and black tie wriggled his bulk from behind the steering wheel. Spencer and Pandora suspended their conversation to investigate their important visitor.

The driver hauled a short fat man from the car by pulling on one of the two outstretched stubby arms projecting from the back door. When he was upright on his feet Spencer and Pandora, who were looking down on him, could see five greasy fingers of blond hair plastered down over the top of his head in a futile attempt to hide his baldness. Below his red face a muffin neck bulged over the collar of his expensive striped shirt and tie. As his neck size expanded, he refused to increase his shirt size to keep pace. He was content to endure discomfort and risk a seizure for the sake of vanity. However, those who knew him could argue that his brain was the one organ in his body that had the least potential to profit from a regular flow of oxygen. The tailoring genius behind his handmade suit managed to flatter his cylindrical body. Each of his sausagey fingers carried a display of diamond-studded rings. The high-pitched squeaky quality of his voice startled those hearing him for the first time and, uncannily, made them struggle to resist imitating him. Forcing his words out in a breathless gasp, he produced an eeeking sound at the beginning of each sentence as if his speech centre was located in his stomach. He addressed Spencer who was staring at him with a mixture of dread and wonder.

"Eeeek. I'm looking for the ghost of this college."

"The ghost? Oh. You mean the pro-vost, Professor Rik Wallace. The ghost. Very droll."

"Eeeek. Droll. What do you mean drolling?" the man asked, taking an ironed and folded white linen handkerchief from his pocket, dabbing his mouth, and inspecting the result. The driver took up a position behind his shoulder with his legs apart and his hands clasped over his stomach.

"Eeeek. He is my brother."

"Who? The ghost. I mean, the provost?"

"Yes. He is my brother, which makes me his brother. I'm Larry Wallace. Did he tell you he has a successful brother, Larry? Rik is not the only one in the family with a meta bellum," he said tapping the side of his forehead.

Spencer looked blankly at him. Larry suspected he was dealing with a simpleton. "Rik isn't the only one with a brain. I could have stayed in school if I'd wanted. My mother never appreciated the one who did everything for her."

"Who was that?"

"Eeeek. Me. It was me! I did everything she wanted, but it was always Rik this and Rik that. She escapes from prison to be with him. I'll kill them both when I catch up with them. Metallurgically speaking, of course. Ha ha."

"Rik doesn't tell us much about himself. He is modest, which is the way of all great men."

Larry grunted and squeezed Spencer's hand between his rings and watched the silent scream coming out through his eyes with calm satisfaction.

"What do you do, Larry?" Pandora asked. She didn't risk shaking hands when she saw Spencer clamping his into his armpit. She correctly guessed Larry wasn't sexist when it came to inflicting pain.

"I'm an entrepreneur." This was a word he had rehearsed just for such introductions, having learned his rivals had used it to describe him on the rare occasions when they were being complimentary. "I entrepreneur things."

"An entrepreneur? Imagine that – a man of business. Welcome to CAT College, which you may be aware, is one of the leading business schools in the city. You should feel at home here?"

"How many other business schools are in this city?"

"None. But as we say in our brochures, that isn't the point."

"My mother was here."

"Your mother? Was in the college? Was she in the secretarial school?" Spencer asked.

"Eeeek. My mother was here after she escaped from prison."

"I know Patricia the provost's grandmother took anyone who applied back then. She had to. She was desperate for numbers. This is the first time I have heard of her taking in a jailbird. Things must have been tougher than we thought back in the good old days."

"Eeeek. For smart-ass academicals, you're not that bright, are you. My mother came here to see my brother, Rik. The little shit didn't even tell me. I was worried out of my mind."

Larry Wallace wiped his hands with his white handkerchief and handed it to the driver. "Someone from the college wrote unanimously to tell me my mother had been here for Rik's big lecher."

"Oh, that lecher … I mean, lecture. An unforgettable occasion. A memorable night. Your brother is a genius."

"Were you there? Did you see my mother?" Larry asked becoming redder.

Spencer raised his hands in front of him. "No. I didn't," he said. "I had to leave to take my daughter to something. What was it? Swimming?"

"Teacher–parent meeting," Pandora corrected him.

"Wonderful memory, Pandora."

"I remember all your daughter's movements."

"I didn't even know you had a mother until now," Spencer told Larry, who was scowling at him.

"You seem to be a successful entrepreneur," Pandora put in to change the subject. She was studying the car and impressively mute driver. "What kind of business are you in?"

"A bit of this and a bit of that. I buy and sell. Buy low. Sell high. Farms and suitables."

"Farms and what?" Spencer asked. He found it impossible to shut up even though he was certain he should.

"Do you have business qualifications?" Pandora asked.

"I have this," Larry Wallace said, holding up a diamond-encrusted clenched fist. "And if that isn't suff—enough, I have this," he said, holding up the other. He executed a lithe boxer's shuffle, weaved and ducked, and hit Spencer a playful jab in the chest to emphasize his point. Spencer sank onto his knees on the gravel beside the car, gasping for air before either Pandora or Larry could react. Pandora suspected Larry's massive driver had lightening reflexes, but he hadn't moved a muscle, giving the impression he often witnessed people dropping to their knees in front of Larry.

"Fuck me. What a wimp. Horse, pick him up," Larry instructed his driver. Horse bent down and placed one arm under Spencer's neck and the other behind his knees and raised him with the care of a mother carrying a precious purchase.

"I didn't mean to discommode him. I'm sorry. I don't know my own strength, or the weakness of others. Where can we take him to get his wind back?"

"Your brother's office," Pandora said. "You can surprise him."

Pandora and Larry walked beside Horse who carried a groaning Spencer the short distance to the provost's office. On the way, Pandora kept glancing sideways at Larry, assessing him as a potential candidate to fill the vacancy in the commerce faculty and any other available roles. Compared to Spencer slumped in Horse's arms, he appeared to her as someone who wouldn't have far to go to transform himself into a savage: maybe not even a noble one. She imagined he would have his own body hair and wouldn't be put off by a little soap. He probably had his own clubs. She didn't notice her feet were drawing her closer to him with each step.

Rik Wallace wasn't in his office. He was in the library

reading Kant's *Critique of Practical Reason,* which, on this occasion, was proving to be an opportune, if not practical, diversion. Spencer sat in Wallace's swivel chair massaging the ring-shaped indents in his sternum. Pandora and Larry sat at the other side of the desk, smoking. She was experiencing strange inner stirrings of emotion that she was struggling to control. Perhaps she was falling in love with Larry in that limited way one megalomaniac might love another. She fantasized about how a pair of monomaniacs might live together.

"I admire a man who smokes," Pandora heard herself saying out loud.

"Eeeeek. I'm not sure I fancy a woman who wears sunglasses inside."

She removed them, folded the temples, and placed them on the desk. She blinked in the dazzle of the unfamiliar daylight. Her varicose eyes watered.

"That's better," Larry said.

"The faculty of commerce has a vacancy. We need a real man – a real business man – and not just … er …women like Maddox the Man or Eddy Cashman to teach our students something practical about the actual business world." Pandora's words were coming out of her mouth without her having formed the thoughts to go with them. "Our students get too much theory about marketing strategies, sales, and spreadsheet nonsense. Old-fashioned rough and tumble is what they need. What you call entrepreneurship. I bet you could teach them a few sales techniques in pharmaceuticals."

"What pharmaceuticals? Oh. Farms and suitables, of course. Okay. Forget I said anything," Spencer said, wrapping his arms to protect his chest. "I thought we agreed we would have more abstract ideas in commerce, not less," he croaked, beginning to find both his breath and courage again. "What do you know about philosophy, Larry?"

"Oh, shut up. You philosophers would drive anyone crazy," Pandora said.

"My brother is a fucking philosopher," Larry said, turning his attention back to Spencer. "He's not just full of shit. He's overflowing with it."

"I know. I mean, I know he's a *philosopher*," Spencer said with a little defiance but he was relieved when Larry lost interest in him.

"You want me to get involved in your business school racket? Oh, Mister High-and-Mighty Rik would love that! What would I have to do?"

"Nothing. We would handle all the details, marking exams, that kind of thing. You would be head of the faculty. In time we could call something after you. *The Wallace Enterprise Centre.* How does that sound? We would pay a generous stipend for your co-operation and the value of your business name."

"Before doing anything rash I think we should discuss the proposal at our next Academic Council meeting," Spencer said, bracing for another blow that didn't come.

"Spencer is too modest. We run the council. We run the college," Pandora boasted. "And we don't need to consult Acting Head, Eddy Cashman, about what happens in her faculty."

There was a loud knock.

"Come in," Spencer shouted before anything else could be said. The door opened. "Ah Julie. Come in," Spencer commanded.

"I just called by to remind Rik that I'm officially still not speaking to him."

"This is Rik's brother, Larry. Someone in the college wrote to him about his mother who has escaped from prison and here he is."

"How do you do, Larry? Pleased to meet you. Rik told us nothing about you."

"Larry is going to run *The Wallace Enterprise Centre* when he becomes head of the commerce faculty. Imagine that? An on-campus business incubator. A nerve-centre of excellence fostering entrepreneurship to allow our graduates to develop real-world business skills under Larry's supervision," Pandora said, already composing the promotional materials in her imagination.

"Wow. That's amazing. The head of a centre with your own name. That's more than anything Rik ever achieved. He will be incredibly jealous. Serves him right the way he treats his students."

"Eeeek. Yah. I'm dying to see the look on his sour face when I tell him."

"Are you going to be supervising students? You wouldn't know this, but I have always been interested in the concept of enterprise from both a philosophical and commercial point of view. My doctoral research has stalled again. I was thinking of changing my topic. I thought I should become more business-focused. Will you be supervising doctoral students in your enterprise centre?"

He looked her up and down.

"I plan to surprise a lot of students," he said.

She smiled. "But you're sweet. Rik told me you were an arsehole."

"He said that? I will teach him some manners when I see him." Larry rotated his rings.

"I think we both know who the real arsehole in your family is?"

"Who?"

"Rik. Rik is the real arsehole."

"Why don't you walk me to my car? You can tell me all about Rik. I'll see you two later when we can make some more plans for doing business together."

"But Larry, you're not leaving already," Pandora pleaded. "We have only begun to discuss our future. Can't you get lost Progress, or find one of your philosophers to supervise your research if haven't already slept with all of them?"

"All this talk of sleep is making me tired," Larry said, stretching his arms above his head. "I think I need to lie down."

Julie Progress walked Larry to his car. Horse was standing beside the driver's door where he had returned after depositing Spencer in Wallace's swivel chair.

"I wrote you that letter, Larry."

"The unanimous one?"

"The what?" Progress studied Larry for a moment. She was unaware that her unconscious was registering doubts about him that it refused to communicate to her consciousness. Typical unconscious: selfish.

"Did Rik tell you where I was?"

"No. Rik doesn't talk about you. He doesn't know I contacted you. I was hoping to surprise him. I owe him a surprise because he gave me one recently. The police were here looking for your mother. I looked her up on the Internet and saw you were offering a reward for information leading to her whereabouts."

"Money is no concern to me."

"I'm not concerned about money either. I'm interested in ideas."

"I have ideas."

"I'll tell you everything, Larry. I have my own reasons for helping you. You can trust me."

"I don't trust anyone."

Again, unknown to Progress, her unconscious self was drawing its own conclusions, but her conscious self was too busy planning revenge on Rik. Progress's unconscious was regretting the letter that her conscious self had posted. We know from Sigmund Freud that the unconscious can be a frustrated part of the mind having no direct control over our limbs and often waiting, days, weeks, and sometimes even years for its views to be heard. The one satisfaction the unconscious has is that it gets to say "I told you so".

"When was my mother here?" Larry asked.

"The night after she escaped."

"Did you talk with her?"

"Briefly."

"Did she stay the night?"

"Yes."

"With Rik?"

"Yes."

"Where did she go afterwards?"

"You won't find her without my help. We can't talk here," she told him, telling herself she still had to work out the details of a version of events that would keep her in the clear with Larry. She planned to give Rik full credit for killing Larry's mother. After all, he was the one who killed her the first time around. In her version, she would make it a one-time murder that happened once. But she had some psychological training, which meant she could make herself remember any interpretation of the past she liked. She was already starting to believe her new memories.

"Let me take you to dinner. This evening," Larry said.

"Oh, I can't. I have a meeting tonight. It's a secret society. You know? A college thing."

"Pity. I was hoping we could do – what do you call it – some super vision together. I would need to build up my strength for that in the best restaurant in the city."

"I suppose I could give my society meeting a miss. I need to get changed. I have a new suit I can wear. What time?"

"Seven thirty. I'll pick you up. Where do you live?"

"It's a dump. I'll take you there when you know everything. Pick me up here under the college arch."

Progress ran the tips of her fingers down the lapel of Horse's jacket and onto the gleaming bonnet of the car as part of an empirical test to confirm they were real. She was reluctant to rely on the evidence of her eyes alone because at some philosophical level she was an idealist.

"Seven thirty. Don't be late."

Horse held the door open while Larry climbed into the back of the long, black shiny car. He didn't realize that since he first placed his feet onto the ground of CAT College two women had just fallen into what they each, in their different ways, considered to be love with him. But while Larry was the object of their affections, he wasn't an expert on romance. He didn't read poetry nor hum love songs to himself. Neither would he have benefitted from consulting philosophy because love has been a neglected topic in the history of that discipline. It was perhaps a heart versus brain thing, with the head winning out. Even in psychology the heart has not been subjected to the same scrutiny that the brain has had to endure. And then the confusion that conflates love and sex. Progress did know a lot about sex from her fickle proclivity for doctorate supervisors but not much about Platonic affection that transcends desire invented by the unhappily married Socrates.

Pandora was familiar with the separation of the concepts of love and sex: she loved her cat.

Meanwhile, back in the provost's office Spencer and Pandora were experiencing yet another significant divergence in college strategy. Following their recent disagreement over who might be next to exit the academic population, they were now arguing over who should be next to join.

"I can't put my finger on it but something is odd about Larry Wallace. I have an instinct for detecting personal foibles," Spencer was telling Pandora. "I know people. It's what I'm good at, and I know something is wrong with Larry."

"He is a wealthy, powerful businessman. We need more men of his type around here. You are jealous because you are weedy. He almost killed you with just one little pat of his hand."

"That was no little pat. He broke my chest bone."

"All the academics in this college are wimps."

"That's not the point. Our leader Rik must have had a sound philosophical reason for never mentioning his brother, Larry."

"Maybe Rik is embarrassed because his brother is successful.

He would make a distinguished head of commerce. Maybe we should ask Larry to come to our secret meetings. Perhaps I could persuade him to agree with me about Progress's future."

"From the way he was leering at her when they left here together, I don't think so. I may be a wimp, but you know I'm your wimp."

"Get off me. Progress jumps on every man that turns up in this college. Funny how she never jumped on you. She has good taste."

Pandora ground a cigarette into Wallace's desk and lit another. She put on her glasses and walked towards the door.

Spencer ran after her. "Pandora, you are taking all these decisions too fast. You just react to your feelings. You need to think things through. You should use your head more and your heart less. That's something you would learn from philosophy, if you ever gave it a chance."

"No thanks. I'll stick with my instincts, which have served me well to date. We need Larry."

"You mean *you* need Larry. Why didn't Rik tell us about his rich brother? I'm going to find him and tell him Larry is here looking for his mother."

"Don't forget we have a CATfish meeting this evening. I think I'll nominate Larry as a new member. He could be useful. And Horse. He could be handy too for carrying stuff instead of that weedy Goth, Doolittle."

"I'll look in the library for Rik. I'll take him straight to the meeting at Jim's place. I'll see you there."

"Don't be late. We have a lot to discuss."

Spencer ran to the library.

Pandora was feeling herself again. It should be a simple

matter, she thought, to get Larry in and Progress out. There was no need for the others to know her irreconcilable emotions for both.

XXXVII

Ars Dissimulationis
The Art of Keeping Secrets

Professors Rik Wallace and Maurice Spencer together approached the ideal symbiotic relationship where one side takes on the burden of most of the talking and the other does most of the ignoring what's being said. In this mode they arrived together for the secret CATfish meeting towards the end of Spencer's wide-ranging monologue. Perhaps from years of lecturing Spencer had become indifferent to whether or not his audience was listening. However, on this occasion he was eager that Wallace acknowledge the importance of his observations. They stood at the front door waiting to be admitted to the home of Jim formerly a porter and currently striving to be a trainee librarian and Rose who was still a cleaner despite her recent foray into physics.

"Thank God you are always studying in the library. Otherwise, I would not have found you before you got here," Spencer repeated for at least the fifth time. Wallace wasn't counting. "Though I can't imagine what you need to learn at this stage. Remember what I said. We must stick together or Pandora will ruin everything for the arts. Don't tell her that I warned you about her plans to set your brother Larry up as head of the commerce faculty and in charge of an eponymous *Wallace Enterprise Centre* or she will kill me. Try to look surprised when she brings it up."

"What? Oh yeah. I'll try."

"I should be at home making dinner for Samantha. Poor child. She will be starving but this is an emergency. I don't like your brother Larry. I don't think Larry likes you."

"I'm guessing we don't have much in common."

"For what my philosophical opinion is worth, your brother is an idiot. Pandora wants him in the college for his brawn, which is a novel approach to pedagogy. She is a woman with unconventional ideas and tastes. Trust me, I know. Progress had better be careful not to get in the way of that relationship. You should try to convince her to leave Larry alone for her own safety. She doesn't want a jealous Pandora on her trail. Trust me, I know. You should try to win Progress back for all of us."

"Progress won't listen. She's not even talking to me."

"Pandora likes people as long as she doesn't get to know them well. After that she hates them because, fundamentally, she hates everyone. She is a genuine misanthrope. I don't know how I have survived this long."

"Maybe she has something special in mind for you. Do you have relatives she could hire to upset you?"

"Oh God." Spencer was running through the possibilities in his mind. "If only you had given Progress that job. If only you had never heard of Kant. If only—"

"We would still be in this mess."

"You are on your own when we get inside. Don't drag me into conflict with Pandora, because I want her to believe that I can follow her orders."

"I'm not afraid of Pandora. Oh God, I hope she is in a good mood tonight. Okay, I am terrified of her, but she isn't going to run my life. I have principles."

"Pandora believes she is ruining everyone's life."

"I said running, not ruining."

"Same thing with her. Remember she wants to make Larry a member of CATfish. She won't stop until she has replaced you with him as provost. Right now, she still likes you, but she doesn't trust philosophers, especially moral ones."

"That's fair, because I replaced his brother with me."

"What are you talking about? You're speaking in metaphysical riddles."

"I don't think Pandora will get the chance to ruin my life if Larry catches up with me first, because he thinks I killed his mother."

"Sibling's often have crazy ideas about each other. My sister always believed that I killed our brother. Crazy nonsense. What happened with that chainsaw was an accident."

Spencer stopped talking and stepped away from Wallace when Rose opened the door.

Spencer sat at the opposite end of the cluttered kitchen table to Wallace trying to give Pandora the impression that they hadn't been conspiring before the meeting.

"Where is Progress?" Pandora asked. "She's late. We cannot run a committee if we don't meet on time. We are already fifteen minutes behind schedule waiting for the two of you to arrive *together*."

"She is having dinner with Rik's brother, Larry," Doolittle told her. "She rang me to ask me to ask you to accept her apologies."

"I will note that in the minutes," the librarian said.

"Maybe we should throw her out if she can't turn up for meetings," Pandora suggested. "It was a mistake to allow her to join in the first place."

"Anyone can miss a meeting," Wallace said. "We can't expel someone for missing one meeting. Can we?"

"We will need to consider it if she misses any more," Pandora said, studying Wallace behind her glasses. She blew a warning shot of smoke over his shoulder.

"Are the rest of us present now?" the librarian asked.

"Who is that?" Spencer asked, pointing to a non-member sitting at the end of the table behind Jim's new computer terminal.

Doolittle took the stranger's hand in hers, squeezed it, and smiling said, "Everyone. This is Maximilien Thierry. He is a French student visiting CAT College on an exchange programme. I translate his name as Maximum Theory. Isn't that wonderful? It's a philosophical miracle that we met. I am incredibly happy."

"But what is he doing here? We are a secret society. We can't be secret if every outsider who just walks by is taken in off the street," Pandora objected.

"Oh. It's okay. Maxi doesn't understand a word of English." Doolittle squeezed his hand again. Maximilien smiled at each in turn and waved.

"Couldn't we ask him to stand outside in the garden for the meeting?" Spencer said.

"I don't know how to ask him to do that in French."

"Couldn't we just push him outside?"

"We don't have time for this," Pandora said. "Let's get on

with the agenda."

"I won't put him in the minutes as a full member yet," the librarian said. "I will describe him as an associate member. How is that?"

"Yes. But we don't want more people wandering in," Pandora snapped. She immediately regretted her comment because she had planned to propose Larry Wallace as a new CATfish member. She rammed a cigarette between her pursed lips. Damned imbeciles, she thought. I should be more careful. They have distracted me from my grand plan.

"I want … I mean, it would be beneficial for our group if Larry Wallace – that is Rik's brother – became the next head of the commerce faculty." Pandora read aloud from her notes. "He could run a business enterprise centre because that is what that faculty needs to remain competitive and relevant in an ever-changing, real-world business environment requiring the constant up-skilling of our learners. I was impressed by Larry's business acumen when I met him today," she continued, searching for the word on the page. Pandora looked up from the paper in front of her. She pushed her black glasses up her nose with an index finger. "Look. He is a successful businessman. He is richer and stronger than any of you."

"Why would he want to work at CAT College?" Jim asked.

"Vanity. How could he resist having his own centre named after him? And, who knows, maybe he admires his potential colleagues and sees a value in spending time with them," Pandora said, looking at the shelves of books on the far wall without seeing individual titles.

"Can he teach?" Spencer asked.

"What difference does that make?"

"He may be rich and strong, but he has no teaching experience. What about our students, or learners, or whatever they are called?"

"What about them? They suffer with you, don't they?"

"What about Larry?" Wallace asked.

"What do you mean?"

"It's not fair on Larry to ask him to teach if he won't feel fulfilled doing it. We should think of his happiness and not the … learners. You don't want Larry to become stressed and unhappy in CAT College, and worse, unhappy with those who hired him, because he can't teach. He would take his frustration out on you, Pandora. Believe me. I know him better than anyone," he lied. "He is my brother," he lied again, getting on a roll. "You don't want Larry taking anything out on you."

Pandora inhaled the tobacco smoke from her glowing cigarette in silence, allowing the blast of nicotine to fuel her brain.

"We could ask him to deliver a trial lecture to a business class. We could sit in the back of the hall and assess his performance and then decide," Rose interrupted.

"We?"

"Yes. The members of CATfish. That is what colleges do all the time."

Pandora stared at Rose. She was smoking and thinking. She was wondering what these morons could be plotting now. "Okay. I agree. But only one short lecture to satisfy your curiosity, and I will be the main judge."

"I don't think I should be there because he is my brother. It would be unethical. What we moral philosophers call a conflict of interest."

"Good point, Professor Wallace," Jim said. "The rest of us will be there. Pandora can arrange it."

"Can I bring Maxi?" Doolittle asked, squeezing his hand again, causing him to smile at the members of CATfish who could barely see each other past the columns of books on the kitchen table that were now, unlike those sitting around it, protected against crime.

XXXVIII

Paranoia Est In Mente Sola
Paranoia is Only Mental

While the CATfish committee was deciding Larry Wallace's future, he was having dinner with Julie Progress behind the enormous window of the most expensive restaurant in the city, L'intestin Grêle. The owner had installed the glass on the reasonable assumption his customers wanted to be seen eating such expensive food. They sat alone, angled at 160 degrees to each other at the circular table that Progress guessed was more than six feet in diameter. Larry dabbed his protruding lips with the large white starched linen napkin that matched the tablecloth. He belched, threw his dessertspoon into the now empty rectangular plate, and leaned back in his reproduction Regency chair.

"That was scrumptious," Progress said. "Such tiny portions and such huge prices. My favourite was the smoked eel terrine, which I never had before. Not at all as slippery as you might expect. The wine was delicious," she said draining her glass.

"Yes. Very professional. I'm starving."

Progress had been wondering how to get Mrs Wallace into the conversation. She saw an opening in the topic of culinary skills. "Rik and I never eat – I mean, ate – like this. We had take-out meals. Did your mother teach you to cook when you were a child?" Was this, she wondered, a good time to tell him his mother was dead.

"No. She didn't. She wasn't domestic. You can eat posh food every night if you stick with me. Think how skinny you would be then."

"But I am thin. Do you think I need to lose weight? Rik never told me I was fat. Maybe it's all that junk food he forced me to eat."

"Eeeeeek. It's all Rik this and Rik that with you. Don't you ever stop talking about him? You're with me now, and with these prices, I expect you to be obsessed with me, not him."

"I'm not obsessed with Rik. You know better than anyone how horrible he is." She paused to steer the conversation back to the essential subject: her need to confess Rik's role in his brother's mother's murder. "It's just that he hurt me, and I need to talk to someone who understands my pain."

"Who's that?"

"You, Larry. It's you. The way he treated you when you were growing up together. The way he treated his mother when—"

"Shut up. Change the subject quick. The waiter is coming."

Progress jerked back in fright into the cushioned upholstery of her reproduction Regency chair because her conscious self didn't see that coming.

The waiter picked up the empty dessert plates as if they were the infectious limbs of a leper and, ignoring Progress, asked Larry if they wanted a *digestif*."

"Do you have indigestion?" Larry asked Progress. "No. No. Just leave us alone. Go away."

"Very good, sir. Excellent choice." The waiter strolled away, carrying the plates in one hand and Progress's empty wineglass in the other, with the solemnity of an undertaker following the coffin of a respected head of state.

"He meant a drink, Larry, not indigestion tablets. I need a drink. Maybe a brandy. Will you call the waiter back?"

"He has been hovering around our table all night. I'm sure he is bugged."

"Hovering? Bugged?"

"Yeah. Wearing a bug. You know. A wire. I can't be too careful. Anyone could be wearing a bug."

Progress saw that Larry was studying her chest with a forensic rather than an erotic leer.

"What? Do you think I'm wearing a wire? Do you want me to strip?"

"Yes. I mean, no. Look. I'm under pressure. The cops have been after me for years."

"The cops?"

"Just unpaid taxes … that sort of thing. No one in their right mind would pay tax. For what? Shissssh. He is passing by again."

"But the police couldn't know you were coming here this evening. How could they get an agent in here so fast? I rang the restaurant less than an hour before we got here."

"I bet your phone is tapped. Besides, I know they have teams of people who can take on parts instantly, such as being a waiter, or a taxi driver, or even a student." He had resumed his forensic staring at her breasts. "They have a place where they train their agents to do all kinds of jobs."

Progress stood up and began to unbutton her blouse.

"Eeeeek. What are you doing?"

"You are paranoid, Larry. I want to show you that I'm not bugged."

"Sit down. Sit down. Stop making a scene."

Progress sat down. "You are paranoid, Larry. But that's genetically exciting because your brother, Rik, suffers from pronoia." She blinked back at his blank stare. "He gets upset when people try to help him," she explained. "I'm never doing anything for him again. Remarkable how much you two complement each other. You're not twins, are you? Psychologists are interested in twins who have been separated at birth. Apparently, it's unethical to separate them just for the sake of research. Did you know that? Maybe I could write my doctorate on you both."

But Larry was too preoccupied in his study of the waiter to hear what she was saying.

"How do you know he is a real waiter? Have you seen him waiting in here before?" he asked.

"No."

"See?"

"I've never been in here before because I'm a student. I can't afford to eat this kind of food."

They were both silent for a few minutes. Progress was wondering how to get Larry's mother back into the conversation. Larry was trying to do the calming exercises that Horse had taught him. He felt he could speak again when his heart slowed down. Now, where was he? Ah yes. Progress said she was poor. If he didn't know digestives, he understood business.

"Couldn't you make some money on the side. You know. Go on the game to pay your way through college? A good-looking student like you could make a fortune."

"That's disgusting. I couldn't take money for sex. Is that what you are saying? Theoretically, how much do you think I could charge?"

"I don't know. I'm just making neutered conversation, you know; innocent dinner chit-chat for anyone listening in. That one over there is a cop. I can smell him. The chef is also a cop who is planting listening devices all around us."

Progress studied the single flower in the tiny vase on the middle of the huge table. She couldn't imagine how anyone could hide anything in that. In the oblique edge of her vision, she saw the waiter was studying Larry from a discreet alcove with an expression of easy well-practised contempt that she imagined only a seasoned professional could master. "I know a lot about psychology, Larry. I understand how stress can cause people to imagine things. I want you to know I know professional listeners if you ever need to talk. In the meantime, I want to tell you about your mother. Let's get out of here. We could go to your hotel where I can tell you all about your mother's visit."

"The hotel will be bugged by now."

Progress blew out her breath and waved at the waiter. "Two extremely large brandies, please."

"I don't want anything."

"They're both for me. Have you ever found an actual bug, Larry?"

"No. They are too small. You would never find one. They are tiny."

Progress watched as the drinks drew nearer to the table on a round tray held high in the hand of the funereal waiter. She was proud that she resisted running towards him, but the moment the two round cut-glass bases touched down on the white table cloth she poured one drink into the other and brought the glass to her lips.

"Let's go and pay a visit to Rik. I'm in the mood for a family reunion," Larry said.

"He might still be at his secret society meeting."

"Maybe I should do a reconnaissance first. Form a plan. Let's go through his files in his office. Mess the place up a bit." Larry started giggling.

"Yes. Let's do that. But remember. You won't be able to say that Rik's office is bugged when you get there because this is your idea. You agree? Then can I tell you about your mother?"

"Shissssh. Stop mentioning my mother here."

Horse drove Larry Wallace and Julie Progress to CAT College.

"Will the building be locked this time of night? Horse has tools if we need to break in."

"It won't be locked. No one wants to steal philosophical or any other kind of academic secrets. Is it safe to talk in the back of your car?"

"No, but I feel better now. The air helps. I'm trying to deal with the pressures of success."

When they arrived, Horse took a flashlight from the boot and guided them across the quadrangle of lawn illuminated by a full moon. Inside, they walked down the hall to the provost's office in the light from the torch that Horse shone along the floor in front of them.

"We don't need the torch. The lights work," Progress said.

"I don't want anyone to see us."

Progress rolled her eyes in the dark. Was her unconscious

making signals?

They stopped outside Pandora's office. Horse ran the light over a collection of photographs on the wall depicting the images of the leaders of CAT College. Someone had drawn a Hitler moustache on Pandora's face. A pair of small round glasses had been added to a smiling Maurice Spencer and one of his front teeth had been blacked out.

"That's Spencer," Progress said. "The head of philosophy. You met him today with Pandora. The one with the imaginary daughter I was telling you about over dinner. Who knows? She might exist. I can't be certain. Do you know the philosopher Bertrand Russell used the example of a teapot orbiting the earth to show that you shouldn't expect people to believe you just because they can't prove you are wrong? Russell would argue that Spencer should prove that Samantha exists before demanding the rest of us to believe in her. But most people don't expect to have to do that with their children. I know from studying logic that the majority of people are wrong about most things all the time, which makes them normal. What do you think, Larry? Would you rather be right or normal? Do you think parents should prove they have children or should they hide them, just to confuse us?"

Larry wasn't listening. He had no interest in being logical. Progress was starting to suspect he might not be as good a listener as his brother. The voice of her unconscious was maintaining a smug silence inside her head.

"Give me that," Larry said, taking the torch from Horse and shining it from one picture to another, resting the light on each face for several seconds. He stopped on a photograph that was so blurred it appeared to be several images superimposed on top of each other.

"That's Rik. I took that picture. He wouldn't stop moving. You would think he didn't want to be recognized. But I believe I captured his essential features, don't you?"

Larry placed his face just inches from that in the photograph to scrutinize it. He stopped breathing and turned even whiter than he was in the torchlight.

"My God. It's him. He's here," Larry muttered to himself. "How does he know my every move? How did he know I would come here? What is going on? It's as if he can read my mind. He must have superpowers."

"Larry. What's wrong now?" Progress asked.

"It's my – what do you call him, Horse? – my nemesis. He has been after me for years. Sitting in his car outside my house. Going through my rubbish bins. Talking to everyone I know. Sleeping with my ex-wife. I would recognize him anywhere. Horse, look at him. It's him, isn't it?"

"It's not your nemesis. It's your brother Rik," Progress shouted, rending the shroud of secretiveness that hung over the dark former-asylum corridor as her shrill voice echoed up and down the empty hall. "Yes. I agree the image could be in focus, but I'm not a professional photographer, and Rik wouldn't sit still. Come to the house with me now and see for yourself; it's your brother Rik."

"Get me out of here, Horse. Get me out of here. I can't stand this," Larry moaned, covering his head with his hands. The beam of light from his torch picked out spiders caught on invisible treads in mid-dangle. Embarrassed to be unmasked in the act of abseiling towards the floor, they stopped and dragged themselves back towards the ceiling.

"Larry, come with me, and you can meet Rik yourself. I live in the house with him. He knows nothing about being a nemesis. He's a moral philosopher."

"You're living with him. You're in this with him. What did I tell you at dinner? Did I tell you my business? Nothing. I told you nothing. I knew it. I can't trust anyone. Horse, take me back to the hotel. No take me to another hotel. Eeeeeek. Pick one at random."

Horse grasped Larry by the shoulders and guided him along the dark corridor.

"Horse. It's his brother Rik. I know it. I took the picture myself. Horse, tell him it's his brother," Progress shouted after the retreating shadows.

Julie Progress walked to the house on Love Street where she found Rik Wallace sleeping, balanced on a row of dining chairs. There was a half-empty foil tray of noodles on the table beside an empty bottle of wine and an ashtray overflowing with cigarette butts. She watched as his chest rose and fell in rhythm with his gentle snoring. She decided, if he woke, she would take him by the hand and lead him to her bed: his bed. They wouldn't utter a word. Her unconscious was screaming, not at Progress but at Wallace, begging him to wake up, for God's sake. But if we can't hear the voices inside our own heads, how can we hope to hear those inside the heads of others even if they are shouting? He slept on. More minutes passed. She picked up the half-eaten tray and a fork, turned off the light, and closed the bedroom door behind her.

XXXIX

Vitans Pugnas
Avoiding Confrontation

In the library, students came and went. Rik Wallace was browsing books on existentialism on a shelf opposite the main doors when he saw Horse come in. Rik recognized him from the description Maurice Spencer had given him when recounting how Horse had carried him to Rik's office after Larry Wallace thumped him in the chest. He assumed the shorter, fatter man accompanying Horse was Larry because he hadn't been able to find a way to ask Spencer to provide a detailed portrait of his brother without arousing suspicion. Spencer had confined his description of Larry to general abstract personality attributes such as goon, idiot, and bully. Rik ducked behind the shelf and peered out through the gap between a row of book-tops and the next shelf up. Even when it dawned on him Larry wouldn't recognize him, he decided to stay where he was, just in case.

Larry approached the library desk with Horse trailing behind him carrying a brand-new brown leather briefcase that still had a label on the handle. Rik took a copy of Albert Camus's *The Myth of Sisyphus* from just in front of his eyes where he was crouching, opened a page at random, and held it front of his face. Thus disguised, he strolled towards the issuing desk to eavesdrop on Larry's business.

"I'm lechering this week," Larry told the library assistant at the desk. "I need books on—" He turned to Horse. Horse whispered in Larry's ear.

"Entering something," Larry guessed.

Horse leaned over and whispered again.

"Enter prize. I'm presenting a lecher on enter prize."

"Do you have a library ID card?"

"Horse, do I have a library ID card?"

Horse shook his head.

"No. I don't. I just want to read some books."

"You will need an ID. Do you have a photograph on you?"

"Of who?"

"Of you?"

"No. I don't."

"That's no problem. I can photograph you in the office over there."

Larry was turning pale. "Why do you need my photograph to read a book?"

"I don't know. It's one of the library rules. If you can wait just a moment, I will deal with this gentleman first. Yes, sir? How can I help you?" she asked turning her attention to the next in line.

"I want to return these books to the senior librarian."

"I can take them for you."

"I would prefer to hand them back in person. It's a private matter. Can you tell her I am here?"

"What is your name, sir?"

"Inspector Jackson. She knows me. I'm the policeman investigating the recent crime wave on campus," he said glancing sideways at Larry and Horse.

"Wait a moment. I will tell her you are here."

Rik saw Larry's back when he raised his eyes from the page of Camus that he was pretending to read. He wasn't quite running, because he didn't want to attract attention, but he was definitely waddling towards the exit. Horse was striding along behind him, swinging the new briefcase by his side. Rik was distracted by the text on the top of the page of the book that he was still holding in front of his face. He read that integrity doesn't need rules. But because he wasn't pedantic, despite his best recent efforts, he decided not to run after Larry to tell him.

XL

Probatio
On Trial

The black spiders in CAT College had siblings, grandparents, parents, cousins, uncles, and aunts – kin of all sorts – living in every hall, room, and office. The ones in the most used lecture theatre in the commerce faculty were gathering on the ceiling as if word had been telegraphed through their vibrating silk threads that Larry Wallace was about to impart his practical knowledge to the second-year commerce students assembling below. Perhaps these arachnids were business-minded.

Horse sat on his own in the front row with a notebook open on his knees. The members of CATfish, with the exception of Rik Wallace, occupied the back row. Doolittle handed Maximilien Thierry a page on which there was a grid of categories for marking Larry's lecturing performance. She passed the rest of the sheets along the line to her fellow conspirators. Rose had found a paper twisted into a knot in Sidney the Sycophant's wastepaper bin. On straightening it out as part of her routine nocturnal investigations, she smiled with delight to discover it was a lecturer's performance assessment form. She wouldn't have found it if she had been looking for one. She spent ten minutes ironing it flat with the heat of her hand. When it was as wrinkle-free as she could hope to make it, she Tippexed out Sidney the Sycophant's name, his low scores, and the abusive lines in the comments box. She carried the doctored page between her thumb and forefinger to the photocopier in the secretary of psychology's empty office. She programmed the machine to make twelve copies just in case someone made a mistake and needed a new sheet. The light from under the lid of the copier ran over and back Rose's lined face as she concentrated on her important administrative role.

Larry stood at the lectern with pages of notes written out in large letters for him by Horse. Confronted by the mountain of books on business he discovered when he found the courage to return to the library, he had despaired of the value of his practical knowledge when confronted by the mass of learning in the commerce faculty. In desperation Larry had instructed Horse to compile the lecture for him from the Internet. Horse had tried in vain to persuade him that he should speak from experience, which was his advantage. His audience could have told him that this practical experience was his unique selling point, or USP as the students had learned to say by second year. Fortunately, Larry was unburdened by any awareness of his extensive lack of theoretical business knowledge. He was even oblivious to the fact that he would have been made aware of his epistemological shortcomings had he attended Rik's first-year lectures on Socrates. Larry was holding a laser pointer in his hand while behind him on a screen the words "The Key Attributes of Entrepreneurship" were spelled out in large yellow italic lettering on a blue rectangular background. Along the bottom of the screen in smaller font, not to distract from the headline, were the words "A lecture by Larry Wallace, boss and entrepreneur." Horse gazed with pride on the product of his PowerPoint skills.

"Good afternoon, class. My name is Larry Wallace, and my lecher today will be on the tributes of entre … enter prize."

While Larry was still trying to work out how to use the laser pointer, a learner in the middle of the third row shot his arm into the air and asked, "Is this on the exam?"

Larry was flummoxed but regained his composure. "What exam? There's no exam. This is a sample lecher, you idiot."

"No exam? So why am I here?" the learner asked, perhaps rhetorically or even existentially, while grinning and looking around for the approval of his classmates. Then he, along with most of two rows of learners, stood up to leave.

"Sit down, or you will need a medical exam."

The two rows paused, looked at each other, and sat down again.

"Everyone comfortable? Good. I begin with a question," Larry said. He pressed the button on the pointer. Horse held his breath. The screen turned from blue to pink with a column of lettering in a darker pink running down the middle listing the attributes of entrepreneurship in no particular order. Horse blew out his breath in relief.

A hand shot up again.

"What now?" Larry growled.

"What are you going to be talking about?"

"Eeeeeek. You will find out if you shut up. That goes for all of you. Just shut up and listen. Give me a chance to get going, will you? You can ask questions at the end."

Larry cleared his throat and began reading. "What are the five most important tributes of a successful enter-pruner?"

"Self-starter," a learner in the fourth row volunteered.

"Risk-taker," another shouted.

"Ability to think outside the box," came from the middle of the hall.

"What box?" Larry asked, looking up from his notes.

Horse held his head in his hands.

"Shut up everybody. Eeeeeek. The five most important tributes, in no particular order, of a successful enter-pruner are …" He pressed the button on the laser with his thumb for emphasis. The words "self-motivation" appeared above the figure of a stick man running across a row of green pointed waves. With another press of his thumb "creativity" was illustrated by a bunch of flowers. Then there was a line drawing of a head with a speech bubble coming out of its mouth into which Horse had almost fitted the words "good communicator". A stick man pole-vaulting illustrated a risk-taker, while a muscled arm represented the concept of strong-willed. The attribute of being able to challenge negative thinking was illustrated by a closed fist from which Horse had managed, before running out of time, to remove just the letter L from the word "love" tattooed on the knuckles by pasting a black rectangle over it.

"That's six," a smug learner volunteered, consulting his notes.

"It's five."

"Six. It's six."

Larry counted back through his notes. "Scrap 'challenge negative thinking'. For fuck's sake, Horse. Can't you count?"

"I have another question?"

"What? What now? I've got twenty minutes, and you little fuckers are wasting all my time." Larry was turning red. Horse waved his arms in an attempt to orchestrate Larry's hysterical pace from *allegro* to *adagio*. The calming conducting had an instant effect. Larry stopped rotating the rings on his fingers.

"Breathe in," Larry told himself aloud. "Breathe in!" He inhaled through his nostrils. After thirty seconds in which he had turned a lighter shade of red, in a quiet voice he asked the learner who had his hand up in the middle of the third row, "What? What is it now?"

"Does your notion of entrepreneurship address the problem of nurture versus nature?"

"What nurture? What are you talking about?" Larry searched through Horse's notes for a reference to this unexpected word that threatened to throw him off balance.

"Don't you need to be born with some or all of these five or six attributes? I mean, if you are not a risk-taker, how can you learn to start taking risks just like that? Isn't it a mistake to believe that you can teach us how to think outside the box?"

"The box. Eeeeek. That box again. What is in that box? Horse you haven't mentioned that box anywhere. For God's sake. Even a second-year enter-pruner knows all about that fucking box."

"Is that your box, Pandora?" Spencer whispered into her ear.

"Shut up," she said, digging him hard in his ribs with her elbow.

He sank down behind the desk.

Larry was speaking again. "Listen, smart-arse. You will be sorry if you fuck this lecher up. You will be in that box and that box will be six feet – not five – *six* feet under the ground if you open your mouth again. *Comprendo* or maybe you don't speak French."

"That's Spanish."

"What is?"

The learner beside the one asking questions whispered loudly to his friend that he would be wise to shut up. His friend ignored him, demonstrating one of the essential attributes of entrepreneurship in his willingness to take risks.

"*Comprendo* – to understand – is Spanish. I'm taking Spanish with business studies for my degree."

The air rushing through Larry's hairy nasal passages could be heard at the back of the hall by the members of the CATfish assessment panel who were conscientiously studying their forms.

Larry expended a full minute of his allotted twenty in a meditative silence. He turned a page and said, "For a business to succeed it must eliminate the opposition."

"Don't you mean successfully compete in the market?" the learner studying Spanish and business studies asked.

"No. I mean eliminate the opposition."

Larry turned another page and resumed reading. "You should remember that being an enter— the boss … is stressful, and to maintain optimum performance, you should be willing to recruit a capable team. You must never take your team for granted. You should boost their confidence, and thereby their efficiency, with well-timed and regular praise. Don't be afraid to acknowledge the contribution of your team members and tell them how much you value them."

Larry stopped reading and picked up the page of notes, turned it over, inspecting it from all angles. "Where did you get this shit, Horse? This has nothing to do with the topic." He placed the offending page on the "read" pile. "Anyway, where was I?" Reading from the top of the next page he said, "You should nurture your team." Just before he threw that page away in contempt he latched onto the word. "See that word 'nurture'. I knew it was in here somewhere. There you are, smart-arse," he said addressing the student of Spanish and business studies. "Are you happy now, amigo? Does that answer your question?" Larry was shouting. "You nurture your fucking team for optimum performance!" Then he was muttering. "Being the boss is stressful. You can only rely on yourself. The boss is on his own."

"What was that? I missed that for my notes," one of the learners near the back asked.

"I haven't bothered taking notes because there is no exam," the student of Spanish and business studies said, leaning back in his seat and interlocking his fingers behind his head to signify his cool indifference to learning.

Larry looked at his watch. He skipped to the last page of his presentation, pressing the laser button over and over until he reached a picture of a computer screen.

"To guarantee the long-term success of your new enterprise you must know how to optimize the transfer of technology solutions to the marketplace."

"What does that mean?" the student of Spanish and business studies asked, sitting upright and rotating left and right to allow his classmates to get a better view of his broad grin.

Larry put down his notes. He pressed his hands together as if in prayer and brought his joined fingers to his mouth. "Breathe," he told himself. The student of Spanish and business studies high-fived the student of French and marketing sitting beside him. Larry got all the way from behind the lectern to the middle of the third row of seats, passing over the front row and the occupied second row on the way, and had the student of Spanish and business studies' head locked in the crook of his elbow before Horse could move. By the time Horse was able to join in the scrum, four of the learner's classmates were hanging from Larry's neck, attempting to unfasten his death grip on the young entrepreneur. Horse flicked them off one at a time, and with both arms, opened Larry's embrace just as the student of Spanish and business studies blacked out.

The members of CATfish waited in the back row until Larry Wallace, Horse, the acting head of faculty, Eddy Cashman – who had popped in as she happened to be passing outside – the stretcher bearers carrying the unconscious student of Spanish and business studies, and all the other learners had left the room before commencing their deliberations on the lecturing performance they had just witnessed.

"Do you have time to do this, Professor Spencer?" Rose the cleaner asked. "You're not rushing off someplace: the cinema, party, ballet, the orthodontist, or a graduation?"

"No. I'm going nowhere. Samantha is visiting her mother."

"That will be a treat for her … mother. For both of them. Now. We are supposed to assign numbers from one to five for the six listed criteria that we are to use to assess Larry's performance, where one is unimpressive and five is excellent," Rose advised her fellow judges. "Are we all clear on what is required?"

Everyone confirmed their understanding by saying, "Yes". A "Oui" followed this from Maximilien after Doolittle elbowed him in the ribs.

"First, we fill in the name of the lecher— I mean, lecturer. That's easy. That's Larry Wallace."

"Does he have a title?" the librarian asked.

"Not yet," Rose said. "The first question is 'Did the lecture meet its stated aims?' You must put a number from one to five in the box depending on what you thought of Larry's presentation."

"I'm giving him a five," Pandora volunteered. "He did more than he said he would. We got six rather than five attributes. Those students are never satisfied."

"I agree," Progress said. "At least a five. Can we give him six?"

"Marks are out of *five*," Rose confirmed.

Everyone wrote a number in the assigned box. Maximilien copied Doolittle's number, and smiled.

"The next question is 'How would you rate the knowledge of the presenter in the field?'" Rose announced, even though the panel of judges could read it on their own form.

"I am giving him a zero," Spencer said. "The students knew more about the topic than he did."

"He understood technology transfers. I have no idea what they are, which makes me think he is a genius," Progress said. "I am giving him a six if you are giving him a zero."

"Use one to five or I will ask you to fill in the form again. Anyone not using the proper numbers will have their forms handed back," Rose said.

"Who put you in charge?"

Rose ignored the question. "Have we all assigned a number?" She looked along the row and nodded in satisfaction. "Sally Doolittle. Will you tell Maximum to come up with his own numbers and to stop copying yours? We should each make our own independent judgements for the assessment to be fair and meaningful. No cheating. The next question is 'Was the content of the lecture consistent with the stated aims?'"

"What aims?" Spencer asked. "I'm giving him a very generous one."

"I agree he could have been better on the aims, but that is a tiny criticism. I will give him a four to prove that I am impartial," Pandora said.

"Next. 'Did the speaker respond well to questions?'"

"I thought he was strong on this," Pandora said. "That little shit from Spanish and business studies was asking for it. That is a clear five."

"A zero from me," Spencer said. "That student will sue the college when he regains consciousness. I wouldn't be surprised if the entire class sues for emotional distress. In fact, I am considering suing myself."

"That's not fair. You can't give him zeros if we can't give him sixes. Rose, Spencer is cheating."

"No zeros, Professor Spencer. Do it properly. Quality assurance is a serious matter. Are we ready? Next. 'Was the content appropriate to its intended audience?'"

"Why is that asshole in Spanish and business studies in college in the first place if he knows so much?" Pandora asked. "Why isn't he running his own successful business? Why doesn't he have a big loud car and silent driver?"

"Good point," Progress said.

"Next. 'Did the presentation include a relevant array of communication tools and appropriate teaching methods?'"

"Spencer, even you must admit that those PowerPoint

slides were amazing. He knows all about technology, and he used a lot of methods."

"I admit the slides were impressive, but I would have used different colours."

"That is an aesthetic argument," Progress objected. "You know art is relative. You cannot hold his choice of colours against him. He is colour-blind. We cannot mark him down for that. That is a clear five across the board."

"And finally, can you please fill in the comment box at the end and make sure you write your own name on the top of the page before handing your completed forms back to me."

When Rose had collected the assessment sheets, she added up the scores with Jim's help. They double-checked their numbers. Rose tapped on the desk with her pen for attention, cleared her throat. "We have a verdict," she announced. "Here are the results of the deliberations of the CATfish jury. Out of a total possible score of 240, which is made up of eight possible scores of thirty, Larry got 110."

"That's less than half," Spencer said.

"It's almost half," Pandora said.

"Oh no, Rose didn't get us to agree what score would be acceptable before we began," the librarian said.

"There wasn't anything about that on the form. The lecturer – I won't name names, but you all know him – scored thirty-five on the page I found in his wastepaper bin. If that was enough for him to keep his job, I think 110 should be sufficient for Larry to get his."

"We must consult Professor Rik Wallace. He is the provost after all. He will know what the minimum acceptable number is. It must be written down somewhere. There has to be a ruling

on this. He is in administration now. That's his responsibility,"
the librarian said. "We will ask Professor Wallace at our next
meeting. I will put that on the agenda."

"No one in the college has ever been fired for a crap score,"
Pandora said, lighting up a cigarette. "I need to get some fresh
air. Can we get out of here?"

XLI

Practica Consulendo
Practical Counselling

Maybe a Freudian interpretation was the correct one: perhaps Rik Wallace was unconsciously trying to build a nest all along because he lost interest in the renovation on Love Street when Julie Progress technically stopped talking to him. The technicality, she explained, allowed her to communicate what she thought about his betrayal of her trust any time she felt like it, while he was not allowed to speak in his defence. Despite this novel uneven muteness, they were able to concur in the division of the spaces within the house. They assigned half the dining table to each for their separate take-out dinners. They agreed to share the kitchen sink into which they both dumped the take-out cartons without regard for sides. Now they sat opposite each other at the table, chewing. He was having Chinese. She was having Indian. A large framed engraving of Immanuel Kant was facing Wallace, propped against an empty wine bottle. Kant's neat powdered wig receded from his forehead in curves that paralleled the lines of his raised eyebrows. If Kant was having doubts about the nutritional value of Wallace's diet, or the decline in table manners since his day, he didn't say.

"The special dinner for two on the Chinese menu is cheaper than two separate meals which demonstrates the economic advantage of conversation," Wallace told Kant in the picture frame.

"I don't care. Not talking is worth the extra expense," Progress said, "and I'm not contradicting myself because I am addressing Kant too."

"Maurice Spencer told me Larry's lecture didn't go well yesterday," Rik told the picture while sucking noodles into his mouth. "It's a pity you couldn't have been there to make one of your famous judgements. I imagine the shock may have killed you if you weren't already dead."

"Your brother has much better table manners than you," Progress said, lapsing into addressing Rik.

"But Spencer says it was good enough that half the members of CATfish could give him high marks," Wallace assured Kant, ignoring her. "Spencer told me how the votes went. Julie must be pleased. Her new best friend Larry is going up in the world of academia. You should watch out. He might replace you as the most formidable intellect, ever. That is, unless I can change their minds this evening at our secret CATfish meeting."

"He was a little rusty, that's all. Rose and Jim liked the lecture. Jim thought he managed the students with natural authority. Pandora thought he was brilliant. I did too. You should have been there if you want to have an opinion on his performance."

"Professor Kant, or may I call you Immanuel? Too informal? No? Immanuel, then. I am exhausted from trying to stay out of Larry's way."

"You don't need to try so hard because he is avoiding you.

He is terrified since he saw your photograph in the hall outside your office. He believes you are his nemesis."

"Tell me, Immanuel, can two people both be each other's nemesis? Mutual nemeses? Is there such a thing? He is mine."

"Rik, I know we're not officially on speaking terms, but I must ask you something directly. It's a medical emergency. Why didn't you tell me your brother Larry has mental problems? He thinks everyone is trying to destroy him."

"I don't know anything about his mental problems, but I hope he is right: I hope people are out to get him," he replied, finally directing his words at Progress.

She shovelled a spoonful of rice into her mouth as a prelude to speaking. "I think I have convinced him his fears are imaginary. I think he is stressed from success. Being an entrepreneur must be nerve-racking. I learned that at his lecture."

"Did you tell him that you killed his mother?"

"No. I didn't. I haven't been able to find the right moment. Anyway, you did that. Not me. At least, that's what I am going to tell him. I have been trying to persuade him that since he will be around the college lecturing and running his enterprise centre, he should meet with you to work out your small differences. You must talk to him, Rik. You are identical. I don't mean in the sense that you look alike on the surface. You know? Height, hair, eyes. People who appear to be different on the outside can be the same underneath at the level of their *real* selves. I told him how much you complement each other. In Lambe's psychology lectures he taught us the importance of ignoring appearances."

Wallace turned to the engraving. "Immanuel, you were a

genius of epistemology, but Lambe was a genius for ignoring things. What are your views on silence as someone who seems to have a talent for that as well? Larry and I should talk, but Progress shouldn't speak to me. Don't you think there is too much talk in general? Don't you think we tell each other far too much about ourselves? Maybe I could get into this not-talking business too. Take it to your level. I could promote a general silence here and in my lectures. Can you imagine me standing there in my first-year class not saying anything? A whole hour of silence with my students worrying how I was going to examine them on that."

Progress slammed the engraving face down onto the table. "I'm talking to you now for Larry's sake – for both your sakes. Brothers shouldn't be fighting. It's not fair on me, stuck in the middle. I need to consider what is best for me. He will start to trust me if I can cure his mental illness. He will stop believing that I am conspiring with you, his nemesis, to bring about his ruin. I can tell from the way he looks at me that he doesn't believe me when I tell him that I am on his side."

"His instincts seem to be working okay. But what about me? Did you ever think that perhaps I don't want to be reconciled with him?"

"Oh Rik, you really are selfish. Always thinking about yourself. You never stop to consider what I want, which co-incidentally is also what is best for your brother, Larry. I can't stay living in this shack forever. I am sure Larry will find a super-modern place on the hill overlooking the city when he relocates here, and I can move in with him."

As Wallace concentrated on sucking noodles into his mouth there was a loud knock at the front door. He stood up, and gathering the tin foil cartons into a pile, he carried them to the sink. He threw them in on top of the previous week's dinner trays that were starting to pong. "It's your turn to empty the sink."

"If you want me to do that I will. No problem."

"Are you feeling okay?" He stepped back to study her face. "What's wrong?"

"What do you mean?" she asked, nervously shaking her head.

"I mean you just agreed to empty the sink without screaming at me that it wasn't your turn. Why are you trying to be pleasant?"

"Nothing is wrong. How are you feeling?"

"What do you mean?"

"How are you feeling now? Good mood? Bad mood?" She waggled her shoulders.

"Medium mood. I feel medium. I'll get the door. That will be Spencer who is picking me up here for the CATfish meeting. Do you want a lift? You can sit in the back. You don't have to talk in front of witnesses."

"Medium mood. Not as good as a good mood, but it could be worse."

This time the knock was louder.

"Remember, Rik. Whatever happens you are in a medium mood."

"What are you talking about? What is wrong with you? Why are you so nervous? It's only Spencer."

Progress was standing just behind Wallace when he opened the door. Larry was standing outside on the footpath where he had spent ten minutes walking up and down muttering to himself about the superior cunning of his arch-rival. By now he had worked out that his nemesis must have lured his mother to CAT College confident that he would follow her straight into his trap. He twisted the rings on his fingers in an effort to ratchet up his courage. Twice he had lost his nerve and gone back to the car. Twice Horse, who supported Progress's advice on the benefits of talking things through, led him back to the door. It was Horse who had knocked before running back to the car. He mimed at Larry to knock again when no one answered because Progress had assured them that they would both be home.

Rik and Larry realized Progress was babbling, but neither of them was taking in the meaning of her words.

"Surprise. Larry. Look it's your brother, Rik. Just as I promised it would be. See? Rik, I didn't want to tell you Larry was calling around because I was afraid that you would run away. I convinced Larry to overcome his fears and meet you, and be friends like good brothers should. Ta-da," she sang in satisfaction. "I *am* a brilliant psychologist." She smiled and opened her arms to grasp a hand of each brother as a link in a chain of healing.

"Eeeeek. Who the fuck are you?" Larry asked, his face turning red and beginning to swell. His courage came back in a flash of relief at not recognizing the man standing in front of him.

Progress pushed her way in front of Rik and held Larry back with her hands on his chest. "Larry. Larry. I told you. It's your brother Rik. It's not a nemesis. Forget those photographs in the college. Spencer has all his teeth, and Pandora isn't Hitler. Look, Rik, it's Larry. Larry, remember your breathing exercises. Deep breaths, Larry. In. And out."

Rik didn't speak. In slow motion he saw Progress falling backwards into the hall when Larry shoved her aside as he charged into his mother's mausoleum, bellowing. Larry was holding his fat-ringed fist out in front of him aimed at Rik's face.

XLII

Identitatem Crisi
Identity Crisis

Professor Maurice Spencer swerved his ancient Saab 900 on the sharp corner leading into Love Street where a green hedge hung over the wall of the first house on the right. He cursed, straightened the car up, and slowed down. He saw Rik Wallace running towards him along the white line in the centre of the road. Behind him a limousine was reversing out of the drive of Wallace's house. Smoke was coming off the tyres that he could hear squealing in delight all the way from the end of the cul-de-sac. Spencer stood on the worn brakes. The car juddered to a stop when Rik had his palms on the bonnet. He ran to the passenger side and jumped in.

"Quick. Get the hell out of here now. Reverse. Reverse, for God's sake, or I'm dead. My brother has had some sort of homicidal seizure at the front door."

Spencer dragged the stiff gear stick into reverse with a metallic clank. "The gears are a bit dodgy," he explained apologetically.

The Saab began to reverse away from the long black car that was now rocketing straight towards them down the middle of Love Street. Spencer and Wallace both stared straight ahead even though the car was accelerating backwards. Just before the Saab reached the overgrown hedge that marked the junction between Love Street and the main road, Spencer pulled hard on the handbrake with one hand as he spun the steering wheel with the other. The Saab executed a perfect 180-degree pirouette within its own length, throwing the impressed Rik against the passenger door. After some fumbling, Spencer found first gear and shot off down the busy road leaving a cloud of burning oil and rubber behind. Horse, who was not prepared for the corner, braked hard in panic. The limousine lost most of the shine along its side where it scraped two parked cars that were half-hidden under the hedge. Horse could be forgiven for not noticing them: they hadn't been noticed by anyone, including their owners, for years.

"Don't panic. I could have driven getaway cars for bank robberies in another life. That's what I wanted to do when I was a kid before I decided to become a philosopher. What kind of a child wants to become a philosopher, anyway? When did I decide that? Find some fast music on the radio I can drive to. Something very fast."

Wallace turned a knob on the worn dashboard. The sound of Coldplay's "Yellow" competed for airtime with the roar of the Saab's engine.

"We can't escape to that. Find something faster," Spencer shouted at him over the noise.

Wallace turned the knob again until "The Flight of The Bumblebee" by Rimsky-Korsakov filled the car.

"Leave that on. I love that." Spencer started to hum. "Do you know it was written as part of an opera?"

"For Christ's sake, just drive," Wallace screamed.

"Do you know there is over a quarter million miles on this beauty?" Spencer said, breaking off humming to pat the dashboard. "She won't let us down now." The old Saab responded by speeding up. "What happened back there?"

"Julie decided to use her counselling skills to reconcile the Wallace brothers. Larry took one look at me and went crazy."

"Where is she?"

"Last time I saw her she was on her back in the hallway while Larry was running for the car. My God, for a fat bastard, that man can run." Wallace paused. "He is not even my brother," he said deciding to confess.

"I would disown him too. Siblings can be a source of embarrassment, especially when you are younger. My sister was tall when we were in school. Six feet. Can you imagine how I felt when I was thirteen with her towering over me everywhere I went? Yes. Sisters can be a pain in the arse."

"Will you shut up and drive."

By now Spencer was in fifth and speeding through a series of red lights. The long black car had caught up and was bouncing against the rear of the Saab as crossing traffic dived into poles and onto footpaths to get out of their way.

"He is not my brother," Wallace shouted above the intermittent sound of screams from outside. "I am not Rik Wallace. Doesn't anyone understand that? Look. Look at me. Look at me! No. Don't look at me. Keep your eyes on the road. I'm not the person you interviewed."

A pedestrian rolled across the bonnet of the Saab.

"How should I know who or what you are supposed to look like? You keep changing. You are a chameleon blending in with the latest trend you come across. Like Kant."

"Kant isn't a trend. His ideas have been around for over two hundred and fifty years. Besides, Kant doesn't affect the way I look. I'm not me. I'm not Rik Wallace."

"You change your mind about everything we manage to agree on. I may be the greatest living follower in the world, but you make it practically impossible to follow you. I can't keep up with your whims."

"Don't you remember the person you met at interview? It's not me. I'm not Rik Wallace."

"But you had that deer disease. You lost all that weight."

"It wasn't me, you idiot. I killed that person months ago."

"Oh, this is confusing. You killed the person with the deer disease? Were you afraid of catching something? I can understand that."

"I killed myself."

Spencer said nothing for another mile that passed in 18 seconds. Then he had what he thought might be a transcendental idea. "Did you kill yourself as part of your moral improvement scheme? To produce a better consequence?"

"I killed Rik Wallace, and no, it wasn't for a better consequence."

"This business with Kant has me confused. I sympathise with our students. I'm never going to understand him, but I promise you I will try."

"I'm not a Kantian. I'm not even a philosopher. I'm *not* Rik Wallace."

Spencer wasn't an ordinary person: he was a philosopher consumed by his own thoughts. Therefore, even while driving a car at high speed he wasn't much of a listener. That was a common side effect of philosophizing. In theory, everything he heard in his ears could be converted into evidence for his pre-formed worldview before ever being sent to his brain. Spencer knew that if his passenger said he wasn't Rik Wallace he didn't literally mean he *wasn't* Rik Wallace, and he didn't literally mean he killed himself because philosophers never took anything literally.

Spencer felt his brain filling up with the information coming from his ears. "Look. I am *not* a metaphysician. I find all those ontological questions about space, time, being, and identity confusing. While we are confessing, the truth is, I'm not a brilliant philosopher. I cheated in my exams. There I said it. I cheated. I cheated. Just drop all the metaphysical mumbo jumbo, and tell me what you mean in a way even I can understand."

"That's fine with me. My name is— Watch out for that woman with the pram!"

Spencer hit the brakes, spun the steering wheel, and slammed down on the accelerator in a sequence of slick moves that took the Saab around the pram in an arc with the wheel rims digging into the road, throwing parallel waves of sparks behind them. The woman instinctively let go of the pram and threw herself backwards to save herself. Horse drove straight through the widening gap between her and the rolling pram.

"Did he hit her?" Wallace asked, trying to see into the rear-view mirror.

"He may have a big fancy car, but Horse can't drive for shit. Obviously, Larry keeps him for his muscles and carrying the people he hits around, not for his driving skills."

Spencer leaned over as the Saab took a sharp corner at speed. Something under the bonnet exploded when it straightened up and smoke began to stream through the dashboard. The Saab cruised to a halt, hissing and popping in a black cloud. "The Flight of The Bumblebee" ended to be replaced by the practised calm voice of someone giving the details of an upcoming Schubert concert. Spencer turned off the radio. "I think we have blown the turbo in this old wreck."

Behind them Horse failed to make the corner, and the limousine slammed into a telephone pole, broke it in two like a twig, and turned over on a grass verge. Spencer and Wallace had an intermittent view of the events in the rear-view mirror through the billowing smoke that seemed to be coming out of the road underneath the Saab. They saw Horse totter from the car and fall into a hedge with no concern for his boss. Seconds later Larry came through the back door with the agility of a high-board diver before plunging into the bushes after Horse. Then the car burst into flames.

"I hope they roast in hell," Spencer said.

"Hell? Since when have you become so judgmental? My God. There's the hotel. Come on I'll help you push this wreck into the car park before that psycho climbs out of those bushes."

Spencer and Wallace shoved the car into a shadow beneath a far wall in the hotel car park. The Saab creaked and spluttered before expiring forever.

"Oh, my poor car?" Spencer said, forlornly.

"Get out of here. Get a bus or a taxi, but just leave. I give you permission to follow whomever you choose, but you must stop following me."

"Where will you go?"

"It doesn't matter. Just don't follow me. Goodbye, Maurice.

It was interesting knowing you. Look out for yourself back at CAT College."

Before Spencer could reply Wallace ran towards the hotel entrance leaving him with his dead Saab. The sound of approaching sirens made Spencer decide to stroll down the street as casually as he could, not to call attention to himself. In fact, his nonchalance made him stand out because everyone else was running in the direction of the overturned burning limousine. He looked at his watch. It was eight forty. He was late for the CATfish meeting. He realized he didn't care because he had lost interest in promoting philosophy amongst business students now that his guru was gone.

"I don't give a shit about thinking anymore," he told himself out loud. He looked back at the hotel and saw Wallace disappear inside. "Rik is right. I am one of life's great followers. Why stop now? Maybe I should start a movement to promote the teachings of Rik Wallace to a broader audience. He is the perfect subject for a new religion because his life has all the necessary ambiguities that only I could decipher as his first disciple. For example, what did he mean when he said he killed himself? What did he mean when he said he wasn't Rik Wallace? He was about to tell me his – metaphysical? – name when that bloody woman pushed her pram out in front of us. Couldn't she have looked where she was going, especially with a baby?" He sighed. "But all great gurus leave mysteries to be unravelled when they go. That's what they are supposed to do so that us disciples have something to interpret. I see it now. I might not be such an idiot if I had studied harder and read more in college. But I'm the best Rik Wallace has got. I will start by recruiting Julie Progress to the cause. After all, she was his first true love."

This monologue fuelled Spencer's feet on the long physical and metaphysical journey back to CAT College.

XLIII

Omen De Supero
Sign from Above

The wind wrapped itself like a bandage round and round Jim the trainee librarian and Rose the cleaner's house. Finding so many wounds in the windows and doors, it soon lost hope and rushed on to the neighbours' house. Inside, five of the members of the influential CATfish had assembled by 8 p.m. sharp, as instructed, to decide Larry Wallace's future in CAT College.

"Where is everyone else?" Pandora demanded, stubbing her cigarette butt out on the ashtray balanced on top of an unstable column of books on the kitchen table. "How are we supposed to run a secret society if no one turns up on time?" She strummed her fingers on the small free space in front of her.

"We're here," Sally Doolittle said, holding Maximilien Thierry's hand.

Jim was beginning to suspect that they might be super-glued together. "Are you afraid he might run away if you let go of him for a minute?" he asked.

"Bonsoir," Maximilien said to no one in particular and smiled.

"Right," Pandora muttered. "Where is that idiot Maurice Spencer?"

"Don't know," the librarian said.

"I suppose he is spouting philosophical gibberish someplace. And Rik Wallace?"

"Don't know. Maybe they are talking philosophy together."

"Rose?"

"Oh. I do know where Rose is," Jim put in. "She has to work tonight sorting out Bacon's office for the next occupant. Apparently, crime scene tape, bloodstains, and dead bodies make a poor impression on new employees."

"Julie Progress?"

"Rose told me she is meeting Larry Wallace."

Pandora lit a fresh cigarette. She exhaled a thick grey cylinder of smoke towards the mosaic of hairline cracks on the kitchen ceiling. "I don't trust Progress. She has no real commitment to our cause. She wasn't a founding member of our group when we had to bump off Maddox the Man and Lambe. It wouldn't surprise me if she was with the police right now telling them all about us."

"Why would she do that? She's in this with the rest of us."

"No. She's not. She hasn't killed anyone. She got into our gang only because of Rik Wallace. She is not genuinely one of us."

"On that basis neither is Rik, Doolittle, nor Maximilien," Jim said.

"I promised Patricia I would look after Rik. The rest had better be careful because I didn't promise anyone that I would look out for them. Progress is going to ruin everything for us – and by us, I mean me. She will break Larry's heart as she did Rik's. I like him the way he is now: strong and independent."

"You're right, Pandora. Progress doesn't belong, but my

Maxi does – and me," Doolittle interrupted.

"What about your friend, Inspector Jackson?" Pandora asked the librarian, ignoring Doolittle. "Maybe you should sleep with him to find out what he knows about us."

The librarian gasped. "Pandora. What a thing to say? I can't just seduce him. Killing people is one thing but sleeping with them is another. I am not sure I approve."

"What about the other detective? He seems much more enthusiastic than Jackson for solving Lambe's disappearance. Maybe you should sleep with him, Pandora," Doolittle put in.

"He is not my type. I suspect Jackson is dragging his police feet because he doesn't want our librarian here going to jail. You should think about it. For God's sake, do something with your hair. And wear a more revealing top. He would want to be into sheep with all the wool you are wrapped up in."

"What do you recommend?" the librarian asked, pushing her hair back from her forehead with one hand while plucking at the mohair on her cardigan with the other.

"Get your boobs out. Maybe a leather mini-skirt instead of those long drab trousers. Put on some mascara and a bit of rouge. You look like a corpse."

The librarian wrote down Pandora's style tips in the notebook she used for taking the minutes of the CATfish meetings. "We have a dress code for library staff. You know? Rules. We don't want the students to get the impression they are reading in a bordello."

"We were supposed to discuss Larry Wallace becoming the new head of the commerce faculty," Pandora said changing the topic. "That decision is urgent. I propose we take a vote even if the rest of the committee aren't here. Anyway, it's their responsibility to get to the meetings when important decisions have to be made."

"Rik was supposed to tell us what an acceptable score in Larry's trial lecture would be. It's not fair to decide without the official input of the provost after all the work Rose put into the assessment procedure," Jim said.

"Unlike some I could name, I do respect Rose's efforts. She is practical and focused, in contrast to the philosophers. I am sure she wouldn't mind us going ahead with a vote," Pandora said.

"Do you think Rik wants his brother to have a job in the college? You know some people can be peculiar about working with their siblings? I wouldn't want to work with my brother after that summer when we were both supposed to—"

"Shut up, Doolittle."

"Do we have a quorum?" the librarian asked.

"I'm a quorum," Pandora insisted.

"I think we should wait for the others," Jim said.

"I think we shouldn't. Let's vote," Pandora said. "All in favour of Larry Wallace becoming head of the commerce faculty say aye."

A detonation, as if someone had fired a cannon in one of the bedrooms upstairs, prevented Pandora hearing the response to her undemocratic appeal. A ribbon of smoke from the tip of Pandora's cigarette hung upside down in the four seconds of total silence that followed the explosion: the kind of comprehensive quiet that must prevail for those who find themselves in outer space where there is no atmosphere to carry sound waves. The five members of CATfish didn't notice the walls bending inwards in response to the vacuum created as the air was sucked out under the kitchen door. They did notice the door blowing off its hinges with the sound of a cork popping out of a giant champagne bottle. In unison, they turned their faces to the ceiling to watch a black crack unzip along its length. A fine sprinkling of white dust, like seasoning from the fracturing plaster, was shaken onto their heads before the house, that had had enough, swallowed them up.

Part III

Usus Et Abuses Wallace
The Use and Abuse of Wallace

XLIV

Magicam Relationem
Magical Relationship

Rik Wallace ran towards the hotel with its grille of dramatic balconies overhanging the street. When he looked back, he saw Maurice Spencer striding with long steps away from the burning wreck, flashing fire brigade engines, wailing ambulances and glittering police cars. Even from that distance Wallace could see Spencer was holding an animated conversation with himself. Perhaps he had banged his head during the car chase?

Turning back to the hotel Wallace saw the neon sign for Momma's Pasta House flashing above the spot where his frantic adventures had begun. He recognized the blond receptionist on duty from the morning when he first tried on his new identity in the form of an oversized suit when he stepped through the automatic doors. She pretended to recognize him as part of her customer services training.

"Good evening, sir. Welcome." She smiled with a set of super-white symmetrical teeth.

Wallace was out of breath from running. He gasped for air, unable to reply. He placed his palms on top of the desk and tried to slow his breathing.

"Do you have a reservation, sir?"

"No," he panted.

"Bags?"

"No bags," he managed to get out.

She wasn't impressed. "Have you stayed with us before?"

Wallace hesitated before confessing that he had indeed stayed in the hotel on another occasion.

With this the receptionist's mood improved. "Our return customers are entitled to a free room upgrade. Our offer is valid for the next three weeks from yesterday."

"I don't want a room. I'm looking for someone who might be staying here."

"What's the name, sir?"

"Della. I don't know her last name. She often stays here when she is in the city."

"It's against hotel policy to divulge details of any guests who are fully or partially unknown to the enquirer, sir."

"I know Della. I just don't know her name. I've seen her naked, for God's sake. In this hotel." He was shouting between gasps and looking back towards the front door expecting a smouldering Larry and Horse to appear at any moment.

"It's against hotel policy to shout at the staff, sir."

"I promise I will recommend your hotel to all my friends and acquaintances if you help me find Della."

"Will you write a positive review for our website?"

"Yes. Yes. Anything you need, if you help me."

Her fingers flew over the keyboard while she gazed at the screen. "I do have a Della who is one of our regular guests. She is entitled to an upgrade, but she never avails of our offers. She always uses the same room.

"514," he shouted. "Is she there now?"

"I couldn't say, sir."

"Say. For Christ's sake, *say*. It's a matter of life or death. Do you remember the man who was killed outside when he landed on the roof of the car?"

"Of course, sir. It was horrific. That's not a normal occurrence in this hotel."

"I know. I know. It's against regulations. That man was me."

"You were killed, sir?" She knew this night would come. She had asked the hotel manager a million times for an alarm button under the counter that would allow her to summon help on just such an occasion when a nutcase presented himself at reception. Her fingers searched in vain for the button that wasn't in the location she had already identified as being the most convenient to discretely reach in a potential emergency.

"Yes. That was me, and if you don't tell me if Della's here, I will kill myself again. I will jump off the roof."

While she was trying to articulate what she imagined the hotel's policy on repeat suicides might be, he had reached the lift and was pressing the Up button.

Wallace heard the throb of music coming from room 514 when the lift doors opened. "She is still partying in there," he sighed to himself. Once more he found himself pounding on the door. This time his motives were different: this time he was desperate to join the party.

The door opened, and Della appeared on cue in front of him. Again, she was ludicrously dressed: this time in a tie-dyed shirt over a shiny white leotard with red tights. She towered above him on a pair of tinfoil platform boots. She was wearing the metal frames of aviator sunglasses without the glass.

"Hey. Come in. Welcome to the seventies," she screamed.

Behind her the crowd were waving their arms in the air, singing along to Don McLean's "American Pie". "You have to move with the times," she screamed, pulling him towards the balcony. "No fun being trapped in the same decade forever. We just go from one to another whenever we wish. Christ, I love the seventies." She whooped, joining in the end of the chorus. "This is where you partied on the last night of your old life," Della told Wallace, sliding the balcony door closed behind them. "This is where your new life began."

"You know what happened out here?" he asked, looking down at the street below, which was now filled with flashing lights. He saw Spencer's Saab smoking in the car park. From up there he couldn't see Larry's car because it was out of sight around the corner of the hotel. He didn't know if Larry and Horse had survived. "You knew I wasn't Rik Wallace all along. You manipulated me into being him with that letter from the college you found in his briefcase."

Della shrugged. "I thought it might be fun. I saw what happened on the balcony. I saw you taking his wallet and keys. I was just trying to help you find yourself."

"My new life is a disaster. I was even thinking of strangling you that night, but your neck is too thick."

"I can take care of myself," Della said, flexing her biceps. "I might have strangled you, since your neck is so skinny."

"I don't know how many are dead as a result of my efforts to become a moral authority."

"How many have *you* killed yourself, in person? I'm just curious."

"Apart from Rik Wallace here on this balcony – none. Well, I did try to kill myself when I thought I killed my mother–

that is Rik Wallace's mother – which was before Julie Progress actually killed her. But that's not a moral defence, because it's the thought that counts. As you can see, I didn't manage to kill myself either. Soon after I arrived at the college my new colleagues formed a group called CATfish dedicated to killing Maddox the Man whom they imagined might get in the way of my being promoted after they killed Lambe. Even though everyone thinks Maddox the Man was hit by lightning, it was Rose the cleaner made the lightning. They might have killed Bacon too. I don't know. Inspector Jackson, the policeman who was here that night, might have killed him because he fancies the librarian. Or he may have died of natural causes. God knows, maybe my new girlfriend— I mean, student, Julie Progress – the one who killed my mother – murdered Bacon to get his job, but I don't know because she isn't even talking to me. Jackson's partner is trying to work out my motivation. Good luck with that, because I don't know what I am doing. Professor Spencer has left a trail of dead and maimed pedestrians down there on the streets while trying to save me tonight from Rik Wallace's brother, Larry. Lambe probably killed his wife, Patricia the Provost; although no one even knew they were married apart from Sally Doolittle. I do know CATfish killed Lambe because they woke me up when they were burying him in my garden. They tried to gas him, but they had to hit him with a champagne bottle. And I'm smoking like a chimney and drinking too much."

"I thought you were doing fine when I saw you at your public lecture. Your audience seemed to think you knew what you were talking about. I can't say I was listening. It's not my sort of thing. But it was fun to see you in action."

"That night was the beginning of the end. My new mother turned up. My colleagues went mad. Now my new brother, Larry, is trying to kill me; if he isn't dead himself down there in a ball of flames, which I hope he is. He could be out there somewhere now searching for me with his goon, Horse. I'm on the run from both the police and the criminals."

"Is it possible you have become a better person since you tried to be moral. I think you are a nicer person."

"Better? Nicer? God knows how much misery I have caused trying to do the right thing. Never again. Anyway, I can't be someone else. I have to be my real self."

"I think being our real selves is overrated. What if your real self is an asshole, which I suspect you used to be?"

"Oh, I'm still an asshole. But don't you start with philosophy. I've had it up to here," he said pointing to his neck. "I don't want to hear or read or think about another idea again for the rest of my life, which will not be long if Larry finds me."

"Weren't you happy as a philosopher?"

"Yes, I was for a while, but then disaster struck."

"I think it's more important to be happy rather than to be right. These days we have an explanation for everything that happens to us: genetics, DNA, psychology, sociology, religion, whether our parents loved us too much or didn't love us enough when we were growing up. Wouldn't you imagine the point in all this knowledge is to increase happiness? But are we happier? Have you noticed happy people never cause much harm to others? Has any moral philosopher ever considered happiness as the goal of life instead of the truth?"

"Aristotle."

"Astonishing. You have learned so much in a such a

short time."

"I was even becoming a Kantian before I had to run away. I didn't have much time to study Aristotle. I do know he thought happiness was being all you could be, and that that kind of happy person is virtuous – or something along those lines. Anyway, I hate the ancient Greeks. It takes years just to understand the Greek language. I only had a few months to cover everyone in the entire two-thousand-year-history of philosophy. There are a few gaps in my knowledge. Not that my students ever noticed. Another year or two, and I could have been a genius."

"It's never too late. You can still be happy. When we were children, we wanted to join the circus because kids know better than adults how to be happy."

"I have left a trail of bodies behind me."

"You should look forward. Not back. That's what we say in the circus. Since you seem to be running away, maybe you should join us. People join the circus to change their lives. Now is your opportunity, and we are very discreet."

"What are you talking about?"

"Us," she said, waving at those dancing inside the glass balcony doors. "We are circus people. Everyone deserves second, third, fourth, fifth, chances."

"Don't you want to know my real name?"

"We are not interested in real names or the real you. But you will need a stage name. The ringmaster has to choose. My brother is the ringmaster at Circus Amaro. He often helps people who are on the run from the law, as any respectable ringmaster should. Maybe you can be a clown, as you seem to have some natural talent for that because most of his clowns are criminals. I might be able to persuade him to take on a failed serial murderer. I will ask what he can do for you when he wakes up. That's him in there," Della said, pointing into the room.

Wallace shaded his eyes with his hand and pressed his face against the glass. He saw a man in a black top hat, red tailcoat, and long black boots, still clutching a whip, lying face down across the end of the bed.

"In the meantime, you can stay here with me, but we won't be alone," she said gesturing to the crowd inside. "How do you like the seventies? Dance, or we will kick you back onto the streets where your new brother can get you. Dance or die," she said and laughed. She slid open the glass door and dragged him inside where everyone was making shapes to the Bee Gee's "Stayin' Alive". Della pushed him into the throng. He held his hands in a pose he remembered John Travolta adopting in *Saturday Night Fever* and began to move his hips to the music.

"Dance or diiiieeeeeee," he sang at a woman bopping in front of him in a pair of blue dungarees.

XLV

Regressus Rosae
Rose Returns

Rose the cleaner transferred the weight of the *Complete Works of William Shakespeare* in the plastic supermarket bag from one hand to the other. She was listening to the Rolling Stone's "Gimme Shelter" turned up to full volume on her headphones as she walked home from her shift at 7.15 a.m. It had been a long night of experimenting with chemicals to remove the bloodstains from the carpet in Doctor Bacon's office, because Rose believed in never throwing anything out if it could be cleaned. The seldom-used room was ready again for occupancy.

Rose had worried that Jim would decline in his retirement. Now she reflected on how surprised she was by how busy he was keeping himself. He had CATfish, but he had also found his true vocation as a private librarian. He drank less and watched fewer trashy science programmes on television. He didn't even complain about her cooking because he was anxious to get back to his index after dinner. He planned to open his library to the public when his catalogue was ready, but Rose put that idea down to the dope-smoking, which he hadn't given up yet. But even if he didn't go public during his own lifetime, she saw no reason why he couldn't bequeath his collection to the nation. She turned into her road. The flashing lights from two fire engines, two ambulances, and a row of police cars provided an unplanned light show accompaniment to the words Mick Jagger was screaming into her ears. Yellow plastic tape with the word "Caution" printed in black letters was strung across the street blocking her way.

"I'm sorry, madam. There's been an accident. It's too dangerous. You can't go any further," Detective Sullivan, who was unable to disguise his excitement, told her.

Rose didn't hear the words because the music was blaring in her ears. "I live here," she said, lifting the tape over her head and walking on. Sullivan followed, shouting at her back that it was too dangerous. As Rose approached her house a man in orange and blue overalls turned off a bank of halogen lights set up in the garden because daylight had strengthened enough to allow the rescuers to see what they were doing. The front door lay face down on the footpath. Behind that Jim's new book security scanner was all that remained upright. The heroic house was a smouldering pyramid of roof tiles, books, bricks, beams, window frames, broken glass, and charred debris. More men in orange and blue overalls were standing on the ruins. Dogs in orange waistcoats were darting in and out of crevices and small tunnels between the fallen walls, their noses sniffing up and down and their tails whipping over and back. Rose dropped the volume of Shakespeare on the path. She saw Inspector Jackson standing in front of her. He seemed to be talking. She removed the earpieces from her ears.

"I live here," she told him. "This is – *was* – my house."

She didn't need to be told what had happened. Looking at the rubble, she realized it was inevitable. Her unconscious voice made itself heard inside her head. Yes. She had known all along. This was not an accident. It was a conclusion.

"At this stage, we can't rule out the possibility of an explosion. Maybe gas or even a bomb. Do you have enemies?"

"It wasn't a bomb. It was the books. The house couldn't take it anymore. It was the books. It was my fault."

"Are you saying you caused some sort of explosion with books?"

"Yes. I suppose I did."

Sullivan, who had abandoned his post at the tape, caught up with her. He took out his notebook. "Can you tell me who was living in the house besides yourself, madam?"

"Just me and Jim."

"We have already recovered two bodies and the dogs indicate there are more," Inspector Jackson said.

"There was a meeting here last night."

"How many people were at this meeting?" Sullivan asked scribbling notes.

"Six. Maybe seven. Depending on new members. It's hard to know because it was a gathering of a secret society. Maybe a French student. I think his name is Maximum Theory. I can't remember. He smiles a lot. I was supposed to be here, but I had to go in to work. There was a cleaning emergency in CAT College."

"A cleaning emergency? You're a cleaner in the college?" Jackson asked.

"Yes. One of the best. You know one of the academics got a knife through his neck. Not easy to get blood out of the carpets. You need to know what you're doing. We can use the office again now, which we need, because the academics are always looking for new offices. They imagine all their problems will be solved if they can move offices. Someone made a real mess dusting for fingerprints on all the surfaces."

Sullivan cleared his throat and continued scribbling notes.

"So, you know a lot about cleaning?" Jackson asked.

"I imagine I know as much as anyone alive about cleaning."

"Have you ever cleaned the Reverend Professor Lambe's house?"

Rose paused before answering. "Once upon a time. Yes."

"So, your house here is connected with CAT College. And surprise, surprise, now we have exploding books and more bodies. Do you recognize these?" Jackson asked, handing Rose a pair of black sunglasses. "Sullivan found them in the wreckage."

"They belong to Pandora. She runs the college."

"Is she the provost, or the chancellor, or something?"

"No. She is just a secretary."

"Would you mind identifying her for us. We have bodies in the ambulance over there."

Jackson and Rose walked to the yellow vehicle and climbed through the open double doors in the back while Sullivan studied the ruin, despairing of getting usable fingerprints from the rubble. Inside, there were two bodies. One lay on the stretcher on the left under a light blue woollen blanket that was tucked under her chin. Her hair was covered in an even layer of white dust. She looked as if she was sleeping, which Rose found disconcerting because, up until that moment, she had never imagined that she slept.

"That's Sally Doolittle," Rose said.

"Does she have family we can inform?" Jackson asked. He

was crouching beside her under the low roof of the ambulance.

"She had a boyfriend. The French student, Maximum. After that, I don't remember."

Rose turned to the other stretcher. She held the hand sticking out from under the light blue blanket that covered that corpse. She squeezed Jim's familiar calloused fingers between her own and allowed the tears to trickle down her worn cheeks. "I think Pandora and Julie Progress might be buried in there along with Professors Maurice Spencer and Rik Wallace," Rose told Jackson in a low voice. "I don't know for sure, because some of them would have arrived after I had left for work."

By now Sullivan was standing at the back of the ambulance. He wrote the names in his notebook. "Don't worry, madam. We will find everyone."

"And the librarian. She *is* in there. She arrived while I was still there."

Inspector Jackson straightened up banging his head on a piece of medical equipment attached to the roof of the ambulance.

A shout from the ruin outside caused everyone in the rescue team to stand perfectly still. The generator shut down throwing a quilt of silence over the mound. An orange-and-blue-clad man probed the aggregate of bricks and books with a camera and microphone mounted on a flexible tube. Beside him a dog whined and danced around in a circle. "I think we have a live one over here," he called to Jackson, who was already running towards the flattened front door.

XLVI

Unitatis Response Subitis
Emergency Response Unit

Pandora's eyes burned in the glare of the neon strip lights on the ceiling above her face. Her varicose eyeballs were full of dust as if a conscientious sculptor had sandpapered them. "Where are my glasses?" she groaned, searching through her hair with her fingers.

"I have them, here," Detective Sullivan said, handing her the sunglasses he had picked out of the rubble.

Pandora was plunged into comforting darkness when she put them on. "Help me sit up," she demanded.

Sullivan placed the white shoebox he was holding on the end of the bed to heave her into a sitting position with one hand, while cramming pillows behind her head with the other.

"Where am I?" she asked when she was upright.

"You are in the emergency response unit for major disasters in Saint Drogo's Hospital. The house you were visiting blew up. You have been out cold since. I'm Detective Sullivan. I'm investigating the explosion. Do you remember what happened?"

"I dreamt I was dead. I met Lambe. He asked me why I had to be dead too so soon after him, and why I couldn't leave him alone. He looked self-satisfied for someone roasting in hell. He said it wasn't half as bad as he expected it to be. The place is full of entertaining people. I'm not dead, am I?" she asked looking around.

"You are lucky to be alive. They found you under the body of a French student. He broke the fall of the kitchen wall on top of you. He saved your life."

"Doolittle's French friend, Maximilien. And I thought he had nothing to offer our group. He did more than anyone. What about the others?"

Sullivan was desperate to change the topic because he wasn't yet comfortable imparting fatal news. Then he remembered the box. "Your colleague from the commerce faculty left this downstairs at reception for you. She wouldn't come up." He handed her the shoebox. It had a row of holes along each side.

"What is this?" she asked shaking it beside her ear, listening for a clue to its contents. The box meowed.

"I don't know. I didn't look inside. Probably chocolates."

"Chocolates don't meow, you idiot. What kind of a detective are you?"

"Patients are not allowed presents in here. I persuaded them to make an exception. I told them it was police business," he said, proud of his intervention. He learned the theory of the value of keeping victims on your side at the police academy.

Pandora ripped off the tape holding the lid in place and opened the shoebox. From inside a very shaken Marley looked out with relief at the familiar black glasses. He was sitting on a bed of shredded newspaper. There was an envelope along one side of the box. Pandora lifted out the cat, kissed him with her dry dust-covered lips, and placed him on the bed. She removed the envelope, opened it, and read the handwritten note.

"Hold Marley," Pandora said, handing the cat to Sullivan. Then she emptied the box onto the bed and rummaged through the shredded paper for the cigarettes.

"You can't smoke in here," Sullivan said, appalled by his role in a potential crime.

Pandora ignored him while ripping open the cigarette packet with her teeth. She searched in vain for a lighter amongst the debris from the box around her on the bed.

"Stupid cow. She forgot to put in a lighter. I suppose you don't have a light, do you?"

Sullivan backed away in dread while Marley crawled onto his shoulder.

In the bed beside Pandora's the librarian was sitting with her plastered leg elevated in a sling. Her arm hung from her neck in another sling. Inspector Jackson was sitting on a plywood and steel chair holding her free hand in his, grinning at her with his upside-down smile.

"How are you feeling now?" he asked.

"The painkillers are working. I hope those drugs don't make me crazy. I don't normally take drugs. You must come across a lot of people on drugs in your business, but that's not me. Ignore me if I start babbling. Imagine a librarian that couldn't stop talking," she babbled. "All the silence signs in the world wouldn't make a difference."

"I was amazed at how relieved I was that you were alive."

"Me too. I mean, not that *you* were alive, but that *I* was alive. Not that I'm not delighted that you are alive too. I am. Oh dear. I don't know what I am saying." She was silent for a moment. "I feel bad about poor Jim. I should have warned him that libraries could be dangerous places without the proper training. I helped him with the catalogue and security, but I should have done more with health and safety."

"It wasn't your fault. The problem had been building up for years."

"Were any of the books saved?"

"The rescue team are still going through the debris. It appears that the house sort of … burst. It will be days before we know anything definite. Perhaps we can go over there together and see what books we can rescue when the site has been made safe. Would you like that? I know how much books mean to you."

"The thought of them exposed to the elements is depressing."

"In the meantime, I can get someone to spread plastic

sheeting over the place to keep the rain off."

"What do you think of my hairstyle?" she asked, freeing her hand from his to pat her dust-encrusted head. "I mean my normal style. Not now. Do you think I should grow it longer?"

"I think your hair is beautiful."

"And my clothes. How do you feel about wool?"

"Ah, wool is nice. Wool is good. Wool suits you."

Rose the cleaner was sitting on a chair on the far side of the librarian's bed. She was wrapped in a foil blanket. She had both hands around a large mug the way she saw victims of disasters hold tea on the television.

"I'm sorry about Jim, Rose, but I'm glad you are okay," the librarian told her when she saw Rose staring at her.

"Is there news of the whereabouts of the others: Professor Spencer, Julie Progress, and Professor Wallace?" Rose asked Jackson.

"We haven't been able to account for everyone yet. There were two incidents last night: your house blowing up and a major traffic accident. That is why Saint Drogo's had to implement their emergency response protocol and open up this special ward. We didn't know how many bodies and injured we would be dealing with. Professor Spencer's car was found abandoned in a hotel car park near the scene of a burned-out wreck, but there was no sign of him. Professor Wallace has vanished. We didn't find his body in the ruins of your house. He is not at his place. Julie Progress is also missing. We think maybe those two lovebirds ran away together. There are more victims behind that screen we still need to process," he told her, nodding towards a nylon curtain drawn halfway across the ward separating the victims of the collapsed house from those brought in from the car chase.

A bin under the librarian's bed caught Rose's eye. Her mind drifted. She wondered if people threw anything interesting away in hospitals. The charts at the end of the beds were a better source of information. A tear painted another stripe down her streaked face when she remembered that she wouldn't be able to share any unearthed secrets with Jim. "Why bother?" she thought. "What was the point in a secret you couldn't tell anyone? That's what secrets were for – sharing."

A fat nurse appeared from behind the curtain and pulled it open, exposing a row of beds containing a variety of gauze-wrapped patients. She moved with caution because she was wearing a uniform that she borrowed from a colleague for this emergency that was much too small for her. Already a button had shot off the bulging front, missing the nice young policeman's head by inches before ricocheting off the wall. She walked down the row of beds trying not to breathe. Two beds down, Horse sat beside a patient whose head was swaddled in white bandages. Both sleeves were burned off Horse's black suit along with his eyebrows that were no longer available for him to raise as he read a magazine. Otherwise, he appeared unscathed.

"That's Horse," Rose shouted. "Look, it's Horse. Look Pandora. It's Horse from Larry Wallace's trial lecture." Her foil wrap fell to the floor when she stood up.

Rose's cry distracted Pandora from a tender moment with Marley, whom she had demanded back from Sullivan. She dropped her unlit cigarette and looked down the rows of beds to where Rose was pointing. She saw Horse, who had stopped reading, and was looking along the beds to see who was calling his name. Pandora handed the cat back to Sullivan, pushed the bed covers off her legs and swung them onto the floor. She saw she was wearing a short hospital gown. Her thin legs were covered in bruises where they were sticking out underneath. "Don't you dare look," she snarled at Sullivan who covered his eyes with the cat as he scrambled to get out of her way. "Come here and help me," she said, grabbing hold of Sullivan. "Let's see what is happening down there." She tucked the policeman into the crook of her arm. He tucked Marley under his opposite arm. She waddled on her discoloured legs between the beds to where Horse was sitting. Arriving at the foot of Larry Wallace's bed, she recognized his rings under the bandages. "It's Larry," she shouted back to the others. "It's Larry. What is he doing here?"

"He was found in a hedge beside his burning limousine," Sullivan told her.

Horse stood up and rolled up his magazine as if prepared to bludgeon anyone disturbing his boss with the hospital's copy of *Homes & Antiques*. When she leaned over Larry, a triangle of naked back and buttocks emerged from between the flaps of Pandora's gown, which was tied behind her neck with a single fastener. Horse stared at her back and then at his paper club. He thought better of hitting a naked woman.

"Larry. Dear Larry. Are you okay?"

Larry opened his eyes and stared at Pandora sunglasses just inches from his face.

"Eeeek."

"He seems to be fine," Pandora told Horse whose face

appeared beside hers as they leaned over the patient together.

"Who are you? Where am I? What am I doing here?" Larry burbled. "I want to go home. I want my mammy. I want to go home."

Horse looked terrified.

"Horse. It's okay," Pandora assured him. "A natural response for anyone coming out of a coma is to lose their mind." She paused. "Maybe not me, but anyone else. Don't worry. I know all about these medical matters. It's normal. All he needs is a little time. Here. You hold Marley. He is getting too fond of the police," she said, pulling the cat from Sullivan's grip and handing him to Horse. Then she grabbed Larry by the front of his hospital gown and started to bounce his bandaged head up and down on the pillow.

"Larry. Larry. Snap out of it. We need you now at CAT College. I need you. This is no time for you to lose your mind. Think of other people, Larry, instead of always thinking of yourself. Think of me, Larry. What am I going to do? Don't ruin everything for me now, Larry. Larry, come back. I *need* you. Come back. Oh Horse. What are we going to do?" she sobbed.

Horse would have dragged Pandora off Larry if he hadn't been certain she was practising a recognized medical technique used on recovering coma patients. Besides Marley was trying to rip the flesh from the back of his sleeveless arms.

Sullivan and the fat nurse were hauling Pandora away by the time Horse had decided which part of her naked flesh to hit with his rolled-up magazine.

Back in her own bed, Pandora wept in frustration that her plans for CAT College were unravelling around her. "Horse.

Give me back my cat. He is mine. You can't keep him," she shouted across the ward. Horse, who had abandoned his magazine in favour of scratching a now-calm Marley's head, reluctantly returned the cat to Pandora. "Whatever about all these unreliable humans, I always have you," she told the cat, squeezing him tight. "We are stuck with each other whether we like it or not." Marley mewed and squirted a runny green shit onto the bed cover as a token of his loyalty.

Professor Maurice Spencer arrived in the ward just as Sullivan and the nurse were covering their mouths in horror. "What's going on here?" he asked.

"Do you have a light? I have cigarettes and no light. I'm going crazy."

"You're not allowed to smoke in this hospital," the nurse told Pandora.

"I know that," Pandora hissed. "I was knocked out, but I'm not stupid like poor Larry over there. Oh Spencer. Have you seen what's happened to Larry?"

"Is he here? Is he alive? The last time I saw him he was rolling out of the back of his car and into a hedge."

"May we have some privacy please?" Pandora asked Sullivan and the nurse. "Can you go away? *Now*?" She flicked her unlit cigarette at them to shoo them from her bedside.

"What did you do to him?" she asked Spencer in a whisper.

"It wasn't me. It was Julie Progress's fault. She was the one who decided to get Rik and Larry together for a fraternal reunion. They don't get on. I had no idea things were so bad between them. Larry went crazy and chased us in his limousine. Horse crashed. I was sort of hoping Larry was dead."

"That stupid bitch. I told you she would cause trouble. But

no. You wouldn't listen. I'll get her for what she's done to my Larry."

"Your Larry?"

"Yes, my Larry. At least, he would have been my Larry if he hadn't lost his mind or his memory or whatever is wrong with him. Where is Progress?"

"I don't know. I came here to look for her. I thought she might have been in the limousine with Larry or in the house when it blew up. It's all over the news."

"Bitch. Unfortunately, she wasn't with us when the ceiling collapsed. Where is Rik Wallace?"

"I don't know. He ran away. He told me to stop following him."

"At least he has demonstrated some sense at last."

"I'm going to set up a movement in the college to promote his teachings. Do you want to join?"

"No, I do not."

"There is no record of Progress being admitted downstairs, but I will look through the beds for her myself while I am here." Spencer went from one bed to another scanning the bandaged victims, oblivious of the fact that he had put the majority of them in hospital. He went back to Pandora's bed. "She's not here," he told her.

"I'll find her and sort her out for good. Where are my clothes? I can't leave in this," she said plucking at the front of her gown.

"Maybe you could wear a nurse's uniform, and I could be a patient, or even a doct—"

"Where are my clothes?" Pandora shouted at the fat nurse who was chatting with Sullivan. "I need to get out of here now."

"We had to cut your clothes off you. Everything was destroyed."

"Just find me something to wear."

"I will look for Progress at the college," Spencer told her.

"Who is missing now?" Sullivan enquired. He had been trying to ignore what the nurse was telling him about her attempts to lose weight in favour of eavesdropping on his suspects.

"Julie Progress. She is a postgraduate student at CAT College. One of our best."

"Yes. I have seen the bed where she does her research. I need to find any missing person who may be a potential witness," Sullivan said. "Do you have a photograph of her?"

"No, he doesn't. You two do what you want. I am going to find her myself. Nurse. Bring me someone else's clothes," Pandora screamed.

Spencer left the emergency response unit almost at a run to get a head start on Pandora who was already out of bed and shouting again at the nurse.

Jackson sat holding the librarian's hand, ignoring the drama around him.

"I thought you might help me to set up a library when you get out of here," he told her.

"Do you have a large house?"

"No, but I can get one."

"Make sure it has strong floors."

Outside the hospital Spencer hailed a passing taxi. "Where to?" the driver asked.

"CAT College."

As the taxi was about to pull out from the kerb Sullivan drove past with a flashing blue lamp fixed to the roof of his car. The race was on to find Progress.

Inside the hospital, in the emergency response ward, Horse approached Pandora carrying a dressing gown and a pair of slippers he had stolen from a changing cubicle in the X-ray department. He held them out to her.

"Thank you, Horse. Can you steal us a car outside?"

Horse nodded.

"You don't say much, but at least you don't talk philosophy, which is a bonus. You and I together – we must look out for Larry's interests until he recovers his senses. I assume you know his business associates?"

Horse nodded again.

"Do you have a light?"

Horse reached into the pocket of his battered jacket, took out a lighter, and flicked his large thumb against the flint wheel. A two-inch flame sprung out of his fist.

"I think you and I are going to get on," Pandora said, lighting her cigarette with one hand while plunging the other into the sleeve of the stolen dressing gown. Marley jumped off the bed and strutted down the middle of the emergency response unit, tail in the air the way a cat that came third in his breed should.

XLVII

Via Wallaciana
The Wallacian Way

Professor Maurice Spencer was squatting in a hedge across the road from Rik Wallace's house, waiting for Detective Sullivan to leave. He had spent most of the day searching the college in vain for Julie Progress when she wouldn't answer her phone. He wasted much of the evening searching student hangouts before he thought of the house on Love Street. From his hiding place deep in the foliage, Spencer could hear Sullivan knock on the door and ask at the top of his voice if anyone was home. There was no response.

As Sullivan's car reached the top of the road and disappeared, Spencer stepped into the circular light of a street lamp and climbed through another hedge into the back garden. Imagine, he thought, this old house will become a monument to philosophy. No doubt intellectual tourists will come here in the future to retrace Rik Wallace's steps.

As he approached the patio doors, he remembered where he was stepping and who lay beneath. He skipped over the spot where Lambe was buried. He blinkered his eyes by cupping his hands to the side of his head and pressed his face to the glass of the patio door. In the gloom inside, he saw Progress lying on her back, her hands stretched out by her sides as if worshipping the sun that was just then hauling itself into the sky behind his head with the reluctance of a fat student getting out of bed in the afternoon. A glowing lava lamp lay on its side at her feet.

"Oh Pandora, what have you done?" Spencer exclaimed. He stepped back and threw himself at the patio doors with such force that he bounced, landing on his back. The spade used to dig Lambe's grave was still standing by the wall. Spencer got back on his feet, took the spade in both hands, and began to smash the small panes of glass on each side of the lock. He reached inside and searched with his fingers for a key or a bolt. He found nothing. He withdrew his hand and pulled on the handle. The door swung out. He sighed as he realized it hadn't been locked. He threw the spade onto the patio and went inside.

He stood over Progress's body.

"I know she was a cow, but why come here and do this?" he asked an imaginary Pandora. "I agree. She was annoying, but I needed her for my Wallacian mission. She knew Rik as well as anyone, and now all that precious knowledge is lost to posterity. She could have written a pamphlet about their time together. What a waste." He looked around the room. "What am I going to do?" he asked over and over. "Maybe you are still here and hiding from the police. Pandora? Pandora? It's me, Maurice. It's Professor Spencer. Your noble savage," he shouted moving from one room to another. "It's okay. You can come out now."

He waited, listening. The old house was as still as a cemetery at dawn when all the ghosts have returned to their coffins. "She is not here," he concluded. "What would Rik do with the body?

Think in the manner of Rik Wallace. He put me in charge of his legacy. What is the Wallacian way? What would Rik do in this situation?" He looked around. He picked up the lamp at Progress's feet and placed it upright on a low table. Then he walked into the hall looking for philosophical inspiration. It came in the form of the wooden stepladder leaning against the wall beneath the trapdoor in the ceiling.

As Professor Spencer's head cleared the opening to the attic a voice asked him what he was doing. He screamed and fell backwards down the ladder into the hall. His landing was cushioned by Progress who had been dangling over his shoulder like a carpet. As he lay on the floor entwined in her legs, he heard the same voice command him, "Get off me, you idiot." He winced when Progress kicked him in the spine. "I said get *off* me." He turned over and knelt on the floor as she dragged herself on her backside down the hall.

"I thought you were dead. I thought Pandora had killed you."

"I wasn't dead. I was drunk. Don't look at me like that. I have been very stressed recently."

"I'm sorry. I was hiding you in the attic because I thought you were already dead. You looked dead."

"Ever think of taking a pulse? The attic? You are the same as Rik."

"Really? You are only saying that to flatter me. Do you really think so?"

"Can't you come up with an idea of your own?"

"What do you mean?"

"The attic," she said pointing at the ceiling. "That's where Rik would have put me if I was dead. Which I'm not."

"Rik would have put you in the attic? Wow. It worked."

"What worked?"

"I concentrated hard on having a Wallacian thought. You know? How would Rik have gone about hiding your body? Then I saw the ladder, and the idea of the attic just came to me. I must be in tune with his thinking processes: I am a real disciple."

"Stay at that end of the hall. Don't come near me."

"I said I was sorry. You did look dead. It's none of my business, but if I were you, I might review my drinking habits. Not that I am judging you. You know the last thing a moral philosopher would do is judge anyone – unless it was another philosopher, but you're not qualified yet so—"

"Shut up. You wanted to shove me up there, which is what Rik did with that hag of a mother of his when she wasn't dead either."

"What are you talking about?"

"Rik killed his mother and put her in the attic. I had to kill her again when she fell through the ceiling, which doesn't count, because as far as Rik was concerned, she was dead already, morally speaking."

"Rik killed his mother? Metaphorically, you mean? In some sort of Freudian ritual?"

"Not metaphorically. Literally," Progress hissed.

"But he had a fantastic relationship with his mother. I saw how close they were at his inaugural lecture."

"No. You didn't. You left to take your daughter somewhere."

"Yes. That's right. We went skiing or was it fishing?"

"Rik killed her."

"I can't believe it. It would go against all of his moral

principles. Even Kant wouldn't kill his own mother. I know the way Rik's mind works. I don't believe you."

"Rik did it. I saw her bounce off the bed with my own eyes. No better empirical proof exists than that."

"He must have had a good philosophical reason for killing her. After all, he is a genius. He occupies a different realm from the rest of us mere mortals. I will work hard to make sense of his ideas before I impart them to the world."

"I can't remember anything about last night," Progress said, holding her head.

"Larry came over here and attacked Rik because of your psychological meddling. I know because he told me when I had to drive him out of here at a hundred miles an hour with Larry chasing us."

"Oh God. It's coming back now. Larry jumped in his limousine. He wouldn't wait. I was begging him to let me help with the mediation, but he wouldn't listen. Is he all right?"

"Who Larry or Rik?"

"Both of them. They are so alike. They are brothers, after all. To the untrained eye they appear to be quite different, but I can see through their superficial differences to their fundamental similarities. Hard to be attracted to the one without being infatuated with the other. It's common for people to fall in love with an entire family."

"Where does that happen?"

"I can't remember, but I know it does. Somewhere in the jungle. I read it in an anthropology book."

"Larry lost his mind when his limousine blew up."

"You mean he is angry?"

"I mean he has literally lost his mind, and Rik has run away."

While Progress's conscious self was struggling with the after-effects of a wave of alcohol that swept across it the night before like a tsunami racing over a one-coconut tree island, her unconscious took advantage of the mental devastation to make itself heard. It was shouting at her how she knew all along Larry was crazy. "I told you so," it was saying over and over again with predictable smugness. The idea of Larry's fading appeal, especially now that he had lost his mind, was starting to crawl into the cracks in her brain where it began to put down roots.

"Is Rik okay? When he left here last night, I realized how much I still care about him, even though he didn't give me my job."

"Oh no. Speaking of jobs. Fischer, you know the one who got your job, is supposed to be here today to check us out. He is trying to decide whether he should join CAT College. It seems he has had several offers. Rik was right. He must be good. I had better go home and get cleaned up to try to make a proper Kantian impression. I still cannot believe Rik has embraced Kant."

"Typical. Fischer is offered loads of positions, and I can't even get my own job. Why couldn't Rik have offered me that post? You wouldn't have had to persuade me to take it." She pressed the sides of her skull with the palms of her hands and moaned. "It's my fault Rik has run off. My counselling went slightly wrong. From now on, I'm sticking with neurotics. Larry is a psychotic. Poor honest, neurotic Rik. How is he? Did Larry hurt him?"

"Rik is not physically hurt. He abandoned me to pursue his own solitary journey. He is a real prophet. I would do anything, absolutely anything, Rik asked of me."

"Would you stop following him?"

"Anything except that. I was hoping he might have changed his mind and come home. I was hoping he was here with you." He worried Rik might be annoyed if he caught up with him so soon, but he also knew that Rik didn't mean he should *literally* stop following him; metaphorically perhaps, but not literally. "He left me in charge of his legacy. I'm starting a movement based on his beliefs. My daughter Samantha has almost grown up. Soon she won't need me. I will need an interest of my own when she leaves home."

"You're starting a cult based around Rik Wallace?"

"Yes. The Wallacian Way."

"That's preposterous."

"Don't you mean 'postposterous'? Like 'postmodernism'?"

"I mean 'preposterous', as in contrary to reason."

"But whose version of reason do you mean? I've had it with the reason of conventional philosophy."

"Postposterous isn't a word."

"It is now. I declare Wallacianism to be about the promotion of postposterousness, everywhere possible. I was hoping you would be my first recruit."

"Will you be providing places for followers to stay?"

"Yes."

"Okay, I'm in."

"Let's get out of here before Pandora shows up."

"What about Fischer?"

"Oh, to hell with Fischer. I'm already following a Kantian. One is enough."

XLVIII

Caelestia Corpora
Heavenly Bodies

The seven-piece circus band were belting out their brass-inspired version of Phil Collins's "In the Air Tonight" to dramatize the daring of the Fabulous Flying Biscotti Brothers high on the trapeze in the big top. Bosco the Clown was sweating under his heavy face paint as he filled in for the regular drummer, Cubic the Clown, who was unconscious in a tiny caravan at the far end of the field in which Circus Amaro had assembled. But Bosco didn't complain because in this circus, as Rik Wallace now knew, everyone had to be flexible.

Wallace, who was now Biscotto, the newest member of the fabulous Biscotti brothers, was trying to reconcile himself to his death as he closed his eyes in terror. Also, he was in agony because his leotard was bunching around his crotch. Carlo, hanging by the back of his knees, held Biscotto's wrists in an iron grip as he swung him through the first arc across the length of the canvas roof. The small faces below shone with excitement as they furiously licked ice-cream cones or hysterically sucked the floss from wooden sticks waiting to see Biscotto, in his red sequined leotard, fly through the air in what everyone except Biscotto himself, expected to be a graceful somersault. Some prudent parents placed their hands over the eyes of their gaping children as Biscotto completed his first pendulum.

Biscotto knew that there was nothing to prevent him breaking every bone in his sequined body in the probable event of a non-choreographed descent from the trapeze that would conform to the law of gravity because there was no net between him and the sawdust-strewn ground below. At least, the red leotard wouldn't emphasize the blood, he thought. The ringmaster had assured him that nets were for fucking cowards and that his audience, especially the younger ones, didn't pay to see fucking cowards flying through the air. There were no fucking cowards amongst the fabulous Biscotti brothers. Wallace had assured the ringmaster that he had the wrong genetic make-up to be a Biscotti, being a craven coward. Wallace had discovered almost immediately on his arrival at Circus Amaro that the ringmaster was a violent drunk, who had once been the circus strongman, specializing in lifting Shetland ponies above his head.

To Biscotto, commencing his next pendulum in Carlo's now sweaty grip, it did indeed seem fabulous that at his age and in his shape, he was flying through the air as Bosco beat out the drum solo below. In the middle of the swing, Carlo struggled to build up enough momentum to throw Biscotto in the direction of the catcher, Marcello, who was just then swinging out of view trying to co-ordinate his own oscillation in the hope of grabbing whatever limb presented itself.

Below the children licked their cones faster, sucked the floss with more efficiency, and chewed their sweets with ever-faster rotating jaws as Bosco broke into the traditional drum roll that by custom precedes all acts of improbable acrobatic dexterity. Bosco made an extra effort drumming, because he was aware this was a more improbable ambition than the average implausible circus act. The sweat was causing his red eyes to run down his yellow cheeks. The faster drum roll added to the anxiety of the audience, though they were unaware what it was they feared. They should have been terrified of Biscotto landing on top of them.

A swarm of shiny-faced children sucked harder on the sweets in their mouths. They were sucking with terror: their collective mood swinging from fear to delight in time with Biscotto above them.

At the end of the arc, Biscotto glimpsed Marcello's inverted grinning face as it swung into his line of vision. Marcello held up a thumb, smiled, waved, and clapped his powdered hands together in anticipation of the important catch. Then he was gone. "Oh God," Biscotto groaned. "Why wasn't I able to be a clown?" His short career as a clown had ended in a stampede: perhaps a first in that profession. His face with large red lips, round black eyes, floppy hat and body suit produced an implicit sinister effect rather than the explicit humour he had hoped for. He had landed on his oversized nose in the middle of the ring to a ripple of approving applause when he was kicked on his padded backside by a two-man mule. The audience groaned when he bounced from a trampoline through a sheet of sugar glass. His discomfort was greeted by a silence: the kind that descends on a noisy jungle with the arrival of an unseen predator. When he ran towards the children at the front of the ringside waving a large rubber snake the way Beano the Clown had done just minutes before, the children didn't cling to each other and scream in delighted terror as they had for Beano.

Instead, they stood up in their seats, screamed in horror, and ran en masse towards the back of the tent, unconcerned that they were trampling on each other and their parents.

Therefore, it was up on the trapeze for him. The ringmaster dismissed his protests with a dramatic crack of his whip and handed him the red leotard with the words, "You can be a Fabulous Flying Biscotti Brother because my sister tells me you have a fabulous talent for survival. You might break your neck up there, but I will break it down here if you don't get the fuck up that rope ladder. Now I must go and tame some lions." With this he turned away and shouted, "Huppah, huppah" while cracking his whip in preparation for his encounter with the ill-tempered lions, who were muttering conspiracies to each other in their own secret feline language.

On the next swing Biscotto thought that there was some karmic justice to his current predicament. After all, he had become Rik Wallace when he knocked the real one off the hotel balcony, where there wasn't even a Marcello swinging upside down outside on a trapeze with a miniscule prospect of catching him. If he was to die tonight, it was fitting that he should be killed falling through the air. He couldn't decide if he should try to aim for the middle of the central ring or hope to cushion his fall on the children below who were staring up at him in fascinated horror. Maybe he wasn't yet finished causing death. At least for a fraction of a second, he thought, in their eyes, as he plunged towards them, he would be a Fabulous Flying Biscotti Brother. He hoped he wouldn't land on Della. But Della wasn't in the tent risking death by Biscotto. She was outside getting the string of small Indian elephants ready to run around the centre ring, each holding the tail of the one in front in the grip of a supportive trunk.

Fabulous Biscotto clamped his eyes shut, and stretched his arms out into space as far as he could reach in the direction of Marcello. Out of sight just beyond his fingertips, he could hear Marcello shouting encouragement. "Come on, Carlo. Let him go. I'll catch him." Carlo released his grip on the fabulous Biscotto, formerly known in philosophy circles as Professor Rik Wallace, and before that, known as a control freak. If ever there was an appropriate occasion when swearing might be justified, Biscotto believed that this was it.

Few of the children below had ever seen a trapeze act before. Those few who had, and many of the parents, knew from experience that trapezing protocol demanded that the acrobats fly through the air maintaining a dignified silence and not swearing in the way Biscotto was now doing above them. The children shrieked in terrified delight at the sounds emanating from the red sequined acrobat flying through the air with the grace of a side of bacon. Some parents moved their hands from their children's eyes to their ears to protect their innocence from the swearing coming from on high. Other parents covered their own ears and looked away.

Above the din of Bosco's rolling drum, the squeals of children, the frantic slurping of ice-cream cones and the groans of terrified parents, a roar was audible, "Ooooooooooh fuuuuuucccccccckkkk."

XLIX

Philosophicas Aemulatio
Philosophical Rivalry

Rik Wallace tugged on the crotch of his red sequined leotard to improve the circulation in his legs. The smoke from his cigarette ricocheted back off the passenger window. The streets outside went by in a parallax blur between the steam on the inside of the glass and a layer of yellow grease on the outside. Beside him the ringmaster was driving in his long red coat and high boots – he had placed his precious whip across the back seat. Being unconscious for the night meant Wallace hadn't been able to change his clothes before the ringmaster had forced him into the car. Now he was sulking.

"How long was I in your circus?" Wallace asked, unaware whether the words were in his head or coming out of his mouth.

"Too long," the ringmaster answered. "Never mind a lion eating one or two lackeys behind the scenes, but stampeding the paying customers twice? Fuck me. I thought I had seen it all until I saw those terrified children running. But I don't know which was worse: you on terra firma in that clown costume or up on the trapeze. You can't swing for shit."

"Della sewed all these sequins to help me fit in," Wallace said, touching the few pieces of glittering plastic still clinging to the front of his soiled leotard.

"She should have sewn on some wings. I would have thought you had some pride or even a sense of shame. Hollering like a baby. I can't see a thing with this low fucking sun," he said breaking off his flow of abuse to cover his eyes with his hand. "Where did you say this college is?"

"Turn left at the top of this road."

"I said to Della, I said as soon as that bollix wakes up, he's going back to wherever he came from, pronto. Here, take a slug of this." The ringmaster passed Wallace a half-full bottle of whiskey. Wallace sipped and handed it back. His cracked lips stung from the liquid. He pulled down again on the leotard. His legs were going numb.

"They didn't design those costumes with balls in mind," the ringmaster said nodding towards Wallace's crotch. "I'm guessing they were invented by a woman. I know fuck all about philosophy, but I'll tell you this much. Stick with it, whatever it is. You're not going to kill yourself or me doing philosophy. You missed me by inches when you came off that swing last night. By that much," he said holding up his thumb and forefinger, causing the car to swerve into the oncoming traffic. A passing truck honked as it swerved to avoid a collision. "Fuck you," the ringmaster shouted through the window. "You're lucky Bosco's drums broke your fall."

For a second, Wallace imagined the ringmaster was addressing the truck driver. He winced. He didn't need to be reminded of his undignified landing. As an aide-memoire, his ribs burned when he inhaled. He had a blue-and-purple semicircle across his chest from the edge of the drum shell. He even had a dent in his leg where it hit the top of the cymbal stand.

"I mean, for fuck's sake. Of all the places you could have landed. To knock out the band. They weren't even able to play something distracting while you were being stretchered out. I'll say it again. I've seen a lot in my years in the circus, but never anyone as fucking bad as you. Don't take this the wrong way, but you are the single most talentless idiot ever hired in the history of spectacle. You could have tried lion-taming if Della hadn't stopped me. I told her those fucking lions would have run for their lives when they saw you." Big cats and children had extraordinary instincts that there was no point in analysing. "You were the worst clown we ever had."

"It wasn't my fault. Della designed my face and costume."

"Yeah, but it was you underneath. Imagine ballsing up being a clown. That's a first in my extensive experience. You frightened the shit out of those children. That's the kind of thing the health and safety people would shut me down over. Is this it?" he asked, skidding to a halt under the main archway into CAT College.

"Thank you for the lift," Wallace said.

"You are most welcome. If I find out Della came looking for you, I will fire her too, even if she is my sister. I've had enough of her miserable misfits. Fuck off back to wherever you came from." He blew a gust of breath between his whiskers and lower lip, and studied Wallace. "Do you need money?"

"There are no pockets in this outfit," Wallace said, plucking at the soiled leotard.

"Take this and buy yourself some clothes," the ringmaster said, pressing a bunch of notes into Wallace's hand.

"Are you sure?"

"Just stay away from Circus Amaro. Agreed? Don't come back even to see the show. Don't bring your friends or family – ever."

"Don't worry. I have neither friends nor family."

"Am I surprised? Just don't bring anyone, even strangers."

Wallace eased himself out of the greasy car. He closed the door behind him with a sullen thump. The ringmaster sped away, spraying mud from under the wheels onto Wallace's red legs. He looked around pondering what he might do now, holding the money in one hand, and his crotch in the other. He felt he had reached the end of the momentum he had set in motion when he first knocked Rik Wallace from the balcony; he felt too exhausted to feel depressed, too numb to feel despondent. His limbs had been stretched beyond their normal elasticity to allow them to spring back into place. He felt the effects of the unnatural lengthening in every joint when he moved. The thought of killing himself involved more energy than he felt he could muster. Besides, he reflected, his last attempt hadn't been worth the pain. "What now?" he muttered looking up at the lettering spelling out CAT College above the archway.

"Rik. Rik. What amazing timing. A miracle your appearing out of the blue like this, just when we need you. You truly are a prophet. What are you wearing? Is that some kind of religious vestment?"

Wallace turned around and saw Maurice Spencer striding towards him with a placard over his shoulder. He was wearing a blue T-shirt stretched on over his overcoat. Behind him a triangle of people, some holding banners extended between two and some carrying placards, were all squeezed into blue

T-shirts bearing the words "The Wallacian Way". Spencer's placard read: "The Past is *PRE*-posterous. The Future is *POST*-posterous".

Julie Progress stepped out from behind Spencer. She was holding a pole that supported one end of a long blue banner bearing the words: "Down with *PRE*-posterousness and the Commerce Faculty. Give *POST*-posterousness a chance".

"Oh, Rik. Rik. You're okay. You're alive. I was worried about you." She rushed at him and wrapped her free arm around his neck, kissing him all over his still greasepainted face. "Darling Rik. I'm sorry for stopping talking to you, for doubting you, for being mean to you and, you know – not appreciating your mother while she was alive. I'm thrilled you have come back." She passed the banner-pole to a student beside her so she could clap her hands together in delight as if in compensation for the children at the circus who were unable to appreciate his hidden talents. "We all missed you."

"Pandora didn't," Spencer put in. "She has gone stark raving mad. She has joined forces with Horse and your brother Larry's gang to form the Wallace Enterprise Centre. Did you know he was a gangster with his own mob? Pandora has been running his gang since Larry lost his mind."

"Larry has lost his mind?"

"He smashed his head when his limousine crashed when he was chasing us. Pandora has taken over the commerce faculty and now she wants to run the college as provost. I don't think she has ever read a book in her life, but she is full of opinions on what we should teach. She even wants to start a Medicine Faculty to try to prove that smoking is good for you. Can you imagine that?"

"Yes, I can."

"She is trying to put that new guy, the Kantian, Ernst Fischer, that you hired, in charge of the philosophy department instead of me. I knew he was a lunatic from the moment I first laid eyes on his hair. Pandora is assembling a mob of like-minded staff and students right now in the quad for a rally. That's where we are headed. To bust it up. She has to be stopped."

"I told you I quit. I can't philosophize anymore. Find someone else. I am a failure at everything. Even this mess with Larry and Pandora is my fault."

"Yes, that's true, because this was a relatively normal campus before you showed up. But now that you have reappeared you can help save us. With you on our side, we cannot lose. You wouldn't believe the number of followers I have recruited since you disappeared. Half the college is behind Pandora, Horse and Fischer, but the other half is behind you."

"Behind me?"

"Yes, behind you. I started a cult in your honour. It was as if everyone was just waiting for something meaningful to believe in. We have been signing up followers, day and night."

"Come on Rik. Let's get them," Progress said, waving her hands over her head in a gesture of encouragement to those bunching into the arch behind her. She grabbed a fist of sequins on his chest and pulled Rik towards her. She kissed him fiercely on the lips. "Oh Rik, I love you. I passed out from drink after Larry chased you – it's a long story – but when I woke up, I realized that deep down inside I always loved you. I have started to listen to my unconscious. I love you, Rik. And you can give me Fischer's job when *you* take care of him."

Many hands grabbed Wallace and spun him around. He was hoisted into the air and onto the shoulders of two large learners squeezed into medium-sized T-shirts bearing the Wallacian slogan. The mob of Wallacians roared their collective joy at having secured their figurehead on the eve of combat. They thought they recognized him from the copies of the blurry photograph that Spencer had handed out at his Wallacian recruitment drives. Off they marched under the arch with Wallace held high like a shiny red sequined battle standard.

The noise of the passing crowd woke Rose the bum where she dozed under a mound of coats and blankets under the arch. She peeked out through a slit between the greasy collar of Jim's old overcoat and a dust-encrusted grey blanket that she had taken from the ruin of her former home. Grey was recolonizing her dyed shoe-brown hair from the roots out. Under her woollen house, she still wore her tin foil wrapping from the hospital. She observed the knees of the followers of Wallace going past without curiosity. She had lost interest in the world now that she had no one with whom to share her observations. She pulled her tortoise neck back into the layers of her woollen shell.

At night she foraged through the bins outside the college canteen, squatting on the grass to mark her territory. At dawn she returned to her pile of coats and blankets. Yesterday morning she had spied on Young Rose at the window of the reception hut, holding her fella's hand, while talking with the new young porter: the replacement Jim. Young Rose was asking him if anyone had seen her mother.

"I don't have time to be looking out for strays," replacement Jim replied. "The college is falling apart. Bags of rubbish piling up everywhere. I'm not moving them. It's not my job. Everyone complaining about the length of the grass. It's not my job to sort out the cleaners or cut the lawns. That's what I'd tell whoever it is I am supposed to complain to if I knew who that was. It's anarchy."

"Do you need some help?" Young Rose's fella asked. "I have an almost-new sit-on mower. I wouldn't mind cutting the grass, and Young Rose here knows everything about the cleaning game. It's what you might call a family business."

"I'm sure you could ask, but I don't know who is in charge."

Rose couldn't hear or see what happened next because she had sunk back into her husk of rags. Her clothes crackled. She wriggled to move the *Complete Works of Shakespeare* from under her buttock that was still in the plastic bag in which she had carried it home, when she thought she still had a home.

From his position above the crowd as he emerged from under the arch, Rik Wallace saw Larry Wallace wandering in front of the opposing mob with a prominent white bandage swaddling his head. He was meandering over and back on an invisible metaphysical dividing line between the two factions. He smiled when he saw Rik and started to amble towards him. Someone had pulled a pink T-shirt down over his suit with black lettering across the chest to signify that he was a member of the commerce faculty. Horse, who was also wearing one of the too-small T-shirts, grabbed Larry by the collar and pulled him back into the ranks.

Just behind Horse, Casper Wall was holding a placard in one hand while reading a text messages on his smartphone in the other. He wasn't wearing a T-shirt. Beside him, Sidney the Sycophant was wearing a pink T-shirt on his chest and a blue one wrapped around his head like a turban, just in case. Rik could see Sydney the Sycophant's lips moving as he counted aloud to himself the number of approaching Wallacians. He was still trying to estimate the odds of his being on the winning side of this impending ontological conflict when his faction pushed forward with Pandora leading her troops from the front taking her example from Boadicea.

Towards the back of the bunch Rik saw a group of thick-set, bald, sun-tanned men with sunglasses in black suits, white shirts, and skinny black ties. These he assumed were the members of Larry's mob who now formed the Wallace Enterprise Centre. They were all wielding baseball bats one-handed, which they beat into the other in gleeful anticipation of cracking the heads of the learners of any faculty.

Rik, high on the shoulders of the Wallacians, shouted over and over again for silence. Spencer raised his hand to bring the mob to a halt, and yelled, "Quiet. Shut up. Our leader desires to say something. Let us be silent for his inspirational words."

The hubbub died down like the vanguard winds of a coming storm. Rik directed his speech towards Fischer who was just visible over Pandora's shoulder. While trying to form his opening words he was distracted by the fact that the Kantian expert had taken the advice of the interview panel with regard to his hair. Gone were the long greasy strings, replaced by short shiny curls.

"Is that a perm?" Rik asked, still trying to order his thoughts that he found at last. "Couldn't you at least divide yourselves along intelligible fault lines that make some historical sense within the discipline if you're going to kill each other over a philosophical dispute? Kant wasn't mortally opposed to anyone. He tried to bring about an epistemological revolution by reconciling the opposite approaches of idealism and realism. Not a violent revolution. Kant wasn't a violent man. Boring, perhaps. Without doubt, obsessive-compulsive. But not violent. Kant was promoting, yes, a new approach, but in the areas of epistemology and metaphysics, not ethics; and definitely not in commerce."

"Welcome back, Rik," Pandora shouted. "I don't have a dispute with you. In fact, what do I care? You can have your old job back as provost. My fight is with Progress. Just hand her over, and you can go."

"You don't have a real dispute with Progress or any of these Wallacians," Wallace said, sweeping his arm over the learners propping him up. "I support Kant's ideas; at least, those few I can understand. Divide along old-fashioned empiricist versus idealist lines, if you must. Or continental versus analytical approaches. Yes, those two camps hate each other, but not because of personal animosities. Jealousies and personality clashes are not morally coherent justifications for philosophical conflict."

"How naïve," Fischer muttered.

"Besides, Progress doesn't love Larry anymore. Not since he lost his mind."

Larry gurgled and tried to walk towards the lone voice of reason, but Horse held him back by the collar of his overcoat.

"Enough philosophy," Pandora shouted. This was followed by a roar as both sides rushed towards each other. Progress crashed into Pandora with such force the impact knocked both of them onto the ground. As they grabbed at each other's thrashing limbs to regain their feet, a ring of rebels formed around them. The circle began to chant "Fight, fight, fight," which soon evolved into the more precise chorus of "Girl fight, girl fight, girl fight."

Pandora and Progress were back on their feet with their fingers rigid like claws in front of them as they revolved around each other in the clearing. Sidney the Sycophant danced in and out between the two combatants. He was holding his bat over his head with both hands. He had decided to deliver the coup de grâce to the weaker party, thereby ingratiating himself with the victor. But then he thought that maybe he should poleaxe the stronger one, endearing himself to the improbable victor. But which one was that? Progress or Pandora? He was trying to decide who to hit when Horse hit him from behind, putting him out of his dilemma as he sank unconscious to his knees and keeled over sideways. Horse threw his bat to Pandora.

"That's not fair," someone in the crowd protested. "Here take this," Spencer said, throwing his placard at Progress. It landed at her feet. Pandora swung her bat at Progress's head as she bent down to pick it up. Progress pitched forward onto her face and lay dead still. Both her conscious and unconscious selves said nothing. The crowd went silent. Those at the front stared at Progress inert on the grass and then at Pandora who was panting, holding the bat in front of her heaving chest. "What?" she asked. "What did I do wrong?" The silence persisted. Then someone in the back shouted, "Get her." Bats seemed to blossom in every hand and Pandora went down under a hail of blows. Then bat-wielders, regardless of which colour T-shirt they were wearing, began to hit whoever was in front of them. An experienced philosophical observer would have recognized that the new porter had been correct in his observation of the ideology that had come to dominate the campus: indeed, this was anarchy.

Professor Maurice Spencer was lying face down on the grass in the first quadrangle of CAT College with his hands clamped over his head protecting himself from the kicks of Doctor Ernest Fischer. He was thinking how it was such a rare sight to see an angry Kantian, and rarer still, so many of them gathered together in one place. He was distracted from his thoughts trying to satisfy his urgent curiosity that perhaps someone had pissed on the grass beneath him. He pressed his fingers into the damp soil and held them under his nose and sniffed. Phew. Barbarians. Just my luck, he thought, caught up in the first major student riot in fifty years.

For his part, Doctor Ernst Fischer didn't know why he was kicking Professor Spencer. Things had gotten out of control for him since arriving at CAT College. He made a mental note to look up mob morality when he was next in the library.

"Stop kicking me," Spencer shouted at him. "I'm a father. My daughter needs me. She will be home from school any minute. I have to make her dinner."

L

Per Scaenam Sinistra Exitus
Exit Stage Left

The gang of learners shouldering Rik Wallace cast him aside in order to better attack each other. He bounced on the grass, rolled over, and crawled away on his hands and knees unnoticed between a forest of denim-clad learners' legs. Reaching the building enclosing the east side of the quadrangle, he stood up and made his way along the stone wall to the next arch that led further into the labyrinthine college. There he dodged a cluster of commerce students beating two classicists with their own plywood signs advertising their support for Kant.

Emerging into the next quadrangle he found himself free of the rioters. He hurried towards the meadow at the back of the college seeking refuge inside the philosophy department where he hoped to find peace because everyone seemed to be practising their philosophizing al fresco this morning. Just as he approached the road that crossed in front of the gloomy sad-eyed department with the aluminium extension ladder still leaning against its side wall, a car with a flashing blue light on the roof pulled up in front of him in a spray of gravel. A red-faced Sullivan jumped out, excited to have cut him off in flight. He folded his arms on the roof of the car, smiling the predatory sneer of the policeman who has trapped his prey.

The nearside back door creaked open. A boy who was an exact miniature Rik Wallace bounced out carrying a football under his arm. "Daddy. Daddy," the boy said as he ran towards him. Behind him a smaller, fatter red-faced boy was grasping the doorframe with his sausage fingers to lever himself out of the car. Behind him again a tiny girl wearing a pair of red plastic sunglasses with white daisies in the frame knelt on the black plastic seat waiting her turn to get out of the car. Her tiny mouth crinkled around the stick of a lollipop. It was as if she had been taking lessons in sucking from Pandora. Wallace could hear his pulse pounding above the repeated shouts of "Daddy".

Then the passenger door opened, which was also on Wallace's side – as if Sullivan had deliberately approached from the most dramatic angle. A woman with short dark hair swung her stomach sideways, using her front-loaded weight to propel herself halfway out of the car. She managed to achieve a sitting position with her feet on the road. She ran her palms up and down her bulge as if to persuade her unborn child within that the order of things in the world outside was now as it should be. Suddenly shy, the children halted a few feet in front of Wallace and began to jump up and down in place. They had stopped shouting. They muttered the words "Daddy, Daddy", as if starting to forget again who he was.

"What were you thinking? We thought you were dead," the woman said from behind the heads of her children. "If it wasn't for this policeman here," she said waving her hand over her shoulder in the vague direction of Sullivan, "I can't remember his name. Anyway, he checked all the fingerprints, DNA, blood types, mobile phones, clothes left in the hotel, that sort of thing – which the other policeman ignored – and here you are." She paused to study him. "What are you wearing? Is that some kind of academic gown?"

From the accumulated impact of his philosophical studies, perhaps from the ignition of a spark of shock rather than intellect, Rik Wallace had an epiphany. He realized he had exhausted all of his moral options but one: the one that he kept on the walls of the corridors of his deepest subconscious self with the words "In Case of Extreme Emergency Break Glass" written on it with underneath in smaller letters "Use Only Once" in a lifetime. From trauma rather than the practice of meditation it was as if he had attained Buddhism's final *arahant* stage of enlightenment when his archetypal family confronted him. He didn't think about it: this moral choice was beyond thought. He didn't need to reflect on the proper course of action. He didn't want to draw up a table of moral consequences, nor would it help to consult Nietzsche or Kant. He was indifferent to interpreting God's will, his horoscope, Freud, or even what the law might consider just. He had reached a place of pure *un*mediated moral enlightenment because, at last, he could act by animal instinct rather than *un*natural philosophical reason. His choice went to the true core of his moral being.

He rotated on his red sequined ballet slipper heels and ran.

He ran when his nicotine-weakened lungs started to hurt.

He ran when his bruised ribs speared his sides and the drum hole in his leg throbbed in protest.

He ran when his feet came through the flimsy soles of his

red slippers.

He ran when the white greasepaint melted down his face and flowed onto his chest.

He ran on after he stopped feeling any pain.

He ran out of the college and down the street, his arms pumping up and down, driving him on. Now he was certain he should have run on that first night he knocked Rik Wallace from the balcony. "What an idiot I am. Seems obvious now," he gasped to himself.

As he ran past a grey block of student accommodation his feet slowed to the languorous rhythm of Chet Baker's trumpet playing "Exitus" from inside an open window on the ground floor. He was jazz-running when the car drew up beside him. The passenger window rolled down. He heard the librarian shouting at him. Glancing sideways between breaths he saw that Jackson was driving.

"Get in, Rik," the librarian shouted. We're starting a new library far from here. Get in the back. Inspector Jackson knew you were a fraud all along. He's not an idiot, you know. He's a smart detective. He has amazing instincts. Get in."

The car moved ahead of him when Jackson mistimed the pace, bringing Della's face behind the glass of the back window in line with his. For the first time since he had first seen her, he thought she looked worried.

"Get in the car, Rik," the librarian shouted again.

He started to laugh out loud: a laugh that had begun somewhere deep inside that was pouring out through his mouth, stretched open as far as his jaws could reach.

Wallace understood that he had learned one moral law during his time in philosophy at CAT College: despite the cigarettes, he could run, but he couldn't hide.

"I think he's lost it," Jackson told the librarian.

This is where we take leave of our hero for the time being: running down the middle of the street, laughing, in a once-sparkly outfit now torn, worn, and splattered with mud and grass. If we are going to judge him, we might consider what the renowned Socrates did when faced with a moral dilemma. He was fat, old, and out of shape. No wonder he chose to kill himself rather than run through the streets of ancient Athens in a flashy toga.

Intermissio
Intermission